UNDER ATTACK

My words were cut off by the sound of a blade slicing through the air. I felt a body make contact with mine, then the wind as it left my chest when I fell onto the cold, damp concrete. I only knew Alex had been hit when I heard the strangled sound of his groan.

"Sophie, run!"

Everything seemed to be happening in slow motion and Alex's command didn't even sound like him. It was higher, more menacing, and I kicked my feet, sliding on the concrete until I got some traction, then stopped dead, seeing the dark figure in front of Alex.

Our attacker was dressed entirely in black and stood a half-head taller than Alex, his face obscured by a black knit ski mask that only revealed sinister hooded eyes, which remained fixed on us.

He held his blade aloft once more and I heard my own scream when I saw the blood—Alex's blood—dripping from the cold steel . . .

Books by Hannah Jayne

UNDER WRAPS

UNDER ATTACK

Published by Kensington Publishing Corporation

UNDER ATTACK

The Underworld Detection Agency Chronicles

>-I-◆-I-<

HANNAH JAYNE

KENSINGTON BOOKS

http://www.kensingtonbooks.com

KENSINGTON BOOKS are published by

Kensington Publishing Corp.
119 West 40th Street
New York, NY 10018

All Kensington titles, imprints, and distributed lines are available at special quantity discounts for bulk purchases for sales promotion, premiums, fund-raising, educational, or institutional use.

Special book excerpts or customized printings can also be created to fit specific needs. For details, write or phone the office of the Kensington Special Sales Manager: Attn. Special Sales Department. Kensington Publishing Corp., 119 West 40th Street, New York, NY 10018. Phone: 1-800-221-2647.

Kensington and the K logo Reg. U.S. Pat. & TM Off.

ISBN-13: 978-0-7582-5893-9
ISBN-10: 0-7582-5893-3

First Printing: November 2011

10 9 8 7 6 5 4 3 2 1

Printed in the United States of America

*To my fifth grade teacher Suzanne Nunes
who let me retest when I failed the language arts
portion of my CBETs test;
to my eighth grade teacher Cynthia Gore
who awarded me language arts Student of the Year;
and to my eleventh grade teacher JoEllen Victoreen
who told me that my book report sounded like I copied
it from the book's back cover (I totally didn't).*

You made a difference.

Acknowledgments

First and foremost thank you to my amazing agent Amberly Finarelli for believing, listening, inspiring—and showing me pictures of Ruby when things get too dark in the Underworld. And to John Scognamiglio—you've ruined me for other editors—you are the best! Many thanks to my copyeditor Erin who humbles me with her red pencil and eagle eye. For you, I will rein in my cocky half-smiles and beelines. A big thank you to Lee Lofland and the entire staff of WPA, the Greensboro Police and Fire Departments for locking me in the slammer for "research." Thank you to Dr. Jonathan Hayes for answering my questions on strangling, drowning and the menu at Gotham. Every woman should be lucky enough to have a gastronome/medical examiner on speed dial. To authors Juliet Blackwell, Sophie Littlefield, Penny Warner and Diana Orgain, thanks for showing me the ropes. A big thank-you to my Beta readers/cheering section at Club One: Shirley, Nadine and Penne.

Thank you to everyone in the city who knowingly (or not) supported me—especially Mike from Recycle Books, the staffs of the Pruneyard Barnes & Noble, M is for Mystery, Bay Books, Towne Books and especially, unequivocally, the gang from Crema Coffee in San Jose. There is no better place to get inspired.

Thank you is not big enough to express my gratitude to John and Joan Wendt for letting me hoard laundry quarters and stuff my purse with Google snacks. Thanks for being expert Beta readers and even better friends. We'll be in Hawaii soon! To Oscar Varela—thank you for everything you do on a daily basis, but most of all for telling me to quit my job four years ago. I wouldn't have done it without you.

To my best stalker fan (now friend and often room-mate) Marina Chappie: thank you for reading, listening, plastering, and plotting with and for me. I can't wait to share shelf space with Elle!

A very special thanks to my entire family, especially my parents for their unyielding and enthusiastic support, Dana and Officer Cousin for offering book tour security and to oil me up, and to my brother Trevor for under-standing that not every novel can center around a quick-witted stockbroker with a heart of gold. And fi-nally, to CTS—now I really mean it when I say "the check's in the mail."

Chapter One

It's nearly impossible to get hobgoblin slobber out of raw silk.

I know this because I had been standing in the bathroom, furiously scrubbing at the stubborn stain for at least forty-five minutes. If I could do magic, I would have zapped the stain out. Heck, if I could do magic I would zap away the whole hobgoblin afternoon and be sinking my toes in the sand somewhere while a tanned god named Carlos rubbed suntan lotion on my back. But no, I was stuck in the Underworld Detection Agency women's restroom—a horrible, echoey room tiled in Pepto pink with four regular stalls and a single tiny one for pixies—when my coworker Nina popped her head in, wrinkled her cute ski-jump nose, and said, "I smell hobgoblin slobber."

Did I mention vampires have a ridiculously good sense of smell?

Nina came in, letting the door snap shut behind her. She used one angled fang to pierce the blood bag she was holding and settled herself onto the sink next to me.

"You're never going to get that out, you know," she said between slurps.

I huffed and wrung the water from my dress, glaring at Nina as I stood there in my baby-pink slip and heels. "Did you come in here just to tell me that?"

Nina extended one long, marble-white leg and examined her complicated Jimmy Choo stilettos. "No, I also came in to tell you that Lorraine is on the warpath, Nelson used his trident to tack a pixie to the corkboard, and Vlad is holding a VERM meeting in the lunch room."

I frowned. "This job bites."

Nina smiled, bared her fangs, and snapped her jaws.

Nina and I work together at the Underworld Detection Agency—the UDA for those in the know. And very few people are in the know. Our branch is located thirty-seven floors below the San Francisco Police Department, but we have physical and satellite offices nationwide—word is the Savannah office gets the most ghosts but has the best food. The Manhattan office gets the best crossovers (curious humans wandering down) and the good ol' San Francisco office is famous for our unruly hordes of the magnificent undead, mostly dead, and back from the dead. However, we're rapidly becoming *in*famous for a management breakdown that tends to make incidents like the fairy stuck to the corkboard barely worth mentioning. Some demons blame the breakdown of Underworld morals. I blame the fact that my boss and former head of the UDA, Pete Sampson, disappeared last year and has yet to be replaced. Thus, we've been privy to a semipermanent parade of interim management made up of everything from werewolves and vampires to goblins and one (mercifully short) stint with a screaming banshee.

So am I a demon? Nope. I'm a plain, one hundred

percent first-life, air breathing, magic-free human being. I don't have fangs, wings, or hooves. I'm five-foot-two on a good day, topped with a ridiculous mess of curly red hair on a bad day, and my eyes are the exact hue of lime Jell-O. My super powers are that I can consume a whole pizza in twelve minutes flat and sing the fifty states in alphabetical order. And that I'm alive. Which makes me a weird, freakish anomaly in an Underworld office that keeps blood in the office fridge and offers life insurance that you can collect should you get the opportunity to come back to life.

"There you both are!"

My head swung to the open doorway where Lorraine stood, eyebrows raised and arched, her blue-green eyes narrowed. Lorraine is a Gestault witch of the green order, which means that her magiks are in kind with nature and are deeply humane. Usually.

Her honey-blond hair hangs past her waist and her fluttery, earth-toned wardrobe reflects her solidarity with natural harmony.

Unless you got on her bad side, which, today, I was.

Lorraine glared at my slip. "Can you wrap up your little lingerie fashion show and meet me in my office, please? And you"—Lorraine swung her head toward Nina, who was holding my damp dress under the hand dryer—"can you please break up Vlad's empowerment meeting and get out to the main floor? Vlad's got nine vamps singing "We Shall Overcome" in the lunch room and I've got sixteen minotaurs in the overflow waiting room."

I looked at Nina. "Vlad is still into the Vampire Empowerment Movement?"

Nina gave me her patented "Don't even start" look,

punched her fist in the air, and bellowed "*Viva la revalución!*" while slipping out the bathroom door.

I pulled my dress over my head under Lorraine's annoyed stare, and then worked quickly to rearrange my hair. When Lorraine sighed—loudly—I wadded my curls into a bun and secured them with a binder clip, then followed her down the hall.

"Okay," I told her as I tried to keep pace with her. "What's up?"

Lorraine didn't miss a step. She pushed a manila file folder in my hand with the blue tag—*Wizards*—sticking out.

"Nicholias Rayburn," I read as I scanned the thick file. "Ring a bell?"

I frowned. "No. Should it?"

"How about 'Three Headed Dog Ravages Noe Valley Neighborhood'?"

I felt myself pale. "Mr. Rayburn did that?"

"No," Lorraine said flatly. "You did."

I raised my eyebrows and Lorraine let out another annoyed sigh. "Nicholias Rayburn was here last week. Old guy, blue robe, pointy hat?"

I cocked my head. "Oh yeah. Now I remember him."

"You should, because you allowed him to renew his magiks license."

My stomach started to sink.

"Yeah. With his three-inch-thick cataracts and mild senility. You were supposed to *withdraw* his license and strip him of his magiks, but you didn't, and he walked home, thought a fire hydrant was following him, and unleashed the hound of Hell on the land of the soccer mom. Not exactly great for our reputation."

I felt my usually pale skin flush. "Whoops."

Lorraine stopped walking and faced me, the hard line of her lips softening. "Look, Sophie, I know you've had a hard time. I understand that with all you've been through you're going to make some mistakes, but you've got to be more aware."

The events of the last year of my life flooded over me, and I blinked rapidly, trying to dispel the imminent rush of tears.

It *had* been rough.

While I had gone for more than thirty-three years with nothing so much as an overdue library book to raise any eyebrows, in the last twelve months I had become involved in a gory murder investigation, been kidnapped, attacked, hung by my ankles as someone attempted to bleed me dry—

"And I know it's got to be hard, what with Alex out of the picture and all."

And I had fallen in love with a fallen angel who had the annoying habit of dropping into my life with a pizza and a six-pack when things were supernaturally awful, and dropping out when things shifted into relatively normal gear.

I sniffed, hugging Mr. Rayburn's file to my chest. "Thanks. It won't happen again. I promise."

"Let's hope not. But why don't you head out a little early today?" she said, squeezing my shoulder. "Get some rest and regroup." Lorraine bit her lip and danced from foot to foot, then leaned in close to me. "Okay. I'm really not supposed to say anything but I'm about to burst, so this is just between you and me, okay?" Lorraine sucked in an excited breath. "The main offices have found Sampson's replacement. We're supposed to have the new management in place by the end of the week. But it's super hush-hush so don't tell a soul, okay?"

I nodded, feeling a fresh pang of emotion washing over me. In the half-second it took to close my eyes I saw Pete Sampson's cocoa-brown office walls, his worn leather chair, the orderly stack of files he always had on his desk. I felt the familiar lump in the back of my throat and swallowed furiously. Pete Sampson wasn't coming back to the Underworld Detection Agency. Pete Sampson was dead. The realization was hard enough to face; knowing someone else would be sitting at Pete's desk was almost too much to bear.

I cleared my throat and winced when my voice came out quiet and choked. "Your secret is safe with me. I'm going to go check in with Nina."

I walked slowly down the hall, taking great gulps of airs and using my index fingers to dab at my moist eyes.

Nina was perched on the end of her desk when I found her, legs crossed seductively, her shoe dangling from one toe. She was winding her long black hair around and around her index finger and interviewing a werevamp who was sitting in her visitor's chair. Nina was the only person I'd ever met who could make the sentence "please tell me about your previous employment history" sound sordid. She was nearly purring as the werevamp—who looked dashing in a steel-grey suit and had the chiseled profile of James Bond—ticked off a forty-seven-decade-long employment history that included working as a tax collector for King Henry the VIII and ended with software programmer.

I tried to catch Nina's eye but she glared at me—nothing is icier than a vampire glare—and I rolled my eyes, heading down the hall toward the elevator. I was skirting the hole in the linoleum where a High witch blew herself up when I ran chest to chest into Vlad and his Fang Gang—the nine vampire staff members of UDA who were currently enraptured by the Vampire Empowerment and Restoration Movement. Loosely put, VERM members were dead-set on bringing vamps back to their glory days (think Dracula, graveyard dirt, and ascots). Though UDA code was adamant about vampire/human relationships (the former was not allowed to eat the latter), I generally tried to steer clear of VERMers—Vlad, being Nina's nephew (and a longtime resident of our couch), was the exception. Vlad and Nina shared the same fine-boned structure and elegant limbs that seemed to be signature of the LaShay family; both had pronounced, inky-black widow's peaks under their sheaths of glossy hair. But fashion-wise, the relatives couldn't have been farther apart.

Vlad fell in step with me, his ankle-length black duster coat floating behind him. I looked at it skeptically.

"Isn't it a little warm for the coat?"

Vlad just shrugged his thin shoulders and straightened his paisley ascot. "Vampire mystique."

"Of course."

"Have you seen Aunt Nina? I've been looking all over for her. She was going to bring the snacks for the meeting."

"I thought she was anti-VERM?"

I watched Vlad's nostrils flare; the members of the Vampire Empowerment and Restoration Movement loathed being belittled by their lame acronym. "She is, but you know Auntie."

I nodded. "Right. Pro-snacks." I gestured toward Nina's office door that had mysteriously closed. "She's interviewing a werevamp."

Vlad smoothed his perfect hair. "I didn't think we had any open positions."

I shrugged. "I'm pretty sure we don't. So, how are things with the movement?"

Vlad grinned, his fangs pressing over his lower lip. "Nice of you to ask. They're going well. We've been able to reach out to more key figures in the Underworld lately, but our next hurdle is our biggest."

I looked at Vlad who raised his eyebrows. "Hollywood," he supplied.

"VERM is going after Hollywood?" I asked, skeptical.

Vlad stiffened. "It's the Vampire Empowerment and Restoration Movement. As for Hollywood, we are against the way vampires are being portrayed in modern media." He shook his head. "It's awful."

I raised my eyebrows and met Vlad's dark eyes. He blew out an exasperated sigh. "Oh, come on; according to Hollywood—and now according to every woman south of forty-five—vampires are misunderstood nightwalkers who are really just looking for someone to love."

I glanced again toward Nina's office door.

"Trust me; she's not interested in *loving* him," Vlad said with a disgusted shudder. "I mean, have you seen television lately? They've got us going to high school, using jewelry to go out into sunlight. If a new vamp tries to mimic what he sees on television, he's going to get burned to a crisp. And don't even get me started on how they're screwing with our legendry!"

I nodded. "Yep. Best to go back to the good old days of Bela Lugosi, Nosferatu, and the Count from *Sesame Street*."

Vlad rolled his eyes but continued to stroll beside me. "So, did you hear about that three-headed dog in Noe last week?"

"No," I said quickly, stepping into the elevator.

My apartment is a little more than six blocks away from the San Francisco Police Department/Underworld Detection Agency offices, but this being the Bay Area, six blocks on foot equaled twenty-five minutes in the car. By the time I pulled into my apartment building's underground parking garage the vein over my left eye was throbbing—whether it was from the midafternoon stop-and-go or from very nearly running down a clutch of tourists wearing I ESCAPED ALCATRAZ sweatshirts, I wasn't sure. Either way, I knew psychologically that there were only two things that could help the kind of day I was having, so a good forty-five seconds after pushing the key into the lock at my second-story walk-up, I had a bottle of chardonnay in one hand and a package of marsh-mallow Pinwheels in the other. The surge of chocolate and alcohol helped but not enough, so I beelined for the bathroom, filling my mouth with cookies and peeling my clothes off as I went.

I drew a bath as hot as I could stand it and upturned a bottle of cucumber-melon bath goo under the tap. Then I positioned my wineglass next to the remaining marsh-mallow Pinwheels and eased myself into the tub.

"Ahh," I moaned, closing my eyes, breathing in the heady scent of cucumber and chocolate as the hot water washed over me. "Much better."

I dunked a washcloth, wrung it out, and placed it over my eyes, then sipped contentedly at my wine. I was reaching out for another Pinwheel cookie when I heard the rustle of cellophane and felt a cold prickle of fear creep up my neck, despite the hot water. I stiffened and froze, arm outstretched, palm upward.

Someone placed a Pinwheel in my open hand and I sat bolt upright in the tub, the washcloth falling from my eyes, the poor Pinwheel reduced to chocolaty, marshmal-low ooze as I gripped it. Bits of bathwater-doused marsh-mallow dripped through my fingers.

"Didn't mean to scare you," Alex said, perched on the side of my tub, his pincher finger and thumb hovering above my half-empty Pinwheel package. "May I?"

Alex Grace was gooey, chocolaty goodness if ever there was. And he had disappeared without a word six months ago.

I felt my eyes bulge and the speedup of my heart was so immediate it hurt. "Alex?" My tone was that rare mix of Christmas-morning excitement, beautiful-man proximity, and ex-boyfriend angst. I felt the burn of anger, the hurt of loss, and the wild rush of pure animal attraction as Alex Grace looked down at me, Pinwheel held aloft, luscious pink-tinged lips pushed up in the cocky half-smile I had started to remember in my dreams.

He was an angel—of the fallen sort—with sky-blue eyes and hair the color of dark chocolate, swirling in wondrous, luxurious curls over his forehead, snaking over ears just perfect for nibbling. He had the high cheekbones and feather-long lashes that women would do naughty things for, and the square jaw and puckered pink lips that could do naughty things. His build was fairly slight but wrought with wiry, rock-hard muscles that made his jeans look mouthwateringly comfortable, and stretched out the chest and arms of his T-shirts mercilessly.

"What the hell—why are you—" I fluttered and floundered, splashing bits of cucumber melon–scented fluff, chocolate pieces, and bathwater all around. Alex just grinned that familiar half-smile that I found so annoyingly erotic; he crossed his arms and relaxed against my towel rack, clearly enjoying my spastic discomfort. That angered me even more so I worked to get my panicked breathing under control. Alex and I had shared some steamy moments and every glance or touch of his skin electrified me. This moment was no exception—but he was bad news. Fallen angels always are. And his whole disappearing/reappearing thing really got on my last nerve.

And then I realized I was naked.

I sunk lower into the water, pushing the bubbles over my girly bits and glowering at Alex who looked at me, that obnoxious, adorable half-smile still playing on his lips. He helped himself to a cookie.

"What are you doing here?" I snapped.

He chewed thoughtfully. "I needed to talk to you."

"I have a phone. Or an e-mail address. Or, hell, a carrier pigeon. Do you always have to show up in the bathroom?"

"I needed your undivided attention."

I raised an annoyed brow. "Or you needed a naked-lady fix. And did you lose your ability to knock along with your wings?"

He grinned, took a swig from my wineglass. "Ooh." His blue eyes looked up, raked the ceiling. "Is that an oh-eight? It's buttery."

"Get out!" I screamed, pointing a sopping, bubble-laden arm at the bathroom door. "I'm not going to talk to you while I'm naked."

Alex's grin widened. "So you are naked . . . ?"

"I'm in the bathtub," I snarled. "What did you expect?" I was sitting forward now and vaguely aware of the cool air touching my breasts. I hunkered down in the water again. "You're a pervert."

Alex shrugged, finished my wine, and poured himself some more. "Hey, I'm no angel."

I rolled my eyes and snatched my wineglass out of his hand. "Get out."

Alex's eyes went puppy-dog round. "I still need to talk to you."

I held my ground, though it wasn't easy; my heart—with its sudden, mile-a-minute beat—was betraying me. "And I still need you to get out."

"Can I have another cookie?"

That did it.

"Out!"

Once Alex was safely on the other side of the bath-room door I slipped out of the tub, hastily dried off, and wrapped myself in my sky-blue bathrobe. I flounced my hair a bit and patted my cheeks, hoping to get a sem-blance of that innocent-girl pink in my cheeks; instead I had the bright red imprint of my own hands. I swiped on some Sugar Kiss lip gloss in hopes that sexy, glossy lips would detract from my cheeks. I was tightening the belt and padding into the kitchen when I was treated to a view of Alex's rump poking out of my fridge.

"Can I help you with something?" I asked his butt.

Alex backed out of the fridge, frowning. "There's nothing in here to eat. Are there any more Pinwheels?"

I crossed my arms in front of my chest. "No. I threw them away." *Threw them down my throat was more like it.*

I nudged Alex aside and peered into the fridge, coming out with a half loaf of cracked-wheat bread and a stack of Polaroid-thin cheese slices. "Grilled cheese?"

"Tres gourmet."

"You'd better believe it."

Alex handed me a frying pan and got to work butter-ing the bread.

I slowly peeled a piece of cheese, careful to keep my eyes away from Alex, lest my bathrobe fall off or I find myself climbing him like a stepladder. "So, what are you doing here anyway? I mean here, here." I pointed with a spatula to the floor. "In this realm. In my kitchen."

Alex peeled the filmy cellophane from a piece of cheese and crumpled it in his hand, popping the cheese ball in his mouth.

"Go ahead," I said. "Make yourself at home."

Alex gave me a sarcastic smile and snagged a couple of beers from the fridge. He opened them both, then handed one over, clinked mine, and took a long pull. I did the same.

"Can't a guy just pop in to talk to a friend?"

The word *friend* sent my hackles up, but I pretended it was from a draft and tightened the belt on my robe.

"A guy could. You couldn't."

Alex shrugged, smiled, and remained quiet.

"Okay, what do you want to talk about?"

Alex wasted no time. He put down his beer and looked at me, cobalt eyes piercing and suddenly serious. I pretended not to notice. "I need your help," he said simply.

I raised my eyebrows. "Is that so?"

"Remember when I told you about the Vessel?"

"The Vessel of Souls? The one that got you banned from Heaven? Stripped of your wings? That Vessel?"

Alex pursed his lips in annoyance. "Are you through?"

I sniffed. "I guess. What about it?"

"I need to find it."

"I know that. But why now? And why do you suddenly need me to help?"

Alex let out a long sigh. "The Vessel of Souls houses all human souls that are in limbo. If the fallen angels get their hands on it they can take over everything: the angelic plane, the human plane—even the Underworld. We need to keep the Vessel out of the hands of the fallen."

I looked at Alex. "You're fallen. Why should I help you get it?"

"You know that if I can restore the balance of the planes and get the Vessel back, I can get my wings restored. I'm not going to jeopardize that . . . again."

I picked up the spatula again, used it to peek underneath my sandwich. "And you need me why?"

Alex raised his eyebrows expectantly and I flipped the sandwich, sighing. "Because the Vessel is charmed," I said, answering my own question.

"Even the angelic plane uses magic. They like to hide things in plain sight."

"Really?"

Alex nodded and took a swig from his bottle. "Yeah. Last I heard the Holy Grail was actually a tanning bed in Manhattan Beach."

I narrowed my eyes at Alex's little-boy grin. "Really, Lawson. You're the only one I know who will be able to see through the charm."

Along with my superior pizza-eating and state-reciting powers, I am also magically immune. My grandmother was a seer, my mother was a mind-melder, and my specialty? Nothing. In a good way. Nothing magical can be used on me. Veils, charms, spells, happy endings—anything that could be conjured, wanded, or abracadab-raed was lost on me. The magical immunity helped working in the Underworld. The occasional fire-breathing dragon singe or High witch explosion rolled off me like water off a duck's back. Warlocks couldn't use glamour spells to make me fall in love with them and give them extra magiks freedoms or process their paperwork any faster, and I could share a cup of coffee with Medusa and stay perfectly, humanly pink.

I flipped the second sandwich onto a plate and handed it to Alex.

"Okay," I said. "Where do we start?"

Chapter Two

I was sprawled on the couch, eating the peanut-butter part of a peanut butter and jelly sandwich when I heard the lock tumble and Nina walked in, dropping her shoulder bag in a heap. Vlad loped in behind her, his shoulders slumped in his black velvet sport coat, earbuds securely clipped in his ears, iPod turned up so loud we could hear the white-noise whir of his music.

"Turn that crap down!" Nina snarled.

Vlad rolled his eyes and snatched his laptop from the kitchen table, then slunk off to the fire escape.

Nina wagged her head as she looked after him, then rubbed her temples. "I just don't know what I'm going to do with him." Though Vlad was technically one hundred and thirteen, he was forever sixteen.

He poked his head back into the living room and eyed Nina and me. "Do we have any of that AB negative left?"

Moody, grunty, hungry sixteen.

"Check the fridge," Nina said to Vlad without taking her eyes off me. "You look like you've seen a ghost," she said to me with a frown.

Nina was my coworker, my roommate, and my very best friend. She was ballerina slim and elegantly tall, with waist-length gorgeous black hair that tumbled over her defined shoulders and highlighted her deep, coal-black eyes. She was the kind of friend I could tell anything to, the kind of girl who always took your side, would stay up nights sharing secrets with you.

And also, she was dead.

Well, undead.

Nina was a one hundred and sixty-eight-year-old vampire and had the pale complexion, penchant for type O neg, and the pointed incisors to prove it.

She was born—the first time—in 1842 and as a twenty-nine-year-old party-girl heiress, she climbed out her bedroom window one night to meet a dark-eyed stranger. Three days and two punctured arteries later, she caused the massacre of the Elpistones army. That was a long time ago and her bloodlust had long ago subsided, being replaced by an insatiable urge for high-end couture. Tonight she was wearing a vintage Guy Laroche cocktail dress with a pair of nosebleed-high leather boots, paired with an Old Navy hoodie and a felt cloche hat. She looked like a page out of *Vogue*; in the same outfit, I would have looked like a college kid on laundry day.

"No ghosts," I said, still studying my sandwich. "Alex."

Nina sat down with a start on the coffee table. "Alex Grace?" She whipped her head around. "Where is he? Is he here now? I want to kick that son of a bitch's—" She paused. "Unless you're back together, then we should all go out and get drinks." She grinned, her small fangs pressing against her bloodstained lips.

I clicked off the TV. "He wants my help."

Nina's eyebrows shot up. "Another mystery? Ooh, I want in." She clapped her hands. "What's going on now? Murder? Mayhem? General mystical unruliness?"

"Heaven stuff."

"Boo." Nina cocked her head, considering. "Well, I guess that could be fun. So, where's Alex now?"

I shrugged. "Wherever angels go when they're not here. Or, back to the police station. I don't know."

Being a fallen angel came with all sorts of otherworld perks, but it didn't come with a paycheck. To keep himself in cloud pillows and ambrosia (okay, beer and pizza), Alex kept his bank account padded with occasional work with the San Francisco Police Department. To them he was an undercover FBI field agent whose long disappearances were chalked up to hush-hush cases in the field; to me he was just annoyingly undependable.

Currently, San Francisco was Alex's home base. His paychecks and credit card bills went to an apartment he kept in the Richmond district; I happened to notice the address on a piece of mail that was inadvertently left in my apartment (after it fell out of Alex's office). When I happened to drive by the Turk Street address, I found it was an empty storefront with newspaper-covered windows and a heap of Target ads and Safeway circulars jammed in the mail slot. I hadn't gotten around to asking Alex about his fake address—mainly because he never asked me if I'd stolen any of his mail.

"I just don't know if I want to get involved," I said.

At one time I had considered Alex and my dead/undead relationship passionate and romantically star-crossed; now I considered it hopelessly dead-end.

Mostly.

There was something about his sexy half-smile, his lush, pink-tinged lips, and my dating drought that made me swoon in a way that brought a blush to my cheeks, a tingle to my nether regions, and made me deeply consider the benefit of one-night stands.

I readjusted myself on the couch and tried to remind myself that losing Alex the first time was gut-wrenchingly, Lifetime-television bad. I didn't know if I could—or wanted to—go through it again.

Nina cocked her head, picked a glob of jelly off the lapel of my bathrobe. "You mean because you're so busy here."

I tried to glare. "I mean I'm not sure if I want to get involved with Alex again. The last year has been so . . ." I let the word trail off and tried to avoid Nina's annoyed stare as self-pity ballooned in my chest.

"The last year has been so what? Ordinary? You may not have been hung up by your ankles lately, but you've also managed to watch the entire seven seasons of *The Golden Girls* multiple times. And"—Nina held up a single index finger—"you've alphabetized our spice rack. Twice. If that's not a body calling out for a little extracurricular activity, I don't know what is."

I remained unconvinced—and gun shy. I had fallen hook, line, and sinker for Alex's baby blues once, and after a few steamy scenes he disappeared for six months without a word. When I finally got over the heartbreak and stopped listening to mopey love songs, Alex popped back into my life—this time, with bad news.

"It's not like the relationship is going to go anywhere. He wants to go—" I paused, looking for the right word. "Back." I sighed miserably. "Last I heard Heaven-to-Earth long-distance relationships didn't ever pan out too well."

"So it's destined to be a dead-end relationship?"

I nodded.

"Even more reason to jump in with both feet and no panties on!"

I licked some peanut butter off my index finger and blew out a tortured sigh. "Why even bother if you know a relationship is doomed from the get-go? It's just asking for heartbreak."

"And a few steamy months of hot, sweaty monkey love."

I raised my eyebrows.

Nina stuck out her tongue. "Oh, come on. All my relationships are doomed. Or damned. Besides, just working with the guy isn't going to get you all hot and bothered. Is it?"

I avoided Nina's gaze but couldn't avoid the telltale blush that crept over my cheeks.

"Slut!" I eyed Nina's gleeful face and she rolled her eyes. "Really, Sophie. What's there to be worried about? He's a lovely specimen of manhood; you're a museum-quality specimen of undersexed womanhood. Don't they say—what is it?—better to have gotten a little and lost, than never to have gotten a little at all."

"Poetic."

Nina poked her foot in between the couch cushion and wiggled her toes underneath my backside. "Whew. Just checking. Wanted to make sure you and the couch weren't sharing a bloodline. Ooh, that reminds me, I'm hungry."

I swatted Nina's foot away and stood up. "You suck."

"It's what we do." She grinned. "So we're helping?"

I pursed my lips. "He's coming over tomorrow night."

I watched as Nina's libido-meter went up to her ears. "We'll have to go to Victoria's Secret at lunch."

"It's purely a business meeting," I said. And then, with a quick lick of my lips, "For now."

Nina grinned and socked me in the shoulder. "That's my slutty friend."

I rolled my eyes and Nina prattled on. "We need to get all our excitement in while we can. This is just between you and me, but I heard that the new UDA management will be in place soon."

"Hey! That was supposed to be between me and Lorraine!"

Nina tugged her ear "Vampire perk. It's not like I can turn off the supersonic hearing."

I glared and she relented. "Okay, fine. Just between you and me and Lorraine. And Vlad. And the operations staff. And I guess some of the VERMers. Anyway, I'm going to find out everything I can about this new management guy. I have worked too long and too hard to let some new demon come in and tell me how to do my job."

I grinned, both at Nina's stern determination and her belief that she worked either long or hard.

The next morning I was out the door before Nina came home from her night out. I hurried to my favorite Philz Coffee and let the scent of roasted beans and caffeine wash over me when I pulled open the door. By the time I got to the front of the line, the warm, comforting feeling of coffee and croissants was replaced by the eerie feeling that I was being watched.

While most women would get the "someone's watching me" feeling and scan the room for the hot barista or the well-dressed businessman giving her the eye, this was *my* life, which meant my first reaction was to search for a fire-breathing dragon, homicidal vamp wannabe, or a three-foot-high troll hell-bent on making me his wife. Oddly enough, it was none of the above. The staff and clientele of Philz was above-ground normal—dog walkers with rolls of plastic poop bags sticking out of their pockets, pseudo-exercise gurus in track suits and pristine Coach sneakers, businessmen with slick striped ties and impeccable hair. No one seemed to be paying me any mind, but I still couldn't shake the feeling. My whole body hummed with an uncomfortable awareness, and when the barista asked again to take my order I jumped, then bit my lip and offered him a shy smile.

"Sorry, I just . . ."

The barista seemed far more interested in the blond woman behind me so I forwent the explanation and ordered my coffee, then offered him a crumpled bill. I shuffled to the end of the bar and waited for my drink, the awkward, uncomfortable feeling not waning.

"Customer service is really not his strong point," the guy beside me said, nudging his head of ash-blond hair toward the barista.

I jumped, and the guy grinned, his smile wide and comforting. "Tell me you're getting a decaf," he said, his English accent clipping his words.

I felt a blush creep over my cheeks. "I'm sorry, I guess I'm a little jumpy. And it's a vanilla latte, full caff, so . . ."

"So I guess they'll be scraping you off the ceiling by lunchtime." The guy picked up his coffee, gave me a friendly head nod, and zigzagged through the crowded coffeehouse. When he turned, I noticed the back of his well-fitting navy-blue T-shirt had the red and white San Francisco Fire Department logo on it.

When the barista handed over my cup, I took my coffee and pushed out of the shop. I looked over my shoulder hoping for a second glance at the fire guy, but the blond woman who was behind me in line was blocking my line of sight. She was staring at me through the plate-glass window, her face half-obscured by the lid of her takeout cup as she sipped slowly. Finally, she pulled the cup away from her face and grinned at me, a dazzling, beatific smile that shook me right to the bone.

* * *

I pushed open the door to Nina's office and slumped into her visitor's chair, balancing my Philz cup in my hand.

"So, I just had a weird experience."

Nina raised her eyebrows, dropping her sparkly Hannah Montana pen. "Demon weird or mortal weird?"

"Mortal, I guess, but you never really can be sure anymore."

"So you say," Nina quipped. "What happened?"

I filled Nina in on my non-run-in with the blonde, and how the heebie-jeebie feeling of discomfort was just now beginning to subside. Nina listened intently, drumming her fingers on her desk, then chewing the end of her pen. I winced when her left fang pierced Hannah Montana's smiling face.

"I have no idea why it bothered me so much, Nina," I explained. "She just smiled. A friendly, nice smile and it was like I had been hit in the head with a sledgehammer. It was weird." I shuddered. "Beyond weird."

Nina dropped her pen, then steepled her fingers psychologist style. "She was probably an old friend from college who recognized you or something. Or, you probably stand in front of her at Philz like, every day and just noticed her now. Or"—Nina waggled her eyebrows salaciously—"she totally has the hots for you and has been stalking you for ages, and is just waiting to bonk you over the head and drag you back to her chick cave."

I frowned and Nina sighed. "Really, Sophie, you're being too paranoid, even for you. You act like every time Alex comes into your life, the world becomes full of goblins or gooblygooks all out to get you."

I rolled my eyes and downed the last of my coffee, tossing the empty into Nina's trashcan. "Who—or *what*-

ever she was, she gave me the heebie-jeebies. And then when I turned around again, she was gone."

"Ooh, spooky. A woman gets her coffee and then mysteriously leaves the coffee shop afterward. How chillingly bizarre."

"Remind me again why we're friends?" I asked.

"Because I pay half the rent and you can't kill me." Nina grinned, her fangs pressed against her lower lip. "So what happened after that? Oh, let me guess—you found Excalibur in your blueberry scone?"

"Fine. Then I won't tell you that I ran into a hot fireman."

Nina dropped her pen and her eyes went big and round. I thought I saw a bit of drool at the side of her mouth. "A fireman? Really?" Her eyes narrowed. "I love firemen. They taste so smoky and good."

I sighed. "And that's why I can't have breather friends."

Nina frowned. "You act like I eat everyone I meet." She brightened. "Now, do you want to hear my news?"

I held up my hands, resigned. "Do I have a choice?"

"Of course not." She stood up and closed the door softly. I grinned at the 1950s-style strapless satin cocktail dress that she wore over a Smelly Mel's T-shirt and topped with a beaded black bolero. She walked noiselessly on Manolo Blahnick cutout stilettos that I know cost more than my car. "I heard about the new staff. They're going to be here later this afternoon."

I leaned forward in my seat. "There's a whole staff? I thought it was just one guy."

Nina shook her head. "Nope. Latest intel says it's a whole staff."

"Intel?"

"Pierre overheard it in the restroom."

"So it's reliable."

Nina nodded.

I sat back, considering. "Wow. So, what did you hear?"

Nina sat on the edge of her desk. "Well, first of all, they're pro-vamp."

"Really?"

She nodded. "Yeah, from what I heard, the new management team is actually all vamp. All men, too, I think."

"You must be in seventh heaven."

Nina looked stunned. "Are you kidding? Vamp men can be such control freaks. And they are so twelfth century when it comes to women in the workplace! Mark my words: This new head-honcho guy thinks he's going to have all the women here wrapped around his bloodless little finger. No way. I'm going to let him *think* he's the boss and then show him who's really in charge here."

"And I'm guessing that would be you?"

"Of course it's me!" Nina exploded. "If that vamp thinks I'm going to give him one extra inch"—she held her thumb and forefinger the appropriate distance apart—"well then, he's got another thing coming."

"Noted," I said, pushing open the office door. "Whoa!"

A swarm of UDA employees ambled down the hall outside Nina's office door. Nina poked her head over my shoulder and frowned. "What's going on?"

Pierre, our resident centaur/file clerk, paused in front of us. "Didn't you hear? Staff meeting. They're introducing the new management."

Nina and I shared an eyebrows-up glance. "Really? Already?"

I stepped out into the crowd and Nina followed behind me, hiking up the green satin skirt on her evening gown so she showed an extra inch of firm, pale thigh.

"I thought you were against wrapping people and things around fingers."

Nina grinned salaciously, repositioning her breasts. "I

said he couldn't wrap *me* around his little finger. I didn't say anything about what I'd wrap him around."

I giggled and linked arms with Nina. We stepped into the demon stream, found Lorraine in the crowd, and glommed on to her.

"So, is there a big announcement or just an intro?" I wanted to know.

Lorraine shrugged, her thin shoulders dusting the bottoms of her dangly jade earrings. "I don't know, but I heard reorg."

Nina and I gulped.

"I swear, if I get moved to licensing, I am so out of here." Lorraine's emerald eyes were wide and defiant—with just a hint of worry.

Licensing was the bane of the UDA employee's existence. The licensing department handled all new demon breeds, half-breeds, and cross breeds, plus was the dumping ground for newly made vampires, werevamps, and werewolves. Newcomers—licensed or otherwise—had the tendency to fly off the handle, testing their new powers in weird and damaging ways, which was why the licensing department had an unlimited budget for new waiting-room chairs, curtains, and carpets, since they were set on fire, chewed, or torn on a regular basis.

"You're accounts receivable. There is no way the new management is going to demote you to licensing," I told her.

"I don't know," Lorraine said, hugging herself with crossed arms. "I heard these guys are pretty shrewd. They really like to shake things up."

"Please," Nina said, checking her eternally perfect cuticles. "You've got nothing to worry about. I have been through so many reorgs. Hell, most of these guys have no idea what they're doing anyway. They'll bring in a couple of old buddies from their pre-vamp college days,

add a few big-busted breather girls for fang candy, and
fire the mail guy so it looks like they're doing something." Nina yawned as if the whole situation bored her.
"We're probably dealing with some pasty, round, Pillsbury dough-vamp on a power trip. Small penis, big car,
everything back to Hell-on-Earth normal in five days,
guaranteed."

"I hope you're right," Lorraine said, rubbing her arms.

"Shh," I hissed. "Here they come."

The whole of the staff straightened as the back-office
doors slid open and the new head of the UDA stepped
out, flanked on either side by well-dressed henchmen
whose dark eyes scanned the assembled crowd, their
faces betraying nothing.

One of the henchmen stepped forward, straightening
his impeccable tie. He leaned against the podium,
cleared his throat into the microphone. "Ladies and gen-
tlemen, please welcome Mr. Dixon Andrade."

There was a smattering of polite applause as Dixon
stepped forward, looking all at once politician slick and
businessman savvy.

To say Dixon was a commanding presence was an
understatement. He was at least six feet tall with strong
swimmer's shoulders and a long, lean body that gave the
impression of careful control. His longish brown hair
was carefully slicked back from a wide forehead that was
punctuated by thick, dark eyebrows that seemed very
comfortably formed into a constant V of consternation
and distaste. His pale skin was taut and perfect; his
square jaw was set hard but offset by ruby red lips that
were pressed into a thin line as he surveyed the UDA
staff. Suddenly, his lips broke into a welcoming grin, and
a slight hint of color washed over his cheeks.

"So this is the San Francisco staff of the Underworld
Detection Agency. Nice-looking group of demons."

Dixon nodded slowly, appraisingly, as the crowd hummed, pleased. I just swallowed and did my best to fade into the background.

It's not that I was any way ashamed of my non-demon status, nor was it much of a secret around the office—I tended to stick out like a sore thumb, as I routinely bypassed the freeze-dried blood in the office vending machine and opted for the Rice Krispies Treats and Kit Kat bars. I just considered that until the new management got to know me, it might be best to blend into the whole of the group—which is not that easy, considering the majority of the group sported horns, fangs, or hooves. I sported a dress with a slobber stain and a Swatch watch.

"Now I know a lot of you might be worried about a so-called shake-up around here. I am here today to put you all at ease. I know my predecessor, Pete Sampson, ran a tight ship around here and you all have the profit margins"—Dixon held a thick stack of documents aloft—"to prove it."

A whoosh of relief whipped through the crowd and suddenly the UDA employees were showing signs of everyday life: Pierre was shifting from hoof to hoof, bored. Kale, the mega-pierced apprentice witch to Lorraine was batting her eyes at Nina's nephew Vlad, who was working hard to ignore her. Eliot, a newly hired werevamp was nonchalantly texting on his iPhone.

"Now, now," Dixon went on, pale palms up to appease the crowd. "That doesn't mean there won't be *some* changes. Nothing drastic, I assure you. But I do want to get a feel for what you all *do* around here." Dixon stressed certain words like an overly sincere politician. I didn't warm to him.

"I want to know *you,* your job descriptions, what a day in the life is like for *you* as a UDA employee." Dixon flashed a brilliant grin, his teeth impossibly white, his incisors sharpened to terrifying points. I felt my eyebrows shoot up and I stole a glance over at Nina.

Her eyebrows were raised, too; her dark eyes were wide as saucers and transfixed—but it wasn't the surprise of seeing a pair of sharpened fangs.

It was love.

Pure, unadulterated, "I'd follow you anywhere, Dixon Andrade" love.

"Aw, geez," I muttered under my breath. "Nina!"

She was leaning forward on her toes, her sky-high Manolo Blahniks raising her up four inches already. Her hands were clasped in front of her heart and every inch of her was still, waiting, watching, like a cat ready to pounce.

"He. Is. Beautiful," she said, her voice coming out high-pitched and breathy.

"I intend to get to know each and every one of you, and to do that"—Dixon's eyes scanned the crowd—"I am hoping to enlist the help of the Underworld Detection Agency's human resources staff."

Nina thrust her chest out with so much pride that I thought her rib cage would come sputtering out of her. She offered a brilliant, toothy grin—her fangs not nearly as spiked as Dixon's—and raised one thin arm, waving proudly, Nadia Comaneci-winning-the-gold style. I felt myself cringe, and I was vaguely concerned that Nina might explode with a supernatural combination of horniness and joy.

"I am thrilled to be of service, Mr. Andrade," Nina purred, her voice a sweet, tender pitch that was usually reserved for puppy dogs and enormous favors.

I leaned forward, whispering in Nina's ear, "I thought he was a useless Pillsbury dough-vamp?"

Nina looked at me incredulously. "Can't you see? He's brilliant!" Nina's eyes went from stunned wonder to naked want. I thought I saw a drop of saliva teeter on her lower lip.

"I will have . . ." Dixon frowned, scanned his stack of papers "Nina, is it?"

Nina nodded with all the restraint of a bobblehead on a dashboard.

"Nina will be scheduling one-on-one interviews with me, which will commence immediately. And with that, the Underworld Detection Agency is ready for business. Demons, man your stations!"

The crowd slowly began to dissipate, a low chorus of grumbles with them, but Nina stood perched, erect, her small hands clapping spastically. "Wonderful speech, Mr. Andrade, just—motivating!" she said.

Dixon grinned at her as he stepped down from the podium and patted Nina gingerly on the shoulder. "You can call me Dixon, Nina."

Again, Nina's chest puffed and I vaguely wondered how that was possible, given that the woman hadn't taken a breath in over a hundred years.

Dixon's brown eyes set on me and I was entranced by the flecks of gold that danced in them. Though my magical immunity rendered me untouchable by the usual glamours that vampires use to mesmerize humans, I wasn't above falling under the spell of a good-looking man—undead or otherwise.

"I don't believe we've met," Dixon said in his satin-sleek voice. He extended a slim, pale hand. "Dixon Andrade. And you are?"

I took his hand, the bloodless cold of his palm going all the way up to my shoulder. "I'm Sophie Lawson," I said, pumping his arm.

"Sophie Lawson," Dixon drew out the words, seemed to savor my name on his tongue. A knowing look flitted across his sharp features. "You were Mr. Sampson's executive assistant, were you not?"

"That's right."

"And she was wonderful with Mr. Sampson," Nina said, butting in between Dixon and me. "He was absolutely crazy about her."

Dixon raised one black eyebrow and Nina licked her lips. "In a purely professional way."

Dixon nodded slowly, his eyes still on me. "Good to know. And lovely to meet you, Sophie. I'll be seeing you around and looking forward to our interview."

"Likewise," I said, my voice sounding thin and weak as Dixon nodded to Nina, then turned on his heel, his henchmen following closely behind him.

"Oh. My. God," Nina said when Dixon was out of earshot. "I thought I was going to explode."

I stepped back. "Well, don't do it anywhere near me."

"Do you not think that Dixon Andrade is downright yummy? I mean, look at him!" Nina gestured wildly as Dixon got smaller and smaller as he headed down one of UDA's long hallways. "That is some delicious vamp candy!"

I crossed my arms. "I suppose he's pretty hot. If you're into that hot, good-looking, brooding type."

"With a smile that could melt butter!"

And fangs that could cut glass. "I guess he's okay," I finished.

Chapter Three

The plastic bag loaded with takeout Chinese was cutting off the circulation in my fingertips as I tried to shift my stuff—coat, laptop case, purse—and get my key into the lock. After four tries and an impressive show of inner-thigh muscle as I clenched the sliding bags between my knees, I got the apartment door open, grunting the whole time but managing to keep the mu shu upright. I dropped everything—except the takeout bag—in a heap on the floor when I saw what greeted me: a living room full of vampires, their faces pale and perfect, eyes narrowed, bee-stung lips full and dyed blood red. The house was in disarray and little droplets of blood spattered the coffee table, along with discarded bits of clothing and glasses knocked on their sides, plasma starting to congeal inside. Despite the blood on their lips, these vampires looked hungry. I blew out a sigh.

"Really, Vlad?"

Vlad sprung up from the flower-print easy chair and strode across the room toward me. His cold fingers chilled my arm as he steered me into the hall.

"We're having an Empowerment meeting."

"You didn't tell me you guys have become the Slob Empowerment Movement."

"Geez, Sophie, you're as bad as Aunt Nina. I'll clean up when we're done. Promise."

"Good. I have a meeting, too." I swung the takeout bag in front of him.

"Another meeting of the Mu Shu Pork Society?" Vlad asked, crossing his arms and jutting out one hip.

I narrowed my eyes. "Just clean it up. You didn't tell me you guys were meeting here today."

"Do I have to tell you everything?"

I held my glare steady.

Vlad fluffed up his ascot. "We were chased out of the UDA by Lorraine. We need a place to meet. The Empowerment Movement is currently only in its infantile stages, so this is when we are most in need of a nurturing environment." He smiled, a sweet, boyish smile that reminded me of the earnest kid he must have been—back in the eighteen hundreds or so.

"Shouldn't you be meeting in a cemetery or something?"

Vlad's eyes widened. "Do you know one with mausoleum space?"

"Look, just wrap it up and give me fair warning the next time you plan on bringing the fang gang around." I looked over his shoulder, eyeing the assembled vamps as they flipped through magazines and stuck skinny straws into their blood bags, à la Capri Sun. "You know I'm pro-vamp and I support the movement," I glanced back at Vlad's ascot and black-painted fingernails. "At least most of it. But Alex and I have some important business to discuss tonight."

"The angel is back?"

Vlad's eyebrows went up, but I stopped him before he

could comment. "Yes. But this is just business—another case. So, can you wrap it up?"

"Geez," Vlad said with an eye roll. "I can't wait until I get my own place."

"Not until you're two hundred," I muttered parentally as I followed him back into the apartment.

I set my bag down and nodded—graciously, though nervously—to Vlad's vampire friends as they gathered up their trash and filed out the front door, Vlad in tow. I gave them a polite finger wave and then raced to the bathroom, telling myself that I was freshening up as a polite hostess and nothing more as I dabbed on a drywall layer of deodorant and slapped on some Siena Sunset lip stain. I undid the bun on the top of my head and my hair fell in soft, curled tendrils that swooped romantically around my face and stuck up like wheat grass in the back. I spent the next eight minutes pleading with said wheat-grass hair and finally finagled it in a downward direction with a handful of centuries-old Dippity-do that I found in the back of the medicine cabinet.

Deeming myself cosmetically presentable, I went back to the kitchen and unloaded the armful of takeout containers onto the dining room table, trying to arrange them artfully. If I couldn't cook, the least I could do was arrange takeout beautifully. I finished off my Hang chow bounty with a meager-looking daisy stuck in a water glass. Not exactly The Slanted Door, but it would do.

I sucked in an anxious breath when I heard the lock tumble on the front door. My heart gave a little pitter of warmth that dropped down into my nether regions and I imagined myself gripping Alex by the lapels and dragging him into the living room, lip to passionate lip. Instead, I crossed my legs and forced myself to look nonchalant.

"Oh," I sighed when I opened the door. "It's you."

Nina gave me a sour look. "Nice way to greet your roommate."

I wrung my hands. "It's just that I was expecting Alex."

Nina gaped. "Don't tell me you gave him a key now, too!"

I wagged my head and Nina arched an eyebrow. "I thought you weren't sure you were interested in getting involved with him again."

"What are you talking about? We're just two old friends meeting for dinner."

Nina sniffed at the air. "Hang chow?" She sniffed again. "And you sprang for the prawns chow fun."

"I like prawns."

Nina squinted and pointed at my pursed lips. "And that's Siena Sunset. That's name-brand product. You don't shell out for shrimp and name-brand product for someone you're not getting involved with. I bet you even shaved your legs."

I bit my lip—whoops.

I sighed, a meager attempt to center myself. "I'm not exactly getting involved. I'm helping him with a case." *And possibly out of his clothes.* . . . I put my hands on my hips. "And I thought you were anti-Alex."

"I'm not anti-Alex. I'm pro-love. You'd be surprised how pro-love one becomes when they're not getting enough blood to their personal parts."

"So love is all about what gets to your personal parts?"

Nina licked her lips and winked. "Honey, love can be about anything having to do with the personal parts."

"Silly me. I thought it was about the heart and all that malarkey."

Nina waved a dismissive hand, twisting her glossy dark hair around her finger. "Eh, it's all the same after a while." She yanked open the fridge door and rooted around for a blood bag, then pulled herself up onto the kitchen counter and kicked off her shoes, aiming them into the dining room.

"So"—she took a long sip that crumpled her blood bag—"back to you and Alex."

"A case," I reiterated. "That's all this is about. Shrimp chow fun, name-brand lip gloss—which was a free sample by the way—and that's it. Just a case." I was talking so loudly I was beginning to convince myself. "He's coming over so we can discuss the particulars."

"Discuss the particulars?" Nina's lips went into a sleazy half-grin. "Something tells me I know the particulars you're interested in. . . ."

"Uh, hello?"

Alex was standing in the open doorway, head cocked, eyebrows raised. I sucked in a traumatic breath, my body not knowing whether to die of embarrassment or of sheer desire.

Tonight, Alex Grace looked good enough to eat.

His pale grey T-shirt looked soft and was fraying a little at the collar. It stretched across his broad shoulders and the short sleeves were pulled taut against his thick, ropey muscles. His arms were crossed and the bottom edge of his tattoo—a single angel's wing—poked out from underneath the fabric covering his left bicep. I worked hard to keep my eyes welcoming and friendly, but they kept slipping to Alex's slim waist, to the way his well-worn jeans hung on him, and visions of him stepping out of those jeans clouded my "friendly" stance.

Alex held up a six-pack of beer and stepped into the apartment, kicking the door shut behind him. The click of the door and the clink of the beer bottles shook me out of my revelry.

"Hi. Nina and I, we were just . . ."

There was a playful look of knowing in Alex's eyes and I felt the heat of embarrassment wash over me. I looked down and went to work opening the beer, certain that my face was flushed as red as a midlife-crisis Corvette.

"So," Nina began, "Sophie tells me there's another mystery to be solved. Count me in."

"Great." Alex walloped the backpack I didn't realize he was carrying onto the dining-room table, making the Chinese food and my pitiful flower jump.

I handed Alex his beer, our fingertips brushing in the exchange. My stomach did a little butterfly flutter and I took a quick pull from my beer, gulping a mouthful of foam.

"Is that mu shu?" Alex asked, sniffing at the air.

"Yes," I said. Then I pointed at the backpack. "Is that your homework?"

Alex took a pair of chopsticks and the takeout box of mu shu. "I guess it's our homework."

Nina frowned. "There's going to be reading in this one? I don't know if I want to play anymore." She pierced her blood bag with a single angled fang, sucked earnestly on what remained and then looked up, her full lips stained a deep red. "What are we after, anyway?"

"The Vessel of Souls," Alex said in between bites.

I took my own takeout box and chopsticks and dug into some Kung Pao. "Hey, how do we even know the Vessel is here anyway? Shouldn't it be like, in Europe—like Vatican City or something?"

Nina looked up from her second blood bag, eyebrows raised. "Rome? Okay, I'm back in."

"The Vessel is definitely here. I'm sure of it."

"Is your angel sense tingling?" I asked.

A flash of darkness skittered across Alex's cobalt eyes and his smile dropped. "I know it's here because Ophelia is here."

I felt like I had been kicked in the stomach. Alex and I weren't exclusive or even dating, really—and I had no idea where he went when he wasn't stretched out drinking a beer on my couch or eating day-old donuts at the police station—but I still felt a sudden, illogical pang of jealousy.

"Who's Ophelia?" *Please say your mother, please say your mother, please say your mother*, I silently prayed.

"Ophelia is a fallen angel."

"Like you," Nina said.

"No." Alex shook his head, holding a piece of mu shu pork between poised chopsticks. "Not like me at all. She's currently the head of the fallen and she's very bad news. Evil bad."

I had a faint sliver of hope that her being the head of the fallen meant she was horned or cross-eyed or wore gaucho pants.

"The head of the baddies?" Nina looked impressed. "Who do you have to kill to get that gig?"

Alex looked away. "Ophelia was why I left here—why I left San Francisco—the first time."

I swallowed, not tasting my food. Instead I imagined Alex and his fallen-angel friend Ophelia frolicking on clouds and harmoniously strumming harps while I had spent those solitary six months after he disappeared in elastic-waist pants trolling the ice cream aisle at Cala Foods.

"Oh." My voice came out a choked whisper.

"No—it wasn't—wasn't like that. The word got out that she was looking for me. So I decided I'd better find her first."

"And did you find her?" Nina asked, toes tapping angrily, eyes narrowed in the ultra-protective best-friend mode.

"No."

I felt remotely better. "So why is she here? And why does that mean the Vessel is, too?"

"Ophelia has been tracking the Vessel ever since—" Alex looked down at his hands, ashamed. "Ever since I lost it. She wants it for herself. She's desperate for it—has been the whole time I've known her. Ophelia is the kind of woman who gets off on power. Lots of power." Alex looked at Nina and me. "She'll kill for it. And if she's here, then the Vessel can't be far off."

I felt a breeze—like icy breath—creep up the back of my neck and I shivered. Hollow laughter rang out in my ear and I frowned, going to the kitchen window and scanning for errant, laughing kids. There was nothing but darkness and the occasional sound of horns honking so I slammed the window shut. The breeze went away, but the chill and the sound of laughter hung in my head for another few seconds.

"How do you know she's back here? Have you"—I paused, tasting the bitterness of my words—"seen her?"

Alex wagged his head again, his dark curls bobbing. "No, thank God. But I've heard things. I know she's here."

I swallowed, waiting for the feeling of relief to wash over me. It didn't.

Alex placed a thick file folder flat on the table and pushed it toward me. I glanced down. "Something tells me this isn't the complete files of the Lolcats."

I opened the file and the front page of a week-old *San Francisco Chronicle* was folded neatly on top. The headline blared HUNGARIAN DIPLOMAT AMONG CESSNA DEATHS.

There was a full-color picture of the wreckage of the small plane in a shallow section of the bay; someone had drawn a red circle around a smudge of black on the wing of the plane. "Did you circle this?" I pointed to the smudge and Alex nodded.

"What is it?"

Alex took the file from me and rummaged past a few pages, then pulled out a tattered-looking Ziploc bag with a single black feather locked inside. I raised my eyebrows, squinted back at the circled smudge.

"*That* is that?" I asked skeptically.

"No. This"—Alex dangled the bag—"is from a different crime scene." He pulled a sheaf of papers from the folder and dropped them in front of me. "But that," he said, gesturing toward the circled smudge, "is also a black feather."

Nina stood up. "Are you saying that both of these murders were committed by crows?" She slammed her fist into her palm. "Damn birds!"

I continued looking through the file. "Homicide," I read, flipping through a thin file with another Ziploced black feather enclosed. "Accidental drowning . . . victim was recovered on shore near Crissy Field, DOA, five-inch black feather was—ugh"—I shuddered—"recovered from victim's throat. Murder-suicide in Portola Valley, one dead in fiery crash on Devil's Canyon Slide." I scanned the last article. "Brendan Joel found dead when his car went off the road. . . . Three-to-four-inch black crow feather found in the victim's right hand." I shook my head. "I don't get it. What's with the black feather?"

I held up my hand to silence Nina before she could answer.

"It's like a sign. Every time the angelic plane crosses the human plane—"

Nina crossed her arms in front of her chest. "In non-Heaven speak, please."

"Every time an angel touches a human, something is left behind."

"I don't remember any black feathers," I said.

"I don't have my wings, remember?"

"Well, if Ophelia is a fallen angel, too, how come she's got hers to toss around all crazy?"

Alex's eyes were downcast. "She's embraced the darkness."

"You mean she's playing on Team Satan, right?" Nina asked.

"We try not to mention it."

"So bad-good angels, like you, don't leave anything behind?" I shrugged. "I guess that's good."

Alex took my hand, turned my wrist so it faced upward. There was a tiny red dot—as though from a ballpoint pen—on the pale flesh of my wrist. He smiled; I gawked.

"That's from you?"

He dropped my hand. "You don't have to look entirely disgusted."

"I'm not, it's just—"

"You were expecting a halo burn?"

I put my hands on my hips, tapped my foot angrily on the floor. "No, you make it hard to forget you're a *fallen* angel."

"Just be glad you're not covered with those stupid crow feathers." Nina shuddered. "Birds totally freak me out."

Alex raised an eyebrow. "Doesn't vampire trump fowl?"

"It was a pre-vamp thing," I said, using my hand to partially cover my mouth. "She's still not over it. So, this?" I brushed my index finger over the tiny strawberry-colored spot.

Alex shrugged, suddenly looking slightly bashful. "Yeah, sorry."

"No, it's . . . kind of nice." I felt the blush creep over my cheeks. "Anyway, back to the crime scene."

"And the Vessel."

"And the crow queen."

Alex and I both swung to face Nina, who held her hands palm up and hunched her shoulders. "Sorry, sorry—just trying to help."

I tapped my index finger against my chin. "So, Ophelia comes into town and just starts randomly killing people and that means the Vessel is here? That's weird."

Alex wagged his head. "I don't think they're random."

I fanned out the photographs and newspaper clippings in front of me on the table. "A diplomat, a couple, a teacher . . . some of these are outright murders, some of these look like accidents. I don't get it; what's the connection?"

Alex sank onto one of the dining room chairs and began stacking the photos. "I think they were all guardians."

Nina raised her black brows. "Of who?"

"Not who, what." Alex looked at me. "The Vessel has seven guardians."

"And there are six incidents with Ophelia's trademark," I said.

"She's picking off the guardians?"

I eyed the fat stack. "Apparently, she's pretty good at it. So, where's the last guardian?"

"Lucky number seven?" Alex shrugged. "Don't know. But I plan on finding him before Ophelia does."

"And finding the Vessel."

Nina came and sat at the table with us, leaning closer. "So back to this Ophelia chick. How do you know all this stuff about her?"

I saw the muscle twitch in Alex's jaw. "Ophelia and I had a history."

"Define history," Nina said, one black eyebrow arched.

"Nina!" I hissed, secretly thankful for my best friend's reliable nosiness.

"I'm asking because 'history' could mean a lot of things to people like us." Nina gestured to herself and to Alex. "Like, we used to hit the movies together, or we assisted in overthrowing the Soviet power structure together."

Alex looked at Nina, alarmed.

"She's always had a thing for Russians," I explained. "So, just for clarity's sake, which was it? Dating or . . . history?"

Alex suddenly became very interested in spearing his next bite of dinner. "The first one," he finally murmured.

I swallowed, suddenly very aware of my stomach, of the mu shu pork that sat like a steel fist at the bottom of my gut. I forced a wan smile anyway. "How nice" was all I could muster.

Nina sat back in her chair. "So, this seems pretty cut and dry to me. Ophelia follows the Vessel, we follow Ophelia, nick the Vessel from her, and, bada-bing, bada-bang"—Nina slapped her hands together—"we hightail it to Rome to do some shoe shopping."

"It's not that easy. We need to find the Vessel before Ophelia does. That's the bottom line. Once it's in her hands, this world is as good as over."

"Dramatic."

I glared at Nina and let Alex continue.

"I figure I can hold off Ophelia while you go after the Vessel."

Nina crossed her arms, shaking her head decidedly. "We don't do minion work."

Alex's eyes were set hard as he glanced at Nina and me. "You need to stay away from Ophelia. She's—she's not like anything you've ever seen at the UDA." I opened my mouth to protest, but Alex held up a silencing hand. "She's evil incarnate."

"But you don't need to stay away from her?" I asked.

"She's not going to expect me coming after her when the Vessel is near. I think she'll assume I'm after the Vessel, too. Again."

Nina arched an eyebrow. "Again?"

"Alex, um, was responsible . . ."

Alex shrugged. "I lost the Vessel the first time. I went after it, found it, and then lost it."

"How do you lose an ancient artifact stuffed with human souls? Did you leave it at the donut shop? Maybe trade it for a couple of maple glazed?"

I watched Alex's jaw tighten. The taking—and losing—of the Vessel of Souls was a sore subject for him. I cleared my throat and tried to give Nina the look of death—loosely translated as "shut up already"—but she persisted.

"I mean, if I'm going to risk my afterlife to help you . . ."

"You don't have to risk anything. I asked for Sophie's help."

"Okay, if my best friend is going to risk her first life to help you . . ."

"When Alex was in favor—" I started.

"I got duped, okay?" Alex said. "I heard about the

Vessel, I lusted for it, I stole it, and then someone stole it from me."

Nina sat back, impressed. "Way to get your wings cut off, lust monster."

The look of sadness in Alex's eyes stung. I wanted to slip my arms around him, to brush the clutch of curls that lolled over his forehead, but the air suddenly seemed heavy and charged. Somehow, a heartfelt "there, there" didn't seem to suffice for someone who had stolen the Vessel that could change the fate of the world, had been thrown out of Heaven for it, and was now relegated to a life of day-old donuts and subpar mu shu in the earthly realm.

"What about the guy who stole it from you? Are you sure it's not on his mantle somewhere? Maybe holding the remains of his Aunt Fanny or something?" Nina asked.

I watched Alex's Adam's apple bob as he swallowed thickly. "I'm sure. He was destroyed. The Vessel wasn't recovered."

"Destroyed?" I asked, my voice coming out in a harsh whisper.

"I'm just lucky I got what I did. And a second chance. I can actually go back if I return the Vessel. It would prove that I no longer lust for power." Alex's eyes held mine. He blinked, those soft eyelashes batting, and I would have scoured the world for him, right there in that moment.

"Yeah, see right there—I'd be out of the angelic realm in a heartbeat." Nina licked her fingers. "So, you've got me. We'll do it. Heck, I'll even go a few rounds with your ex. I can take her." Nina flexed a nonexistent bicep.

"No," Alex said firmly.

"What's she going to do? Kill me again?" Nina grinned at her own cleverness.

I rolled my eyes, but Alex's look stayed hard. "I mean it."

The same chill seemed to creep up my spine and I hugged my arms across my chest. "Is anyone else freezing?"

Nina and Alex stared at me and I yanked the afghan off the couch. "Oh. Right."

Nina yawned, exposing sharp incisors. "Evil, schmevil. How bad can a fallen angel be? And what'd she do to you? Break your heart? Cheat on you with Cupid?"

"Just stay away from her, okay?"

I pushed away my dinner, suddenly feeling very full. I wanted to believe Alex. I wanted to believe that he had our best interests at heart. Ophelia could be bad news. Fallen angels always are. So was Ophelia really that bad—or did Alex really have something to hide?

I looked at him sideways, my appraisal hidden by a few strands of hair that fell over my forehead. I didn't want to love him, didn't want to feel that rush of adrenaline that washed over me whenever he walked through my door, whenever he walked back into my life. I wanted to believe all the best about him. In the Underworld I could see through magical veils. Horns, fangs, tails, bad intentions—everything that could be hidden with a charm or a spell was hung out in clear sight to me, but when it came to Alex Grace—and love—everything was as clear as mud.

"Do you think she'd really try and come after us?" I asked.

"Maybe. She might consider you an enemy, especially if you were standing in the way of her getting what she wanted. But believe me, you'd know if Ophelia was after you. She's never been one to keep a secret."

Nina snorted. "Does she travel with a marching band

or something? Like, the fallen angel's equivalent of the angelic trumpets?" She grinned, her fangs catching the light.

I narrowed my eyes at her. "You really have a way of comforting people."

"Hello? Vampire, remember? Empathy has never really been our strong point."

The thought of Alex's psycho-killer ex-girlfriend rattled me a little, but with the entire Underworld behind me, I wasn't *that* concerned.

"I don't think she'd be able to find us." I jutted my chin toward Nina. "Nina doesn't have a paper trail above ground and mine's pretty limited. We're pretty far off the grid."

Nina held up a finger. "Except for my Facebook page." She whipped out her iPhone and started mumbling to herself while she typed. *"Am embarking on a Heaven and Earth scavenger hunt."*

"Way to keep under the radar," I said.

Alex bit his lip, considering whether or not to share his information. Finally he sighed and said, "Ophelia—and fallen angels in general—can read minds. They don't really need to go looking for anyone—at least not the conventional way."

Heat surged from my toes to the frazzled red hair follicles on my head. I thought of all the nights I had lain awake, thinking of Alex's firm chest, the way he tasted, those soft, full lips pressed up against mine. "All the time?" I asked meekly.

Alex grinned, breaking the somberness in the room. "If we so choose."

I promptly tried to erase all further thoughts of Alex in anything other than wholesome activities—including the velvety sweet tone of his voice as he murmured in my ear. It wasn't working, so I urged my inner voice into a loud rendition of the *Gilligan's Island* theme song. And then I imagined Alex's smooth chest glistened up with coconut butter as he reclined on the beach.

"Damn," I muttered.

Less than thirty minutes later, two sets of chopsticks poked out of a host of empty takeout boxes and a few fat grains of fried rice and packets of soy sauce littered the table. I eyed the backpack Alex had left untouched on the dining-room table and pointed to it.

"So, what's in there?"

I really hoped it wasn't a scrapbook of Alex's past relationship with Ophelia. I knew it was childish, but I earnestly prayed that in the time since they had been apart, Ophelia had sprouted a tail, horns, a unibrow, or a beer belly—anything that might render her patently undatable—as though Alex's description of her imminent evil wasn't enough.

Alex unzipped the pack and slid out a stack of leatherbound books. Nina wrinkled her nose, and I coughed, covering my nose over the dusty smell of old paper. "What are those?"

"Various accounts of the history of the Vessel."

I picked up one of the books, squinting at the worn gold writing on the spine. "There are books about it? I thought it was supposed to be hush-hush."

"Well, you can't exactly get them on Amazon."

"*The Vessel of Souls and the Origin of Evil,*" Nina read. "Ooh, I'll take this one."

I poked through the stack. "Looks like people have been searching for this thing for years."

"Eons," Alex said without looking up. "Searching for it, documenting the things they know about it, even the things they just think they know."

I slid a thin volume out from Alex's backpack and

opened it, leafing through the handwritten pages. "This one looks more like a journal," I said.

Alex looked over my shoulder. "That's the journal of the last guy who was seeking the Vessel."

"What happened to him?"

Alex shrugged. "Don't know. I didn't get a lot of back-story with the books."

Nina kicked her feet up on the table and crossed her ankles. "Hmm. I'm guessing that means you didn't pick these up at our local Barnes and Noble?"

I watched Alex's Adam's apple bob as he swallowed. "No. I sort of took them. From Ophelia."

I felt myself gape. "You 'sort of' took them?"

"Okay, I completely took them. And pretty soon she'll come looking for them." Alex poked the journal I held in my hand. "Especially that one."

I flipped the journal to the first page and froze, my eyes set on the name inscribed. "Lucas Szabo," I murmured.

"Yeah, that's the guy. He's some mortal guy who obviously has a serious desire for some power. There's no other reason to seek out the Vessel. Apparently, he got pretty close. It should help us. The guy was really detailed. He listed who guarded the Vessel, included drawings, pictures—where he last tracked it. Everything."

My heart started to beat in the rapid thud-thud-thud of a panic attack. My palms started to sweat and the inscription on the yellowed page swirled as tears started to pool.

"Are you okay, Sophie?"

"Sophie?" I felt Alex's hand on my shoulder, but his voice sounded far away.

"Lucas Szabo," I murmured again.

"Yeah, he was the hunter who was looking for the Vessel."

I shook my head and with leaden hands, pulled the book toward me. I tried to form saliva to lick my parched lips, but I couldn't. All I could do was choke out the name "Lucas Szabo."

"Sophie, what's wrong? You're scaring me." Nina was standing up, rushing toward me, her coal-black eyes the size of saucers. I heard her voice, but it was a million miles away—distant—like the feeling of Alex's hand on my shoulder.

"Lucas Szabo is my father," I answered.

Chapter Four

Nina's eyes widened. "Your father?"

I felt the sickening weight in my stomach again.

I knew my father by name only.

He had only spent four days with me—the first four days I was alive—but his identity had never been a secret. The fact that he was tracking the Vessel of Souls, however, had.

"I don't understand though," I said, resting the journal on the table. "Mom was looking for someone normal when she found Lucas, someone who had nothing to do with the supernatural realm."

Like my grandmother, my mother was a seer. But unlike my grandmother, my mother hated what she could do. She shut out her powers in any way she could—first with drugs and alcohol, and finally, with Lucas Szabo. The way Grandma told it, my mother and Lucas fell in love immediately. To Lucas, my mother was a classic beauty, a strong-willed woman who guarded her privacy and her serenity with everything she had. To my mother, Lucas Szabo was a stable man who wore cardigans rather than capes, who drove a sensible Ford Taurus and had a pantry full of cream of mushroom soup and Ovaltine rather than our standard eye of newt and freeze-dried bat. He taught mythological studies at the University of San Francisco, but rather than conjure or cohabitate with magicks, he debunked them. One by one Lucas went after the fake fortune tellers and mystics that pandered to the Pier 39 tourists. My mother thought his disdain for the mystical world was perfect and envisioned a future attending Junior League meetings and eating deviled egg sandwiches at Crissy Field. The perfect, normal family.

Nine months later I came along, and four days after that, Lucas Szabo disappeared.

Alex's hand closed over mine and squeezed gently. His touch was comforting but did little to dispel the surge of emotions roiling through me.

"He left her because of me."

"That's not true, Lawson."

I shook Alex's hand off mine. "Yes, it is. Apparently, he was looking for a kid that had some powers. After four days of gurgling and sucking on my toes I wasn't able to pull a rabbit out of my hat, so daddy dearest took off."

"If he didn't believe in any of the supernatural stuff, why would your lack of abilities be a problem?" Nina wanted to know.

I shrugged. "I don't know. That's just the way the story goes. I don't know anything else about him. According to my grandmother, he never tried to contact me, not even after my mother died. He didn't even come to her funeral."

I felt a stab of pain mixed with the sting of anger. *What kind of father abandons his child?*

"Well, maybe there was something more to it," Nina said hopefully. "The rest of these books are super old. Maybe that one is, too. Maybe—maybe your dad died. I mean, not that that's necessarily a good thing but . . . do you even know if he's still alive?"

Nina and I both looked at Alex.

"What are you looking at me for?"

"Don't you have some kind of, I don't know, list of the dead?" Nina asked. "I mean, you know . . ."

Alex frowned. "You're dead, too. Do *you* have a list?"

Nina held up a finger. "Technically, I'm undead. You, my friend, are dead-dead. And we don't deal in ghosts."

Alex raised a challenging eyebrow. "I have a heartbeat. And a pulse. If anyone is dead here, it's you. You're way deader than I am. And we don't deal with ghosts, either. We work strictly souls. Well, angels and souls."

"Okay! Now that we know that everyone is dead—or undead—can we get back to this? Can we get back to searching for the Vessel? There's got to be something informative in the journal." I sounded a lot cooler and more aloof than I felt. In actuality, my fingers were twitching, anxious to devour the journal, to study every nuance of my father that could be culled from his writings. I wanted to know how he dotted his i's, how he crossed his t's. I wanted to know if there were long entries thinking about the daughter that he left behind; wanted to know if he wrote about my mother. My memories of her were fuzzy at best, the majority having been fed to me by my grandmother, who raised me after my mother's passing.

Nina leafed through the journal. "We don't even know why your father was searching for the Vessel." Nina paused, cocked her head. "Sophie?"

I looked over my shoulder and Nina held the book open. I read the date—June 16, 1982. "That was eleven days before I was born." I took the book from her, smoothed my palm over the image sketched on the page. "And that's my mother."

Nina came beside me. "Then that must be you."

Lucas had drawn a very detailed sketch of my mother. She had the same slight smile on her face that I dreamed of. Her long, delicate curls were tied at the nape of her neck and her slim hands held the full swell of a very pregnant belly. Inside the round swell, Lucas had drawn a baby.

"I guess," I said, trying my best to distance myself from my mother's familiar eyes.

Nina flipped the page and I blinked. "You again," she said.

Another baby drawing, this one me, without my mother.

"Why was he drawing pictures of me if he was just going to leave? Why was he drawing *me* in a journal that he used to log his searches for the Vessel?"

Alex squeezed my hand. "I don't know, Lawson."

Nina hugged me to her.

Alex looked from her to me. "I think the real question is—how did Ophelia end up with your father's journal?"

I peeled Alex's hand from mine and brushed my fingers through my hair, my eyes still fixed on the journal, on the sketch of me.

"Maybe you should sit down." Nina's cold hands pressing against my shoulders rattled me and I stepped away. "Maybe this journal will help answer some questions you have about your father, you know? It could be a good thing." Nina tried to smile and I forced a nod.

"You know, I think I just need some air," I said.

"That's a good idea," Alex said. "We can go for a walk."

"Actually, I think I'd like to be alone right now." I

pulled my keys from the ring by the door. "I'm just going to go for a drive."

I went down to the underground garage and slipped behind the wheel of my new-to-me '91 Honda Accord. I'd always considered myself more of a rough-and-tumble SUV kind of girl, but since I'd written "My CRV was peeled open like a tin can by a power-crazed wannabe mystic" on my auto policy form—well, eyebrows at my insurance company were raised. After that, I figured a fairly nondescript sedan was a good way to go for a replacement car.

I sunk into my seat and practiced a little bit of deep breathing, determined not to cry. Or scream, or punch the steering wheel, or yell profanities to a man whom I'd never known and who would never hear them. Instead, I turned on the radio and pulled out of the garage into the inky black night, humming along to some throbbing new Lady Gaga beat.

The gentle flow of post-rush-hour traffic went to an immediate, brake-squealing stop-and-go when the sky opened up and started to dump quarter-sized raindrops onto the cement. I groaned and pulled around a soccer mom in an SUV the size of my apartment, angling onto the 280 Freeway exit. I had no idea where I was going, but according to the blurry green freeway sign, I was on my way south to San Jose.

I flipped on my headlights and thought about my father, thought about his careful script in the yellowing pages of the old notebook.

Nina was right; there could be things in that journal that answered my questions about him. If I knew enough about him to have questions.

As a little girl I imagined him tall and slim with a

dashing career that kept him out of my life—perhaps a mild-mannered college professor by day, a continent-hopping James Bond type by night. He was supposed to *want* to be with me, to want to know his only daughter, but circumstances kept him at bay.

Now I knew what those circumstances were—greed. Power. My father wanted to find the Vessel of Souls. A Vessel that controlled the balance of good and evil in the world.

I wasn't any use to him. . . .

The thought entered my head on its own and I felt a lump forming in my throat. I clenched my teeth and felt the leaden weight in my foot as I pressed the gas pedal harder, my little car zipping past the minivans and eco-conscious carpoolers.

He could have found me anytime. . . .

My eyes stung and I took my hands off the wheel, pressing them over my ears. Why was I doing this to myself? The car pulled a little to the left and I jerked it back, then stared at the road in front of me. Somewhere along my drive I had turned onto a deserted strip of highway. The fat raindrops had now turned into a sad, constant drizzle that thundered on the hood of my car. I wiped the tears that poured down my cheeks. I sniffed, then squinted as a pair of halogen headlights beamed in my rearview mirror. I frowned. We were the only two cars on the road, yet Mr. Bright Lights apparently felt honor bound to drive directly behind me.

"If you're in such a hurry, go around!" I mumbled to the car's reflection. "It's not like there aren't three other lanes to choose from."

In response, the headlights drew closer, filling the interior of my car with a glaring blue-white light. I snapped on my blinker and coasted into the slow lane. As Mr. Bright Lights pulled even with me, I shot him a dirty look, but the interior of his black SUV was dark. All I could make out was a figure hunched in the driver's seat.

"Jerk," I muttered, my tears drying in my cheeks.

Mr. Bright Lights sped up again, showering a spray of water onto my windshield. I kicked my wipers onto high; with the first whoosh of water I saw the blurry glare of Mr. Bright Lights's taillights, directly in front of me.

"Holy shit!" I screamed, slamming on my brakes and yanking the wheel. My heart hammered as my tires spun and slid helplessly on the wet road. I felt my seat belt tighten and cut across my chest as the dark scenery outside swirled into a blurry, circling mess. I felt the prickling heat of sweat on my upper lip and down my back, and I let out a gurgling, wailing cry until my car glided to a gentle stop, just inches from the highway retaining wall. With shaking hands I killed the engine and bit back the feeling of hot adrenaline as it roared through my body.

There was no sound except the drumming of rain on metal and the thundering beat of my heart. I peeled my aching hands from the steering wheel and gulped lungfuls of air, waiting impatiently for the imminent posttraumatic-experience heart attack. When it didn't come I clicked off my seat belt and pressed my forehead against the cool window glass, my gaze sweeping over the desolate highway. Mr. Bright Lights was long gone.

I looked at the cement wall a hairbreadth from my car and realized that I could have been gone, too. Gone—dead.

The tears started to pool again and I rested my head on my steering wheel, crying until my heartbeat had resumed its normal, steady beat, until I was numb to the horror of a complete stranger in an SUV trying to kill me on a deserted stretch of San Francisco highway.

I started my car and exited the freeway, turning around and heading home. My arms felt as though I had just completed a marathon workout session; it felt like it took hours to drive the eleven miles back to my apartment. I don't think I took a breath until my car was parked in my designated spot and my feet were back on solid ground.

"My God, what happened to you? You look horrible!" Nina shrieked when I pushed open the apartment door.

I watched Alex give her an annoyed look, gently flicking her shoulder. "I mean, are you feeling better?" she corrected with a forced smile.

I dumped my sweatshirt on the floor and flopped onto the couch, Nina and Alex surrounding me, looking concerned but confused.

"Look, Lawson," Alex started, taking his hand in mine. "This thing about your dad . . . well, we don't know for sure that he was hunting the Vessel. Or why."

I pulled my hand away from his. "It's not that—at least not right now." I looked from Alex's cobalt eyes to Nina's coal-black ones. "Someone just tried to kill me!"

Nina frowned, halfway through tucking a fuzzy pink blanket over my shoulders. "Again?"

I ignored her. "On 280. I was driving . . . thinking . . . and this guy slammed on his brakes right in front of me! I spun out and almost hit the wall. I was this close," I held my thumb and forefinger a miniscule distance apart. "And then he just drove away. I guess he thought he accomplished his mission." I felt my lower lip pop out crybaby style.

Nina looked slightly skeptical. "His mission being to kill you?"

I nodded, feeling the familiar lump in my throat.

My eyes searched Alex's. "Why does everyone want to kill me?"

"No one wants to kill you," Alex said, rubbing my arm.

"Right," Nina agreed, rubbing my other arm. "You know that most people have no idea how to drive. He probably didn't even notice you were on the road."

I shook away from both their patronizing arm rubs. "I was the *only* person on the road!" I snapped. "He knew I was there. He saw me. He looked directly at me—he glared at me."

Alex sat back. "He glared at you? You saw him? What did he look like?"

I bit my lip. "Well, it was dark, so I couldn't really see his expression *that* clearly. Or him. But I could *feel* he was glaring at me."

"Through his car window."

"Yes," I said solemnly.

"In the dark."

I nodded again.

Nina snorted, her effort to quell her laughter failing miserably. "I'm sorry!" she said.

I watched Alex's bent head as he looked down; I watched the gentle vibration of his shoulders as he laughed silently. "Thank you both for your heartfelt concern." I kicked the blanket off me and stood up, hands on hips. "Please remember it when you're scraping me off two-eighty."

I started to stomp toward my bedroom when I felt Alex's soft hand on my shoulder. He squeezed gently and pulled me toward him, curling me into his chest. I kept my stern, angry composure for all of a millisecond while I melted into his warm, firm curves, while his arms slid around me, hands resting at the small of my back. Alex inclined his head so the tip of his chin brushed against my nose. His familiar cocoa-bean and cut-grass scent comforted me and I tried to remind myself that it was the safety of a trusted friend that was warming my heart; that the slow, delicious churning in my stomach had nothing to do with the way his body molded so perfectly against my curves. I stiffened immediately when I felt the hard coldness of Nina pressing up against me, her arms splayed in group-hug format, her head resting on my shoulder. "This moment is just so beautiful," she murmured.

I broke away from our threesome and stared at Nina.

"You know, I think I am going to take this warm, fuzzy feeling outside." She grabbed her purse and disappeared out the door, leaving Alex and I alone together in the silent apartment. We were still in a loose hug. I flushed and Alex straightened, then smiled. He pulled me close.

"This feels good," he murmured.

I wanted to resist, but his arms around me were like warm chocolate. "It does," I said finally.

"Look, Lawson, I—" Alex looked down at me and his cobalt eyes were deep, and soft. He licked his lips. "I just couldn't take it if anything ever happened to you."

I smiled. "I think I've proven I'm pretty resilient."

Alex's lips pushed up into his trademark half-smile and my stomach fluttered. He brushed my bangs from my forehead. "That, you have." Alex leaned close to me, his soft curls lolling over his forehead. I drank in his warm scent and rolled up on my toes as his arms tightened around my waist, his lips brushed against mine, and then he was kissing me.

My head spun in delicious chaos as Alex's palms caressed my back and he kissed and nibbled my lips, my ears, my neck. My heart thumped and I started to lose my breath and Alex broke away, raking a hand through his hair. His curls resettled in that perfectly tousled way.

"I should go," he said quickly.

I looked at him, deflated, rejected. "Oh. Okay."

He took my hand, squeezed it softly. His eyes were warm, sad. "I'm sorry, I just—I need to go."

I hugged my arms to my chest, forced a smile. "Hey, no problem. Thanks for the information. I should go to bed now anyway."

"That's a good idea. We can take this up tomorrow." Alex strode to the dining room table, began unzipping his backpack and stacking the books to go inside.

"Alex," I started, once his back was to me. "What's it like?"

He turned slowly. "What's what like?"

I studied the carpet. "Heaven."

The slow smile of memory spread across his lips, but his eyes were far away. "I can't describe it."

I sat down at the table and Alex followed suit. "Why?" I asked. "Are you not allowed or something?"

Alex slowly wagged his head from side to side and then looked at me. "There are no words."

"Do you miss it?" I asked, my voice sounding small. "So you miss Heaven?"

Alex slid the leftover Chinese food boxes closer to him and plucked out a fortune cookie. He broke it, popped a piece in his mouth, and chewed thoughtfully. "Of course. It's home. It's all I've known for"—he shrugged, swallowed—"forever."

"Oh." I picked at a glob of solid grease on the dining-room table. "Is there anything you like about being here?"

One corner of Alex's mouth turned up into a wry grin. "I like you."

I blushed, went back to studying my table. "Thanks."

"And the food." Alex pushed the last bit of fortune

cookie into his mouth. "I absolutely love the food. We didn't have Chinese takeout like this when I was there last."

I crumpled up a napkin and threw it across the table at him. He started sliding the books into his pack again until I put my hand flat on the table, pinning a single volume under my palm. "I'm keeping this one," I said, my eyes firm and holding his.

Alex looked at the book. "You don't need to . . ."

I picked up my father's journal and held it against my chest. "Yes, I do."

Chapter Five

I slammed my hand against the nightstand again, trying to quell the infernal racket of the morning-show DJs cackling on my alarm clock. Instead I managed to knock the whole thing over. "Crap," I muttered, sitting up in my bed.

It was just after six-thirty and the last time I looked at the clock—just before I fell asleep in the greying light of dawn—it was five-forty. My eyes stung and my eyelashes were clumped with bits of post-sleep goo. My cheeks felt tight from the hours of inexhaustible tears and the spine of my father's journal was wedged into my rib cage, leaving an angry—though impressive—red indentation.

I made it to the bathroom without completely opening my eyes and yawned through a hot shower. It wasn't until I was showered and pink and standing in front of my fogged-over bathroom mirror that I noticed it. In the snatches of clear mirror my reflection looked odd—my fire-engine red hair had a noticeably silver hue and rather than the usual wet-rat look of my post-shower curls, my hair fell in elegant long waves. I yanked off my towel and used it to scrub the steam from the mirror.

I looked at my reflection.

It looked back at me.

I ran a hand through my hair, patted my cheeks, leaned forward, and scrutinized myself.

My reflection did the same, and then it started laughing.

I jumped back, slipped on my discarded towel and steadied myself by ripping down the shower curtain. I landed in a naked vinyl heap on the bathroom floor, jaunty electric-blue shower-curtain fish swimming over my naked stomach.

"What the hell?" I screamed.

"Now, Sophie Annemarie Lawson. Watch your mouth. Hell is a heck of a place and you don't want to mention it too much."

I scrambled to my feet, steadying myself with both hands against the bathroom sink, then used one finger to poke at the offending mirror.

"That is so annoying. Now I know what all those poor fish feel like at the dentist's office. Poke, poke, poke."

I watched my grandmother's index finger poke against the mirror glass, watched the windy ridges of her fingerprints smudge the inside of my mirror.

"Grandma?"

"Ah!" Grandma said from behind the glass. "She remembers me!"

I rubbed my head, looking behind me, trying to recall if my naked acrobatics had resulted in a head wound.

No such luck.

"Grandma, are you in the mirror?"

Grandma nodded slowly, her expression a combination of amusement and annoyance that I remembered from breaking curfew in my teen years.

I swallowed. "But you're dead."

"That's my Sophie," Grandma said, snapping her fingers. "Smart as a whip."

"No," I said again, my hands on hips. "You're not here. You're dead."

Grandma crossed her arms in front of her chest, her lips set, her expression indignant. "And you're naked. Really, Sophie, you amaze me. Is seeing your dead grandmother in your bathroom mirror really all that unbelievable? Really? Maybe we should ask your vampire roommate. Nina, is it? Nina . . ."

Witches, I'm used to. Banshees, vampires, were-wolves, trolls, hobgoblins, and *other*—provided that "other" was a corporeal being. My dead grandmother showing up in my bathroom mirror (and me being buck naked to receive her)—was odd. Very, very odd.

I pulled my bathrobe from the hook and yanked the belt tight around my waist. "What are you doing here?" I asked as I wrapped my hair in a towel turban. "Not that I'm not thrilled to see you. Where are you?" I leaned in closer, peering around the sides of the mirror, trying to see behind her. "Are you in Heaven?"

Grandma raised an eyebrow. "No, I'm in your bathroom mirror." She dragged another finger across the glass. "Which could use a very good cleaning, by the way. Really, Sophie, I haven't been gone that long. I know I didn't teach you to clean house like this," she tsked.

"Can you come out here?" I stepped back, offering her a space.

"No. Specters—that's what we are, specters—isn't that just a darling way to refer to us? So much better than dead or afterlifers or life-retired. Anywho, specters can only be seen on shiny surfaces."

"But why now?" I felt the sting of tears beginning to

pool behind my eyes, and I leaned in toward the mirror again. "Grandma, I've needed you for so long. The last year of my life has been so . . ."

"Oh, honey, I know. I have been there; you just weren't able to see me. It's a different magic that allows this"— Grandma indicated herself and the mirror—"than you're used to. This one you might actually not be immune to. I tried to appear before—in stainless steel dishes, in your rearview mirror. Even on a sunny day on the back of Mr. Matsura's head. That poor man has been balding since he was twenty-three. Took me a little while to get the knack for it."

"You showed up on Mr. Matsura?"

Mr. Matsura was the kindly old man who lived across the hall from me and walked his toy poodle Pickle three times a day.

"My grandmother appears in my bathroom mirror and on my neighbor's bald head." I sat down on the edge of my tub, rubbing my temples. "And now I know why I was driven to drink." Seeing your dead grandmother projected on the bald head of an aging Japanese man would do that to you. "I guess this is a relief. I thought I was going crazy."

"This seems like a really inopportune moment to say, 'Gotcha!'" Grandma grinned her trademark toothy smile, both her wrinkled hands held shotgun style in front of her.

"Are you here to tell my I'm in mortal danger?" I asked warily.

"Now that would be cliché, wouldn't it? Dead grandmother appears in bathroom mirror, warning of the evil to come. Wooooo, whooooo!" Grandma did ghostly hands, her wrinkled lips forming an ominous O.

I laughed. "Yeah, I guess it would be."

"But really, Sophie," my grandma said, the smile dropping from her voice, "you are in danger."

"You said you weren't going to do that!"

"No, I said it would be cliché. Cliché, but necessary. Now listen to me, Sophie. You are in serious danger. Have you ever heard of the Vessel of Souls?"

"Yup. You missed it. Alex Grace, fallen angel. Filled me in on the whole thing."

Grandma appeared to be thinking. "Alex Grace? You mean that hot ball of cheesecake you had over last night?"

"How did you know?"

Grandma shrugged. "The man had to use the bathroom."

"Grandma! Did you look?"

"Oh honey, I might be old, but I'm not—well, that phrase doesn't work anymore, now does it? Anywho, enough about Alex. You need to know that you're being tailed, watched. Someone is looking for you and believe you me it's not Ed McMahon with one of those big Publishers Clearinghouse checks."

"So the driver last night—that was real? Someone really was trying to kill me?" I felt my heart flutter when I thought back to his headlights piercing through the dark night.

Grandma nodded solemnly.

"Do you know who it is? Also, Ed McMahon is dead."

Grandma looked pleased as she clapped her hands in front of her chest. "Really? Dead? I should look him up, maybe invite him to bingo. Oh, honey, I've got to run." Grandma looked over her shoulder. "That's the breakfast bell. You have to move quickly around here or you're the only specter without a waffle."

I sprang up, pressed my hands against the mirror.

"Grandma, no! Wait! Who is it? Who's tracking me? I have so many questions!"

"I'll be back, sweetie. I promise."

I pressed my forehead against the mirror and sighed when my own reflection stared back at me.

I dressed quickly and drove to work, considering what was more odd: that my dead grandmother had appeared to me in my bathroom mirror or that I wasn't more freaked out about it. There was also the idea of her playing bingo with Ed McMahon and the issue of a waffle shortage in Heaven, but those rang in at a distant third, what with the apparition and the ominous warning.

Someone's out to get you. . . .

It was a singsongy voice ringing in my ear. A thought I didn't realize I was having.

Someone's going to get you. . . .

I pulled to a four-way stop and scrunched my eyes shut, willing the voices and the ghosts to go away until the man behind me angrily laid on the horn, making me jump in my car seat and slosh a wave of black coffee across my pale-blue button-down.

"Oh, crap," I said, pulling into the intersection, driving with my knees, licking the coffee from my wrist.

I managed to make it the UDA offices coffee-scented yet otherwise unscathed, and I was greeted by Nina at the front desk. She was wearing rhinestone-studded horn-rimmed glasses and carrying a clipboard, her long hair wound into a tight bun. She was tucked into a pencil skirt that made her appear as wide as—well, a pencil— and she had an embroidered pink cardigan that I swore once belonged to Donna Reed resting on her shoulders. Her crisp white blouse was unbuttoned just enough to reveal a tiny peek of her white lace bra, and somehow, she had hoisted her breasts to just under her lifted chin. She looked like a porn star for library fetishists. I stared at her breasts.

"Where did you get those?" I asked them.

Nina waved dismissively. "They came with the bra. Where have you been? Dixon wants to interview everyone today."

"Everyone?" I asked.

Nina fell in step with me as I snagged a bagel and headed toward my office. "Okay, that's no big deal. I'm comfortable with my job performance," I told her.

In my last four years at the UDA, I never failed to lock up my werewolf boss once. After Mr. Sampson, I kept the interim bosses abreast of standard operating procedure, and I acted as the go-between for the under and upper worlds when the banshee was filling in. Whoever had given her the job had failed to realize the fact that for mortals, laying eyes on a banshee means instant death— hence the usual warning scream. The upper world lost two baristas and a meter maid before that little snafu was fixed.

I took a big bite of bagel and spoke with my mouth full. "The interview will be cake."

"Yeah," Nina said, looking disgusted, "as you are a veritable poster child for the proper businesswoman."

I looked down at my coffee-stained blouse that was now spotted black with poppy seeds. "I had a bit of a rough morning," I said, swallowing.

"Well, it's about to get rougher," Nina said, eyes trailing.

"Steve," I said with a grimace.

As usual, I smelled him before I saw him. Steve was a troll and one thing that everyone should know is that trolls smell—badly. Like a slightly more pungent combination of bleu cheese and belly button. At one point, Steve and I had one of those love-hate relationships. He loved me and I hated him. At least I did hate him. That's not to say that I loved him now—far from it. But when someone saves your life, you tend to have a soft spot for him.

"Never fear, ladies and demonettes, Steve is here." Steve's small grey troll hands clutched his lapels and he grinned up at Nina and me, his yellow snaggled teeth glistening in the harsh fluorescent overhead lights.

"Wow, Steve, you look nice," I said.

Steve was wearing a slick sharkskin suit. Shiny, pointed black wingtips stuck out from underneath his stubby pant legs and his pink-and-grey striped tie sat lop-sided over his stout stomach. What remained of his bushy black hair was oiled down into a careful comb-over that did little to conceal the overwhelming baldness on his ill-shapen head.

"Steve thinks Sophie likes what she sees," Steve said, waggling his bushy caterpillar brows. "Too bad that ship has sailed."

Steve's affections for me had been replaced—immediately and irrevocably—when he met Sasha, a busty paramedic who had a thing for short guys. She had lost her sense of smell over a previous Zicam addiction, so she and Steve were an odd, weird-looking match made in Underworld heaven.

"Steve is meeting with the new bigwig today."

"With Dixon? Why?" I wanted to know.

"Good business practice," Steve said assuredly. "Steve wants Mr. Andrade to put the face with the name Elpher Brothers Moving."

Steve and his three-foot-high troll brothers ran the moving and operations company that serviced the UDA. While his height and smell didn't exactly promote a sense of well-being or ability when it came to large furniture moving, Steve and his brothers had a surprising way of getting things done. I just hadn't been able to figure out what it was.

"Steve would love to stay and chat, but business calls." He jabbed a pudgy finger at the gleaming face of his gold watch. "Time is money," he said as he strutted toward Mr. Andrade's office. Nina and I peered down the hall as Steve reached his destination. We watched him arch up on his tiptoes, small arm extended, his fingertips just missing the doorknob. Undeterred, Steve sank back onto flat feet and swiftly began kicking the door until one of Dixon's henchmen pulled it open.

"That little troll's got—"

I clamped my hands over my ears and shook my head. "Don't say it! I don't want to hear about anything that Steve has."

"I was going to say 'an appointment,' little Miss Mind in the Gutter. So what was so rough about your morning?"

"My grandmother appeared to me. In the bathroom mirror."

Nina's eyes went wide. "Shut up! You are so Jennifer Love Hewitt ghost whispering right now! Did you lead her to the white light, cross her over?"

"I'm serious!"

Nina thrust out her lower lip and pouted. "Me, too. It's not like I have a whole lot of ghostly experience. What'd she look like? All skeletal and stuff?"

I glanced at Nina, who looked positively titillated. "I always wished I could talk to dead people," she said. I held up a finger and Nina grabbed it, glared. "Oh, you know what I mean."

"She said I was in grave danger."

"Original. What does she know?"

"She didn't tell me much; basically, you know, 'hey, how you doing?' and 'you're in grave danger.'"

Nina's eyes were far away. "And then she crossed over into the light . . ."

"No, she went to breakfast. Possibly with Ed McMahon."

"We can learn so much from the dead."

I had barely settled into my chair when I blinked up at an impossibly tall vampire in an elegant suit who seemed to materialize in my office doorway. He smiled down at me, a calm, disarming smile, and stayed silent for a moment.

"May I help you?" I asked.

"Ms. Lawson, correct?"

I nodded, scooting forward in my chair, my eyes glancing over my desk calendar, the stack of unopened files in my in-box. "I'm sorry. Did we have an appointment Mr.—"

"Rosenthal," the man supplied politely. "May I sit?" He did so without me answering. His movements were fluid and he settled in comfortably, his eyes focused on mine, his legs crossed, hands folded in his lap. I chanced a look over his head, one of those "What the hell is going on here?" looks that best friends share, but Nina—who had been standing just outside my office door—had just as silently dematerialized.

"I don't have an appointment. Don't worry, you're not in trouble." Mr. Rosenthal kept smiling. "I'm just here to observe."

I gulped. "Observe what?"

"Mr. Andrade would just like to get a better feel for what it is all of his key staff members do." His smile, meant to be disarming, was starting to give me the creeps.

"Oh. Oh . . .'kay."

"Just go ahead, go about your business. Pretend I'm not even here."

I took another look at Mr. Rosenthal, who now had a small notebook resting in his lap. He nodded encouragingly. I looked helplessly over his left shoulder, where Vlad was parading his team of VERM supporters down the hall, TAKE BACK YOUR AFTERLIFE! signs waving. I wondered if it would reflect poorly on me if I threw a blood bag into the hallway and let Mr. Rosenthal and the VERMers duke it out while I slipped out the back door.

I clicked on my computer and dragged a few files from my in-box closer to me, hearing the deafening pulse of my heart.

I have no reason to be nervous, I told myself. *I'm good at my job.*

I flipped open the file on top of my stack labeled *Active Vamps—Sunset*—and the thick red cover knocked over my teacup, dousing the remaining files and two stacks of Post-it notes with day-old tea. I felt my face flush as I pillaged through a box of Kleenex, dabbing at the mess. Mr. Rosenthal remained silent and smiled serenely as he leaned down and wrote something on his notepad.

I cocked my head, trying to hear Mr. Rosenthal's low murmur. "I'm sorry, I didn't hear you," I said.

Mr. Rosenthal looked up at me, eyebrows raised. "Excuse me?"

"I didn't hear what you were saying."

"I didn't say anything."

I heard the murmur again and held up an index finger. "That! Someone must be outside. . . ." I concentrated, hearing a low snicker.

Mr. Rosenthal's lips eased back into the smile that I

thought was serene, but now I was starting to recognize as patronizing. "I assure you, Miss Lawson, no one is speaking." He tapped his ear. "Supernatural hearing, remember?"

I felt my face flush, felt my blood thicken and rush through my veins. Mr. Rosenthal's smile seemed to take on a more sinister edge.

"I heard *that*," he said with a thirsty smile.

I gulped; few things were more eerie than a fanged office superior who could hear the blood rushing through your veins.

I sunk back into my seat and tried to continue my work.

By the time Mr. Rosenthal stood up and brushed the imaginary creases from his impeccable suit, I had dropped the passport of a centaur who needed a sticker into the shredder, stapled the corner of my blouse to a de-activation request and mixed up the employment files for a Nichi demon and a Sousan demon. Which wouldn't have been so bad if I didn't send a baby eater to a nursery and a protector demon to a demolition site. Luckily, the mistake was caught before the Nichi demon actually ate any babies, but still, Mr. Rosenthal cocked his head and then wrote something down on his notepad. And I'm pretty sure it wasn't *Nice save!*

After Mr. Rosenthal left, I slunk into my coat and buzzed Nina. "I'm leaving for lunch," I said to her. "I need to end this misery at least for a little while. You coming? We could go by that Italian guy you like so much."

I could hear the low murmur of voices on Nina's end of the phone, and then she said, "No, thank you. I'm not through just yet."

I wrinkled my nose. "Nina?"

"Yes," she said, her voice tight. "This is Nina."

"What's wrong with you?"

"Mr. Andrade is here in my office right now as a matter of fact. I'll let him know that you bid him good afternoon."

"I bit him what?"

I heard the clatter of the phone and then the dial tone. "Whatever," I muttered, slinging my bag over my shoulder and slamming my office door behind me.

I stepped into the hallway and Steve stepped out from the shadows, his small troll legs working hard to keep stride with me. "Sophie doesn't look too happy."

"Sophie's not in the mood today, Steve."

"Maybe Sophie would like a massage?" Steve laced his pudgy grey fingers together and stretched his arms over his head, releasing a symphony of pops and cracks and a fresh wave of bleu-cheese odor. "Steve is very good with his hands."

"Pass," I said, pausing at the elevator and working the up button. "Besides, what would Sasha say?"

Steve shrugged, his shoulders brushing the bottom of his long, pointed earlobes. "Sasha knows that she cannot hold Steve down." He pushed out his chest. "Steve is just too much troll for one woman."

I glanced down at him, his wiry hair just brushing the top of my thigh. "I'll say," I murmured. "Really, Steve," I said as the elevator door slid open with aching slowness, "I appreciate the offer, but maybe some other time."

Steve shrugged his troll shoulders, and dug his hands into his pants pockets. "Suit yourself. But just so you know, Steve won't be around forever."

If only.

The elevator doors opened on the police station vestibule and I was halfway out the front doors when I heard someone calling my name. I whirled and Alex caught the back of my shirt.

"Hello to you, too."

Alex smoothed the part of my shirt he had gripped, the gentle touch of his fingers sending shock waves down my spine, making my knees go wonky. I shrugged out of his grip, afraid of dissolving into a pool of quivering Jell-O right there in the police station. "What do you want?"

"Do you like baseball?"

I raised an eyebrow. "That's what you want? To know if I like baseball?"

Alex narrowed his eyes. "Geez, Lawson, can you give a guy a break?" He pulled two orange and black Giants tickets from his shirt pocket. I saw the fat baseball logo and felt my grin go all the way to my ears. I snatched the tickets.

"These are behind home plate!"

Alex looked blank. "And that's good?"

I gaped. "What do you mean, is that good?"

Alex just shrugged.

"You don't like baseball?"

He lowered his voice. "Let's just say it was not the pastime it is now when I was around."

My mouth formed a small O. "Well, then you have to go with me."

Alex crossed his arms and grinned. "Is that so? You're inviting me to a game?"

I waggled the tickets. "Behind home plate. You can't miss it."

He pulled the tickets from my fingers. "And you must have missed that these are still *my* tickets."

I felt myself flush head to toe. "Oh, right. So, you wanted to know if I like baseball, right?"

Alex nodded, his eyes playful, smile wide.

"Yeah." I kicked at an invisible speck of dirt on the linoleum. "I could take it or leave it."

"So you don't mind if I give the tickets to . . ." Alex scanned the offices, tickets in hand, and I pummeled him.

"I'll drive. And buy you popcorn. And beer," I said eagerly.

"Throw in one of those giant foam fingers and you're on."

"Done!"

Chapter Six

I squinted in the midday sun and followed the crowd of businesspeople down the block toward Loco Legs sandwich shop, skipping a little, working to contain my giddiness. A Giants game—and a date. A date! There may be romantic touching. And kissing. Kissing Alex . . .

I felt a low heat start in my belly and spread downward. I bit the inside of my cheek to keep from breaking into maniacal giggles and focused on a list of pre-date activities—shave, pluck, tweeze. . . . It was somewhere between tweeze and spritz when I glanced across the street while waiting for the light to change and caught the eye of a man standing on the opposite corner. His eyes were small, lime Jell-O green—like mine. He raked a pale, freckled hand across what remained of his red hair—a frazzled mess of unruly curls.

Like mine.

He looked at me from across the street, and I saw him blink, saw his lips tighten, felt the thunderbolt of realization that must have gone through him roil through me.

"Lucas Szabo." The name settled on my dry lips and I was focused, rushing out into the intersection toward him. I felt someone clawing at my shoulder, felt someone try and grab the back of my jacket.

"Stop, lady!" I heard.

"What's she doing?" someone yelled. "There's a car coming!"

"Idiot," someone groaned.

The admonishments seemed miles away.

I stumbled into the street, my eyes never leaving Lucas Szabo's, until the raging howl of a Muni bus hurtling toward me gave me pause. I was rooted to the cement, the scream of the bus's horn all around me. I felt the warm puff of smog as the driver yanked the bus to the side and the bus narrowly missed me.

Suddenly everything was really loud. The city came back to life and I was standing in the middle of a San Francisco intersection. Cars whirled by me, honking, drivers glaring at me from their tinted windows. Pedestrians shook their heads at me, chalked my suicidal jaunt into the intersection up to drug use, to being one of those "city crazies."

Lucas Szabo wasn't on the corner anymore.

He wasn't anywhere.

My saliva tasted metallic; my head felt heavy, as if I had just come out of a drug-induced fog. I rubbed my eyes and ducked into the nearest café, abandoning my plan to eat at Loco Legs.

I didn't want anyone to see me.

I flopped down in the nearest booth and hung my head, my fingertips making small circular motions at my temples. *Am I seeing things now?*

No. He was there. He *had been* there, standing on the street corner, his eyes trained on mine.

My father.

"What can I get you?"

I looked up to see a pierced, pale waitress snapping her gum at me. She couldn't have been more than seventeen, and when she wound her ink-black hair around her index finger, I saw that she had a series of navy-blue stars tattooed on her hand.

"Uh," I said, "a burger. Cheeseburger, actually. And fries. And a Diet Coke, please."

The waitress scrawled my order on her pad and snapped her gum. "Coming right up."

When she was safely out of view I reached into my shoulder bag and took out my cell. I flipped it open to dial, but it shook in my hand. My entire body was quaking. I took several deep breaths and a few calming gulps of ice water. By this time the waitress returned, carrying my lunch.

"Are you okay, hon?" she asked me.

"Fine," I said without looking up.

"Sure thing," she said, sliding the plate in front of me.

Suddenly, I was ravenous. I took one bite of my burger and chewed hungrily, but when I tried to swallow, the meat stuck in my throat. I felt a prick go up the back of my neck, felt the cold sting of sweat as it beaded along my hairline and then blanketed my skin. The whole café dropped into silence; all I could hear was the heaving beat of my heart, the whoosh of my own breath as it filled my lungs. I looked around slowly, my whole body feeling leaden and foreign. I turned a quarter inch to my left and I saw her, perched on a bar stool, her body facing me. Her posture was ramrod straight and her hands were folded daintily in her lap, her knees bolted together, legs crossed at the ankle. Her blond hair was nearly waist length and hung in brilliant waves over one shoulder. She smiled and her lips were full and berry-stained; her chin was defined and defiant. She stared at me with eyes that were an icy, piercing blue.

She was the same woman from the coffee shop, and suddenly I knew without having to ask—she was Ophelia.

It was as though she knew exactly what I was thinking. The second I came to the realization, her lips parted into a smile that was part sweet, part bone-chillingly sly and she raised one hand, arching her fingers into a prim finger wave.

Ice water filled my veins.

Ophelia turned around on her bar stool so she was facing away from me. I turned back to my lunch and the sounds of the café crashed over me. I looked down at my plate and clamped my hand over my mouth. My eyes watered, my stomach heaved.

The top bun of my burger moved slowly, jerkily. My fries were covered with fat, yellow-white maggots writhing, falling off my French fries, dripping onto the table. I poked my burger bun with my fingernail and it fell aside, revealing my hamburger patty, my arched bite mark, and a hundred pulsing bugs.

I let out a howl and stood up, scratching the electric-blue vinyl of the booth as I clawed for my shoulder bag. I knocked over my Diet Coke, heard the clatter of my plate as it crashed to the floor.

"You've got to pay for that," I heard as I ran through the café. "Hey, lady!"

I fished a few bills out of my purse and tossed them onto the counter—right at the empty spot where Ophelia had been sitting a half second ago. I paused and looked over my shoulder at my lunch: my burger bun spilled open, the grilled brown patty lay on the floor in a pool of gelling grease. My fries scattered in a thousand directions. There wasn't a maggot anywhere.

I pushed out of the café and ran the entire way back to

the UDA, my tears making cold, wet tracks down my cheeks. I was heaving and hiccuping by the time I barreled through the doors of the police station, by the time I ran full force into Alex's chest. He instinctively wrapped his arms around me and I was enveloped in his soothing warmth.

"Whoa, Lawson! Slow down! Hey, sweetie, what's wrong?" he was saying. "It's okay, calm down." He pressed his lips into my hair, and I buried my damp face into the warm skin of his neck, breathing in his familiar, calming scent of cut grass and cocoa. When I was assured that my heart wouldn't beat out of my chest, I loosened my grip on Alex, sniffed, and looked up at him.

"It was Ophelia," I said, my voice sounding very small. "And my father. And maggots."

Alex held me at arm's length, his eyes going wide. "You saw Ophelia?"

I nodded and began to tremble again as the image of her wry smile blazed in my memory.

"Did she hurt you?"

"No," I said, breaking away from Alex and running my fingers through my hair. "She didn't have to." I flopped into the vinyl waiting-room chair in the police station vestibule and looked up at him. "Alex, I think I'm going crazy. I'm hearing things, seeing things. . . ." I shrugged miserably, cradling my head in my hands.

Alex sat down next to me, his thigh brushing against mine. "Crazy?" His mouth pushed up into that sweet half-smile. "From the girl who spends forty hours a week with the dead and horned among us?"

I tried not to smile but gave in—slightly. It wasn't easy to focus on my bizarre upside-down life with Alex sitting so close to me, but I reminded myself that thanks to him—my bizarre life *was* upside down—and maybe even in danger.

"So, crazy is relative. But seeing maggots? And my father? And Ophelia—all in the same day? Heck, all in the same lunch hour. That's not weird?"

Alex put his hand on mine, his thumb stroking my skin. "Ophelia is trying to get to you."

"Well, she did."

Alex wagged his head, the muscle in his jaw jumping. "This isn't good. She could have hurt you. Ophelia's intentions are never good."

"If she was so into me, why didn't she attack me just now at the café?"

"She did. Your father, the maggots—she can make you see things. She can get in your head—if you let her."

I pulled my hand away from Alex's, squeezing my fingers into fists, feeling my nails digging into my palms. "The maggots, maybe. But my father? You think that was Ophelia playing with my head? That he wasn't really"— I swallowed a sob that I had no reason to have—"here?"

"No, Lawson, I don't think your father was really there. I don't think he was walking down the street in the middle of the day."

I tried to blink back the sting of tears. "What?"

Alex swallowed; his voice was soft. "You haven't seen him in more than thirty years—and suddenly you see him walking down the street? I'm not saying it's impossible, I just think it's unlikely."

"But it was him. I know it was. How would Ophelia know what my father looks like?"

"Angels draw strong influence. And with Ophelia—if you let her—she'll get in your mind and show you anything you want to see. And probably a lot of things you don't want to see, too."

I paused, considering. "Why do you keep saying that, 'if I let her'?"

Alex shrugged. "Relax, Lawson. I'm not trying to attack you."

"Well, you seem to be pretty sure of your ex-girlfriend's skill set."

"You know that's not what I'm saying."

"No, it kind of is. You think Ophelia is stronger than me."

Alex inched away from me and drew in a breath. "All I am saying is that the human mind is very easily influenced. You react well to suggestion. It's not a dig, it's a fact."

I stood up. "Easily influenced? React to suggestion? I am not making this up, Alex. I saw what I saw. It wasn't a suggestion, it was maggots. Fat, creepy, crawly maggots on my plate, on my French fries, everywhere. I *don't* see things, remember? I am magically immune."

Alex bit his lip. "It's not magic. It's powers. We have powers. Angels and demons, we're . . . it's different."

I shook my head, working to block out Alex's words "It was my father. I saw him, and I just knew it was him—your angelic superpowers or not."

"Lawson." Alex's voice was low, his eyes scanning the police station, where people had started to notice us, to drop their papers and swing their heads to the girl with the fire-engine-red hair stomping and screaming in the waiting room.

"I don't know how she did it or why she did it, but your girlfriend"—I spat the word—"tried to poison me. Or freak me out. Or whatever."

Alex rolled his eyes. "She's not my girlfriend. And could you keep your voice down?"

I growled, turned on my heel, and jabbed at the elevator's down button. "I have to get back to work."

The elevator bell dinged and the heavy metal doors slid open. I jumped inside and kicked the CLOSE DOOR button, Alex's face with its mix of anger and concern getting narrower and narrower as the doors eeked shut.

When I got downstairs, the UDA was buzzing. Demons stood hoof-to-hoof in long lines, mildly held in place by swooping velvet ropes. I tried to keep my head down and my eyes low, but I wasn't two feet into the office when Mrs. Henderson—our resident busybody and fire-breathing dragon—stomped over to me, a thick sheaf of papers clutched in her manicured claw.

"Sophie—finally, someone who knows what she's doing. I tell you, that—that—*vampire* that you have working behind the counter is completely useless. Has she ever heard of customer service? I don't think so." Mrs. Henderson turned up her nose, tiny tendrils of black smoke trailing from each nostril. I stepped aside.

"It's nice to see you again, Mrs. Henderson."

Mrs. Henderson and Nina had a long history of glaring at each other and mild name calling, usually culminating with someone (Nina) being set on fire and someone else (me) coming in to diffuse the situation and sign off on whatever dingbat issue was cheesing Mrs. Henderson off at the moment. Apparently, this afternoon it was Mrs. Henderson's inability to collect alimony from Mr. Henderson, who took up with a showgirl he met on a dragon's weekend in Vegas.

"We've got little ones, you know. How am I supposed to feed them?" Mrs. Henderson clutched at her pashmina scarf with her jeweled hand and batted her eyelashes.

"The UDA was supposed to serve him with the papers and garnish his wages. I know for a fact he's making very good money over there at the Luxor, that louse. I'm just so concerned about my little ones." She choked a manufactured wailing sob.

Mrs. Henderson's little ones—two ornery, grey-scaled teenaged creatures—were stretched out on our waiting-room chairs, madly texting on their matching iPhones, Juicy Couture sweatpants pushed up over their scaly knees.

I took the papers Mrs. Henderson was waving. "I'll get these approved right away for you, Mrs. Henderson. I'll get this request in by the end of the day and we can send out a gargoyle to serve Mr. Henderson tomorrow morning. Your check should be here by the end of the week."

Mrs. Henderson clasped her hands. "Oh, Sophie, you're just a lifesaver! I don't care what they say about you—I really think the UDA is lucky to have you."

"Um, thank you," I started.

She quickly put her finger to her narrow lips and her eyes took on a more sinister hue as they looked off into the distance. "Make sure you have the gargoyle get there early in the morning. I only wish I could see the look on that little showgirl-breather's face when she opens the door to a gargoyle." Mrs. Henderson seemed to remember I was there then and smiled kindly at me, big eyelashes batting. "You know, for the children."

I nodded and Mrs. Henderson turned on her heel, leaving me to skip over her long tail. I stumbled backward and got poked in the shoulder by a pushpin holding up a VERM poster advertising their latest meeting. Then I walked down the hall to find Nina.

"Maggots, ugh!" Nina spit out her pale tongue as she sat across from me at her desk. "That is so gross. I hate when maggots get on my food." She shuddered while I arched my eyebrows. "That's why I stopped eating leftovers."

I shut out the image of a half-drained human wrapped in tinfoil that might have once been in Nina's fridge.

"So, I wonder what Ophelia's deal is."

"I don't know. Just messing with me?"

Nina bit her fingernail. "Yeah, but I thought we were

in a fight to the finish for this vase thing. Why would Ophelia be sitting around tossing bugs on stuff when she could be out trapping souls in the Vase of the Lord?"

"It's the Vessel of Souls. And I have no idea. But I know who might."

Nina looked up at me, interested.

"My father was there, Nina. It was him. I need to find him. I think he might be able to answer some questions, help us out with this Vessel thing."

"Sophie, are you sure about this?"

I stood up, wringing my hands. "No, but I know that I have to. Everything is just getting so weird—and that's saying a lot in my life. Maybe he can help me put some things together."

Nina offered a friendly, understanding smile, showing off her fangs, her bloodstained lips. "If you think he could help."

"I think it might be the only way to find the Vessel. I mean, he was hunting for it. Alex said he was the one who got closest."

Nina frowned. "I wonder what made him stop searching."

"I don't know, but hopefully, he can tell me. And maybe get Ophelia out of my life—and my head."

"Or," Nina started, aiming her pen at me, "it could open up a universal war between good and evil, with Ophelia picking teams first and us ending up with the pasty kids who spent their school lunch hours playing Dungeons and Dragons."

I crossed my arms. "So does this mean you're not going to help me?"

Nina stood up, crossed the room and put her arms around me, squeezing me against her ice-cold chest. "Of course I'm going to help you. You're my best friend. Besides, what's a little danger to me? I'm immortal."

"Thanks. I think. But—for now—this is just between you and me, okay? I don't want Alex to know that I'm looking for Lucas."

Nina held out her pinkie and I hooked it with mine. "Deal," she said.

There was a crackle from Nina's desk, and then a smooth, velvety voice came from the intercom. "Nina, may I see you, please?"

Nina dropped my pinkie and rushed to her desk, leaning close to the telephone, seductively pressing her breasts together.

He can't see you, I mouthed.

"Just one second, Mr. Andrade—I mean, Dixon," Nina said, her voice a vixenish trill. Nina clicked the intercom off and yanked open her top desk drawer, revealing a three-tiered makeup collection that Lancôme would be jealous of. She puckered her lips and painted them a ravishing red, then powdered her cheeks an even paler shade of pale.

"I thought you were going to show the new UDA management who they're dealing with. Weren't you all about keeping the new guy in line?"

Nina snapped her compact shut and blotted her lips, then unbuttoned another button on her blouse. "Oh, I'm all about letting Dixon know who he's dealing with."

I rolled my eyes and Nina grabbed my arm, giving it a quick shake. "Oh, come on, Sophie. You have to admit he is a wonderful piece of dead man candy. I mean, those eyes, those lips, those fangs! You know what it means when a vampire has big fangs, don't you?" Nina waggled her eyebrows and I groaned. "Besides, he's got all the traits I adore in a man: He's tall, dark and demonic." She kicked up a happy leg and sauntered on her sky-high heels out the door, then poked her head back in. "Don't wait up. I have a feeling I'll be working late."

Chapter Seven

The sun was slipping behind the fog when I got into my car and headed home. I was still annoyed with Alex and the prospect of finding—and facing—my father weighed heavily on me. I tried to erase it from my mind, or to call up images of all those wonderful father-daughter reunions on the *Maury Povich Show* and from Disney movies, but nothing helped. By the time I pulled into my designated parking space I was jumpy and grumpy.

I was reaching for my bag when a gentle tap-tap got my attention.

"Christ, Grandma, you scared the—"

Grandma narrowed her eyes, staring out at me from my rearview mirror. "Language, Sophie."

"You scared me. What are you doing here?"

"I'm here to talk some sense into you."

I raised my eyebrows and slumped back into my car seat. "Yeah?" The lady in the mirror was going to talk some sense into me? I didn't know what was more non-sensical: Grandma showing up in my rearview mirror or me holding a conversation with her.

"Word around town is that you're going to go looking for your father."

"Word around town? Like, word in *Heaven*?" I whistled. "Sheesh, news travels fast up there."

Grandma shrugged. "You can only play a harp for so many hours each day."

"I guess."

"Sophie, dear, don't go looking for your father. It won't help."

"What do you know about my father?" I asked, feeling a familiar prick up the back of my neck. "If you know something, you should tell me."

"I know enough about him to know that you should steer clear of him."

"Grandma . . ."

"Look," Grandma said, "I'm not going to tell you what to do, honey, but listen to me: Don't try to find him. It's not worth it. Trust me on this."

"So much for not telling me what to do."

Grandmother's eyes narrowed. "Don't sass me, young lady. Mark my words: Your father is only going to let you down." Grandma's voice softened, and there was a moist wistfulness in her milky eyes. "Just like he let your mother down."

"Grandma, don't I deserve to know my father? At the very least, just to know a few things about him? Why would that be such a bad thing?"

Grandma sucked on her teeth and shook her head, her long dangly earrings jangling against her jawbone.

"I just need to know a few things about myself."

"Like what?" my grandmother huffed. "I can tell you everything you need to know. You learned to ride a bike when you were seven. You're a rubbish card player, you come from good Hungarian stock, and you have a weakness for anything with marshmallow in it."

I rolled my eyes. "That's not what I meant and you know it."

Grandma relented, her shoulders noticeably sagging. "If you're going to look for your father, you need to be prepared for what you find."

I felt my shoulders stiffen. "Like what? What am I going to find out about him? You're not telling me anything about him. No one is!"

"Even if I wanted to tell you about him—which I don't—I couldn't." Grandma looked around, her eyes checking the corners of my rearview mirror. "It's not something I can just talk about all willy-nilly out here."

I was getting frustrated. "*What* can't you talk about?"

My grandmother pursed her lips in an expression that tugged at my heart. I had seen it before whenever she was trying to protect me from something she didn't think I could handle.

"I can handle whatever you tell me, Gram. And isn't it better for me to find out things from you rather than on my own?"

"I'm sorry, Sophie," Grandma said. "I'm sorry, honey, but I just can't."

"Gram? Gram!" I peered into the mirror, my own squinting eyes reflecting back at me.

I got out of the car feeling deflated, the frustrated, grumpy feeling still around me. I walked the entire way to my walk-up looking behind me and jumping at every little sound.

I pushed open my apartment door and stood in the foyer, looking around anxiously. "Hello?" I called out, reminding myself of every character ever killed in horror movies. "Anybody home?"

When no one answered me, I dumped my shoulder

bag onto the couch and then flopped there myself, letting my heartbeat slow to a normal, non-frenetic pace.

I almost swallowed my tongue when I heard the knock on my door.

"Son of a—!" I cursed, rolling off the couch and heading for the door. I popped the chain and inched the door open.

"Sophie Lawson?"

Her eyes were impossibly pale and lined with huge, delicate lashes that cast spiderweb shadows across her ruddy pink cheeks.

"Ophelia," I whispered, without opening the door any wider.

Ophelia's pink lips split into a delighted sweet smile, and she bobbed her shoulders in that cute, sorority-girl way that I couldn't get away with. The movement left the faint scent of her freesia perfume on the air. "You know me!"

I stood there, dumbfounded, trying to work out a plan in my head: let her in, try and talk? I chanced a quick second glance at her through the two-inch gap in the doorway: tall, blond, primly dressed in a melon-colored twin set and pencil skirt, a strand of glazed pearls demurely wrapped around her neck. She looked more like a PTA mom than a crazed supernatural killer.

Then I thought of Alex, his stern eyes and the hard set of his jawline as he warned about Ophelia. Maybe I should slam the door and take off running? I was seriously considering the latter when there was a splitting smack against my cheek. A piercing heat starburst through my nose, up against my forehead. I reeled backward, stumbling into my living room, my eyes watering from the sting. I blinked rapidly and the tears tumbled down my cheeks as I pressed my fingers against the mashed-in spot where my nose once was. Now it stung and started to tickle as the blood came.

Ophelia's eyes still looked wide and innocent; there wasn't a wrinkle or a shard of splintered wood on her twin set, and her pearls had barely moved.

I gaped at Ophelia as she stood in my foyer, arms crossed in front of her, a delicate purse hanging from her pinkie.

My front door hung limply from its hinges just over her left shoulder. I was *so* not going to get my security deposit back.

"I was going to let you in, you know," I said, my hand massaging a new hot spot on my cheek.

Ophelia shrugged. "Patience is a virtue." Her eyes narrowed and sparkled with something that sent a cold chill down my spine. "And I'm not very virtuous. Now come on." She held out her hand, palm up, fingers beckoning. "I don't have all day. And frankly"—she looked around my apartment distastefully—"your decorating is giving me hives."

I crossed my own arms in front of my chest and widened my stance, determined to stare her down. I heard a high-pitched giggle reverberate through my head and then Ophelia's rich voice. *Cute,* I heard her say—although her lips stayed pressed together in a pale pink line. *You think you can stand up to me?*

"Don't do that," I said, my teeth gritted.

"Do what?" she asked, batting her eyelashes innocently.

A second tinkle of laughter swept through my head. I wanted to clench my eyes shut, but I knew better than to take my gaze off Ophelia.

"Stop."

"Then give me what I want."

"I don't—" Before I could finish my sentence, my

thought, Ophelia was nose to nose with me and then her hands were on my chest, shoving me hard. I was off balance, reeling backward, groaning when I felt my back make contact with the floor, my head thumping against the carpet. "Oaf!"

"Don't screw with me!" she snarled, advancing toward me.

I yelped when Ophelia's foot made contact with my thigh and a wallop of pain ached through me.

She lunged for me again and I rolled out of her way, but not before her hand grazed the top of my head, her fingernails raking through my hair. I howled and turned instinctively, and was surprised when I felt the back of my hand make contact with Ophelia's cheek. There was a satisfying crack and I retrieved my stinging hand.

We both stood looking at each other in stunned silence—her rubbing her reddening cheek, me rubbing my new bald spot. She lunged for me again, barely missing me as I crab-crawled to the bookshelf and used it to pull myself up, the ache in my leg tightening like a fist. I used the back of my arm to swipe at my nose, and my stomach lurched when I saw the bright red ribbon of blood on my arm. Other people's blood never bothered me that much, but my own was a different story. I felt woozy and Ophelia seemed to know it, her face breaking into a satisfied half-smile.

"This could go so much more smoothly, you know," she said, picking up a lamp and smashing it on the coffee table Van Damme style. She held the broken shards to me, her baby pink lips distorted into a gruesome snarl. "Give it!"

I shrunk against the bookcase, feeling the wood pressing against my shoulders. Ophelia held the jagged glass edge of the lamp against my neck, pressing the tines in for effect. I winced as I felt them cut my skin.

"Okay, okay, okay," I wailed, my head feeling tender and raw. "The Vessel. I know you want the Vessel." I took a deep breath that made my bruised chest scream with pain and carefully, solemnly slid a pale green milk-glass vase from the lower shelf. I discreetly upturned it and brushed away the parade of crumpled gum wrappers that lived inside of it and then turned around, cuddling the dollar-ninety-nine IKEA vase to my chest reverently.

"Okay, Ophelia. You win." With shaking hands I held the vase out to Ophelia, who stared at it, wide-eyed, wanting. "Here is the Vessel of Souls."

Ophelia raised one sculpted eyebrow and jabbed at the air in front of her. *"That?"*

I nodded. "Yes, this. The angels often charm things so they can be hidden—"

"In plain sight, blah, blah, blah." Ophelia finished. "Don't forget who you're talking to."

I licked my dry lips. "Of course. So, here it is. You win, fair and square."

Ophelia reached out and smacked the vase with the back of her hand, sending it hurtling to the ground, crashing against the hardwood floor. Thick shards of pale green glass splintered in all directions; the one that held the dollar ninety-nine IKEA price tag skidded toward me and landed a quarter-inch from my sneaker.

We heard the gentle *ahhhh* of souls ascending to Heaven.

Ophelia stamped her foot, one hand on her hip. "Stop that!"

I snapped my mouth shut and the wailing *ahhh* stopped. Then Ophelia smiled. A grotesque smile of delight that twisted her normally lovely features into something awful.

You really don't know, do you? Her voice was in my head again.

"Don't know what?" I snarled out loud. "And stop with the head talk!"

"Sophie!"

I cut my eyes to our front door hanging askew, anchored by a single hinge. Nina flung it open and the bent hinge gave way, the door flopping to the ground.

"You stay the hell away from her!" Nina screamed, her dark eyes fierce and intent on Ophelia.

"Oh, wow." Ophelia glanced from me to Nina. "And her toothy pal comes to the rescue. If only you knew what you were guarding."

Nina was between Ophelia and me in a heartbeat, standing nose to nose with Ophelia, the jagged piece of lamp hanging limply at her side. "Don't you have a harp to strum?" Nina spat from between gritted teeth.

Ophelia wrinkled her nose. "A harp, that's cute." She narrowed her eyes and elbowed Nina hard in the chest, sending her skittering to the ground. Nina landed on her back with a thud. I tried to lunge to Nina, but Ophelia clamped her hand on my shoulder. I heard myself cry out as her fingers dug into my muscle, forming heat against my skin.

A low growl escaped from Nina's chest and she flung herself against Ophelia, who deftly stepped aside, taking me with her.

"Knock, knock!"

We all seemed to freeze, openmouthed and panicked, as we looked at Mr. Matsura, who stood in the doorway, his wrinkled lips turned up in a quizzical smile.

Mr. Matsura lived across the hall in an afghan-festooned apartment that was stuck in 1952. He wore a cardigan sweater over his button-up shirt and neatly pressed slacks with his house slippers when he went out at dawn and at dusk for his daily walks. In the waking hours in between, he ate takeout and watched the game-show channel, the volume turned up to an ungodly level. I credit my ability to correctly guess the prices of a cata-maran, a set of Calphalon pans, and an electric skillet to his faulty hearing aid.

He let out a low whistle as he slid his palm over the cracked door frame. "Looks like someone did some damage here."

Mr. Matsura looked like a smiling beacon of hope—or the next victim in Ophelia's domestic destruction.

Without loosening her grip on me, Ophelia grinned, her smile dazzling and welcoming even as her fingertips continued to burrow into my shoulder. "And you are?"

Mr. Matsura jabbed his thumb over his shoulder. "Neighbor. Right across the hall."

My heart started to beat again and the blood was re-turning to my extremities. Nina was pushing herself up from the floor and Ophelia snaked her arm across my shoulders, making our threesome look more like a group of overzealous girlfriends than a battle for the fate of the humankind.

"We just got a little out of control," Ophelia said, sweet innocence dripping from her voice. "Sorry to have bothered you."

Mr. Matsura opened his mouth to speak, his hand ges-turing toward the broken door.

"Sorry to have bothered you," Ophelia said again, this time slowly, her crystal-blue eyes focused hard on Mr. Matsura's. He closed his mouth and nodded, his eyes taking on a dull, vacant glaze. He turned slowly and dis-appeared into his own apartment.

"How did you—"

"Shut up," Ophelia hissed. She frowned. "That really harshed my buzz."

Ophelia loosened her grip on me, and I shrugged away, trying to rub some feeling back into my shoulder.

Nina gaped. "Your buzz?"

Ophelia narrowed her eyes and they glittered a sinister blue. "Violence makes me giddy." She shoved her way between Nina and me and stepped backward, heading toward the front door, the crumbles of our vase and shards of splintered door frame rustling under her feet. She hung in our broken doorway, her hands on what remained of the frame.

"Well, you know what they say about three being a crowd. Nina, it was just precious to meet you in person. Sophie, you and I will pick this up later."

And I can hardly wait for that. Ophelia's voice rang in my brain, her eyes brimming with intent and focused hard on me.

Once Ophelia disappeared out the front door Nina rushed to me, gathering me in her arms and crushing me against her cold, marble chest. "Oaf," I groaned, feeling the bruise from Ophelia's push.

"Oh, I'm so sorry," Nina said, pushing away from me. "Are you hurt? Did she get the Vessel?" Her dark eyes traveled to the shards of broken milk glass on the floor. "Was that it?"

"No. Yes. I mean, I'm fine." I massaged my chest. "Mostly. And no, that's not the Vessel."

Nina crouched down, gathering up the glass pieces. "Well, that's good." She picked up a piece, scrutinized it. "I'd hate to think that God shopped at IKEA." She brushed the rest of the glass into her bloodless palm and dumped it into the trash in the kitchen. "So you're okay?"

"I will be." I went to the kitchen for a wet rag and caught a glimpse of myself in the hall mirror: bald spot slightly visible, black marks already starting to blossom under each eye, blood caking and starting to dry at the corner of my mouth. I checked my neck and groaned at the constellation of tiny bloody pricks there and Nina came up behind me, frowning.

"Wow, she really got you good. Are you sure you're okay? Can I get you something—a Band-Aid, a transfusion?"

I wet a rag and pressed it against my neck, then gingerly laid a package of frozen corn across my head. The sting of the cold seemed to counteract the sting of my lack of hair.

I slumped onto the couch, pulling my knees up to my chest. "Now I'm just confused."

"Confused?" Nina brushed her hands on her skirt and pulled a second package of frozen vegetables from the freezer. She sat down next to me on the couch and carefully laid the bag on the purple handprints peeking out of my shirt. "About what?"

"Ophelia." I pressed the frozen peas to my chest, held the corn against my head.

"She's a class-one nutter. What's there to be confused about?"

"When I handed her the vase—which I tried to pass off as the Vessel—"

Nina grinned. "Nice strategy."

"Thanks. Anyway, she knew right away that that wasn't it."

"So Ophelia knows what the Vessel looks like."

"Yeah." I nodded. "But then she seemed almost amused. She looked me up and down and said, 'You really don't know, do you?' Why does everyone seem to think that I know something I don't, or that I don't need to know something I should? Or you know, maybe should."

Nina shrugged her small shoulders.

"It wasn't even what she said was so weird. It was the *way* she said it. It was like I was a piece of meat. It was weird." I shuddered. "Gave me the heebie jeebies."

"Well, didn't the fallen angels used to drink the blood and eat the flesh of man? So, maybe you were, like, dinner?" Nina grinned triumphantly.

I raised my eyebrows.

"Not that *I've* ever thought of you that way."

"I know. But it wasn't hungry-like; it was . . . appraising, almost."

Nina looked thoughtful. "Well, Alex said the Vessel could be anything or anywhere. Maybe you *do* have it and you don't even know it. Maybe it is here."

I looked around the apartment. "You said yourself you don't think God shops at IKEA. That doesn't leave much else around here."

Nina sprang up from the couch and walked toward the bookcase. "Maybe it's this." She held up a porcelain elephant with gold tusks.

"Doubt it. My college boyfriend gave me that."

She studied the figurine, then dumped it into the trash-can. "It's definitely time to let go of that one. What if it's this?" Nina snatched up a tattered copy of *Lady Chatterley's Lover.* "Wouldn't that be hilarious?"

I stood up and took the paperback from Nina, returning it to its spot on the shelf. "No." I glanced at everything on the bookshelf, my hands on my hips. "I can't imagine it's anything here. And most of this stuff I've had forever or picked up randomly along the way. I would think that the Vessel of Souls would have come into my possession in a more regal way—not from an old boyfriend or from the used bookstore."

"So IKEA is out then?"

"Wow," Alex said from the hallway as he gingerly

stepped over our crumbled front door. "Did I forget to tell you that you put the key in and then turn the knob?"

I rolled my eyes. "Ophelia was here."

"Ophelia?" Alex's eyes widened and he came inside, setting his slick leather jacket on the table. He crossed the living room in one swoop and rested his hands on my shoulders. "Are you okay? Did she hurt you at all?"

"Did she hurt me at all?" I pointed to my mask of bruises. "I look like a prizefighter. Who lost." The frozen corn slid from my head and thunked on the floor.

"You dropped your corn," Alex said, pointing at it. "Really, Lawson, are you going to be okay? Should we take you to the emergency room?"

"No," I said quietly. "I'm okay."

Alex pulled me against him and I melted into his warm chest, shivered as I felt his strong arms slide across my back, encircling me, protecting me, melting the bag of frozen peas between us. "I couldn't stand it if she hurt one hair on your head."

"Well," Nina said from over Alex's left shoulder. "She hurt our vase. Where have you been? We could have been dead! Or, you know, dead . . . *er*. Don't forget, you brought that psychopath into our lives."

Alex ignored Nina, and held me at arm's length, his cobalt eyes intense and locked on mine. "You're sure you're okay?"

I nodded. "I'm okay." For the first time I noticed that Alex was dressed in dark jeans cinched with an expensive-looking brown leather belt. He was wearing a butter-soft deep green cashmere sweater that V'ed at the neck, a bit of his white T-shirt peeking out from underneath. The thin sweater was formfitting, and hugged the muscles across his chest and broad shoulders in all the right places. His hair—a usual jumble of chocolaty dark curls that spilled this way and that—was brushed back and gelled.

"You gelled?"

A flush of crimson went across Alex's cheeks as he reached a hand up to pat his hair. "It's stupid. I—"

"No, it looks nice. You look nice. Why do you look so—?" I slammed my mouth shut, knowing flooding over me.

My date. My big date.

Alex's smile was polite. "You forgot?"

Nina stepped in between us. "Yes, she forgot. Can you blame her? She's been tenderized by hurricane Ophelia!"

Alex looked pained and gingerly tucked a lock of hair behind my ear. "Does it hurt much?"

I rubbed the sore spot on my cheek. "I told you, it's fine. It looks worse than it is. I'm pale; I bruise easily."

"I would feel better if you were protected."

"Like with a bodyguard?" I nodded toward Nina. "I've already got a vampire."

Nina put her hands on her hips. "So that's why you keep me around?"

"Geez! And you say my friends are messy!" We all swung to look as Vlad stood in the doorway, his calf-length velvet coat swirling in a nonexistent breeze, his jacquard ascot puffed against his silk vest.

"Sophie got attacked," Nina filled him in.

Vlad frowned. "Wow! You look terrible."

"Yeah, but you should see what the other guy looks like," I joked.

Nina's eyes were wide. "Yeah, she's really pretty. I love her hair."

I tried to glare, but my face was sore. "Geez, sorry," Nina said, threading her arm through Vlad's. "Come on." She dragged Vlad toward her room. "You're helping me organize."

Alex leaned in toward me. "Do you still have the gun I got you?"

In Alex and my previous relationship incarnation, I found myself the victim of things going bump in the night. Alex's gift of a lethal weapon wasn't just romantic, it was practical.

Still, I would have preferred chocolates.

"Yeah, I still have it."

"Somewhere close by?"

I went to the kitchen and retrieved the gun from its special hiding place in the junk drawer. The slick, black .357 Magnum kept my packets of takeout soy sauce, bubble gum, and twist ties safe.

Alex took the gun and released the magazine. "It's not loaded. Do you still have any bullets?"

I dutifully went to the freezer and scooped a handful of silver-tipped bullets from their hiding place in an ancient box of Skinny Cow ice cream bars—ice cream bars having been eaten to make room for bullets. From the exasperated look on Alex's face as I dumped the frozen ammo into his palm, I figured it was best to keep to myself the fact that I had, on occasion, used the butt of the gun for some light fix-it projects around the house.

Alex frowned down at the butt of the gun, picking at something white stuck into the grooves with his fingernail. "Is that plaster?"

"Either that or the sugar coating from the bubble gum in the junk drawer," I said. And then, noticing the sheer annoyance marching across Alex's face, "I don't know. It's your gun." I batted my eyelashes attractively before Alex had the chance to roll his eyes.

"You know what," he said, putting the gun aside, "we'll deal with firepower later. We have a game to get to. Are you still up for it?"

I slapped my palm to my forehead—then winced. "That's right! My Giants!"

Alex held out a hand. "We don't have to go."

"The hell we don't!" I jumped up and tried to mask the sharp pain I felt by pasting on a home-team grin. Then I looked at Alex and frowned. "You can't go like that."

Alex looked down at himself. "Like what?"

"Like—" I struggled for the right word. Like "every fantasy I've ever had" didn't seem to cut it. Instead, I grabbed his hand and dragged him toward my room. "Come on, let's get you set."

I rummaged through my pajama drawer and grinned, triumphantly holding out a Barry Bonds commemorative T-shirt. "Here, put this on. Just—"

My eyes widened and my mouth went dry as Alex dutifully slipped off his sweater, revealing a tight white T-shirt underneath that hugged his firm chest appreciatively.

"Don't—"

He whipped off the T-shirt next and I was left staring dumbfounded and openmouthed at his smooth chest, his muscles like perfect stair steps down his abdomen. I commanded myself to tear my eyes away but was drawn to his sun-kissed contours like a moth to a flame. He slipped the Barry Bonds T-shirt over his head and grinned at me, caught ogling.

"What was that?"

"Uh, just don't . . . get mustard on it." I gave him a tight-lipped smile.

"How do I look?"

Yummy! I wanted to scream. I bit my lip. "Needs something. Oh, wait." I turned to my closet, rooted around a bit, and turned, sliding a giant orange foam finger onto Alex's left hand. "Perfect!"

Alex looked at the enormous finger, shook it. "You

know, I was going to wear this, but I thought, nah, too formal for a first date."

The word "date" tumbling off his lips gave my heart a little shudder. Normal people went on dates, and normal girls got kisses at the end of their dates. I snuck a glance at Alex's full lips and licked my own.

"Come on," I said, dragging him out the front door by his normal-sized hand.

There was already a heavy mist on the air when we hit the sidewalk. Alex jingled his keys and I raised my eyebrows.

"What are you planning on doing with those?"

"I was planning on driving with them."

I shook my head, took his keys, and deposited them in my purse. He stared at his open palm when I laid a dollar bill in it.

"What's this for?"

"Muni. No one drives to the ballpark." I grabbed his sleeve and started tugging. "Come on, the five will be here any minute."

We fed our dollars into the machine and collected our tickets while the bus driver gave us both a broad smile and an enthusiastic thumbs-up. We edged our way down the crowded bus aisle, angled ourselves between the sea of orange and black–clad revelers. Sitting shoulder to shoulder, jostling toward the ballpark, I felt happily normal—scratches, black eye, and visit from one pissed-off angel aside. I looked around and felt as one with my city mates—even though my companion was technically dead. Alex's knee thumped against mine, and he smiled, rubbing his hand over my knee, sending shivers up my spine, making every one of my hormones stand at attention.

Maybe today wouldn't be the crappiest one in recent memory.

Forty-five minutes later we were seated behind home

plate, balancing overpriced beers and trough-sized baskets of garlic fries on our knees. Alex held both our hot dogs in one hand and sipped at his beer while I arranged my jacket and beckoned for the peanut guy as he made his way down the aisle.

"Peanuts, too? When was the last time you ate?"

"It's not a matter of hunger," I reported, fishing some bills out of my back pocket. "It's all about the ballpark experience."

Alex got the peanut guy's attention and pushed my money aside, shelling out for two warm bags of nuts. "Okay, do we have everything?"

I took my hot dog from his hand and took a big bite, nodding happily. "Let's play ball!" I said with a mouthful.

Alex grinned and wiped away a smear of mustard from my chin. I blushed with his touch, blushed when his eyes held mine a moment too long.

Nine innings later we were covered in a fine spray of ocean mist and flushed with the excitement of a tight win. We both oozed garlic and mustard and as we wound through the horde of slow-moving Giants fans, Alex reached out and took my hand, pulling me close against him. His chest was warm and deliciously firm, and I could smell his comforting cocoa scent tinged with a touch of fabric softener and stadium mustard as I leaned against him.

"So, you like baseball?"

He looked down at me, his cobalt eyes bright in the stadium lights, and pulled me closer. "I love it."

I swallowed hard as my mouth watered and my mind was littered with unmentionable things; I felt the pressure on my cheeks from what must have been a four-hour grin.

"Me, too."

It was a hike back to the connecting bus stop and rather than take a cab, we strolled hand in hand in the mist, walking along the deserted streets when suddenly Alex stiffened. I saw the muscle in his jaw tighten, his lips tense. "Did you hear that?"

I cocked my head to one side, listening to the night sounds of the city: the mournful wail of a police siren, the buzz of the yellow streetlight above us.

"Hear what?"

Alex whirled around and I felt a spike of fear start at the base of my spine and prick its way up. My saliva went sour. "I heard that."

It was the raspy sound of sneakers on concrete coming to an abrupt stop. The sound of heavy breathing—distinct, though barely audible on the late-night breeze.

"Maybe it's just—"

My words were cut off by the sound of a blade slicing through the air. I felt a body make contact with mine; then the wind as it left my chest when I made contact with the cold, damp concrete. I only knew Alex had been hit when I heard the strangled sound of his groan.

"Sophie, run!"

Everything seemed to be happening in slow motion and Alex's command didn't even sound like him. It was higher, more menacing, and I kicked my feet, sliding on the concrete until I got some traction, then stopped dead, seeing the dark figure in front of Alex.

Our attacker was dressed entirely in black and stood a half-head taller than Alex, his face obscured by a black knit ski mask that only revealed sinister hooded eyes that remained fixed on us. He held his blade aloft once more and I heard my own scream when I saw the blood—Alex's blood—dripping from the cold steel.

The man dove forward, his body colliding with Alex's with a stomach-churning thud, the blade hacking at the air just behind Alex's left ear. I tried to grab at the assailant, to push away his knife and when Alex got the upper hand I did the only thing I could think of. Within seconds I had my arms around our attacker's neck, my legs flailing wildly as I rode his back. His non-knife hand pulled back to grab at me and I gripped it, and bit down as hard as I could on the fleshy web between his forefinger and thumb. He howled, hunched, and launched me forward. I rammed into Alex's chest and he caught me, sloppily, both of us going down to the concrete and rolling apart. The wail of a police siren sounded somewhere in the distance and droned until it was closer; by the time I looked up, our attacker was long gone.

"Are you okay?" Alex asked breathily.

"I'm fine but you're—" I gaped at the red velvet blood that rippled through his fingers as he clutched his shoulder. "You're hurt. We've got to get you to the hospital." I sprang to my feet and sprinted into the middle of the street, flailing my arms wildly at no one.

"Where is everyone? This is an emergency! We need a doctor! We need an ambulance!" I rolled up on my tiptoes as though the extra half inch would allow me to see over the building tops. "What happened to the police siren?"

Alex lumbered up and put his hand on my shoulder. "I'm fine; it's nothing. It's just a scratch."

"A scratch?" I could smell the metallic scent of his blood and it made me slightly woozy. "We've got to do something! You could lose that arm!" I patted myself. "Oh! Cell phone!"

"It's fine."

Before I could steady my shaking fingers enough to dial, I saw Alex use his good arm to flag down a couple of orbs of white light coming from the dark alley. I felt a little splinter of joy. A cab! We're saved!

The yellow cab stopped in the middle of the street in front of us. I hustled Alex inside and half climbed over the front seat. "SF General and step on it! We've just been mugged." I sat back on the bench seat as the cabbie sped off. "We were mugged, right?"

Alex, still holding his shoulder, shrugged, then winced. "He didn't ask for my wallet. But I lost your foam finger." He looked apologetic and I used both my hands against his chest to push him against the seat. "Don't talk. Relax. We'll get you another foam finger. You've just got to live!" I searched frantically in my purse.

"What are you doing?"

"I'm looking for something to make a tourniquet. We've got to stop the bleeding. I'm not going to let you bleed out in the back of this godforsaken cab." I leaned back over the front seat. "No offense."

"None taken."

I could feel the sweat bead out at my hairline and above my upper lip as I wrung my hands and looked out the front windshield. "Can't you go any faster?"

When I turned back to Alex, he was grinning.

"What?"

"You. I'm fine, really. It's a scratch. Hey, guy, can you just take us back to her house? In the Sunset."

The driver obediently flipped on his blinker and I lurched over the front seat. "No. San Francisco General."

He flipped his blinker in the other direction.

"Lawson, I'm fine."

"You're delirious! We need to call the cops. Did we get anything on the perp?"

Alex pushed me back with his good hand and a slight smile. "*You're* delirious. The perp? Didn't I tell you no more *Law and Order*?" He reached for me, fingered my elbow. "You've got a heck of a scratch there."

I glanced down, shrugged him off, and pointed to the piddly-looking collection of scratches on my arm. "*That* is nothing. That"—I gestured to his gaping wound—"is serious."

"Lawson—"

I touched Alex's hand, and felt his blood on my fingertips. I felt the tears burning behind my eyes. "But you're going to bleed out."

Alex put both hands firmly on my shoulders and stared me in the eye, his an intense, piercing blue. "Lawson, I am not going to bleed out. I am not"—he glanced over the seat and then back at me, dropping his voice—"a normal person."

I don't know if it was divine intervention, angelic persuasion or the post-mustard drunkenness of a Giants win, but I believed him instantly and nodded enthusiastically. "Right. Right."

"So no hospital?" the cab driver wondered.

"No, no." I glanced back at Alex. "It's not as bad as I thought it was."

Alex kept a firm grip on his shoulder as I pushed open the door of the apartment building. "You're sure you're okay?"

"It's going to be fine." His tongue dragged across his bottom lip and I cursed myself for feeling so wildly attracted to this sexy, bleeding man.

"Come upstairs."

I held the apartment door open for Alex and watched Nina go from prone to bolt upright on the couch, an *InStyle* magazine falling onto the floor, her nostrils flaring. "Who's bleeding?" she asked without turning around.

Alex paled and took a step back, ramming into me. I

shoved around him. "Alex. And he's going to be fine. Is the first aid kit still under the sink?"

He grabbed my elbow as I tried to step away. "Is she going to—?"

"Eat you? No." Nina stood in front of us, offered me the first aid kit. While I was impressed by her vampire speed, Alex still seemed unconvinced that he wasn't about to be a vamp snack.

"And Vlad is out with the fang gang, burning copies of *True Blood* or something. So what happened?"

"We were mugged. Take off your shirt."

Alex's eyes nervously trailed to Nina and she rolled hers. "Fine!" She stomped toward her room. "But just so you know, if I were going to eat you, I would have done it a long time ago."

"Good to know."

"Hemophobe." She slammed the door.

"Shirt off."

Alex did as he was told and I went from Florence Nightingale to Jenna Jameson. My mouth watered at the smooth contours of his chest and my body ached, remembering how long it had been since I had seen half-naked man flesh . . . in the flesh. Now it was twice in one night.

"Is something wrong?"

I wagged my head and busied myself soaking a washrag under the faucet and lining up a roll of gauze and surgical tape. "Okay, move your hand."

The blood was smeared from the edge of Alex's collarbone and thickened into a dark red band around his bicep. The thin edges of his tattoo faded into the blood and I used the damp rag to gently wipe it away, careful not to aggravate the open wound. I wiped a little more and Alex's naked skin peeked through, a healthy pink.

More skin, more pink. I grabbed his palm and scrubbed that, then frowned, taking a step back.

"Where is all this blood coming from?" I snatched the discarded Barry Bonds T-shirt he had been wearing and poked my fingers through the neat, blood-soaked hole at the shoulder.

Alex bit his bottom lip. "I told you."

"But it's—gone?"

Alex rung out the rag, wetted it again, and scrubbed his arm. He turned on the coffee-table lamp and beckoned me to look closer. I squinted, and saw a five-inch scar in his skin. It was clean, slightly puckered—a pale remembrance of a slice.

I touched it gently, my fingertips gliding over the glossy, raised surface. "It's healed."

He gave me a tight-lipped smile. "Kind of an above-world perk."

"Right." I cleared my throat and stumbled toward my bedroom. "Let me get your clothes—uh, your shirt. It's—it's late."

I picked up his sweater. It was cold from sitting on my desk, just under my open window all night. I pressed the soft fabric to my face, held it against my nose and breathed, but the scent, the warm, comforting scent of Alex, was gone. All I could get was the distant scent of the ocean on the night air. I felt a lump rise in my throat, felt the frustratingly familiar sting of tears starting to form behind my eyes.

He ate hot dogs. He stepped on popcorn. He slurped when he drank his beer, he howled at the umpire, he slung his arm around my shoulders and belted out "Take Me Out to the Ball Game" with the thousands of other fans in the stadium.

But he wasn't like them.

I glanced down at the scratch on my arm, red and puckered and angry, throbbing with a gentle, warm heat and so distinctly alive.

"Lawson?" Alex called from the living room.

"I'll be right there."

Chapter Eight

When I woke up, my bedroom was blanketed in a warm canary yellow. It was comforting, until I realized it was a Post-it note stuck to my forehead. I peeled it off and read Nina's loopy, bubbled script: *Put some Mercurochrome on that scratch. I can smell you from the living room! xoxo Neens.*

Did I mention that living with a vampire took some getting used to?

I rolled out of bed and trudged, still half asleep, to the kitchen, where I flicked on the coffeemaker and repeated the slow plod to the bathroom.

"Ahem!"

I glanced into the mirror and sighed. "Grandma, I'm really not in the mood."

My grandmother's bushy white brows raised, then furrowed. "What happened to your face?"

"Alex and I got mugged last night."

Grandma's milky blue eyes widened and she pursed her bright red lips, the stain of the lipstick sinking into her wrinkles. "What is that city coming to? Used to be a girl and her beau—" Grandma's eyes flicked back to me.

"He is your beau, isn't he?" I didn't answer and she prattled on, oblivious. "Could spend a night out without fear of being attacked by some animal. Or some dope-head or some criminal all hopped up on—on marijuana."

I shrugged. "It wasn't that bad. This"—I pointed to the purpling mask of bruises under my right eye—"is actually from a different incident."

Another tsking sigh.

I rolled up on my toes and gripped the sides of the sink. "Hey, Gram, can I ask you something?"

"Of course you can, honey. You can ask me anything."

"Why didn't you ever get married?"

Grandma's shoulders stiffened and I could tell that I had caught her off guard. "What are you getting at?"

"Nothing, I just—I don't remember there ever being . . . someone . . . in your life . . . that way. And Mom and Dad didn't work out and . . ."

Grandma raised her brows. "And?"

I sunk back onto the souls of my feet. "And never mind. I have to get ready for work."

I didn't remember dressing myself in charcoal-grey slacks and a black cowl-necked sweater. I didn't remember driving to work or the six hours that passed between getting there and processing the last demon request—a notice of intention to cease terror—offered up by a fanged creature with an unfortunate underbite.

"You understand that by giving up your right to terrify, you are also giving up all under-bed, dark-corner, and closet access?" I mumbled.

"I just don't want to be the boogeyman anymore. I'm hoping to get this underbite worked on and I can't get a dentist to even look at me without the cease notice."

I stamped his form and sent him to the next line over, then hung my head and rubbed my temples.

Suddenly, I had a pounding headache and the fat velvet ropes that held our daily demons in orderly lines were bulging, and everyone was talking at once—a cacophony of groans, growls, and wailing howls. My blood started to pulse in my veins and my heart sped up to a feverish, sickening pace. My hairline started to prick with little beads of sweat.

"I've got to get out of here."

I slid the closed sign across my window and pressed out of my chair so quickly that I left it spinning behind me. I was making my way toward the elevator when I stopped, taking in a lungful of freesia-scented air.

Ophelia.

Every muscle in my body tightened into a painful spasm and I looked around, panicked. I spotted a snatch of blond hair between two tall centaurs. Her elegant, sun-bronzed shoulder standing out against the stark whiteness of a vampire in line. Her laugh, tinkling in my ear. I shook my head and clamped my eyes shut.

"You're not here, you're not here," I whispered.

I flinched when I felt a cold hand encircle my arm. "Sophie?"

Nina was still gripping even as I tried to flail. She was holding a paper cup filled with water and looking concerned. "What's wrong?"

"Ophelia," I managed, my lips dry. "She's here."

"Drink this."

Nina handed me the cup and I stared down into it and then blinked up at Nina. *Is it Nina?* Even my own hand circling the cup looked foreign to me and I dropped it, feeling the water splash against my ankles as I sped for the elevator. I mashed the CLOSE DOOR button and hung my head as the concerned and confused eyes of the demon Underworld bore into me.

I tore out of the elevator and ran with my head down through the police station vestibule, not wanting to be stopped. When I pushed outside the damp air caught in my throat and dripped down my cheeks. It was then I realized that I was crying.

I'm going crazy.

I doubled over and stared at the blacktop while I took in huge gulps of air. I was hiccupping and shivering, and I jumped when I felt a hand on my shoulder. I stumbled until Alex reached out and steadied me.

"Hey, Lawson, are you all right? You took off like a shot from the elevator. Didn't even stop when I called. Hey, are you crying?"

I sniffled, feeling the itch of my runny nose, and then threw myself against Alex's chest, letting out a day's worth of heaving cries. I felt him stiffen and then soften, his arms encircling me, one hand gingerly holding the back of my head, the other patting my back softly.

"Hey, hey, it's going to be okay. We're going to get through this."

I snorted. "I don't even know what *this* is. First you show up, and then Ophelia shows up. And then there's maggots and my door and the mugging and you get stabbed, but you still look like"—I gestured to Alex's perfectly sculpted chest and broad shoulders—"that and I look like, like crap." I sniffled and used the back of my hand to wipe at my eyes, then winced when a starburst of pain set off through the bruise. "Ow!"

"I'm sorry. I'm sorry that I dragged you into this."

"I just"—*hiccup, sniff*—"want to be"—*sniff, sniff*—"normal. Or not normal. But not this in-between, my-butt-gets-kicked-and-stays-kicked human. And I want her out of my head."

Alex pulled me forward, his lips laying feathery kisses across my forehead. "I am so, so sorry, Lawson. I'm going to do everything I can to make it up to you."

I cried myself to exhaustion in Alex's office while he dialed Nina at the UDA and asked her to bring up my things. She rushed in, my coat and purse clutched in her pale hands.

"What happened? Are you okay? Did she come after you again?"

"I'm fine," I whimpered. "My life is just a toilet bowl of despair and I look like a battered wife, but I'm fine. I just want to go home and take a nap."

Nina smiled sympathetically. "Can I drive you?"

I shook my head. "I'll be fine. But can you cover for me?"

Nina's sweet smile turned salacious and she popped a button on her blouse. "You mean distract Dixon until closing? You bet."

I squeezed her hand. "I can always depend on you to be slutty when it counts."

Nina gave me a military salute and sped back downstairs.

"You sure you're okay to drive?"

I nodded again and Alex walked me to the parking lot. "I'm just going to wrap up a few things and then I'll come over. I'll pick up dinner and we can figure this out. Don't answer the door to anyone and don't answer the phone unless it's me or Nina."

I nodded robotically and started to turn, my head a heavy, foggy mess.

"Hey." Alex took my hand, and I turned to stare at him, my eyes feeling like blank saucers. He kissed my palm and looked at me with kind eyes. "Be safe."

* * *

I had just finished watching my third hour of Discovery Health and had diagnosed myself with sarcoidosis, Morton's neuroma, and a mild case of dwarfism when there was a quick rap on the door, followed by someone trying the knob. My heart dropped into my stomach and my blood felt warm as I crept—keeping low to the ground—to the door. "Who is it?" I hissed, keeping my distance.

"It's Alex."

I raised one eyebrow and my hand hovered over the knob. "Are you sure?"

"Look, Lawson, I'm glad you're taking my advice with the whole don't-open-the-door thing, but it's late and the grease from this takeout bag is eating through my sleeve.

"You brought Bambino's?"

"Open the door."

I pushed the door open a few inches and poked my nose toward the opening, sniffing cautiously. The overwhelming scent of garlic and oregano floated up to greet me and my mouth watered. I reached out and snatched the bag, examining it from every angle and sniffing like a patrolling bloodhound.

"Are you satisfied?" Alex asked, coming in and shutting the door behind him. "It's dinner."

I examined the dinner-plate-sized grease stain on the side of the bag. "It certainly looks like Bambino's."

"Lawson . . ."

I put down the bag and put my fists on my hips. "Look, you're the one who told me to be careful. I think you once even said, 'You never can be too careful.' Or maybe that was on Court TV, but either way, I think it's good advice."

Alex cocked his head, a half-smile playing on his full, tasty lips. "You're cute when you're belligerent."

"I'm not belligerent."

Alex opened the bag, removing tinned boxes of marinara-stained takeout. "I'm glad you're being extra careful, but you know you can trust me."

Do I? The thought lodged in my cerebral before I even had a chance to challenge it. I tried to shrug it off, to ply it with hunks of cheese-covered bread, but the nagging thought remained.

Alex pointed at me with a handful of plastic utensils. "Here, sit."

I did as I was told and Alex helped himself to the two plates I owned plus a heap of paper napkins.

"Mangia."

I raised an eyebrow. "Are—were—you Italian?"

It occurred to me then that beyond the cut-glass blue of his eyes and his dark chocolaty hair, beyond his chiseled chest and a light introduction to his supernatural history, I didn't know much about Alex Grace.

He nodded as he chewed. "Half. On my mother's side."

"And your father?"

Alex shrugged, reaching for a fork. "American mutt, I think."

"Didn't you know him well?"

Alex put down his fork. "I don't remember."

I swallowed. "It's been that long?"

"When—when you die and come to grace, the events of your death are erased. You don't remember. The longer you're in grace, the less you remember about your Earthly life."

"Well, that seems kind of lousy—having no memories?"

"You have no bad memories. You don't miss anyone. You just . . . are."

I frowned. "So, how do you know about your parents?"

Alex and I reached for a piece of garlic bread at the same time, our hands touching. He pulled back, then pushed the plate closer to me. "The longer you're fallen or earthbound, the more you start to remember."

I nibbled the edge of my bread. "Isn't that good?"

Alex swung his head. "No. The memories that start to come back—they're the worst ones. You remember the pain, the hate—the miserable way people treated you."

I shuddered. "That's awful."

"It's a powerful way to bring people to the dark side. They can't remember anything good—can't remember ever being at peace. They get angry, violent."

"Like Ophelia."

"Yeah. That's how he persuades you to take the dark path."

"He? He like . . ."

"The devil."

I felt a cold shiver—like a shot of ice water—speed through my veins, piercing my heart. "That sounds awful."

We ate in silence for the next few minutes. I steered clear of the spaghetti—images of maggots kept coming back—but went headfirst into the meat lasagna. I was crunching through my third slice of the ultra-buttery garlic-bread goodness when Nina pushed through the front door, Vlad in tow.

Nina rushed over toward me and threw her arms across my shoulders, tugging me to her marble-cold chest. "Poor thing! Are you doing okay? You looked horrible at the office. Like, like—" I peeled myself away from Nina, wiping my greasy lips on a napkin. "Like that," she finished.

"Thank you for your concern," I said, patting her arm softly.

"What happened?" Vlad asked, keeping his distance from the dinner table.

"Sophie was attacked. And mugged!"

Vlad's eyes widened, and I could see the rise and fall of his paisley silk ascot as he swallowed slowly. "By whom?"

Nina pointed a well-manicured finger in Alex's direction. "His ex-girlfriend attacked her. But we don't know who mugged her."

Alex put down his fork. "We're working on it."

Nina crossed her arms, jutting out a single bony hip. "How are you working on it? Because it looks an awful lot like you're sitting here, stuffing your face, wining and dining my roommate, not out trolling the clouds or galaxies or wherever you angels go when you're not breaking our pottery."

"It was an IKEA vase," I protested.

"How can you just sit there, eating?"

Vlad's nostrils flared. "Is that garlic?"

Nina pierced him with any icy stare. "Go get the donation clothes. The grown-ups are talking."

"Oh what*ever*!" Vlad moaned, stomping all the way to Nina's room.

I took another bite of garlic bread. "What else do you expect us to do?"

Nina stomped her foot.

Vlad poked his head out of Nina's room. "Uh, Auntie?"

Nina held up a silencing hand and glared at Alex and me. "We need to be doing something."

"We're eating."

Vlad stepped out of Nina's room, his arms weighed

down with a monster-sized heap of Nina's discarded couture. "Nina?"

Nina shot him another glare, then focused back on us. "Sophie was practically useless at work today. Can't you see how this is tearing her apart?"

Vlad stepped out and dumped the load of clothes on the living-room floor. He produced an iPod from his pocket and popped in the earbuds, then disappeared back into Nina's room, shutting the door with a slam behind him.

I swallowed while Alex fished around in the Bambino's bag, extracting a handful of red-pepper packets. "We're going to get to it, but first we have to eat. Not all of us are—you know, dead."

I poked at the remains of my lasagna and Caesar salad while Alex and Nina bickered.

"We're close," Alex was saying. "I know we're close to finding the Vessel."

"Yeah, but Ophelia actually has that going-out-and-looking-for-it thing going on. What have we done? Nothing. Nothing!"

"We're researching," Alex said, the muscle flicking in his jaw—the way it does when he is desperately trying to remain calm.

There was the faintest giggle—gentle, like the sound of tinkling bells—trilling in my head. *They can't help you*, Ophelia's voice intoned. *They don't even know where to begin. Your little friends have no idea how to deal with people like us. Us, Sophie . . . you and I are one and the same.*

"I am not dead!" I stood up, my fork clattering to my plate, my chair flopping onto the ground behind me. Nina and Alex's faces swung toward me.

"Um, Sophie?" Nina asked, her dark eyes wide with alarm.

I squeezed my eyes shut and rubbed my temples. "It's Ophelia," I said, "I can hear her."

Alex stood up. "Where? Is she here?"

"Here?" Nina scrambled up on the kitchen table, *eek-a-mouse* style. "As in *here*?" She crouched down fighter style and clenched her fists. "I'll kill her."

"No," I wailed, pushing my palms against my head. "She's in my head. I can—I can hear her in there, talking to me. Taunting me. She's driving me crazy."

That's good. Tell them you're hearing voices. That's just another nail in the nutty-mortal-girl coffin. They're not going to save you, Sophie. Not when they think you're already going crazy.

Nina pointed at me and angrily stared at Alex. "See what I mean?"

"I'm not crazy!" I yelled, feeling the red flush of blood as it rushed to my cheeks. "You're the crazy one, Ophelia!"

Alex swallowed hard, his eyes intent and holding mine. "She's in your mind?"

I felt the tears welling in my eyes. "I'm not crazy," I said, my voice small. "I can hear her."

"I know," Alex said, taking my hand in his. "I know."

I stepped back, shaking my hand from Alex's. "You have to tell me everything," I snapped, "everything that fallen angels can do. I need to know what I'm up against with Ophelia."

Alex sighed. "I already told you."

"You told me mind reading. Now she's *in* my mind." I crossed my arms. "What else?"

"Well . . . we can manipulate your thoughts."

I stepped back, looked Alex up and down, then leaned

close, examining the curve of his chest, the muscular swell of his shoulder.

"What are you doing?" he asked.

I used my index finger to poke his firm stomach. "How do I know you're not manipulating my reality right now? For all I know you could be some eighty-year-old bald guy with gold teeth and liver spots."

Alex grabbed my outstretched index finger and pulled me against him, my breasts pressing against his chiseled chest. We were hip bone to hip bone and I could hear—and feel—the rhythmic beat of his heart. Alex's lips brushed the tip of my ear and I gave a slight, involuntary shiver, relishing the delicious feeling of his closeness, of his breath on my neck. All the pain and fear of Ophelia's visit was melting away.

"Are you willing to give me the benefit of the doubt?"

I shoved away from him. "Don't be sexy when I'm seriously trying to be mad at you."

"Or when your roommate might seriously be in jeopardy of losing her lunch," Nina moaned.

I steeled myself, gazing at Alex. "Anything else I should know?"

Alex sucked in a breath. "Yes. I guess so."

I gave him the universal "Spit it out!" look.

"But it's not about Ophelia. It's about your father."

Nina looked up. "Is he dead? You said you didn't know if he was dead."

"Is he?" I asked.

"I don't know. It's not about that."

"Okay . . ." I said.

Alex avoided my gaze, looked at his hands. "Have you ever considered why you are the way that you are?"

I used the heels of my hands to wipe the last of my tears. "Neurotic? I can think of a few reasons."

Alex raised his eyes. "No, your 'power.'"

"Power?"

"Okay, your lack of power. Both your mother and your grandmother had real powers."

"And I can't do anything."

"Not true," Nina said, finger raised. "I've seen you make a pizza disappear. Ba-dump cha!" She held up her palms, played to an imaginary crowd. "Thank you, thank you, I'll be here all week . . . starting in an hour." Then she disappeared into her room.

"Not that you can't do anything—it's that nothing can be done to you. Magical immunity."

I shrugged. "So? What of it?"

"Look, you get your traits from both parents, right? Red hair, green eyes."

I nodded. "Excellent use of high school biology, thanks."

Alex rolled his eyes.

"Okay, sure, fine, whatever—family traits. But I didn't get mind-reading abilities. So, what's your point?"

I didn't think it was possible for Alex to look even more exasperated, but he did.

"My point is that your father might also be magically immune."

I wagged my head. "No, my father was one hundred percent grade-A normal."

"You think. You look pretty grade-A normal and yet you're magically immune."

"Okay, so how does knowing my father might be magically immune help us? I mean, it's not like it's going to show up on his medical records or on a Google search. And, what does my family tree have to do with finding the Vessel of Souls? Or getting rid of Ophelia?"

Alex looked at the floor and then up at me. "You might want to sit down for this."

I snorted. "I'm talking to an angel about the father that left me four days after I was born, in my apartment where I saw the image of my dead grandmother in the bathroom mirror. And got beaten up by a fallen angel in a sweater set. I really don't think there is anything I need to sit down for."

Alex shrugged. "Suit yourself."

I stared at him. "Well?"

"Lawson, there is only one other known person who is magically immune."

"And that would be . . . ?"

"Satan."

I sat down with a thud on the couch. "What? Satan? Like *the* Satan? Are you saying that I could be related to Satan?" I sprang up, went nose to nose with Alex. "Are you saying Satan could be my father?"

"I told you you might want to sit down."

"Oh, Lord, I need to sit down." I flopped onto the couch, letting my head sink into the pillows.

"What's wrong with Sophie?" Nina asked, coming out of her room.

"Her dad might be Satan," Alex answered.

"Oh. Bummer. Are we out of O neg?"

I sat up and pointed to Nina, who was rooting around in our refrigerator, frowning at a plastic bag of blood. "And that is not the weirdest thing that happened to me today," I said. "Geez."

"Hey, Soph, it's okay." Alex was crouching down, his muscular thighs flexed, his palm on my knee.

"Totally," Nina said, tearing open her snack. "There are worse things than being the spawn of Satan."

"Oh yeah? Like what?"

Nina and Alex exchanged a panicked glance. "Like, uh, you could be . . . help me out here, angel," Nina murmured out of the side of her mouth.

Alex held up his palms. "Hey, you're on your own with this one, Nina. I was going to go with the 'there, there' form of sympathy. Clean, neat, no promises." Alex turned back to me, patting my knee and smiling softly. "There, there," he said.

"At least you know who your father is," Nina said helpfully.

"Might be. We're not sure yet." I looked from Nina to Alex. "Right?"

Alex remained silent and I felt my blood pressure rise. I looked at Alex, aghast. "You knew about this, didn't you? You know that only Satan had the magical immunity thing going on and that I might have some kind of a connection."

Alex stepped back, putting up his hands in case I decided to swing at him. "Look, I'll admit I thought about it—a little. But frankly, it's really hard to consider that your girlfriend might be Satan's kid."

I paused, feeling a tiny prick in my heart. "Girlfriend?"

Alex immediately pinkened and my heart did a double-thump. "I mean . . ."

"No, that's okay." I imagined Alex and me pressed up against each other, stealing kisses, holding hands—doing the things that *couples* did. I imagined my engagement ring and sparkly veil—and my father, Satan, walking me down the aisle.

"Crap," I muttered. "Still, what does this have to do with the Vessel?"

Nina's eyes widened. "He's the other big cheese that wants the Vessel, right?"

Alex nodded slowly and I felt the blood pulsing in my cheeks. "Oh, great. So, not only does Ophelia want to kill me because she thinks I know where this stupid thing is, but now my father, who may or may not be Satan, may or may not want to kill me to get a hold of this thing that I have no idea about." I put my fists on my hips. "You're sure there's not an unsolved murder that we could team up on? You know, maybe work up to this whole fate-of-humanity thing?"

Alex patted me awkwardly on the shoulder. "It's going to be okay. We'll figure something out."

I wasn't so sure. My stomach started to churn and I felt as though my whole world—my whole, Sophie Lawson, demonically normal world—was slipping away. I didn't know my father, I couldn't know my mother. My grandmother was gone and I was alone in the world— and now, somehow, I might not be.

I wondered whether it would be better to be an orphan or the daughter of the dark king.

I stood up, surprised my shaky legs could hold me. "I'll be right back."

I clicked the bathroom door shut behind me and went to the sink, turning the faucet on. I splashed cold water on my face and looked at my reflection in the mirror. Green eyes gone glassy and cold. Miniscule lashes flecked with tiny droplets of water. Pale white cheeks pockmarked with angry red blotches. The face that I had recognized and scrutinized my whole life through—flesh and blood—and now some of that blood belonged to the devil. Maybe.

The tears started involuntarily. The weight of knowing heaved against my chest, seeming to squeeze out every last inch of air.

I thought of all the images of Satan that I had seen in

the past—a sinister, red-faced man with a cleanly cut beard, a prominent widow's peak, and jet-black hair pushed back. I thought of the cloven feet, the pointed tail, the two sharp horns sprouting on his head. Images of evil, of tortured souls writhing in a fiery hell while Satan gleefully watched on. Satan.

My father, the devil.

My round face and bushy brows were courtesy of my mother. Ditto for my diminutive stature, my stubby toes, and what my doctor politely referred to as "child-bearing" hips. What had my father given me?

I bared my teeth—straight, Crest white, supremely human, fang free. I checked my nails—half a manicure, each nail that wasn't chipped or bitten filed into a neat square. No claws. I wiggled my toes—all ten of them. No cloven hooves.

I had no physical traits of my father—in devil form—so I supposed that was good. And I didn't consider myself a sadist or anyone who took pleasure in the pain of others except for the occasional schaudenfraude.

So what did it mean to be Satan's kid?

I glanced back up into the mirror and sucked in a shaky breath, using my index finger to tap the glass.

"Grandma?" My voice sounded small, foreign, and tinny. No one appeared; the only person looking out was me, with red-rimmed eyes and a clutch of fire-red hair. I lifted my hand to knock again, but the thought that my grandmother may have known this weighed on me.

There was a gentle knock on the bathroom door.

I peeled the door open and slipped out, trying to avoid the quiet stares.

Nina looked at me, her eyes registering concern. "We've got to do something. Look at you, Soph, you're upset. This is not okay."

Nina looked from me to Alex and then widened her stance, slamming her fist into her flat-open palm. "We're going to do something. We have to do more than just read books. Sophie, I'm going to find Ophelia and we're going to find out if you're the spawn of Satan if it kills me. Again." She nodded her head definitively, crossed her arms in front of her DUDE, WHERE'S MY COUTURE? shirt and stared both Alex and me down with her black eyes.

"The spawn of Satan?" I repeated meekly.

"Oh." Nina pressed her reverse-French manicured fingers against her mouth. "Satan's kin. Is that better?"

Frankly, with my working in the demon Underworld and sharing a bathroom with a card-carrying member of the soulless undead, I'd always considered myself more Hell-adjacent, rather than directly in line with anything from the actual dark side. Yet here I was, in my living room, being told that daddy dearest might actually be devil dearest.

"Aw, crap," I muttered again, massaging my aching forehead.

"Come on, Soph. You're okay." Nina shrugged toward Alex. "He's an angel, I'm a vampire, and you're—"

I held up a silencing hand and Alex leaned in. "You're Sophie Lawson, regular girl."

I smiled softly in spite of myself, relishing the feeling of delicious warmth as it spread through my body. I didn't even pause to consider that my life was crashing down around me, my father might be responsible for every bad thing that happened in the world, and I was becoming a knock-kneed schoolgirl because a cute boy was being nice to me. "You really think I'm regular?"

Alex cocked his head with that sexy half-smile. "Actually, I think you're way better than regular."

I sat up a little straighter, feeling a lump rise in my throat.

But whether it was from my newfound family tree or the sweet, earnest expression of my friends, I wasn't sure.

Nina's head swayed back and forth like a spectator at a tennis match. "Did we really just have a Hallmark moment right now? Sophie might very well be in the clutches of world-ending evil and you're acting like a couple of eighth graders!"

I shrugged, and Nina used her index finger and thumb to pinch the bridge of her nose and blow out an exasperated sigh. "Am I the only one in the room who isn't thinking with her genitals?"

"Sorry, Nina. What do you suggest we do?"

"There has to be someone who knows something; there has to be some way to find out more," said Nina.

"There is. I think I know where to find help," Alex said solemnly.

"Where?" Nina asked.

"Heaven."

Chapter Nine

"*This* is Heaven?"

I yanked open the door, immediately wrinkling my nose and rubbing my greasy palm on my jeans.

"Yeah," Alex returned. "What did you expect? Clouds and harpsichords?"

Heaven was a dive bar at the mouth of Hayes Valley and nothing about the place reflected its name except for a chipping depiction of God giving life to Adam painted on the wall just in front of the illuminated restrooms sign.

I immediately felt a nervous blush wash over me. "Geez. Why is it that otherworldly information never comes from a stodgy man in a suit at the Burlingame Hilton?"

Though I wasn't a teetotaler by any means, my last bar experience was trying my bloody best to fit in at the vampire bar, Dirt. It didn't seem like I was doing any better at Heaven, where every face swung to scrutinize us once we stepped into the dimly lit place. Alex got the interested once-over from the ladies sipping brightly colored martinis at the table in the corner; Nina was being admired by a drag queen drinking a Sam Adams, and everyone else was focused on me.

"Blend in," Alex ordered.

"With what?" I asked, my eyes sweeping the half-human, half-demon, half-*other* clientele.

I tried to paste on Paris Hilton's patented too-bored-for-this-planet look, but I was having a hard time tearing my eyes from the gentleman at the end of the bar. His amber eyes were almond shaped and deeply focused; he took long, slow pulls from his beer without steering his gaze from me. There was something vaguely familiar about his ash-blond hair, something recognizable about the slope of his nose, his thin lips. My mind reeled as I tried to place him. I was still working on it when Alex nudged me.

"That's Piri," Alex said, gesturing to the man behind the bar.

"That's the pixie you were telling us about?" Nina asked, incredulous.

On our drive to Heaven, Alex had filled us in on Piri, a local pixie who spent most of his time in the "upper world" (that's ours), and was the go-to guy for finding out the seedy goings-ons of human-angel-demon dealings.

Alex looked at Piri, nodded his head. "Yeah, that's him. Why?"

While it's true that very few demons reflect their Disneyized/Wes Craven/Hollywoodized images, pixies were generally fairly well depicted.

Except for this one.

Though he had the same fine-boned features and porcelain skin I was used to with other fairy folk, the stern set of his jaw and his narrowed, beer-bottle brown eyes—eyes that raked over us as we stood in the doorway—generally didn't give off that cutesy Tinkerbelle vibe.

Piri stood behind the bar, his huge mitt-like hands set on the hardwood top, his fingers tapping in a slow, bored rhythm that made the tattooed coiled snake on his forearm jump. His bare, bulging biceps were littered with images of thorny roses and screaming eagles, their talons arched and sharp.

"You know, in the sixteenth century, rose tattoos were given to prisoners sentenced to death," Nina said matter-of-factly.

I studied the burgeoning bush spewing rose blossoms out from under Piri's leather vest and gulped. "Good to know."

Piri's thick eyebrows rose and he eyed our trio with an unwelcome glare. Nina paused when her cell phone trilled a jaunty out-of-place tune.

"I need to get this," she said, pointing to the spastically vibrating jeweled device. "It's Dixon."

"This is Nina," she trilled into the phone.

Nina disappeared out the front door and Alex and I shared a look. I shrugged, pasted on my most welcoming smile, and sauntered over to the bar. I seated myself directly in front of Piri and hopped up onto the cracked Naugahyde stool. "Hi there," I said, all smiles and normalcy. "Can I get a cosmo?"

Piri said nothing; he just blinked, revealing a spider-web tattoo that started at his inner eye and blossomed out toward his temple. I felt myself involuntarily wince.

Alex sat down next to me and faced ol' baldy. "Scotch. Neat. You Piri?"

The bartender lined up two smudged highball glasses and upturned a scotch bottle over each one. He slid the half-full glasses across the bar to us. "Who wants to know?" was his response.

I looked at the amber liquid in my glass and dropped

my voice. "Actually, sir, I ordered a—" I gazed up into unforgiving eyes. "Never mind."

I caught a hint of movement from the corner of my eye and I noticed the guy with the ash-blond hair had moved one stool closer to me. I gave him a closed-lipped smile as he grinned at me and raised his half-full glass in one of those "Hey, how ya doin'?" bar salutes. He inched a small bit closer and opened his mouth to speak, but my whole body was on high alert, focused on Piri and finding my father.

"I'm with someone," I said to the blond-haired stranger.

"Brilliant. I'd like to be with the peanuts if you'd hand them down."

My cheeks burned with embarrassment as I slipped the bowl of peanuts to the guy. He didn't take his eyes off me as he shook a handful of peanuts in his palms, tossed them into his mouth.

"Very smooth," Alex whispered in my ear.

I clutched my glass and narrowed my eyes at him. "Are we just here visiting, or did we actually come for a reason?"

Alex cleared his throat, threw back his entire glass of scotch. He seemed to savor it a minute before swallowing.

Piri raised his eyebrows when Alex slapped the empty glass on the bar. "'Nother?"

Alex nodded and Piri's eyes grazed me and my still-full glass. "I'm good," I said, bringing it to my lips. The wafting scent of the amber liquid burned my nostrils and I worked hard not to cough. "Smells good," I said in a scotch-induced hoarse whisper.

I sipped my drink and tried not to wince as the scotch burned my throat and Alex got Piri to talk.

"I don't recognize you—either of you," Piri said as he worked a bar rag. "Where you from?"

"Not important," Alex said. "You know a Lucas Szabo?"

Piri stopped wiping the bar. "Maybe."

"Well, would you know, maybe, where someone could find him?"

Piri jutted his chin toward me. "Who's the girl?"

"Lucas Szabo," Alex repeated.

I looked around nonchalantly but could feel Piri's dark eyes boring into me, studying me.

"I asked you a question."

I thrust out a hand. "I'm Sophie."

Piri ignored my offer to shake. I watched his lip twitch and I saw that he was fighting a smile.

I heard the tinkle of ice against glass down the bar. "Can I get another?" the blond-haired guy was asking.

Piri regarded his customer disdainfully but still filled his drink.

"You know him?" Alex asked again once Piri returned to us.

"Please?" I asked Piri. "It's important that we find Lucas Szabo."

"Because?" asked Piri—but I had the feeling he already knew.

"Because he's my father," I supplied.

Piri crossed his arms in front of his chest, and I worked not to stare at the troop of scorpions that were tattooed down the front of his arm. "I can help you find him," Piri said finally. He leaned forward, his elbow gently tapping Alex's glass of scotch. Alex watched the glass as it wobbled to the lip of the bar and then dropped gracefully, shattering on the floor. Alex leaned down and Piri bounded over him, clearing the bar in a single smooth motion. A pair of gossamer wings tore through

Piri's leather vest and caught the stolid, beer-soaked stench of the bar and then his hands were around my neck, his thumbs pressing against my windpipe. I hurtled to the floor, Piri on top of me, choking me, and I felt the breath leave my body, but I opened my mouth anyway, gasping, working. The first scrapings of a severe headache blossomed from the back of my head where I hit the ground.

Piri groaned when Alex's body made contact with his; I felt Piri's nails rake across my neck, scrape at the skin on my cheek as Alex dragged him off me. Piri landed with a thud and howled as his head mashed against the shards of broken glass on the floor. Alex had his knee pressed against Piri's chest, his hand on Piri's throat. Piri's short legs and arms flailed under Alex's weight. I gaped at Alex, who wore an expression so fierce, so angry that it startled me.

"Don't you touch her, demon," Alex spat between gritted teeth.

Piri's chest rose and Alex's knee drifted up an inch. Piri cut his eyes to me and they were hard, cold. "She's not even human. She's a thing, a prize—and you want her as badly as I do."

I shuddered at the sound of Alex's knuckles connecting with Piri's jaw.

"Alex!" I shouted.

"He doesn't have anything worthwhile to say."

I stood up, mildly surprised that my shaky legs held me up. "Let's just go."

Alex looked at me and then down at Piri. "If I let him up, he's just going to come after you again."

Piri tried to nod his head, his lips arching into a horrible, grimacing smile. I scrambled behind the bar and pried the pour spout off two bottles of coconut rum. I upended the bottles over Piri, who howled and writhed.

"You can get up now," I told Alex.

Alex looked down, incredulous. "Coconut rum kills pixies? Who knew?"

"It's not the rum," I said, shrugging at Piri, his wings soaked and stuck to the floor. "It's the liquid. Sticks 'em down. And the coconut is just . . . festive."

Alex nodded, carefully stepping off Piri and brushing his palms on his jeans. "I will . . . keep that in mind."

We crossed the bar and left Piri on the floor behind us, wings pinned to the ground, legs and arms floundering wildly. His bald head was red with effort and when I looked back at him he growled, "Your days are numbered, girl. A prize like you isn't safe anywhere."

We stepped out the door, letting it snap shut behind us. Nina clicked her phone off and grinned at us, dropping it into her enormous purse. "What'd I miss?" she asked.

"Nothing," Alex said, his jaw tight.

I used my index fingers to rub little circles on my suddenly pounding temples. "This is just getting weirder and weirder. I'm a prize? A pixie wants to kill me?"

Nina stamped her foot. "Someone wants to kill you? You said I didn't miss anything!"

"Like someone doesn't try to kill me every day," I said. "It gets old."

"Surprisingly, it doesn't," Nina said with a smug grin.

The streets were deserted as we walked back to the car. As I pulled open the door I glanced behind me, the eerie sensation of being watched pressing against my chest. I couldn't be sure, but I thought I saw a clutch of ash-blond hair disappear behind an SUV parked a few spaces behind us. My stomach warbled and I swallowed hard, slinking into the car.

"Everything okay?" Alex asked, his hand on mine.

"I've just been attacked by a pixie. You tell me." I tried to force a smile. As the engine revved I chanced a glance behind me and caught him standing on the sidewalk, hazel eyes fixed, blond hair catching the glint from the streetlight. I shuddered. He got smaller as we drove away, standing, unmoving, and I tried to push the eerie feeling out of my head. There could, after all, be the mild possibility that not everyone wanted to kill me, right? Maybe he was just a regular guy interested in what he thought was a regular girl. It could happen.

Right?

We drove home in complete silence. As we pulled up to the light at Van Ness I blew out a sigh and leaned my forehead against the cool glass of the passenger-side window. "Well, that was a total waste," I said. "We didn't learn anything."

"That's not true," Alex said.

"Right," Nina finished. "We learned that Piri wants to kill you."

I forced a smile. "You're right. I feel so much better now."

We let the elephant stand in the car for a full moment before I started again. "What do you think Piri meant when he said I wasn't human?"

"He doesn't think you're human?" Nina asked, maneuvering her car around a double-parked cab.

"He probably just thought you weren't human because you were with me," Alex said. "He probably knew I wasn't"—a hint of sadness flitted across his chiseled features—"real."

"No," I said. "Humans don't always recognize demons. It's different in reverse. Demons know. . . ."

"We can smell life force. Can't you?" Nina asked Alex, as though it were the most natural thing on earth.

"Uh . . . no."

There was another beat of silence, pregnant with the

statement no one wanted to make: If I really was Satan's daughter, Piri was right—I wouldn't be human. Would I?

I gulped.

"I'm sure it was nothing," Alex said, breaking the silence. "Just the nonsensical ramblings of a rogue pixie." As he said it, he avoided my gaze, his eyes solid and set straight ahead. I watched the muscle in his jaw jump as he stared out the windshield—the muscle in his jaw that only jumped when he was considering something huge. He glanced at me for a quick second and then focused back on the road in front of him. "You should put something on the scrape."

Chapter Ten

I cracked one eye and a bleary face with coal-black eyes, intent on me, came into view. I blinked twice and the face became clear and sharp, angled planes leaning toward me.

"Holy crap!" I sprang out of bed, blankets flying, landing with an inglorious thud on the floor.

"Hey, there, boo," Nina said, her face breaking into a sweet smile. "Didja sleep okay?" She cocked her head, her thick black hair in sweet Shirley Temple curls that bounced over her shoulders.

"What is going on, Nina?"

"I made you some breakfast. Are you hungry?"

Nina's gentle smile, her wide, innocent eyes, and her vintage Donna Reed dress completely creeped me out. Something wasn't right.

"Ophelia?" I whispered. "Is that you?" Nina looked taken aback and I sprung up on bare feet, snatching the closest weapon I could find—a flyswatter in the shape of a flip-flop—and brandished it at this body-snatcher Nina. "What have you done with my best friend?"

"Sophie, it's me!"

"Look, bitch," I spat, teeth gritted, "I know my best

friend and you are *not* her. Nina loves me. She would never cook for me."

Faux Nina stomped her foot and put her small fists on her hips. "Good God, Sophie, would you get your bony ass out of here and eat the breakfast I so lovingly made for you?"

I dropped my flyswatter and leaned closer to Nina, staring into her eyes. I poked her cold marble chest. "It *is* you."

Nina rolled her dark eyes with an exasperated groan and stomped out of my room. I snatched my comforter off my bed, wrapped it around my shoulders, and followed her into the living room.

"Oh my . . ." My eyes were wide, taking in the spread Nina had laid on the dining-room table: bagels, juice, limp bacon, half-raw eggs with runny yolks, a full pineapple, and a chocolate cake with pink icing roses, the words *Happy Birthday, Sophie* in cursive scrawl across the front.

"Ta-da!" Nina shouted, dancing around the table.

I took a tentative step back toward my bedroom. "What is this all about, Nina?" I pointed at the cake. "It's not my birthday. You know that, right?"

Nina shrugged. "I know. But you try and find a cake at nine am. Let's just hope little Stella doesn't miss it today."

I frowned, seeing where the kid's name had been scraped off and replaced by mine. "Oh." I looked at Nina. "And this is for what again?"

Nina bounded toward me, threaded her arm through mine. "What are you talking about, silly? Can't a best friend do something for her fantastically talented best friend?"

"Yes. But you can't. And I'm not talented. So, what's going on?"

Nina was silent, a wide smile on her face. I rubbed my eyes. "Look, Nina, in the last week I was almost killed twice, was introduced to my new mortal enemy, and learned that I very well might be the fruit of Satan's loins. So I'll ask you again: What is going on?"

Nina skipped to her closed bedroom door—bedroom being a loose term as vampires don't sleep, thus don't own beds—and pushed open the door. "Sophie Lawson, meet ChaCha!" Nina said.

I looked down, incredulous, as the little ball of fur vaulted and yapped, throwing his full three-pound body against my ankles. "Oh, Nina, he's adorable!" I said, scooping up the puppy into my arms. I nuzzled the tiny brown terrier against my cheek, and he responded with a series of introductory yips followed by a full-face tongue wash. "He's so cute! Wait—" I held the puppy out and eyed Nina suspiciously. "You're not going to eat him or anything, are you?"

Nina looked horrified. "What kind of monster do you think I am?" She scratched ChaCha on his little puppy head and he rolled his big, chocolate brown eyes skyward, trying to see her. "I don't eat puppies. I got him for you! You know, as a pet. I thought you could use a little cheering up."

I snuggled ChaCha close and pulled Nina into a one-armed hug. "Oh, Nina, thank you! He's so cute! I love him! You are so thoughtful!"

Nina stroked ChaCha once on the head, then took my hand in hers. "Sophie, sit down. I have something to tell you."

I let Nina lead me to the couch. "It's bad news, isn't it?" I looked down at ChaCha and skipped a breath. "It's *puppy-bad* news? Oh Lord, I don't know if I can take any more bad news."

"It's about Dixon."

I looked around. "Are you moving out? Are you moving in with him?"

"No. Not yet. It is about Dixon . . . and you."

I slapped the heel of my hand to my forehead and ChaCha jumped at the sound, then licked my chin. "Don't tell me—he wants to kill me, too?" I looked down into ChaCha's sweet, too-sensitive face. "That's it, right? This is what this is all about? Oh, geez. How about I lay down so you can kick me?"

Nina crossed her arms. "Are you through?"

"No. I can't believe you're trying to make me feel good because someone else wants to kill me. Someone you're in love with! Oh, man!"

Nina took both my hands. "No! No," she said, her voice soft. "I would never be in love with someone who wanted to kill you, Sophie, no matter how long his fangs were. I love you; you're my best friend."

"That's good. I really don't think I could survive another assassination attempt." I paused, swallowed hard, patted ChaCha's velvet-soft nose. "So, what is it?"

"I promise, Sophie, Dixon doesn't want to kill you," Nina said, a relieved smile on her face. "He just wants me to fire you."

Someone let all the air out of the room. I gasped, sputtered, and coughed, and Nina ran toward me with a glass. She held it to my lips and I drank gratefully, then hiccupped.

"What is this?"

"A mimosa," she said with a grin.

I hiccupped again. "I think you forgot the orange juice."

Nina knitted her brows, set the tumbler full of champagne on the coffee table. "So you're okay with this?"

I picked the tumbler back up and downed it. "No, I'm

not okay. I'm fired? Fired?" I felt the sting of tears at the corners of my eyes—but whether they were tears of sadness or anger, I wasn't sure.

"Technically, we're laying you off."

"Is anyone else being laid off?"

She bit her lip. "No. Dixon just thought it would be best for the company."

"What?" I stood up and ChaCha rolled to the floor, then bit down on the leg of my pink pajama pants, growling ferociously.

"Well." Nina stood up, too, and patted my arm affectionately. "I'm sorry, Sophie. I tried to talk him out of it. He just doesn't think you're UDA material."

"Not UDA material? I've been with UDA longer than half the staff!"

"But you're, you know"—Nina lowered her voice to a whisper—"*human*. Dixon thinks an all-demon staff would make our clientele feel more comfortable."

"Our clientele loves me! No one has had any problems with me! Most of them hate you! He wants to fire me because I'm *human*? That's discrimination! That's race—or life—that's lifeism!"

"Is that even a word?"

"No!" I said miserably. "This is because of the VERM movement, isn't it? Dixon is a supporter. I feel so betrayed! I let Vlad sleep on our couch."

Nina held up a finger. "Actually, vampires don't sl—" I snarled and she waved her hand. "Never mind. Vlad had nothing to do with this. It was just Dixon. I don't even think VERM knows about it."

I flopped onto the couch, pulling my comforter over my head. "I've never been fired before."

I sniffed, letting the tears flow freely over my cheeks. Nina patted my head. "We'll find you something else,

Sophie. How about being a doctor? You love those surgery shows on Discovery Health. I'll bet the hospital is hiring."

I threw the blanket off my head and gaped at Nina. "I can't just *be* a doctor. You can't just walk into a hospital and *be* a surgeon!"

Nina crossed her arms. "Not if you're going to be so negative, you're not. We'll find you another job. It's not like the Underworld Detection Agency was your life."

But it kind of was.

My life—even pre-Satan's kid knowledge—had never been white-bread normal. I was raised by a woman who read palms, fortunes, and tea leaves and who advertised that fact with a six-foot neon hand that flashed in our living-room window. Not exactly the stucco-tract home simplicity that high school popularity demanded. I tried to separate my home life from my school life and I had succeeded for a while—until a group of perfect plastic senior girls thought it would be a hoot to have their fortunes read and showed up on my doorstep one Saturday morning. By Monday morning my grandmother's profession was all over school and the fact that I was related to the "crazy palm lady" spread like wildfire. I could no longer stay silent in the back of the cafeteria, masquerading as an exotic foreign exchange student who lived with a host family somewhere in Marin. I was dubbed "Special Sophie" and lived out the rest of my high school existence slinking in the hallways and avoiding crystal-ball and "I see dead people" jokes.

It wasn't any easier once I got home. While most kids can sink into normalcy once the three o'clock bell rang, I usually opened the door on one of Grandma's mahjongg games—her regulars being a pink-haired pixie named Lulabell, a pair of zombie twins who often left fingertips on the game board, and a centaur named Alistair who, I think, was a little light in the hooves.

I attempted a normalcy reinvention in college, but my magical immunity prevented that. While most girls joined sororities and chatted about boys, professors and term papers, I knew that the woman who slopped slaw in the Lone Mountain cafeteria was actually a level-four witch who had had her magiks revoked and that the history professor was, in fact, the expert on the Civil War—having been a general there (pre-vampire bite). For me the supernaturals never crawled out of the woodwork—they always seemed to be in the living room, feet up, drinking a beer out of my mini-fridge. When Grandma introduced me to Pete Sampson and the Underworld Detection Agency, I felt like I finally belonged. It's true that my pumping heart and flesh and blood made me an anomaly among the majority of the UDA staff, but they thought my "issues" were as normal as any other demon issues—like Mrs. Henderson who spent most of her time setting her loved ones on fire (accidentally, of course), or the hobgoblins, who had to have every document laminated to prevent spoilage by hobgoblin slobber. I never had to second-guess at the Underworld Detection Agency and among the other above-world rejects, I was, blissfully, just one of the crowd.

I sniffed. "I'm jobless. Destitute." I pulled my comforter up over my head a second time; ChaCha bounded up and snuggled underneath with me.

"I have something that might make you feel better," Nina said.

"Eggs won't make me feel better. Ditto bacon." I considered. "Maybe the cake, though." I stuck out my hand, hoping she'd bring it to me.

My palm remained empty.

"Oh, Nina! I'm miserable. Unsavable." I stuck out my lower lip. "And cake-less."

I felt Nina tug on my comforter. "Sophie . . ."

I poked out my head, opened one eye. "Did you get me a kitten, too?"

"I hope you still have time to cancel the caterer for your little pity party."

I stuck my tongue out at Nina and went back to my blanket cave.

"Dixon promised to write you a glowing letter of recommendation, you know."

I glared at her from the folds of my comforter and felt the fist of anger settle low in my belly. "A glowing letter from a dead guy is supposed to make me feel better?"

If it were possible for Nina to pale, she did so. Her lips dipped into a sharp frown. "I'm really sorry, Sophie."

"I just want to be alone right now."

"Oh . . . okay." I watched Nina scramble around the apartment, gathering up her purse and coat. She gave me a plaintive look before she slipped out the front door and headed off to work at the UDA.

It was just ChaCha and me alone in the apartment. "Well, ChaCha, it's my first day as an unemployed woman. What should we do?"

ChaCha cocked her little terrier head at me, big brown eyes searching. Then she promptly rolled over and went to sleep. "Lot of help you are," I told her.

There was a soft knock at the door and I stiffened, my heart going from zero to sixty in a millisecond. I crept to the door and pressed one hand against it, holding my body as far away as possible, lest I get another door-in-the-face visitor.

"Who is it?" I hissed.

"It's me, Lawson, open up."

I peeled up on my tiptoes, squinted through the peephole. Alex stood in my hallway, arms crossed in front of his navy-blue T-shirt, jeans cinched with a brown belt, lips pursed and looking slightly annoyed.

My hand hovered above the knob. "How do I know you're Alex and not Ophelia pretending to be Alex?"

I could practically hear Alex's eyes roll through the front door.

"I don't know . . . because I know you like to eat marshmallow Pinwheels in the bathtub."

I crossed my arms, considering. "Lucky guess. What else?"

"Um, okay. I know you have a heart-shaped birthmark on your—"

I threw the lock and tugged the door open, snatching Alex by his shirtfront and pulling him into the apartment.

"Are you crazy? My neighbors already think I'm nutso enough; I don't want them to think I'm a slut showing off my naked body to the world, too."

Alex chuckled. "Your naked body."

"Grow up, deadso. What are you doing here, anyway? How did you even know I would be home?"

Alex followed me to the kitchen. "Nina told me what happened. I'm really sorry about the job."

"Me, too," I said, pulling a box of frozen waffles from the freezer. "Want one?" I shook the box at Alex and he declined, but I popped two in the toaster anyway and stood by with peanut butter and jelly.

"It's going to be okay, though, you know," Alex said, patting me awkwardly on the shoulder.

"Right. Did Nina tell you I was going to be a doctor?"

"Don't you need to go to school—"

I shot him an icy glare.

"You know I would help you out if you needed any money," he said.

"Get an advance on your heavenly paycheck, did you?"

Alex rolled his eyes.

"So, what are you doing here?" I wanted to know.

"Frankly, I'm worried about you being here alone."

My waffles popped up and I slathered them with peanut butter and jelly and slapped them together, sandwich style.

"I have a gun," I said, mouth full of peanut-buttery-waffle goodness.

"I know," Alex said, reaching out for my peanut-butter waffle-wich. He took a big bite. "Your gun smells like grape Hubba Bubba."

I was indignant and snatched my waffle back, then pointed at him with it.

"Look, buddy, living in the city affords me a lot of opportunities where going in packing heat would solve a lot of problems. Like parking during the Christmas season or trying to make a left turn off of Market Street. You should be thankful that I keep the gun in a safe and non-emotionally charged place."

"And the bullets?"

"When I'm stressed, I can reach for bullets or ice cream." I polished off the last of my waffle and licked my fingers, satisfied.

Alex scratched his chin. "I think I've been earthbound for way too long. That's actually starting to make a lot of sense."

I grinned, vindicated.

"But that doesn't mean that I feel better about you being unprotected—frozen ammo or no."

"I told you, I have a vampire, too."

"And Ophelia has the hounds of Hell and an entire army of the fallen behind her. Plus her Nephilim goon squad."

"I have a dog, now, too," I remembered. "Nina got her

for me as a lovely parting gift." I pointed to ChaCha in the living room.

Alex looked at her, snoring away in her Nina-furnished little pink doggie bed, rhinestoned PRINCESS inscription sparkling above her splayed furry belly.

Alex looked unimpressed. "Ophelia has Cerberus and you have . . ."

"ChaCha," I supplied with a smug smile.

"ChaCha. Excellent. Well, despite your obviously iron-clad protection system"—again Alex's eyes scanned my crime-busting paraphernalia: the bubble gum–scented, unloaded gun, the three-pound Chihuahua-terrier mix in her pink leatherette collar—"I think you should have this." Alex produced a hard-sided black plastic case, just a bit smaller than a shoebox. He slid it across the table to me.

I popped the lock on the plastic box and opened it, staring at the device inside, encased in its own red velveteen–molded casing. I took the black-handled device out, and frowned. "You want me to shave Ophelia's legs?"

Alex rolled his eyes. "It's a stun gun, not an electric razor." He cocked his head, taking the gun from my hands. "Although I can see where it does look a little bit like that."

He used his index finger to depress the side trigger and the two metal tines shared a hairline-thin electric blue charge. I involuntarily jumped as the jolt of electricity crackled in his hands.

"That would definitely give you a close shave."

"Do you know how to use one of these?"

The electric current crackled again and my saliva went metallic. Little pinpricks of cold sweat budded on my upper lips and palms and I felt myself go stiff. "I've had one used on me."

Alex squeezed my hand softly. "Even more reason why you need to be prepared."

I took the stun gun from Alex and felt its weight in my hand.

"Flip the trigger," Alex suggested.

I licked my lips and slid my finger over the trigger button without depressing it. "I think I've got the picture."

Alex reached into his pocket and produced two extra cartridges. "Don't keep these in the freezer, okay?"

I nodded and Alex took the stun gun from me and slipped it into the smaller carrying case in the box, then handed the whole thing to me. "And for the love of God, this time, if something or someone comes after you, use the stun gun on them." He raised one brow. "And that doesn't mean throw it at them."

I nodded curtly and slipped the gun case closer toward me. "Noted."

Alex grinned. "Good."

I crossed my arms and glowered. "I still don't see why I need all this. Shouldn't I be okay if I've got you around?" I waggled my eyebrows in an effort to look suggestive and adorable. "Like my guardian angel?"

The muscle in Alex's jaw jumped and I watched his lips purse, nostrils flare. I don't think Alex got either my suggestive or adorable vibe.

"Don't you see, Lawson? That's just it. I'm not always going to be around to protect you. I wanted to stick around here today to look in on you, but the department has me working on a case today out in Hunter's Point."

My heart swelled as I considered Alex's sweet, protective side—but then the nag of anger overlooked it when I thought about Alex's need to "look in" on me as though I were a charge he was babysitting.

"I'm fine, Alex."

Alex ignored me, seemed to be lost in his own thought.

His eyes were focused on the table as he mumbled, "You can't . . . you can't just depend on me all the time."

I was taken aback. "Oh. Right. You mean because you're a fallen angel. And you guys are inherently unreliable."

"I mean because I won't always be here."

I swallowed thickly. "You want to go home."

Alex looked at the ground. "That's what this is about. That's what this has always been about."

"You want to find the Vessel so you'll be restored."

Alex nodded but avoided my gaze.

"So it's never been about us. Or me." I could feel the tears starting, but I refused to let them flow, refused to let Alex know that I had, once again, stupidly fallen in love. "It's always just been about you finding the Vessel."

"No, Lawson, I didn't mean it like that."

"You may not have meant it that way, but that's exactly what it is, right?"

Alex opened his mouth and then closed it, dumbly, still avoiding my gaze. Instead he stood up, plucked his keys from the table where he had left them, and pressed the black plastic Taser box toward me. "Promise me you'll be safe, okay?"

I sat at the table, staring at the plastic box until I heard Alex walk out the front door, clicking it shut behind him. I swallowed the lump in my throat and slid the Taser box into my purse, then brushed all thoughts of Alex and the Vessel aside. ChaCha stood up in her little dog bed and yawned mightily, and then trotted over to me, her toenails making a comforting tap-tap sound on the linoleum. I scooped her up and nuzzled her.

"You're not going anywhere, are you, ChaCha?"

She licked my face agreeably and I smiled, handing her a dog bone and feeling an immediate sense of prideful dog ownership. "Let's go for a walk!"

Chapter Eleven

I pulled on a pair of yoga pants and tossed on a sweat-shirt, winding my bed-head hair into an unemployed-girl updo before yanking on my sneakers and finding ChaCha's leash. I did a few obligatory stretches before striding proudly out the front door with ChaCha pranc-ing in front of me in all her pink-studded-collar glory. We were three-quarters down the first city block when ChaCha abruptly flopped over onto her little doggie side, closed her eyes, and started snoring.

I gently tugged at her collar. "Come on, ChaCha. It's time for a walk, girl! We're still walking! Come on, girl!"

"The little thing is pooped," I heard.

I whirled around and grinned when I saw him: tall, with *Men's Health* muscles, short, ash-blond hair that spiked up around his scalp, a deep olive complexion highlighted by the flecks of gold sparkling in his hazel eyes. If my brand-new dog hadn't been playing dead on the sidewalk I may have recognized him.

"We've hardly gone a block!" I said.

The guy leaned down, his polo shirt sliding back and revealing a strong neck and traps that could choke a pony. He uncapped his water bottle and poured some out;

ChaCha sprang back to life, popped onto all fours, and drank gratefully.

"She was just thirsty."

I felt like a heel. "I feed her and give her water. She had water before we left, I swear. It was even bottled— no tap!" I said, certain that CPS—ChaCha Protective Services—was going to spring out from behind the potted palm and nab me for tiny animal cruelty.

"I'm Will Sherman," the guy said, standing up and offering me a hand to shake. "And I believe that you're a good pet parent."

I shook his hand, oddly grateful for the positive judgment from a complete stranger.

"I'm Sophie. And you've got an accent."

Will smiled, his cheeks tinting a shade redder. "It's that obvious, huh?"

I liked the way he stretched out the words, the relaxed lilt of his voice.

"Yep, it's true. I'm from Oregon." We both did that mildly uncomfortable small-talk chuckle. "By way of England."

"Ah." I smiled into his bright eyes, cocked my head, and then my stomach started to sink. "You look familiar." My mental Rolodex started to go and I tried to place him—with a horn, from the UDA office; with a knife from one of my many near-death experiences; with a frapaccino from the local Starbucks. I prayed for memory to lodge itself in the normalcy of a Starbucks but nothing stuck. "I feel like I know you from somewhere."

Will grinned. "Wow. And I was going to use the 'if I could rearrange the alphabet' line."

I felt my brows furrow. "What?"

"I would put 'u' and 'I' together. You know, if I could rearrange the alphabet."

"What?" I said again.

"You weren't picking me up? You know, with the 'don't I know you?' thing? That wasn't a line?"

I felt the corners of my lips pull down. "No! Geez, no. I really thought I knew you. Or had seen you or something."

Will looked away, sheepish. "Sorry."

"So, do I know you in a non-flirtational, non-coming-on-to-you kind of way?"

Will frowned. "Well, when you say it like that you take all the fun out of it."

"Never mind." I bent to scoop ChaCha up, but Will stopped me with a soft hand on my arm.

"Sorry. You might have seen me around." Will shrugged. "I'm local—now. We've probably run into each other a hundred times and never even noticed. It's a small city." He grinned; his teeth were shockingly white and straight, except for two on the very bottom that crossed a little, giving him a semblance of little-boy cute.

I forced a smile. "I guess. Anyway, thanks for the water. Seems to have done the trick."

ChaCha was nuzzling against Will's pant leg now, sitting on his shoe and looking up adoringly at him.

"Ready to finish our walk, girl?"

ChaCha popped onto all fours and trotted around my ankles, winding her leash around my calves and into a pink-studded tourniquet.

"I think your dog is trying to tell you something."

I looked down at ChaCha, who did indeed look like she was trying to tell me something as she sat down, smugly licking her genitals. I stepped out of my leash lasso and scooped up my traitorous pup.

"You may have won this one, dog," I told her with a nuzzle, "but when we get home, you're hitting the treadmill." I looked back at Will and offered a friendly smile. "Thanks again."

"Sure."

I turned on my heel and started toward my building. Will followed the same direction, a foot or so back. Within a second he had caught up and fallen in step with me.

He offered me a polite smile and my hackles went up. I considered how to juggle my dog and my stun gun when Will decided to plunge a dagger into my heart/rape me/beat me/force me to watch an endless loop of *How Stuff Works*. He seemed like a perfectly normal guy out for a perfectly normal coffee run on a perfectly normal day, which meant, most likely, he was some sort of demon.

But then again, I was the spawn of Satan.

"Are you walking with me?"

"I'm walking near you. I happen to be going in that direction. I live right there." He poked his index finger to the building in front of us. *My* building.

I raised an eyebrow. "Really?" Had he seen me come out? Did he have telepathic powers? "What apartment?"

"3C."

I felt a little flutter in my chest. The previous resident of 3C—a sweet, dirty old man who had a penchant for slightly younger women in leopard-print spandex—had fallen in the stairwell and died. At least that's how the story went.

I stopped in midstride. "How come I've never seen you around the building, then?"

Will took a sip from his paper coffee cup. "Why would you? Wait, is that your building, too?"

I crossed my arms. "Like you didn't already know that."

Will put up his hands. "Whoa, lady, I don't know who you are and I have no idea where you live. I was just getting some coffee and walking back to my place. I'm not some kind of stalker freak."

"Aren't you?"

"No. That's why I said 'I'm not some kind of stalker freak.'"

He looked earnest and offended.

"Sorry," I said. "I'm just a little . . . cautious."

Will grinned, his hazel eyes doing a quick toe-to-head scan. "That's okay. Paranoia looks good on you."

I felt my cheeks flush so I looked at the sidewalk as I hurried back to the apartment vestibule, careful not to look back to see if Will was following me. ChaCha looked up at me and yawned, pushing her paws over my arms. "I'm going to teach you to be an attack dog, ChaCha. I'm going to get you a steak."

I pushed into my apartment and checked the fridge. No steak.

"Okay, ChaCha," I sighed. "How do you feel about Cap'n Crunch?"

I poured us each a bowl and set up my laptop on the kitchen table. I was one day out of a job and in desperate need of another. I eyed the newspaper heaped on the chair next to me, was about to type in the Web address for the Monster job search engine when I felt the tiny prick of anger nag at the edge of my mind.

"No." I thumped my fist on the table and ChaCha jumped. "I am not going to take this lying down, ChaCha."

She cocked her head at me, her velvety brown eyes reflecting my Cap'n Crunch box. "Dixon thinks he can just fire me? He thinks that I—me, of all people—am not UDA material?"

ChaCha leaned down on her forepaws, downward-dog style and growled deep in her throat.

"You're absolutely right, ChaCha! I am the UDA!" I thumped my chest. "I'm going to get my job back. Today. They can't run the Underworld Detection Agency without me. I made that company! Well, I made the color-coded demon filing system—and that is very important to the Underworld." I stood up with a start, my chair flopping to the floor behind me. "I am going to march right now there and tell Dixon that I am taking my job back, and he can take his UDA material and shove it right up his bloodless—" ChaCha blinked up at me with those big doe eyes. "Tush."

I marched into the bathroom, stripping my clothes off and formulating a fierce, wordy speech, pockmarked with profanities and three-syllable words, that I planned to take to Dixon. I imagined myself in a killer pencil skirt and sky-high heels, slapping my palm into my fist while Dixon cowered at his desk, nodding spastically, agreeing to every one of my demands. In my fantasy, I had luscious, waist-length hair and for some reason wore glasses that I whisked off and pointed at him as I narrowed my eyes and called him emasculating names.

In my fantasy, Dixon may not have been a vampire with two-inch long, scalpel-sharp fangs and a penchant for blood sucking and general throat-ripping-outing.

"Sophie!"

"Geez, Grandma!" I crossed my arms over my naked chest and yanked a towel from the peg by the door. "Can't you knock or something?"

Grandma rolled her eyes. "Do you remember who used to diaper and powder that bottom of yours? It's not like it's something I've never seen."

I felt the blood rush to my cheeks. "Can we not talk about my bottom right now?"

Grandma looked indignant. "Well, you brought it up."

"Is there a reason for this visit?"

Grandma's lower lip jutted out. "Can't a dead woman visit her granddaughter without being grilled?"

"I'm sorry, Grandma, it's not that I'm not happy to see

you . . . in my bathroom mirror . . . several years after you've died. It's just that I have an important—thing—to take care of."

"Well, my thing is important, too!"

I wanted to strike at Dixon while the fire still roiled in my belly, while the profanities and words like dedication and commitment to UDA excellence still flitted around in my mind. I leaned over and turned on the bath tap. "You know, Grandma, let's take this up later, okay? Let's make, like, a date. Bathroom mirror, say about seven o'clock? Does that work for you?"

The steam from the tap started to cloud the mirror but not before Grandma's eyes narrowed and she blew out a long sigh. "Fine. Mine can wait. I just hope what you have to do is important. More important than having a conversation with your dead grandmother whose time on this planet may be limited . . ." She sniffed, though her eyes remained dry.

I leaned on my toes and kissed the mirror. "Thanks, Gram, I knew you'd understand. And you're already dead, so the walk-the-earth thing isn't as guilt inducing. Good try, though!"

I jumped in the shower with the sound of Grandma groaning behind me.

I didn't have a pencil skirt or a pair of glasses, but I had the sky-high heels down. Nina had given me a pair of Manolo Blahniks for a birthday two years ago and I had never worn them. I pulled them out of their box now, examining their narrow, chest-piercing heels, and tossed them on with a businessy black skirt and a no-nonsense French blue button-down. I took a few steps, wobbled uncomfortably, and managed to make it to the front door without breaking an ankle or getting a nosebleed.

Things were starting to look up.

I pulled my hair into a severe-looking French twist in

the hallway mirror. I let a few strands fall loose around my face when I thought the look was a little too Russian prison warden, then grabbed my shoulder bag and blew a kiss to ChaCha.

"Wish me lucky, baby girl!"

I practiced my speech the entire way to the UDA but seemed to get less and less confident the closer I got. *I belong at the UDA*, I reminded myself as I pulled into a space.

Do you?

It was barely a voice, a weird flutter in my mind, but it stopped me. I sucked in a deep breath and gave myself the once-over in the rearview mirror, half expecting to see my grandmother's exasperated face glaring back. When I didn't, I straightened my blouse and hopped out of the car, walking—with purpose, as Gram used to say—to the police station vestibule.

"Sophie!"

I whirled and saw Alex over my left shoulder. "Hey, Alex."

"What are you doing here?"

I put both hands on my hips. "Getting my job back."

He strode closer to me. "They're giving you your job back? That's great!" His smile was wide and genuine.

"Not exactly. But I'm taking it back."

The smile fell from his lips. "You don't have the stun gun on you, do you?"

I raised an annoyed eyebrow. "I'm not going to Taser him! Unless he really pisses me off."

Alex looked alarmed.

"I'm kidding. I'm just going to tell Dixon that he made a mistake in letting me go. The UDA needs me. I do good work. And once he reinstates me there will be no hard feelings."

Alex crossed his arms in front of his chest. "So you

promise you won't use the stun gun on him? Not that I care if you want to do a little vamp-shock; I just don't want you to get hurt."

"Why does everyone think I'm going to fly off the handle all the time? I'm a completely rational, calm human being who just happens to want to reclaim her rightful position among San Francisco's undead."

I stopped when I noticed the police station had dropped into silence, all heads turned toward me. I rolled up on my tiptoes and peeked over Alex's shoulder, catching the wary eye of Chief Dugan. I went flat-footed again and shook my finger in Alex's face. "That was your fault. I am calm and rational." The elevator dinged and I jumped inside, watching the door slide shut on the San Francisco Police Department, its clutch of officers and alleged felons staring at me like I was the crazy one.

The closer the elevator dropped to UDA, the farther my heart dropped into my belly. I practiced a few deep-breathing exercises I had learned on a late-night infomercial and went through my speech in my head. When the doors sprang open on the bustling UDA, I was shaking my finger at no one and had worked my anger back up to a frothy lather.

The purple velvet ropes were bulging as all manner of the demon Underworld hopped from foot to foot—or hoof to hoof—waiting for their turn at the windows. Most clutched their paperwork, some passed the time by texting or flipping through the long-expired waiting-room magazines. Mrs. Henderson spun when she saw me, trotting over, her thick dragon tail thumping along behind her.

"Sophie, Sophie, Sophie!" she said, gathering me up in a scaly-armed hug. "They said you weren't here anymore. I'm so glad you are."

"Thanks," I said breathlessly, feeling the crunch of my

ribs against Mrs. Henderson's heavy chest. I tried to squirm away and Mrs. Henderson gave me one of her wide, toothy grins—then thrust a sheaf of papers at me.

"Could you be a dear and process these? The kids are so impatient." Her glass-marble eyes shot to two smaller, younger versions of herself slouched in the orange waiting-room chairs, working hard to look disinterested and bored as they played with his-and-hers Nintendo hand-helds. "I have to get Lola to ballet and Sam to baseball."

I chanced a look at Lola, her slick, green-scaled belly exposed as her belly shirt—imprinted with the word SWEETHEART in tiny rhinestones—rode up. She was wearing a flitty black skirt over pink tights that cut off at the ankle, exposing her wide, flat feet.

As used to demonic life as I was, I had a hard time imagining this kid doing a grande plié.

I handed the sheaf of papers back to Mrs. Henderson.

"I'm sorry, I can't. Maybe you can get Nina to help you."

Mrs. Henderson looked horrified. "That vampire?"

"Sorry," I called over my shoulder, aiming myself toward Dixon's office. I raced down the hall—remembering to skirt a blown-up witch hole in the linoleum—and only slowed when I approached Dixon's office. There was a stab of sadness mixed in with my rage; the old wood desk that sat just outside Dixon's office—where I had spent so many years filing Pete Sampson's papers and processing demon requests—had been replaced by a slick black metal version. In Dixon's few days as head of the Underworld Detection Agency he had managed to do away with the standard visitor chairs and nondescript waiting-room couch and replace everything with slick, metal-and-black leather sling chairs and low glass mini-malist tables. Even the spider plant that Sampson had nursed back from the dead the three times I almost killed it was replaced by a sleeker version in a square black pot.

"May I help you?"

A blond-haired vampire who hadn't been there a half-second ago was sitting primly behind the large black desk, with elbows resting on the desktop, fingers laced. He had a pair of half-glasses perched on his long, narrow nose and looked vaguely familiar—one of Dixon's henchmen, no doubt. The engraved nameplate at the edge of the desk said Anson Hale and I regarded him carefully. He did the same with me.

"I'm here to see Dixon," I said, puffing out my chest a little bit.

Anson stiffened in his desk chair and then dropped his head, pretending to study a calendar. "Do you have an appointment?"

Anson's words dropped off behind me as I stormed past him, heading straight for Dixon's office. I had flung the door open and was staring, openmouthed, at Dixon and Nina when I felt a cold, viselike grip on my shoulder, felt the pinch of Anson's icy fingers against the flesh at my throat. He yanked me backward and I felt his nose brush up against my chin. Then I realized he was poised to sink his large fangs into my neck. I felt my blood pressure drop and my bladder fill up.

"Anson!" Dixon's voice was loud and firm. The second the word was out of his mouth Anson's fingers left my shoulder, and I felt myself slump, my muscles exhausted after clenching so desperately even for those few seconds. My blood slowly restarted to circulate and I panted.

Dixon was still poised and unfazed, but Nina's eyes were huge and desperately black. *What are you doing?* she mouthed.

"You must not bite our visitors," Dixon said as he straightened his cuffs.

Anson's lip curled angrily. "Well, she wasn't listening to me."

Dixon's eyebrows went up sharply and Anson slumped away. I took the opportunity to look around the office—Pete Sampson's old office—and stamp back the flood of emotion. The once chocolate-brown walls were now a deep burgundy. The twelve-foot panel of cement and rebar-reinforced back wall that once housed Mr. Sampson's evening chains was painted over, the holes in the walls patched, the eyebolts replaced by ugly pictures of English foxhunts. I briefly wondered if they were a slight.

"Now, Miss Lawson, please don't take this the wrong way, but your employment has been terminated." Dixon turned to Nina, his thin lips pursed. "Did Nina not make that clear?"

"Oh, no, Nina made it very clear. That, and that you don't think I'm UDA material."

Nina put down the clipboard she was holding and took a few steps toward me. "Sophie, you have to understand—"

"I understand that you are siding with this—this monster over your best friend. I am not just UDA material—I am UDA!"

Chapter Twelve

This seemed to amuse Dixon and he crossed his long arms in front of his chest. "You may have been back when Pete Sampson was alive. This is a whole new era for the Underworld Detection Agency, Sophie. Times are changing." He cocked his head patronizingly. "You understand, don't you, dear?"

I felt a snarl of anger as I looked from Dixon to Nina. "No, I don't understand." My teeth were clenched. My fists were clenched. And suddenly I had no idea what I planned to say to Dixon. All the expletives and polysyllabic words flew out of my head. "You can't fire me," I started.

Dixon's lips and eyebrows resettled to a look somewhere between amusement and surprise.

"The UDA won't run without me."

At that moment Anson came slinking back in, dropping a thick file of demon transfer forms onto Dixon's desktop. Both our eyes skimmed the bulging file.

"You were saying?"

Nina stepped forward and put her hands on my crossed arms. "Sophie," she said, her voice uselessly low, "don't do this."

I shrugged off her cold hands and felt the anger glitter in my narrowed eyes. "Traitor," I spat.

I spun on my heel and sped through the door, leaving a stunned—or amused, I wasn't sure—Dixon and Nina in my wake. I was huffing and my eyes were watering by the time I hit the main hallway and ran into Lorraine, Kale skittering behind her. Lorraine threw her arms around me.

"Sophie! We miss you so much! Are you back?"

I sniffed into Lorraine's shoulder and she pushed me away delicately. "Oh, honey, what happened?"

"I hate that stupid vampire!" I huffed, wiping my eyes on my shirtsleeve. I looked around at the smattering of demon faces and gave Lorraine a quick squeeze and peck on the cheek. "I've got to get out of here."

"Are you coming back?" I heard Lorraine ask the back of my head.

I wagged my head in defeat, and mashed the elevator's up button.

I alternated between tearful rage and tearful defeat as the elevator heaved up floor by floor. When the doors opened on the police office vestibule I was back to hopping mad and I made a beeline for Alex's office.

"I need a job!" I yelled, once I found him at his desk.

He looked up with a sly grin. "And what are your qualifications?"

I flopped down in his visitor's chair and glared at him. He held his hands up, seeming to shrink behind them. "Okay, okay, I'm sorry. But I'm glad you're here. We need to talk about—"

The snarl that I felt roil through me must have been audible because Alex dropped his hands and used one of them to rake through his dark curls.

"Okay, okay; what's going on?"

I frowned. "Dixon fired me."

"Again?"

I felt my eyes tear up again. "Not again. He just wouldn't give me my job back."

Alex sucked in a slow breath and I crossed my arms. "What did you want to talk to me about?" I asked.

"Ophelia."

I felt the anger flail again. "Ophelia? I don't want to talk about Ophelia!"

"I think she has something up her sleeve. I'm worried that she's coming up with something big."

I snorted. "Something big? Look, Alex, I know you're all ghostly pale about your ex-girlfriend's supposed powers, but so far all she's done is throw around a few bugs and kick in my door. If she were really the murderous beast you tell me she is, wouldn't she have done a little more than the hamburger flea circus?"

Alex came around his desk and sat on the arm of my chair, patting my shoulder gingerly. "Look, Lawson, you're pretty worked up. Why don't you just go on home and get yourself together—"

I couldn't hear the rest of what Alex said for the steam blowing out of my ears. "Are you seriously going to patronize me right now?" I stood up, grabbing my shoulder bag and sending Alex wobbling to maintain his balance.

"I swear, you guys are all the same. It's like one giant dead boys' club around here and I can't stand it!" I tore out through Alex's office doorway. "I swear to God I'm going to strangle somebody!"

It was just after lunchtime by the time I got back to my apartment, cried, stomped on Nina's leather jacket, and finished an entire box of Easter chocolates in an egg-shaped box.

Once the nuts-and-chews sugar rush subsided I decided to be proactive and got online. An hour later I had trolled the Internet and applied for jobs anywhere from

Highly Organized Executive Assistant Needed to *Food Tester Wanted*. It wasn't exactly that I lived paycheck to paycheck; it was more that paycheck to paycheck didn't even begin to cover the bills. I huffed out a sigh and rummaged through the cupboards and fridge, hoping to find a leftover Santa-shaped box of chocolates. Finding none, I pulled a half cantaloupe and a carton of cottage cheese out of the fridge. I frowned when I heard someone clear her throat.

"Nina?" I called. "Are you back to stomp on my heart? Maybe you'd like to eat my new puppy?"

"Sophie! Down here!"

ChaCha looked up at the counter, shrieked, and ran out of the room. The last I saw of her was her tiny, rug-rat butt sliding under the couch. I looked down at my cantaloupe and let out an annoyed groan.

"Seriously, Grandma? In my lunch?"

"It's not like I have a lot of options, dear. You really should clean up around here. Trying to find a shiny surface where I can catch your attention is a feat. When was the last time you dusted?"

I assumed that any other person would be thrilled to see the image of a departed loved one wherever she might manifest herself. I, however, preferred my otherworld manifestations to show up after I'd had enough coffee. Or scotch. That, and I wasn't too keen on having my housekeeping judged by a woman in a cantaloupe.

"Do you have more news for me?" I asked, pouring myself a mug of coffee.

"It's good to see you, too, darling," Grandma said haughtily.

I smiled into my cantaloupe. "You, too, Gram. Really. I'm sorry. It's just that this whole thing is horrendous bordering on ridiculous. I got fired, people are trying to kill me. . . ."

"You've been fired?"

Good to see Grandma was concerned with what counted: my employment status over my still-alive status.

"Yup. Apparently I'm not UDA material." I scooped a heap of cottage cheese into my mouth and licked the spoon.

Grandma harrumphed. "Well, I wish I had better news. I've been poking around to try and find some information on this Ophelia character, but everyone is just so— so *pious* here. It's hard to get anyone to shovel any dirt."

"I appreciate you trying, Gram."

"Now about that Alex . . ."

I put my spoon down, could feel the flutter of my stomach. "You have information on Alex?"

"No. I was hoping you could give me some." Grandma grinned, her grey-white eyebrows raised.

I rolled my eyes. "No. But how was your bingo game with Ed McMahon?"

Grandma waved her hand dismissively. "Not everything I thought it would be."

Just then the phone rang and Grandmother gave me a finger wave before disappearing. I eyed the cantaloupe half and then rolled it into the sink, my stomach souring at the thought of chewing on my grandmother's face. I slurped another spoonful of cottage cheese and chewed while I answered the phone.

"'Lo?"

"Sophie Lawson, please."

"May I ask who's calling?"

"My name is Elizabeth Wells. We received your online application this morning and we're hoping you could come in for an interview. This afternoon. I know it's rather short notice. . . ."

"No," I said, swallowing quickly, "not at all. I would love to. What firm did you say you were from?" My mind reeled, counting back over the heap of applications I had filled out this morning. The law firm? The accounting place? The *San Francisco Chronicle*?

"Oh, I'm sorry. I'm calling from People's Pants."

My heart sank. People's Pants was a discount clothing store in China Basin; it was one of the last applications I filled out after I had done the math in my head and realized that my savings account would last me for a good, solid twenty minutes of unemployment.

"Great," I said. "I'll see you in an hour."

The city of San Francisco is technically seven square miles from borders to bay. That means, of course, that it takes a good thirty minutes to get just about anywhere in the city, depending on bus schedules, traffic, weather conditions, and the Earth's magnetic pull. I climbed into my car with a printed Google map in hand and pulled out into traffic, negotiating my way between Muni buses, wide-eyed tourists, and the occasional gruff man in a collar and leash being walked by a dominatrix. My little Honda heaved its way up steep grades, and I bit the inside of my cheek as I hit a stoplight at the top of a straight-up hill, saying a quick prayer and taking the leap of faith that the road would continue as I veered over the edge. I let out my breath and watched the hulking mansions of Pacific Heights slide by, then edged my way around the standstill traffic of cars with out-of-state license plates lined up to traverse the red-bricked switchbacks of Lombard Street. I was enjoying the quiet quaintness of Chestnut Street when I glanced back at my directions and cursed up a blue streak, realizing I had spent the last twenty minutes going in the exact opposite direction of People's Pants.

"Freudian slip?" I murmured to the empty car. I

double-checked the address again and aimed toward China Basin, dreading my destination even as my car crept closer.

China Basin is built on a landfill, and People's Pants seemed to be stocked with garments suitable for said landfill. I wound my way through racks and racks of polyester pants with permanent pleats, stretch pants in colors never found in nature, and heaps of velour track suits in cotton-candy colors, my heart sinking with each gruesome discovery. Though I had given myself a reasonably peppy self-talk in the car, I felt the betraying sting of tears starting to form behind my eyes as I approached the register. I clutched my briefcase a little harder and convinced myself that People's Pants was a mere stepping stone. I might start as a floor manager or some kind of junior buyer, but before long the People's Pants Corporation was bound to applaud my moxie, admire my swift organizational and people skills, and move me up to a position that I wouldn't have to lie about at parties.

By the time I found the cash register, I was feeling quite good about eventually taking over as People's Pants' first female CEO. I put my hands on the counter and beamed at the young woman who was slouching behind it, picking at her cuticles. Her brilliant blue hair was done up in Medusa braids and her pale face was pierced everywhere that wasn't covered with deathly white pancake makeup.

When she didn't look up, I cleared my throat and re-pasted on my newly acquired corporate-friendly smile.

"Everything with a green label is two-for-one. Higher-priced item prevails," Medusa braids said without looking up.

"Oh, no, I'm not a shopper." I stood up a little

straighter, held my briefcase close to my crisp white shirt. "I'm here for an interview. With Elizabeth?"

The human pincushion looked up slowly, revealing flat brown eyes lined with thick black pencil, making her look both whorish and sleep-deprived.

"You're the new girl?" she asked.

"Well, no. Not yet. I just have an interview. Is Elizabeth here?" I looked at my watch. "I was supposed to meet her at—"

"You're the new girl. I'm Avery. Here," Avery leaned under the counter and tossed a blue smock at me. "This is yours."

I glanced up and noticed that underneath the *Dead Milkmen*, *Eat Your TV!*, and *A is for Anarchy* buttons, Avery was wearing a similar smock over her black mesh shirt and just-past-her-butt-length plaid skirt. Her ensemble was completed with over-the-knee striped stockings and shoes with soles the size of loaves of bread. I estimated without them, she'd be about nose-height to me.

"So, I'm hired?" I asked.

Avery blew a bubble and snapped it, shrugged. "Guess so. Elizabeth had to study for a final. She told me to show you the ropes."

"Oh, okay."

Avery looked again at the smock in my hands.

"Right," I said, dropping my briefcase and pulling the hideous thing over my head. Avery leaned forward and clipped a red plastic name tag to my smock. It read TRAINEE in big white letters.

"Excellent," I muttered under my breath.

"Your breaks will be at ten and two, and you can take lunch from twelve to twelve-thirty. You need to vacate the break room between twelve-thirty and one o'clock because that's my lunch and I have to meditate."

Avery tried to pin me with a glare, the brown of her

eyes picking up the faint sparkle of her heavy dark eye-liner. "Got it?"

"Sure." I nodded, my eyes wandering to the hunk of quartz suspended from a leather tie around her neck. She fingered it, tapped it with her black-painted fingernails.

"Do you know about the healing power of crystals?" she asked me in her bored, nasally voice. "They are especially good for keeping away evil. There's a lot of evil in this town, you know."

You mean beyond the rows of size-twenty-four flower-printed rayon pants? I wanted to ask. Instead I said, "Evil, right. Noted." And tried to keep a straight face.

Avery blinked at me. "You seem like someone who is closed to the occult. I can read your disbelief all around you; your aura is white, cloudy. You're lacking a certain consciousness. You have mistrust. People like me"—she closed her bruised-looking eyelids—"are at one with all beings in all worlds."

I thought of the hordes of centaurs, demons, vampires, zombies, dragons, and banshees I had processed in my time at the UDA. I thought of the blood bags in the office fridge, of my evenings spent chaining up Mr. Sampson before nightfall. I looked around the swarm of people's pants, and wanted to cry.

Chapter Thirteen

I had managed to make it through my first day at People's Pants unscathed. I was still mad at Nina and Alex and wavering between giving my grandmother a piece of my mind if she knew about my Satan-as-dad bloodline and breaking it to her gently if she didn't. Either way I wussed out and hid in my bedroom after work, eyes wide open until I heard Nina come in and watch a few late-night episodes of *The Nanny*, murmuring to Vlad, who must have been with her. Eventually I fell asleep and the next morning I skipped out of the house (with my blue smock jammed in my purse) before Nina came out for breakfast.

My cell phone chirped as I navigated the stockroom, wrinkling my nose at the smell of dampness and unnatural fibers. I checked my phone's readout, saw Nina's name, and clicked the silence key, feeling a pang of anger tinged with sadness as I did so. I knew it wasn't her fault that I was spending my afternoon knee deep in polyester rather than knee deep in hobgoblin slobber. I knew she was just doing what Dixon asked of her and she probably felt as miserable as I did, but I wasn't ready to let go of my anger, especially when she went all goo-goo-eyed the second Dixon walked into the room. Nina called two more times and the phone buzzed once more. I was about to thumb the power-off button when I noticed that it was Alex calling. I palmed the phone for three rings before I decided to answer.

"Hello?"

"Are you feeling better?"

Any sense of love or calm I felt from Alex zipped out of the phone and fell flat on the floor. I felt my nostrils flare. "Did you call me just to check up on me? Because as a matter of fact, I'm feeling way better. I'm eating bonbons while reclining on the couch. I'm considering throwing a pot roast in the oven a little later. Does that suit you?"

"Actually, no. I know what happened the last time you tried to cook pot roast."

I stamped my foot against the amusement in his voice.

"So you're still mad at me."

I made a sound halfway between a grunt and a growl.

"Well, fine. All I need you to do is listen, anyway. So, what I said about Ophelia. I really think she has something bad up her—"

"The cellular customer you are trying to reach currently hates you. Please try again later." I slammed the phone shut and jammed it in my smock pocket the same time Avery came into the stockroom, lounging in the stairway, studying me.

"Everything okay?" she asked.

I started to restack the heap of pants I had knocked over. "Yeah, I just need to get these out to the floor."

"No," she said, gesturing to the smock pocket. "Everything okay with your boyfriend?"

I clamped my jaws shut. "He is *not* my boyfriend."

Avery shrugged. "Whatever. It's clock-out time."

I followed her to the break room to clock out and gather my belongings, but before I could leave Avery stopped me at the front door, the keys to People's Pants dangling from a fluorescent pink, squishy cord wound around her wrist. Her purple eyes flashed over my purse.

"What?" I asked.

"We need to do a check before any employee leaves," she said. "It's company policy."

I looked incredulously at our stock. "You think I would steal pants?"

Avery shrugged again—seemingly her standard answer to most questions. I blew out a sigh and handed over my purse. She poked around with a dutiful sense of disinterest and then handed it back to me.

"Who checks yours?" I asked.

She held up a tiny wristlet, big enough for a bus pass (if you folded it long-wise) and a tube of mascara.

"I don't like people pawing through my stuff."

By the time I got to my car I was fuming again and the parking ticket flopping jauntily on my windshield did little to lighten my mood. I looked around my gritty surroundings. Though much of China Basin had been rehabbed with the development of the ballpark and a clutch of waterfront lofts, People's Pants and its industrial neighbors seemed to have been forgotten in the effort. The funky charm of the city was choked out here by aluminum door frames and plate-glass windows pinned with aging iron bars. The nearby waterfront was dotted with palm trees and streetlights, but back here, the ocean fog hung heavy and dark. Even the employee parking lot—a slab of gravel underneath the 101 Freeway—looked grey and sad, cast in shadows from the highway.

I drove home with the radio cranked up, but even the jaunty beat of the pop star du jour did little to soften my bad mood. I was cursing under my breath and had given way to obscene hand gestures by the time I pulled into underground parking.

Hmm. Maybe I did have a little devil in me.

I stepped into the apartment vestibule and Will was there, holding an enormous white Styrofoam Jamba Juice cup to his lips, his other arm lost up to his elbow in the apartment 3C mailbox. The edges of his wide grin poked out on either side of his cup.

"Hey there," he said kindly.

I yanked open my own little silver mailbox and sifted through the handful of weekly mailers and twenty-percent-off coupons. "Hey," I said without meeting his eyes.

"Nice weather we're having, isn't it?"

I looked over Will's left shoulder at the grey sky outside and then back at Will, one eyebrow raised. He looked slightly sheepish. "Okay, so I'm not great at making small talk."

"And I'm still not entirely sure you're not a stalker."

He retrieved a handful of mail—I noticed a few air bills and the red-and-white border of *par avion* envelopes—and slammed the mailbox door. He raised his Jamba Juice to me and spun on his heel. "Nice talking to you."

I stood grumpily in the hallway, tearing my junk mail into violent shreds, then dumped the whole handful into recycling and climbed into the elevator.

I pushed open my apartment door and dropped my things in the hall, crouching down to scoop up ChaCha and let her lick my face and wag her little puppy tail spastically. I started to feel better after I showered off the People's Pants stench, tossed my cell phone into my sock drawer, and ordered a pizza from Mr. Pizza Man. I was dressed in an oversized pair of Giants flannel pants— little orange and black hats scattered all over my legs— and a floppy, thigh-length T-shirt when the doorbell rang and ChaCha went barreling toward it. She jumped up and down at the door, pressing her nose against the frame to get a good pizza-whiff. I grabbed a twenty out of my purse and met the pizza man at the door.

"Oh," I said when I pulled the door open. "Mr. Matsura. Sorry." I patted my damp, unbrushed hair. "I thought you were the pizza man."

Mr. Matsura smiled, his lips pressing his cheeks into round pink apples. "Nonsense," he said with a wave of his hand. "You look lovely. And I'm sorry to bother you at your suppertime. It's just that—would you mind helping me with something? I feel a little like an old coot asking you, but do you know how to tape-record a program on the new recorder?"

The local phone company had been around recently offering great deals and free DVRs if you were willing to switch companies. Nina and I weren't until we learned we could tape four shows at once.

That was six days ago, and we had approximately fifty-seven hours of *Project Runway* and *Criminal Minds* between us.

"Of course I can help you, Mr. M. Let me just leave a note for the pizza man to knock on your door."

I deposited ChaCha into her dog bed—after she got an appreciative head scratch from Mr. Matsura—and scrawled a note to the pizza man, sticking it to my front door with a bit of scotch tape.

"Okay, show me to your DVR."

Mr. Matsura handed over the remote control tentatively. "Are you certain you know how to do this? Because I can call the fellow from AT&T. Or ask the super."

I rolled my eyes good-naturedly. "Mr. Matsura! Your show will probably be off the air by the time you get the super up here. It's easy; let me show you."

* * *

I blinked, my eyes working hard to focus in the dim light. Each time my eyelids fluttered a sharp pain pierced my skull, shooting a dagger-like ache through my eyes. I groaned and pressed my palms flat against my temples; I was surprised to find my fingers sticky. The pounding in my head intensified and I started to make out the things in front of me—an expanse of white, thin blades, an awkward shadow. I was lying on my back, staring up at a ceiling fan, my shoulder blades grinding into the hard wood floor underneath me. I pressed myself to my feet and wobbled a bit, shuffling to get my balance, squinting against the pain in my head that continued to thunder, growing more intense with every breath. I heard a loud thump and I whirled around when the door behind me splintered and blew open. I stumbled backward, shocked, falling hard on my backside, elbows on the floor.

"Sophie Lawson, freeze!"

But I wasn't about to move. I was bolted to the floor, my eyes fixed on what had tripped me. He lay there, his eyes fixed on mine. They were cold, hard, unblinking. He was dead.

Mr. Matsura's head was lolled to the side, his mouth hanging slightly open, lips ashen.

"Oh my God," I heard myself whisper. I wanted to reach out and touch him, to help him. He couldn't be dead; we had just spoken this afternoon.

"Mr. Matsura?"

The officer who had kicked open the door made his way to me now and roughly shoved a meaty hand under my arm, yanking me up.

"Oh, thank God you're here." I looked back at Mr. Matsura, a sob choking in my throat. "Mr. Matsura— we need to call an ambulance."

"The coroner is on his way."

"The coroner? Are you sure?"

"What? You don't trust your own handiwork?"

"What? What are you—"

The officer—whose name badge read Houston—pulled my arms behind me and snapped a pair of cold metal cuffs around my wrists.

"My—oh my God. You think that I did this?"

I glanced back at Mr. Matsura lying silently on his braided rug and felt the tears stinging my eyes. "I didn't do this! I would never hurt anyone—especially not Mr. Matsura. He was my neighbor!"

Officer Houston's radio squawked on his shoulder and he leaned his angled chin, muttering, "Yeah, come up for the body."

The body.

Mr. Matsura was now *the body*.

My stomach heaved. "I didn't do this," I whispered.

Officer Houston looked me full in the face now and I noticed that though he seemed young, his eyes were sunken and dark and his mouth was heavily lined with lips that pulled down at the corners in a natural frown. He regarded me disdainfully.

"If you didn't do this, someone went a long way to make it seem like you did."

"That's it! That's it—I've been framed, I—" I stopped in midsentence, my cuffed wrists raised, my palms facing me. "Oh," I said, my eyes focusing on the dark red streaked across my palms, the rivulets of color seeping over my fingers. "That's blood. I have blood on my hands." I stared down in disbelief, seeing the heavy streaks of color on my jeans, the splatter on the toes of my white sneakers.

Officer Houston pushed me down in a kitchen chair and I slumped, then backed away when I noticed the bloody trail on the clean wood surface of the table. The trail of blood led to a kitchen knife, its blade hanging over the edge of the table, blood drying on it. I gulped.

"Do you recognize that knife, Ms. Lawson?"

"It's mine," I whispered.

The next few hours passed by in a daze. I was shuffled down the stairs of my apartment building and slammed into the backseat of a squad car. I stared out the window, watching the rain-slicked city race by as I was carted to the police station. It was dark, but I didn't know what time. I didn't know what day it was. I looked down again at my white T-shirt, my blood-caked jeans—I didn't even remember changing out of my Giants pajama bottoms and T-shirt.

I scooched forward on the car seat, leaned as close as I dared to the plastic-holed divider. "Do you know Alex Grace?" I asked Officer Houston as he drove, one hand on the wheel, the other resting on the butt of his shotgun. He didn't answer me, just smoothly pulled around a slow-moving minivan and hit the gas.

"Sir? Excuse me?"

I saw Officer Houston's chest go as he blew out a long sigh. "Yeah, I know Detective Grace. Why?"

An immense feeling of relief washed over me. "He's my friend. He'll tell you that I didn't do this. There is someone after me. Her name is Ophelia. Ophelia—well, she doesn't have a last name, at least I don't think she does. Anyway, she did it; Alex—Detective Grace—he'll corroborate my story. Can you just call him, please? Or, don't I get a phone call?"

Officer Houston turned the wheel and maneuvered the squad car into an open space in the police department lot. He opened the back door and clamped his hand on my shoulder, sliding me out.

"You're going to call him, right? Or we could just go see him. He's probably in his office."

Officer Houston pulled me close to him. We were nearly nose to nose and I could see the grit of his yellowed teeth, smell the faint odor of nicotine and sweat on his collar. "Look, girlie. The only thing I hate more than someone who would take advantage of an elderly individual is someone who thinks they have some sort of special privilege because they know someone on the force. I don't care if your best friend is the Queen of fucking Sheba; this isn't a parking ticket. You're not getting out of this one."

"I'm not trying to get out of this," I wailed as Officer Houston shuffled me toward the door. "I want this person caught as much as you do. She's evil. You don't understand what's at stake!"

Officer Houston rolled his eyes and kept walking, shoving me lightly in front of him. "Let me guess: I should set you free, and you'll bring the *real* killer to justice."

"Um, yes, actually."

"You and OJ, sweetie pie."

Officer Houston guided me into the police station vestibule and I looked longingly at the elevators that had so often shuttled me down to the safety and comfort of the Underworld. I clamped my eyes shut, imploring the elevator doors to open, to spit out Nina or Vlad or even Pierre—anyone who could help me.

"Can I call someone?" I asked, my voice sounding small.

Officer Houston just stared at me as he picked up the phone at the registry desk and punched a few numbers. He held the phone to my ear and I felt my lower lip quiver when I heard the recorded voice on the line.

"The customer you have tried to call"—a break, and then a gruff-sounding Alex inserting his name—"has left the calling area. Please try again later." There was a click, then the drone of the dial tone as it wailed mournfully on the line.

"Looks like your detective buddy took the day off."

"She planned that."

Officer Houston's smile was patronizing. "I'm sure she did."

I considered calling Nina and then reminded myself that even if I weren't mad at her, asking a vampire to bail me out of jail for murder was a flawed plan. Bringing Nina to the police station would draw unnecessary attention to the Underworld and plus, she was a vampire— which would also bring unnecessary attention.

But I was desperate.

"Can I call someone else?"

Officer Houston just shook his head, threaded his hand underneath my arm, and led me to booking.

My eyes were wide and moist and my throat was dry as I was strip-searched, fingerprinted, and subjected to three rather unflattering mug shots.

Officer Elia Gonzalez was escorting me around the premises now—she was a pinched woman with slicked-back hair, a deep frown, and a Napoleon complex.

I looked at her and tried my best sisterly grin. "Look, Officer Gonzalez, this is all a big misunderstanding."

"Are you saying Officer Houston isn't doing his job correctly?"

"No, no, I would never say that. He's been more than"—I frowned down at my cuffed wrists—"adequate. And I know how it must have looked, me there in Mr. Matsura's apartment. It's an honest mistake."

Officer Gonzalez studied me, arms crossed in front of her chest, one hip jutted out. "Uh-huh."

She put one hand on the small of my back and used the other to lead me down a long, sterile hallway to an electronically monitored door that said HOLDING CELLS. She dialed in her code and a loud buzz signaled the open door.

"But I'm innocent!" I exclaimed.

Officer Gonzalez's expression didn't change as she led me through the door. "Everyone is."

I tried to struggle away. "No, no—I'm serious. You've got to believe me. This is a setup. I don't even know if this really happened. Has anyone gone back and checked on Mr. Matsura? He's probably alive. She can make you see things!"

"Well, whoever she is, she's making Mr. Matsura see the inside of the morgue."

I blinked back tears. "I'm being framed!"

Officer Gonzalez stopped, her thick-soled black shoes squeaking on the tiled floor. "Really?" Her eyebrows went up.

I took in a relieved breath. "Yes, that's what I've been trying to tell you. I tried to tell Officer Houston, but he wouldn't believe me. I am being framed."

Officer Gonzalez dipped into her pocket and used the key to click off my handcuffs. I rubbed the red rings left on my wrists.

"Thank you. I know who's framing me, too. I don't know where to find her or really, how to contact her, but her name is Ophelia and—"

I stopped in midsentence as Officer Gonzalez put one hand on my shoulder, pushing me gently backward. I took a few steps and she slammed the barred door in my face, clicking the lock.

"Everyone is innocent," she said.

Chapter Fourteen

I shuffled my feet and felt the prick of heat as the terror slipped down my spine. I was *in jail*. A holding cell, yes, but still—jail. I knew what went on in prison. I had seen *Oz*, the final episodes of *Prison Break*. I opened my mouth; felt the lightness in my head as I started to hyperventilate.

"Put your head between your knees."

I whirled around.

"Sit down. Come on, sit down and put your head between your knees."

I gaped at the woman relaxing on the hard metal bench behind me. She was older, probably in her late forties, with a bubbly head of slick black curls and a kindly face. Sitting primly in her housecoat and slippers, she gave off a comforting cookies-and-milk vibe. The woman slid aside, patted an open spot on the bench. I sat next to her and crumbled over, my hair swinging against the concrete as I shoved my head between my knees and tried to take deep, calming breaths while also trying not to suck in the stale air of the holding cell.

"I'm not supposed to be here," I mumbled, feeling the tears slip over my nose and plop onto the ground.

The woman patted the back of my head calmly. "None of us are," she said.

I sat up and looked around, for the first time noticing the other women in the cell. Two girls were chatting in the back corner, dressed in thigh-highs and barely there dresses, giggling as though they were at a frat party instead of in a jail cell.

"They're regulars," the woman on the bench said, following my gaze. "That's Ella and Asia," she said.

The two girls looked at me and gave brief smiles; both were heavily made up with cheery bright red lips and streaky eye makeup in colors not found in nature.

I offered a tight smile. "They look . . . nice." My gaze trailed from Ella and Asia to the cinder-block walls of the cell, messages from past guests—EASTSIDE BITCHES! and DEATH TO PIGS!—scrawled into a semi-fresh coat of steel-grey paint. I felt the color drain from my face and my head went light again.

"Between your knees," the woman next to me commanded. I folded forward and willed myself not to cry, but a fresh round of tears started anyway. I sniffed.

The woman next to me bent over as well, her curly black hair in an unmoving bouffant. "I'm Arletta."

I shook the hand the woman offered and we both straightened up. "Sophie," I said, working hard to smile.

Arletta's dark eyes trailed over me. "Rough night, huh?"

I sniffled again and swallowed wildly, trying to squash down the lump in my throat.

Arletta scooched closer to me on the cold metal bench and patted me gently on the shoulder. "We know you didn't mean to do it, sugar. Sometimes the devil just gets into you."

Arletta's words hit me like a hot stone. I stared down at my hands and gasped—they felt heavy, hot, and when

I blinked, Mr. Matsura's blood was seeping through my fingers, pooling in velvet-red spots on the cement. I gasped and rubbed my palms furiously against my jeans, feeling the friction of the denim on my skin but still unable to get the heat of Mr. Matsura's blood off of them.

Sometimes the devil just gets into you. . . .

The devil wasn't in me—he was part of me.

Arletta took my hand and laced her fingers through mine. I expected her to recoil, to scream at the sight and feel of my bloody palms, but she didn't, and when I looked down, my hand was clean—the only color coming from leftover smears of fingerprint ink.

"You're going to be all right," she said with a matronly pat of my hand.

I wished I could believe her.

I leaned my head against the cold cement wall and blew out a sigh. I tried to close my eyes, to imagine a better scenario, but each time I did my mind was flooded with images of Mr. Matsura, of his gaping mouth, of his ashen lips, the marble glass of his cold, dead eyes.

"I have to get out of here," I mumbled, springing to my feet. "Is there a guard, someone?" I went to the bars at the front of the cell and gripped them, trying my best to rattle them, to make some noise.

"Hello?"

There were answering catcalls from the surrounding holding cells and then the creak of the security door. The catcalls died down, the chatter replaced by the thunk-thunk-thunk of metal against metal, by the click of high heels walking slowly, deliberately, across the hard linoleum floor. I craned my neck, pressing my forehead against the bars, and gasped.

Ophelia.

She was poured into a sexy prison guard uniform that showed off her shapely hips. Her slate-grey top was unzipped to show the top of her breasts and I wondered why the other prisoners weren't reacting. The whole cell-block was deathly quiet; the only sound was the thunk-thunk-thunk of Ophelia as she slowly dragged a tin cup against the jailhouse bars.

Her deliberate walk slowed when she reached my holding cell. As she passed I saw that her icicle-blue eyes were dancing with a sick kind of delight. Her red lips were plumped into a wicked grin. She stopped and we were nose to nose.

"You did this," I spat.

Ophelia just wagged her head and broadened her smile, touching my nose with her index finger. "You did this," she said, unable to keep the glee from her voice. "I have to say, little sis, the orange jumper looks good on you. Really sets off your hair."

Heat surged in my belly.

"Looks like you were made for prison." Ophelia wagged her head sadly. "Have a felon for a child—big disappointment for a lot of parents."

"I didn't do anything wrong."

Ophelia's elegant fingers trailed across her neck. "Tell me, Sophie, have you had any issues with your neck lately?"

"I—" But my voice was immediately choked by the heavy band tightening around my neck. I felt my eyes start to water and I tried to cough, to scratch at the non-existent collar.

"You look so much like your mother when you do that."

The choking feeling intensified and I clamped my eyes shut, seeing stars—and my mother's eyes as she stepped forward and threaded a noose around her neck.

I opened my mouth, sputtering, and tried to step back, out of her reach, and when I did I stumbled, falling hard on my butt. The noose around my neck was gone and I gasped and breathed heavily, feeling tears spill over my cheeks. I blinked and looked around me; the grey blocks of the cell were gone and I was in an attic somewhere. My mother was in front of me, young and soft, just the way I remember. A tear slipped down her cheek. I tried to reach out, to say something to her, but I couldn't move, couldn't get my mouth to form the words. My mother stepped forward and threaded the noose around her neck.

I started to scream.

There were voices all around me. Some laughed, some uttered things like "newbie" and "fresh meat." Someone else told me to can it.

Arletta was kneeling next to me, her arms around me, her dark eyes full of motherly concern. Ella and Asia looked on, Ella's purple-rimmed eyes registering boredom, Asia's a thinly veiled sadness. "Drugs," I heard her mumble.

"Did you see her?" I gasped. "She was here."

"Who was here, honey?"

"Ophelia." I kicked back against the cement floor and struggled to stand up. "And my mother." I felt the warmth from the rope around my neck. "She made me see—she made me . . ."

"No one was here, Sophie. Just the four of us."

Ella and Asia offered patronizing smiles.

"She's making me crazy," I said, rubbing my temples. "She's not going to be happy until I'm in the nuthouse."

"Drugs are a terrible mistress." Arletta shook her head sadly.

"It's not drugs," I said, sinking my hands into my back pockets. My fingers touched a piece of paper and I tugged a business card from my pocket. I gaped at it. "What the—?" I turned the card over in my hand and shook my head at the raised gold lettering: *Will Sherman, Guardian*. I had a vague recollection of seeing him in the vestibule, but I couldn't recall him ever handing me a business card.

And I would have remembered if it had said *Guardian*. I turned the little white card over and over in my hands, then bit my lip.

"I need to make a phone call," I said slowly.

I called out for a guard, praying that Ophelia and her sex-crazed warden outfit wouldn't show up again. I guess I was in luck as Officer Houston ambled down the hall toward me, his arms crossed in front of his chest, his expression wary.

"You need something?"

"Can I make a phone call?"

"You got your one call."

"But there was no answer. That doesn't count. Right?"

"Hey, Trevor!" Asia did a delicate finger wave in Officer Houston's direction. She batted her heavily made-up lashes, raked her talonlike fingernails through her hot-pink hair. "I didn't know you were working tonight."

Officer Houston offered what I supposed was a grin to the ladies. "Didn't know you were working tonight either, Asia. Hey, Ella, Arletta."

"Can I make that phone call now, Trev—er, Officer?" I offered my sweetest smile, batted my eyelashes.

"Got any gum?" Asia asked him, her breasts thrust out in front of her.

Officer Houston pulled a stick of gum from his pocket and fed it through the bars to Asia.

"Look," I whispered, "if you're going to give them special treatment . . ."

"Special treatment? It's a stick of gum. And besides—Asia didn't kill a man."

Asia and Ella stiffened and shrank behind me.

"You killed a man?" Ella asked, her dishwater-blond hair straggly as it fell over her bony shoulder.

"No! No. The phone call, please?"

"Hands."

"What?"

Officer Houston tapped his nightstick on a horizontal opening in the cell bars. "Hands."

I set my hands through the slot and he clamped a set of handcuffs around my wrists, then sunk a key into the lock and escorted me out of the holding cell.

My heart beat with each ring of the phone. *Come on, come on, answer*, I silently prayed.

"'Yello?"

My heart caught in my throat. "Oh, thank God, Will."

"Yes, this is Will. My I ask who's speaking?"

"Will, it's me, Sophie."

"Sophie, Sophie . . . doesn't ring a bell."

"Sophie Lawson!" I shouted into the phone. I lowered my voice trying to cover the mouthpiece with my shoulder. "You know, from your apartment building?"

"Oh, right! How are you, Sophie?"

"Terrible. I'm in jail."

I heard a snort of laughter. "What's that? I didn't hear you. It almost sounded like you said you were in jail."

"I did—I am!"

"In jail?"

"Yes. Look, forget the pleasantries and get me out of here!"

"Calm down, love, I'm on my way."

I listened to the drone of the dial tone for a full minute before I let Officer Houston shuffle me back to the holding cell.

I don't know if it was the damp cigarette smell of the holding cell or my sheer fear of being in the pokey, but it felt like it took hours for Will to arrive. Relief poured over me in waves when the heavy hallway door opened and an annoyed-looking Officer Houston, followed by a grinning Will, pushed through.

I rushed to the bars and gripped them. "Oh, Will, thank God you're here!"

Will looked around, whistled through his teeth. "This is all right, I kind of like it." He grinned at me. "It's a little like picking up a puppy out at the pound, isn't it?"

I ignored his comment and looked at Officer Houston. "He's my friend. Do we get to talk face-to-face?"

"Better n'that," Officer Houston said, sinking his key into the lock. "You're free to go."

Ella, Asia, and Arletta flooded to the front of the cell. Officer Houston held up his hand stop-sign style and inclined his head to me. "Just her."

I beamed, but Officer Houston didn't look happy.

"You got me out? Like, I can go out onto the street? I'm not a fugitive?"

Both men shuffled me out and I cringed in the bright light of the police vestibule, bustling with uniformed cops. "It's so bright. I think my eyes were adjusting to my life without sunlight."

"You were in there for two hours," Will said.

"How did you spring me? Do I owe you for bail?"

"No. It took a lot of smooth talking but"—Will rolled up on the balls of his feet, brushed his nails across his chest—"I've got quite a lot of pull."

Officer Gonzalez, the woman who had shoved me into the cell initially, bustled past us. "And they lost the body," she said without making eye contact.

My eyes widened. "What?"

Officer Houston's nostrils flared. "We didn't lose the body. It just sort of . . ."

"Disappeared. Vanished. Poof." Will grinned.

I thought of the bloody scene, my soiled kitchen knife. "And the crime scene?"

"Completely clean," Will said, while Officer Houston stewed at my shoulder.

"We think it may have been an elaborate prank," he said finally. "But until we get concrete verification that Mr. Matsura is safe and well at his sister's place in Pacifica like he says, don't leave the city."

"I told you I was innocent! It was Ophelia. She can make you see things. She does that. She's gotten into your head, too!"

Officer Houston's chubby cheeks flushed a deeply annoyed red. He looked about to blow, and Will gripped me by the shoulders, pushing me toward the door. "Let's go before they put you on a seventy-two-hour psych hold. I promise, Officer, we'll be of no more problems to you."

I let Will lead me out to the parking lot, my mind working the whole time. "So if everything disappeared—and they talked to Mr. Matsura—that means he's alive, right?"

Will looked at me, brow furrowed. "Of course, love, how many dead people sit up and answer the phone?"

I shot him my patented *Are you kidding me?* look and he smiled sheepishly. "Oh, right. You're all about the walking, talking dead. Fancy a pint?"

I looked around, felt the cool night air, damp with mist from the bay as it rushed over my bare skin. "Yeah, why not. I just got out of the clink. I could go for a beer."

Chapter Fifteen

We stopped at Will's car and just before he opened my door I gawked at him. "Hey. Wait!" I reached into my jeans pocket, felt around for his business card. It wasn't there. I gave myself a brief pat down and tried every pocket twice while Will looked on, his face registering amusement.

"You've only been in jail for two hours and already feeling the need for a little conjugal? It's really unorthodox, but if you need a little loving I guess I could . . ."

"Can it, crumpet. I'm looking for the business card."

"Oh, the nice lady with the tattoo on her neck slipped you her card, did she?"

I put my fists on my hips. "*Your* business card. The one you slipped into my jeans pocket. The one that said *Will Sherman, Guardian.*"

Will clicked open my car door and strode toward the driver's side. "I have no idea what you're talking about."

"The hell you don't!"

Will's eyebrows went up and I rolled my eyes. "Fine. Whatever game you're playing—fine. I don't know how you got the business card in my pocket and I don't know what you did with it, but I want to know why."

"Why what?"

"Why did I have a business card that said *Will Sherman, Guardian*?"

Will rested his hands on the gearshift, his eyes intent on the street in front of the windshield. "Put your seat belt on."

I buckled myself in. "You're the seventh guardian."

He gave me a grave look. "You know what happened to the other six, don't you?"

I nodded.

"So I'd thank you to keep this under wraps."

I mimed locking my lips and throwing away the key. "Your secret is safe. But why wouldn't you have just told me? Why didn't you just say, 'Hi, Sophie, I'm here to protect the Vessel of Souls. Pip-pip, cheerio.'"

He looked annoyed. "Why do all Americans think the English say 'pip-pip' and 'cheerio'? It's really quite obnoxious."

"Fine. No pip-pip. How about just the 'I'm the seventh guardian of the Vessel of Souls.' Would have saved us both a whole heck of a lot of strife."

"Would have saved you a bit of strife. Me, not so much. I have to keep my identity a secret."

"Why? Are you also Superman?"

Will guided the car out of the police department lot and into the smooth flow of late-night traffic. "My job isn't exactly an easy one."

"Because of Ophelia trying to pick you off?"

"Because the item that I am charged with guarding does stupid things like taking up with a fallen angel or getting herself thrown in jail."

I narrowed my eyes. "I am not an item that needs guarding. And how am I even associated with this?"

Will didn't answer and I could feel my frustration turning to a tiny ball of anger. My fingers started to twitch.

"Does everyone up there"—I turned my eyes skyward—
"know about my magical immunity? Do they all know
I'm helping Alex find the Vessel?"

"Blarney Stone all right?"

Will held the door for me as we slipped into the Blarney Stone, a dark pub in Outer Richmond that was illuminated with neon beer signs and was famed for making
the kind of drinks that made normal people wince.

Will grinned as he ordered a shot of something dark
and a beer chaser for each of us. He held the small shot
glass between thumb and forefinger and we cheers'ed—
me looking skeptical, him looking thirsty. He licked his
lips and took the shot.

"That'll put hair on your chest."

I looked down into my glass. "Just what I wanted. A
hairy chest." I shot the liquid and was about to howl when
Will shoved the pint glass in my hand and I grabbed it,
downing half my beer in a huge slurp.

Will looked impressed. "Now that's a brave woman."

I burped softly. "Jail'll do that to you."

Will held up two fingers when the bartender cleared
our empty glasses. Before the liquid had finished sloshing around in my stomach, there was another set of pint
and shot glasses set out in front of us.

I sucked in a nervous breath. "So, you're the seventh
guardian."

Will fingered his glass. "We're back to this again,
are we?"

"Are you going to tell me anything? About being a
guardian? About the Vessel?"

Will didn't answer, just kept his gaze fixed straight
ahead, his fingers working around the rim of his shot
glass.

"You must know where the Vessel is."

He gave an almost imperceptible nod, lifted his glass to his lips, took a small sip. "I do."

"That's amazing. That's perfect! You can get it and take it out of here and Ophelia will disappear. She'll be out of our hair." I looked over at Will's strong profile and felt a tingle of guilt. "She'll be after you, but . . ." My voice sounded small. "We'll be safe."

Will gave a humorless bark of laughter and downed his drink. "It doesn't really work that way, love."

I dropped my voice. "The Vessel. Is it nearby?"

Another tiny nod.

"Is it—" My eyes scanned the small darkened bar, flitting over each neon sign, over the sticky round tables and the small, deserted dance floor. "Is it here?"

Will set his glass on the bar, the glass on wood making a hollow thump. The bartender came immediately back and tended to the empty glass, filling it with a sloshing pour. "It is," Will said finally.

I scooched closer to him on my bar stool, feeling the rising race of my pulse. "Is it *here* here?"

Another sip, another nod.

"Can I see it?"

Will took a sip, focused hard on the row of liquor bottles displayed neatly on the mirrored shelves in front of us. "Look away."

I squinted, reading the bottles, trying to follow his unwavering gaze. "It's a Jack Daniel's bottle?"

Will kept drinking and I frowned, my reflection looking like a sullen child in the mirror. "Give me a hint."

"Fine. Here's your hint." Will did a half turn on his bar stool so he was facing me. His expression was part bored, part exasperated.

"What's my hint?"

He raised his eyebrows and I felt my frown go from sulky to frustrated. "What?"

"Really, Sophie. You have no idea where the Vessel might be?"

I wagged my head.

"None at all? Not even when fallen angels flock to you and a guy as good looking as me comes by and springs you from jail, no questions asked?"

I still wagged my head, was still confused.

"You!" Will's index finger was a quarter inch from my nose.

"Me, what?"

He rolled his eyes, downed the second shot, and then downed mine. He dug into his pocket, slapped some bills on the bar, and took my elbow. I stumbled after him.

"Where are we going? What are we doing? Are we going to see it?"

Will yanked open the car door and I slid inside; he got in across from me and hit the automatic door locks. My heart did a little double-tap and I felt a tiny nervous fist forming in the pit of my gut.

"What are you doing, Will?"

He turned to me. "You're the Vessel, Sophie. How could you not know that?"

I opened my mouth and then closed it dumbly. "Come again?"

"It's you. You're it."

I put my hand to my chest, feeling the regular thump of my heart. "It's me?"

Will just nodded.

"I'm a vessel?" My eyes widened. "So, am I filled with souls in limbo?"

I had an image of opening my mouth, seeing the mournful souls trying to climb over my tongue and teeth, trying to climb over one another to get out.

"I think I'm going to be sick."

I kicked open the car door and leaned out, the familiar

comfort of San Francisco's moist night air rushing over me in waves. I stared down at the concrete until the toes of Will's sneakers came into view. I gradually rose up and Will was hunched next to me, a compassionate grin on his face.

"You okay?"

"I don't understand." Will just shrugged and my emotional pendulum swung back to frustration. "How can I be the Vessel? How could I *be* the Vessel and not know it? I can't even eat sushi without getting a little queasy; how could I possibly have the souls of millions of people inside me? I mean, wouldn't that be a little obvious? Wouldn't it make me—schizophrenic or something?"

Will patted my leg and I was surprised at how comforting the gesture was. "It's going to be okay, Sophie. Knowing you're the Vessel isn't going to change anything. You've probably always been this way."

"Probably? So, there is a chance that I was normal once? And I got, what—infected—with the Vessel?"

"I really don't think it works that way."

"This is nuts. I'm the Vessel and—and—you're the guardian."

Will grinned his cute, boyish grin and did a little hand flourish that really pissed me off.

"You're *my* guardian? No offense, Will, but has anyone ever told you that you're crap at your job?"

Will's smile dropped and he pressed his lips into a thin line, the annoyance obvious. "Thanks for the confidence boost, love, but you don't exactly make my job easy. Getting into desperate situations, living with a vampire, running off to demon bars . . ."

I did a mental head slap. "That's right! You were in Heaven that night."

"That night Arsenal was down two-oh. It wasn't heaven for me."

A thunderbolt of anger roiled through me. "I get pummeled by a pixie in black leather because you were watching a soccer game?"

Will sucked in his cheeks. "It's called football, love."

"Great. Half the immortal world wants to kill me and my guardian is watching"—Will's nostrils flared and I continued smugly—"soccer."

He pushed himself up to a standing position and started to mumble to himself, his grumbling just loud enough for me to hear.

"The past guardians had to watch over things like mayonnaise jars and dinosaur bones. I come up to bat and they stash the ol' Holy Roller in a gorgeous bird with a fallen angel for a boyfriend."

"He's not my boyfriend," I whispered.

Slowly, I felt all the air leave the car. My chest felt heavy with the effort to breathe and I sunk back into the bucket seat.

Had Alex always known?

My throat went dry and when I tried to swallow; I was wracked with a choking cough that turned into uncontrollable sobs. Through my tears, I saw Will looking at me, his face contorted in concern and confusion. I felt his hand on my shoulder, patting softly, if awkwardly.

"Do you think—do you think Alex knew the whole time?"

Will raked a hand through his hair; when he brought the same hand down to rest on his hip I stiffened. Will's gaze followed mine and he jammed his fisted hand in his jeans pocket. I sprang up and grabbed his wrist, glaring at his hand.

"What is this?"

Will shook my hand off and crossed his arms in front of his chest, both hands shoved in his armpits.

"I got a little scratch, so what?"

"That's not a scratch, it's a bite mark." I pulled his hand out again, examined the little purple half-moon between his thumb and forefinger, and remembered the attack after the Giants game. "And it's mine. It was you."

Will shook me off and started to walk around the car, dangling his keys as he went. "So, back to your apartment then?"

I put my hands on my hips. "I'm not going anywhere with you. You tried to kill us."

"Get in the car, love."

Will's sexy English accent was quickly losing its appeal. I crossed my arms. "No."

"Get in the car."

"Not until you tell me why you were trying to kill us."

"I wasn't trying to kill you. I was trying to kill him." He sunk into the driver's seat and leaned toward me. "Now get in the car, love."

I jumped into the passenger seat and turned down the radio that had inexplicably gone up to car-filling volume.

"You attacked us."

"No, I attacked him. I was doing my job. I was saving you."

I gaped. "From a few moments of normalcy?"

"You are the Vessel of Souls. You were alone with a fallen angel. Do the math." He stepped hard on the gas and I flopped back into my seat.

Chapter Sixteen

After Will dropped me off and after I had washed the smell of crime and primal fear out of my hair, I slid into my fuzzy bathrobe and crawled onto the couch. ChaCha obediently jumped onto my lap and snuggled up against my thigh, her warm chest rising and falling as she snoozed comfortably. I stared down longingly at her, wondering if I would ever again feel comfortable enough to close my eyes, to drop off into unconsciousness without waking up in a pool of my neighbor's blood.

Then there was the Vessel.

My stomach roiled each time I considered that Alex might already know about me. Did we actually have a relationship or was it a ploy? Then there was Grandma. . . .

I stood up and ChaCha flopped over on the couch, growling at my bathrobe. I stared at myself in the hall mirror, trying to figure out which part of me was Vessel-esque and trying to formulate what to say to Grandma when I heard the lock tumble on the front door. The door opened a few inches and Nina pushed her fist—clutching her enormous orange leather Marc Jacobs bag—through the opening.

"Uh, Neens," I started, kneading my hands, "I'm really

sorry about the way I—" I pulled open the door and stopped dead in my tracks.

"Oh my God, Nina. What happened?"

Nina brushed past me delicately, holding her arms out tenderly, fingers splayed. Her black sundress billowed all around her, barely touching her thin frame. She continued her uncomfortable, straight-legged walk into the house and blinked out at me from behind enormous black-framed sunglasses. She peeled them off and I tried not to gasp.

"Oh, Nina, what have you done to yourself?"

She gulped. "Is it really that noticeable?"

"What would—why would you—" I picked around for the right words while Nina flopped onto the couch, her full lower lip pressed out and quivering.

"I wanted Dixon to notice me. I just wanted to stand out."

"But Nina—" I looked her up and down. "A spray tan?"

The usual marble sheen of Nina's delicate skin was gone, covered over by a cocoa-butter tan that made the ruddy pink of her bloodstained lips stand out awkwardly, made the glossy black of her hair look inky and unnatural.

"But you're a vampire!"

Nina looked at her arms. "Do I really look that different?"

"You look like a Chicken McNugget!"

She knitted her brows. "And that's bad."

I nodded slowly while Nina pulled up her dress and poked out one long leg, once a brilliant, porcelain pale— now an odd, Shake 'n Bake brown.

"I just wanted to stand out," she said again, her voice soft.

"Nina." I took her hand and sat down next to her. "You do stand out." I turned her hand over in mine, then poked at her arm. "Even without the hard candy shell."

She flopped headfirst onto the pillows. "I knew it! It's horrible!"

"No!" I pulled her up by the arm, trying to reconcile the warm cocoa brown of her skin with the frigid chill of it.

"I'm actually starting to get used to it. It was just a surprise is all." I forced a grin.

Nina cocked her head, a small, thankful smile on her lips. "Oh, Sophie—you are such a good friend. And a bad liar." She wagged her head, staring at her palms. "I'm so sorry about today."

I shrugged. "Nina, the tan will come off in a few days."

"Not about that. About Dixon. The firing."

I felt a pang of sadness, but tried to brush it away. "It's okay. It's not the worst thing that happened to me this week."

"I'm lucky to have you."

"Well, who else would? After all, I'm a felon. Do you want something from the fridge?"

"I'll take a—wait, a felon?" Nina took my hand, examining the leftover black fingerprinting ink that even a good scrub hadn't been able to fade.

"Long story." I stood up, went to the kitchen. "Do you want something to drink? I could pour some O neg into a coconut shell. You know, to keep the Hawaiian Tropic thing going."

Nina ran for the kitchen and was under my nose in a millisecond. "What do you mean, felon?" She shook my ink-stained finger. "Were you in jail?"

I blew out a reluctant sigh—I wasn't happy about reliving the events of the night—but gave Nina the details anyway while she sipped a blood bag and I nursed a Diet Coke. When I finished, Nina's brow was knitted in concern and I was beginning to consider Botox for what I assumed was my new perma-frown.

Nina looked me over, her dark eyes appraising. "So you're the Vessel."

I nodded. "I guess so."

"What did your grandmother say? I mean, she had to know she was raising—"

"Supernatural Tupperware? I don't know; I haven't asked her yet."

Nina's eyes bulged. "Go ask her!"

I went back to the hallway mirror and tapped. My finger tapped back. "Grandma?" I asked into the mirror.

Nina stepped up behind me; she had no reflection, but I could feel the cool air coming off her body in waves. I shivered.

"Do you like, have to say a magic phrase or something?"

I shot Nina an *Are you kidding me?* look and hugged my arms. "She comes out to give me warnings about nothing and to watch Alex in the bathroom, but when I really need her, she's not here." I narrowed my eyes. "I bet she's with Ed McMahon." I paused, an idea edging its way from my periphery. "I'm going to Cala Foods."

Nina blinked. "You're going to the grocery store?"

I snatched my keys from the rack and hiked my shoulder bag up. "Be back in twenty."

I pulled into the parking lot of our local twenty-four-hour grocery, thanking the god of parking and permits that he had allowed Cala Foods the measly six-spot piece of earth where I parked my car. Parking might not mean a lot to most people, but to a city girl like me, a spot within the area code you intended to visit is worthy of celebration.

I dug my hands into my pockets, shuddering against the biting San Francisco summer and entering the store, heading for the produce department and stopping in front of a pyramid of half-priced melon. I slipped one into my basket.

I looked at the cantaloupe I had selected, bit my lip, and then heaved two more in, just in case Grandma was going to be initially uncooperative. I dropped a package of Snausages in there for ChaCha and two more boxes of marshmallow Pinwheels for myself. I paused, and then cleaned out the entire Pinwheel shelf.

I lugged my stash to my car, the solid cantaloupes finding their way to the bottom of my pink canvas shopping bag and bopping painfully against my shins as I hurried. At home, I hefted the melons onto my counter and pulled out a butcher knife, slicing into the first piece of fruit after checking the reflection in the knife's steel blade. I halved the first melon and then leaned in, whispering to the pale orange flesh.

"Grandma?"

I tried the other half. "Grandma?"

I slopped the silent melon halves into the sink and sliced into the next fruit. "Grandma?" I shouted.

"Um, Sophie?"

I whirled around to see Nina standing behind me, her cocoa-butter tan even more outstanding now that she had changed into a hot-pink Juicy Couture tracksuit. "What are you doing?"

I put my melon-soaked hands on my hips and sighed. "What does it look like I'm doing?"

"It looks like you're talking to fruit. Fruit that you've named Grandma. Maybe you want to sit down. Sit down for a bit while I call the doctor?" Nina moved to the wall and picked up the phone.

I frowned. "No. I'm perfectly fine." I looked back at my melons. "Okay, I guess this looks a little weird. It's that . . ."

"Sophie!"

Both Nina and I snapped to look at the face in the fruit as it beckoned to us. Grandma looked from side to side. "What's with all the cantaloupe?"

"I was looking for you everywhere!" I said, as if there were a natural connection between communication and cantaloupe.

Grandma raised her bushy grey eyebrows in the sly, sexy fashion that grandmothers should never use in front of their grandchildren. "Sorry, I was indisposed. Turns out Ed McMahon and I got along better than I expected."

I crossed my arms in front of my chest, my hip jutting out in instinctual irritated-teenager fashion. "You mean you were canoodling with Ed McMahon in my moment of need?"

Grandma sucked her teeth and looked annoyed. "Sophie, you're a grown woman and lately, you have a lot of moments of need." She shrugged her shoulders. "Sometimes your grandma has her own moments of need."

Nina pressed her palms over her ears and clamped her eyes shut. "Okay, I don't know what's weirding me out more: seeing your grandmother in half a cantaloupe, or hearing that Granny's getting it on with Ed McMahon posthumously."

I gave Nina a dirty look and turned back to Gram. "This is serious. Grandma, I met Will Sherman today."

Grandma blinked, her eyes flat in the cantaloupe flesh. "Is he some sort of rapper or something?"

"*Will Sherman*, Grandma," I enunciated. "My guardian? You know, because I'm the Vessel of Souls."

Grandma paled, despite the fleshy orange cantaloupe color. "How do you know that?" she asked, her voice a hoarse rasp.

"Did you know I was the Vessel of Souls, Grandma?"

Grandma nodded very slowly.

"And you didn't tell me?" My voice was rising to near hysterics. "How could you not tell me that I was a Vessel?"

Grandma rolled her cantaloupe-colored eyes. "Please, Sophie. You locked yourself in your bedroom and cried for two months straight when I said you were going to have to get braces. I didn't think telling you that you were a supernatural holding tank would go over all that well. So sue me!"

"I need you to tell me the truth. About everything." My hysteria was giving way to tears and I fought to keep myself from crying. "Did my mother kill herself?"

Grandma pressed her lips together, her eyes rolling upward as if the answer she was looking for was somewhere above her.

"Oh, God, it's true. That's why she doesn't appear to me. She's"—I paused, swallowing saliva that had gone metallic and sour—"not in the same place as you are, right? She can't appear to me."

"Sophie, who told you this?"

"Tell me the truth, Grandma. Did my mother commit suicide?"

"Your mother loved you very much."

"Did she do it?" My voice was barely above a whisper.

I watched the grey-tinged curls on my grandmother's head waggle as she nodded her head, her chin low in defeat. "Yes, it's true. But Sophie, you have to understand—"

"And my father? Lucas Szabo, the college professor. Only he wasn't a college professor, was he? Did Mom know, Grandma? Did Mom know that he was the devil?"

My grandmother looked away and I felt a pang of despair as I watched a glistening tear roll silently down her cheek. "She wasn't sure at first," Grandma said. "She promised me she didn't know."

I gritted my teeth. "She killed herself. If anything

would have happened to you, would my father have taken care of me?"

"We had to keep you safe."

"And suicide was my mother's answer?"

"The Vessel of Souls existed long before you did, Sophie."

I crossed my arms, slumped into a dining room chair. "What does that have to do with anything? My mother took up with the devil. My mother fell in love with Satan."

"To her credit, he was very charming."

"Grandma!"

Grandma's eyes were stern. "You don't know everything, Sophie."

The tears started to spill over my cheeks before I even knew I was crying. "She fell in love with him and then she abandoned me. Is it because she knew what I was? Because she knew I wasn't real—that I was a Vessel?"

"Sophie Lawson, you are as real as any of us in this room."

I stood up angrily. "Forgive me if that doesn't give me much comfort, Grandma. You're a cantaloupe and Nina's been dead for a hundred years!"

I sniffed, storming past Nina, who stood in the kitchen, stunned, and leaving my grandmother, openmouthed, in half a cantaloupe. I was about to walk into my room when I heard my grandmother's voice ring through the apartment.

"Being the Vessel of Souls is not a bad thing, Sophie Lawson. But dying to protect it is!"

I slammed the door behind me and flopped down on my bed, letting the tears come. If it weren't for me, my mother would still be alive. My mother killed herself and Ophelia knew it. I rolled onto my side and curled my knees up into my chest and let the tears shake me. One time in my life the strangest thing was being the only breather in an office full of the undead. Now I had no idea who—or what—I was, though it seemed like the whole world already knew. I hugged my knees, rested my head on my arm, and fell asleep.

I tossed and turned most of the night, staring at the red numbers on my digital clock and finally putting on my iPod to try and drown out the chatter that was going on in my brain. The next morning I awoke with the cord from my headphones wrapped around my neck and my sheets bunched on the floor. I was still achy and tired but did my best to keep the events of the last night—from jail to Vessel to suicide—out of my head. When I padded into the kitchen Nina was still there, sipping from a coffee mug and leaning against the cabinets, ChaCha asleep at her feet.

"You look good today," she said with a cheerful smile.

"I love that I can always count on you to lie to me."

Nina handed me a Starbucks from the fridge and slung her arm across my shoulders. "That's what best friends are for."

I unscrewed my drink and slumped at the kitchen table. Nina sat across from me. "So, speaking of fabulous best friends, I couldn't sleep last night."

"Because you're a vampire?"

"Yeah, and because my best friend feels like her life has been turned upside down." Nina reached out and grabbed my hand, giving it a squeeze.

I felt another lump forming in my throat, but I smiled. Nina's skin may be cold, but her touch warmed me nonetheless.

"You need answers, so I'm going to help you get them."

"And how do you plan on doing that?"

Nina offered me a wide grin that showed off her white teeth—pointed incisors and all. "Close your eyes."

I laid my head against the table and moaned. "No, no

more surprises. From now on, I'm never losing consciousness, never closing my eyes, never opening doors. And I'm only eating clear broths."

I could practically hear Nina's eyes rolling.

"I was in jail!" I wailed.

I looked up as I heard the paper fall onto the table. A piece of folded yellow notepaper lay in front of me. I grabbed it.

"What's this?"

"Open it."

I raised a suspicious eyebrow and Nina snatched the paper out of my hand and unfolded it, smoothing it on the table. At the top of the paper was written Lucas Szabo, and underneath it, his full address. I felt my jaw drop.

"You found my father." My voice was a near whisper. "What? How?"

Growing up without a father, I went through the typical stages of child-abandonment feelings: making believe my father was looking for me, never wanting to see my bastard-making father, assuming he had a good reason for leaving, dating guys who wore blazers and used fatherly expressions like "cotton-pickin'" and "malarkey." At times I pored through old records or did halfhearted Internet searches. As angry as I wanted to be, I couldn't help but feel a meaningful tug around Father's Day or The Men's Wearhouse, but not knowing where my father was—only that he existed somewhere out in the world—gave me a weird sense of comfort. Not anymore.

"Lorraine owed me a favor," Nina said, her voice smug.

I felt a little stab of warmth. "And you used it on me? How? When?"

Nina shrugged. "Turns out Lorraine's as much of an insomniac as I am."

I looked at the paper, pinching it hard between my thumb and forefinger. "Thank you."

Nina threw her arms around me, engulfing me in one of her cold vampire hugs. "I'm really sorry about everything, Soph."

I barely heard her as I stared at my father's address. He lived in Marin County, less than forty-five minutes from my home in San Francisco. I wondered how long he had lived there. I wondered how long he had lived just across the Golden Gate Bridge and had never bothered to see me.

"I want to see him," I finally said.

"What? Now?"

"No, not now. I want to see him, at least see his house. I want to see where he lives, but I don't want him to see me."

"Because he might be Satan?"

I rolled my eyes. "I don't want him to see me because I'm not ready for that. I just want to see where he lives. I want to see what I can find out about him before I actually"—I swallowed hard—"meet him."

Nina and I shared a glance.

"And also, I guess I wouldn't mind finding out if he is actually the devil."

"We can go there. He lives close," Nina said softly.

Too close. My father lived less than an hour away from me, yet made no attempt to find me. Satan or not, shouldn't every father want to check on his little girl? I steeled myself, reminded myself that my so-called father just might be the cornerstone of evil, the King of Darkness, Hell personified. Not the kind of guy you want driving your car pool.

Nina put her hands on her hips. "What are we supposed to find at his house, though? Pictures of his Hell-adjacent condo? Pitchfork in the coat closet?"

I grinned in spite of myself. "Whatever works."

Nina shrugged. "Either way, I guess a little sleuthing couldn't hurt."

"Unless we're found and flayed alive," I said helpfully.

Nina slung an arm over my shoulder. "Sophie, do you really think your dad would flay you alive? And he should be happy to see me. Technically, I'm one of his people." She bared her fangs. "He probably even has my soul somewhere in one of his file cabinets. Alex's, too."

I stood up, my heart hammering in my chest. "Then this isn't a crazy idea?"

"Of course it is. It's downright suicidal." She licked her lips as my stomach sank. "But I love a challenge. It'll be a midnight mission." Nina held out her tanned arms. "And now I won't stand out in the dark. We'll go tonight."

My heart stopped. I tried to swallow, but my throat was suddenly bone dry.

I had spent the last thirty-three years pretending that I didn't care about my father's whereabouts and inwardly hoping that somehow, he was searching for me. Now, in less than twenty-four hours I could be face-to-face with the man who abandoned me, who walked out, leaving behind my mother and a four-day-old infant. I could ask him why and he could tell me. He could tell me that he missed me and that he looked everywhere for me, that he dreamed of me, too. Or he could tell me that he just didn't want me.

"Okay, then," I said, my voice wavering. "Tonight."

Nina put out her pinkie, hooked it with mine. "To your family tree. May it not be growing in Hell."

Chapter Seventeen

At just after four o'clock—my second break, and forty-five minutes after hefting an armload of "slightly irregular" skinny jeans to the front of the store—I slumped into a plastic break-room chair and called Nina.

"So, I got the text! How did I know you'd get hired in a heartbeat? So, what are you doing? Where are you working?"

With the excitement of last night—felonious misunderstandings, a rather invasive strip search, and a vampire with a spray tan—I had forgotten to mention my new career in the retail sector to Nina. I tried to call and tell her over the phone, but for some reason I couldn't make the statement "I work at People's Pants" come out of my mouth. Besides, didn't rayon look better in print? Instead, I had shot her a vague text while holding my cell phone under a round rack of extended-size cargo pants.

I held the phone to my ear and looked around at the bank of metal lockers, most etched with cheerful sayings like *Mike was here* and *Hell=People's Pants*. I glanced at the big row of time cards stuck to one wall.

"Well," I started, "I guess you could say I'm in the fashion industry."

"Oh my God, I am so dying with envy right now! I would give my soul—if I had one—to work around clothes. You are so lucky!"

"Yeah," I said, "but I think I'm going to keep looking. Oh, and I'm apparently closed to the occult, says my seventeen-year-old supervisor."

"Seriously and seriously? You, closed to the occult, and you, with a seventeen-year-old supervisor?"

"I am the lucky one. Look, I'll meet you at home as soon as I leave here."

I heard Nina stammering on her end of the phone. "Um, actually . . . would you mind meeting me here?"

My stomach clenched. "At UDA?"

"It's just that I have a project that I need to finish up and I brought the stuff with me and it would just be way easier to hop on the freeway from here. Besides, Dixon'll probably be gone by the time you get over here. He's getting a haircut at five-thirty."

"I don't know, Neens." My eyes shifted across the break room to Avery, who stood in the doorway pointing at the tattooed spot on her wrist where a watch would be. "Fine. Whatever. I've got to go. I'll see you tonight."

"Can't wait," Nina said.

The sun was setting outside People's Pants when Avery officially dismissed me. I locked my terrible blue smock with the trainee name tag in my newly assigned locker—number forty-three, the one etched with *Hell=People's Pants*—snatched out my purse, and headed for the door. After yesterday's strip search, having Avery paw through my shoulder bag didn't bother me quite so much.

I was sitting in Nina's visitor's chair at the UDA when Dixon poked his head in, his wide, slick-as-leather smile going solid and forced when he saw me. "Ms. Lawson." I'm not sure if it was meant to be a greeting or a question, but the tone of his voice made my hair stand on end.

Nina jumped up, panic crossing her dark eyes. "Sophie is just here to see me. To ride home with me."

Dixon's forced smile faltered minimally. "That's nice." He gave an odd, stiff nod in my direction. "Nice to see you."

I gritted my teeth and returned his approximation of a smile.

"Is there anything you need, Dixon?" Nina shimmied impossibly close to him.

"I'm leaving for the day, actually, but thank you," Dixon said. And then, with a polite glance toward me, "Good night, ladies."

I waited until Dixon was out of earshot before starting. "He is—"

"I know, fantastic, right? I really think he might be the one."

I stood up and shut the door softly. "The one? I'm not even sure he's the one to run the UDA. I mean, what's his background even?"

Nina shrugged. "I don't know. French?"

"I mean his business background. What do you even know about him?"

Nina thought for a second. "I know he's a Leo. You know how well I do with Leos."

"You also know that he fired me. Your best friend."

"Relinquishing you to find an amazing job in the fashion industry."

Amazing. Fashion. People's Pants. Nope.

I shook my head. "So, back to the plan."

Nina rubbed her hands together. "I've been looking forward to it all day."

I stood up, my heart beginning to hammer in my chest. "Then this is something we should do? It's not crazy?"

"Of course it is. But it's par for the course with the whole demon-slash-angelic world looking at you as some sort of cosmic prize." Nina clapped her hand on my arm. "Maybe I should take you for myself."

I gave her a look and she licked her lips, grinned. "Kidding. But as I said before, I love a challenge."

"Okay, then," I said, hands on hips. "I guess we go."

"Wait." Nina stood up and upturned her shoulder bag on her desk, the contents spilling out onto the floor. "You can't just break and enter looking like that." She gestured to my standard sheath dress distastefully.

"Are you kidding me?" I slumped back into my chair. "There's a dress code for breaking and entering?"

"Hello? Watched any *CSI* lately? Black, black, and more black."

"And let me guess? Ski masks?"

Nina's hand went to her silky dark hair and stroked a lock. "No. That would mess up my hair. Anyway, I, obviously, am already dressed." Nina twirled in her black velour Juicy Couture sweat suit, the word *Juicy* bedazzled in rhinestones across her butt.

"The Juicy is a nice touch."

Nina wiggled her butt at me and grinned. "I got to dress down because I was helping Dixon redecorate his office. We had to move some furniture." Nina waggled her eyebrows.

"I'll bet."

"Yeah," Nina said, her eyes trailing over me. "The only problem is that I don't have a whole lot of black in my wardrobe."

I gaped and Nina crossed her arms, one hip jutting out indignantly. "I hate it how you all think that just because I'm a vampire that I have an entire wardrobe of black leather dusters and Elvira dresses."

"I don't think that. I've seen your closet."

She rolled her eyes. "Black is so stereotypical. I don't

like it. It's for amateurs. And besides"—she tossed her hair over her shoulders—"it washes me out."

I raised one eyebrow, focusing hard on Nina's back to lily-white, bloodless complexion. "You're right. It's definitely the black clothing that makes you look so *deathly* pale."

Nina rolled her eyes and handed me a heap of black fabric from her desktop. "Just put this on."

I shimmied out of my dress and stood there in my slip. "You're kidding me," I said, when I shook out the dress.

She shrugged. "I told you, it was all I had. And we're running out of time. It's either that, your slip, or lurk in the shadows in your Jackson Pollack-on-speed sheath dress."

I eyed my multicolored sheath and then slipped into Nina's black dress. "Oh yeah," I said, ekeing the sequined fabric over my hips, "this is definitely made for B and E."

The dress was a one-shoulder, bugle-beaded Romona Keveza cocktail gown with a blush-worthy side slit and a foot of fabric that trailed on the ground behind me.

"Wow," Nina said, examining me, "that dress really is amazing. With the right shoes . . ."

"No. An evening gown for breaking and entering is as far as I go. I am not wearing heels, too."

"Suit yourself." Nina shrugged. "It would really extend the line though."

I blew out a sigh and yanked the extra fabric up, tossing it over my shoulder. Then I hiked the skin-tight skirt to mid-thigh. "I said bring a flashlight, too."

Nina rummaged through her bag again and produced two mini Maglites. "Done."

"And latex gloves?"

Nina bit her lip.

"You forgot the gloves? Well, that's okay. We'll just

have to be very careful. If Lucas Szabo reports a break-in, I don't want anyone to find our prints."

"*Your* prints." Nina waggled her fingers. "I don't have any. And I said I couldn't find *latex* gloves. Besides, they would do nothing for that dress. But I do have gloves. Voila!"

Nina produced two pairs of elbow-length cashmere gloves. She handed me the black pair that had rhinestone-studded ruching up the sides. "Aren't those to die for?" she asked. "I want them back." She slid her own delicate hands into a charcoal-grey pair with a tuft of faux fur around the tops, then stretched her arms elegantly. "Lohman's. After-Christmas sale. Seventy percent off."

"What every good criminal is after," I muttered as I gathered my purse. "A sale. Well, are you ready?"

Nina smiled and nodded, then followed me out the office door.

"You know, a French twist would really offset the one-shoulder neckline of that dress. . . ."

"Nina!" I moaned.

"Sorry!"

She shut the door with a click behind her.

We crossed the bridge in near silence, but once our tires hit the Marin side, I was fairly sure the thunderous beat of my heart was filling the car.

"There's nothing to be nervous about," Nina said, not taking her eyes off the road. "Everything is going to be fine."

"Thanks," I said, grateful, but unconvinced. "If I had known he lived just a few miles away . . ."

"You don't know how long he's lived here. He could have just moved into the area."

"Or he could have been here all along."

"Then he's a huge deadbeat bastard. It's not nice, but it's not rare."

I blew out a sigh, stroked the smooth fabric of my rhinestone-studded breaking-and-entering gloves. "Turn here," I said.

Nina glided her car down a tree-lined street. The moonless darkness was punctuated by the occasional weak streetlight. We rolled slowly down the street until we found number seventy-one, a well kept but otherwise nondescript house set way off from the street at the arc of a cul-de-sac.

"Here it is." Nina said.

"Yeah, here it is."

We parked across the street, then ducked our way to the front of my father's house, positioning ourselves in a thick bank of rosebushes. We hunched low against the moist dirt, our elegant gloves protecting us from the rosebushes' thorns.

"See?" Nina said happily. "Better than latex."

I squinted, frowned in the darkness. "Binoculars. I should have brought binoculars."

"One step ahead of you," Nina said as she leaned forward, her face pressed up against a pair of bejeweled opera glasses.

"See anything?"

"Not really." She glared down at the long-stemmed binoculars. "These aren't the best for this kind of thing."

"Imagine that," I said, my legs aching from my fifteen-minute squat. "This was a bad idea. I don't think we're going to find anything."

"Shh!" Nina's held out her hand, gloved fingers splayed. "What was that?"

"What was what?" I asked, relenting and flopping

down on my butt in the flower garden. "I've got human hearing, remember?"

But then I heard it, too. A gentle rustling in the bushes to the left of us.

Nina sniffed at the air, her eyebrows raised. She furrowed her brow, then frowned, sniffing again. "Alex? Is that you?"

"It's cool and disconcerting that you can do that."

The bushes rustled again and Alex poked his head out, his skin translucent in the pale moonlight.

"Alex?" I asked.

He had a pair of binoculars—real binoculars—in one hand and was tastefully dressed in black cargo pants, black combat-style boots, and a yummy, formfitting long-sleeved henley shirt. He grinned when he saw me. "I guess we both had the same idea here. Of course, my tux was at the cleaners."

"Very funny," I scoffed. "You should be glad I don't have a closet full of breaking-and-entering attire."

"You really shouldn't be here," Nina said, pointing at Alex. "I could smell you from a mile away."

"You shouldn't be here, either." Alex was looking at Nina but talking to me.

"Vampires don't have a smell. *You* have a smell."

"Sophie has a smell," Alex said.

"Sophie is right here and not too crazy about people discussing her smell," I said.

The opening of the garage door silenced our smell discussion. "Look!" Nina hissed. "Who's that?"

I snatched her opera glasses and peered down at the garage, the yellow glow from the overhead light illuminating my father. My stomach dropped. It was him; it was the man I had seen on the corner on my way to Loco Legs, the man I had seen in a picture that my grandmother kept taped to the back of a picture frame.

It angered me to see him flipping his car keys in his palm. It roiled my blood to see him glide effortlessly to his car, to back out and drive away. Somehow, I had hoped that things were difficult for him. That going out to look for me, to *find* me, would be impossible due to paralysis or a lame leg or a rattletrap car. But my father was doing fine, gliding down the street in a midnight blue and perfectly well-running Audi.

"We need to get inside his house," I said.

"We do?" Nina asked.

"Sophie's right. We're not going to find out anything out here. Nina, you stand watch, Sophie and I will go in."

Nina stood up, put her cashmere-covered hands on her hips. "Why do I have to stand watch?"

"Would you rather I asked you to stand smell?"

She stomped out of the bushes and to the curb. "Fine. But I'm smelling from the car."

Alex turned to me. "Are you ready?"

"For breaking and entering?"

Alex's gaze was solid.

"I'm ready," I said.

Alex and I picked our way across the sloping grass, being careful to stay in the shadows. Halfway down, a car drove by and Alex reached behind him, his hand grabbing mine, and we tucked behind a Japanese maple.

It may have been my adrenaline or my hormones on high alert, but the feel of his hand on mine was heavenly, the gentle brushing of our knees while we crouched, sweet.

"Okay," he whispered, "we're safe."

We stood up, but Alex didn't let go of my hand.

"So," I said when we had made it to the front porch, "do you have some sort of magically angelic way of getting through locked doors?"

"Yep." Alex dug in his pocket, revealed a long, skinny

tool, and pushed it into the door lock. After a half-second jiggle we heard the lock click and give, and he pushed the door open, slipping the shim into his pocket.

I put my hands on my hips. "Alex Grace, what would God say?"

Alex rolled his eyes and ushered me into the dark foyer.

I went to turn on the light, but Alex stopped me. "Someone might notice it."

"How are we supposed to see anything?" I asked.

"With my glowing angelic orb."

"You have one of those?"

"In your world, it's called a flashlight. Now come on." Alex clicked on his flashlight and kept the beam low. We edged around the furniture in Szabo's living room and made our way to the bookcases that lined one wall.

"Look for anything that has to do with the Vessel. We need to know what he knows about . . . it."

I fingered the spine of classics (*Moby Dick*, *Gulliver's Travels*) and figured my dad must have been quite the traveler from his collection of *Let's Go!* guides. I passed over the usual stock of *New York Times* bestsellers and John Grisham novels, then stopped on one book—*Stroham's Guide to Angels*. Beside that, *Contacting Angels* and *Communicating After Death*.

"I haven't found anything about the Vessel, but he sure is into angels."

"Makes sense," Alex said, turning to me and showing the carved ivory angel figurine he held in his hand.

I turned back to the bookshelf and bumped a small volume that stuck out from the pack. It was simply titled *Dark Angels*.

I held the book up. "Maybe he was looking for you, too." I thumbed through the book. "It's all about fallen angels. It was probably for work though; my grandmother did say he was a professor of mythological studies at one time."

Alex snorted. "Angels. Mythological. Whatev."

I grinned. "Don't get your wings in a bunch."

Alex scanned the bookshelves, the blue-white light of his flashlight illuminating the spines.

"Communicating with the dead, waking the dead," he murmured, "your dad was sure death-occupied."

I crouched down to get a better look at a stack of papers on the bottom shelf. "Well, that's a plus."

Alex looked at me, confused.

"I would think Satan would know how to talk to the dead, so maybe Lucas is just . . ." I struggled not to say *Dad*. "A guy." I snagged a book off the shelf and wagged it in front of Alex. "Also, I don't think Satan reads Janet Evanovich."

He grinned. "I guess that's good news."

I shoved the book back and continued searching. "Maybe he is just a guy. Maybe he was just trying to contact my mother. Or Ophelia."

"Why would he want to contact—"

"Ophelia," I said again.

I held the yellowed *Chronicle* newspaper clipping in my shaking hands, staring into Ophelia's eyes. She was young, with a printed jumper and pigtails, but her eyes were still the same, vivid, even through the pixilated and fading print. The last time I had looked into those eyes she had vowed to kill me and now there she was, snuggled up against the man who was supposed to be *my* father, the man who was supposed to have been photographed with *me* on his knee.

"Lawson?" Alex whispered.

I dropped the newspaper clipping and took the stairs

two by two. I was vaguely aware that Alex was behind me, calling to me, but something drove me. I darted down the hall, pushing open doors as I went. I paused at the last door and sucked in a breath. Closing my hand on the knob, I pushed the door open.

It was a young woman's room, but still held the pale pink remnants of little-girl life. The frilly lace lampshade was now partly covered by an orange and black Giants baseball cap. The rolling pink teddy bears on the wallpaper were now mostly covered by concert posters, magazine clippings, and photographs of smiling teenagers, their arms entwined, their youth captured forever. The fresh, bright smell of freesias still hung on the air, their sweet scent making me nauseous.

"This was Ophelia's room," I said slowly. "This is where she grew up."

A yearbook was askew on her night table, its binding creased and old, as though someone had leafed through the book often. Alex picked it up and it fell open. He turned the book to face me.

There, with a demure look as she stared over her shoulder, was a full-page photograph of Ophelia. Underneath, it read: *In Memory of Ophelia Szabo: a bright light gone out much too soon.*

"Oh my God," I whispered. "Oh my God. She was my sister."

Chapter Eighteen

I felt a coil of anger in my stomach. "Did you know?"

"No, Sophie, I swear. How would I have known?"

"You dated her, Alex! You dated her and you didn't know where she came from before?"

I was spitting mad now, feeling the emotion roiling through my veins. I was standing up, cornering Alex. "How could you not have known?"

Alex put his hands on my arms, holding me at arm's length. His eyes were hard, cold. "I didn't know, Sophie. Angels in grace don't have any knowledge of the circumstances of their death or anything that happened before it. Time moves differently there. There is no way I could have put this together."

I knew he was right, but I balled my hands into fists anyway, felt the tears spring into my eyes. I looked around the room, looked at the sweet pink sheets on the still-made bed, at the photographs of Ophelia and my father sharing family moments—at the beach, under the Christmas tree.

"He knew me and he didn't want me," I sobbed. "He knew how to be a dad, he just didn't want to be one to me."

Alex put his arms around me and I crumbled into him, sobbing, hiccupping. "I don't care, I swear," I sobbed. "He never even tried to find me."

I gathered myself and used the tail of my black evening gown to wipe my eyes. "I'm sorry," I sniffed.

Alex just squeezed my shoulder and led me out of Ophelia's room. We picked our way down the stairs, peeking in rooms and thumbing through bookshelves until we came to my father's den. Alex was rifling through the top desk drawer when he suddenly stopped and withdrew a large manila envelope. He dumped the contents on the desk.

"Uh, Lawson?"

I dropped the statuette I was holding and went to the desk, sucking in a gasp as I did. I stared down into my own eyes. Into my own face.

"What the—?" I pawed through the heap of photographs—they were all me, from every angle. I was a pudgy, round-eyed baby in some shots, then a toddler, gripping my mother's hand. There was a long gap, and then the next few pictures were more recent.

"Maybe he was looking for you."

But they weren't the photographs of a father longing for his child. There weren't shots of me grinning, shopping at the Farmer's Market, snuggling the family dog. They were banal: shots of daily tasks, close-ups of my face, my hands, slipping into the doors above the UDA.

Four days after I was born . . . I thought. *He was seeking the Vessel; it consumed him. . . .*

I put the photograph I was holding back on the desk. My saliva went sour, my face hot.

"Sophie?"

Alex's voice sounded tinny, far away.

Now don't you see? You're the only one who didn't know. Poor, dumb baby sister . . .

It was Ophelia's voice and it was happy, giggly.

You know the truth, she said. *You know it's there. . . .
You've always known that you weren't right, you never fit
in. . . . But a prize? Nah. Just a thing. You were always
just a thing, Sophie. We know it, Daddy knew it, and now
Alex knows it, too.*

She whispered the last part and her breath echoed in
my mind, ran shivers up my spine.

"You." The word caught in my throat, hung in the air.

"What?"

I took a step back. "You know . . . about me. He knew.
My dad knew."

Alex looked at me, his eyes wide. "What are you talking about? Are you okay? Maybe you should sit down."
Alex reached out for my hand and his touch—usually
warm and comforting—was icy and I pulled my hand
away, stumbling.

"You know about me."

Alex opened his mouth and then closed it, and I
watched the flash of realization cross over his eyes. "*You*
are the Vessel of Souls."

I nodded, every inch of my body tense, on high alert.
I was aware each time my heart beat, was certain of each
pump of blood. I was ready to run but Alex just sat,
stunned.

"You."

I could feel the tears pooling behind my eyes. "You
didn't know?"

Alex wagged his head. "I had no idea. When did—did
you always know?"

"No. Will told me."

"Will? The guy from your apartment building?"

I nodded. "He told me after he bailed me out of jail.
Yesterday."

Alex's eyes flashed. "Geez, Lawson. Jail?"

"It's a long story. I'll tell you later."

Alex rubbed his palm over his forehead. "Okay. So how does this Will guy know anything about you—about you being—"

"The Vessel."

Alex just nodded, wouldn't say the words.

"He's the seventh guardian."

Shock registered across Alex's features. "Well, I'll be. . . ."

I bit my lip. "So, you really didn't know."

"Know? Lawson, I've been chasing my tail around this my whole afterlife. If I knew it was you I'd—"

"You'd what?"

He looked me up and down, slowly, carefully choosing his words. "I—I don't know. I don't even know what this means for . . ." He let the word trail off.

"For you. You don't know what it means for you."

"Come on, Lawson. This is a lot to process. You've got to give me a minute. I mean, first you're Satan's kid, then Ophelia's sister, now this. Are you sure? Absolutely sure?"

"As sure as I can be. I don't know what any of this"— I flung my arms open wide—"means."

Alex opened his mouth and then closed it again. "Plain sight," he murmured.

"Plain sight," I agreed.

"I don't understand."

I shook my head. "Neither do I. But I'm not wrong."

"Okay," Alex said with a monumental sigh. "Now what?"

"Now what? Now we throw a big welcome-home party for my dad. I don't know! I'm a vessel. I'm a *thing*!"

"You're not a thing, Lawson. You're you."

"Eloquent."

There was a soft knock on the office door, and then Nina poked her head in. "Are we done spying? I'm bored."

"Nina! You're supposed to be standing watch!"

Nina looked over one narrow shoulder. "Clear," she said.

I grabbed Alex by the sleeve of his shirt and hustled him toward Nina. "I want to get out of here. I need to get out of here."

Nina followed behind us. "What'd you find out about dear ol' dad? Cross-dresser? Closet masochist? Satan?"

"It wasn't about Szabo," Alex said, his voice steady as he carefully chose his words. "It was about Sophie."

"And Ophelia," I interjected. "Ophelia is my sister."

Nina's eyes widened. "Oh. Lord."

"I need a milkshake."

Nina and Alex nodded and followed me to the car, Nina chattering the whole way. "So, Ophelia, huh? Interesting." She looked from me to Alex. "You've dated sisters. Major no-no in the Dater's Compendium."

"I think the afterlife version might be different," I whispered. Alex reached out and squeezed my hand, and though the move was meant to be comforting, it wasn't. "Wow. I have a sister."

Nina bit her lip. "If Ophelia is your sister and Satan is your dad, who's Ophelia's mom?"

My eyebrows went up, and Nina and I both swung to look at Alex, who shook his head. "I don't know."

"Never got that serious, huh?" Nina said.

I thought of my own mother, her eyes warm, her touch so soft. My throat tightened. "Milkshake. Please."

We slid into the car and drove in silence, until Alex found an In-N-Out Burger. He ran us through the drive-through, handing a chocolate milkshake back to me and balancing a basket of fries on his lap. I snatched a few, pried the lid off my shake, and dipped.

Alex looked at me. "That's gross."

I swallowed a chocolaty, salty mouthful. "I've had a bad night."

"So," Nina said as we coasted back onto the highway, "did you find out if Pops is Satan?"

Alex wagged his head, sipped at his shake. "It didn't seem important anymore."

"Because of the Ophelia thing?"

I took another handful of fries and a big gulp of chocolate shake. I could feel the soul-soothing triumvirate of salt, grease, and fat begin to work through my system.

"And because of the Vessel," Alex said.

Nina's eyes were wide and she tossed me a panicked look, sitting up straighter in the car seat. "What do you know about the Vessel?" she asked Alex.

"It's okay, Nina. I told him."

Nina's shoulders fell a millimeter, but her eyes narrowed angrily. "You might know her secret, angel, but if you lay one hand on Sophie just because she's this tank thing, I swear you'll regret it for all your lives to come."

I watched Alex's Adam's apple bob as he swallowed. "Noted."

I reached across the seat and squeezed Nina's hand. My dad might be Satan, I was thrown in the slammer for a disappearing murder, and I might be some kind of supernatural Tupperware, but I had the best best friend in the world.

I stole a glance over at Alex. His eyes were icicle blue and fiery. He was focused straight ahead on the dark road before us, and the muscle in his jaw was twitching the way it did when he was concentrating. I didn't want to consider what he was thinking, so I sunk down in my seat and tried to close my eyes.

I thought about us lying in bed together, our naked shoulders touching, and him telling me about Heaven. I thought about the way he had talked about being restored to grace—about "going home." And I thought about how *I* was the only way he was going to get there. I swallowed a sob.

The truth hurts, doesn't it? My eyes flashed open. *He doesn't want you. He wants the Vessel. . . .*

I clamped my hands over my ears, trying to silence Ophelia's singsongy voice.

Do us all a favor. . . .

I gritted my teeth. *Did you like seeing photos of Daddy and me? Maybe we can all get together some day . . . go out for ice cream. Doesn't that sound like the perfect family outing? He used to take me out for ice cream all the time. . . .*

Shut up, I thought, closing my eyes, clenching my fists, and going rigid. *Shut up, shut up, shut up.*

There was a faint, echoing giggle, and then she was gone.

I opened my eyes and saw Nina bite her lip, thinking. "So, if Sophie is the Vessel, then . . . how do we get to it?"

Alex was silent, avoiding my gaze. "Alex?" I asked.

"The only way to possess the Vessel in this"—Alex's eyes wandered over me, met mine—"form, is to release it."

"Release it? What does that mean?" Nina asked.

I swallowed, the truth washing over me. "Death," I said, my eyes fixing on Alex's. "He has to kill me."

Now you know what Alex was thinking this whole time. . . . He gets close to you, you fall in love with him, trust him . . . and he kills you.

"No," I murmured under my breath.

"Sophie?" Alex asked.

"That's not true," I whispered.

You think he really cares, don't you? You don't think he knew what you were all along? Come on, little sis, grow up. Alex is only after one thing. He's a fallen angel. He's no better than I am.

I clenched my fists, feeling my nails dig little half-moons into my palms. I felt the sting of sweat on my upper lip.

Alex put his hand on my thigh, leaned close. "Lawson, are you okay?"

"It's Ophelia," I whispered. "She's in my head again."

"Block her out. You have to." Alex's eyes were wide, insistent.

I pressed my palms against my ears. "I'm trying to."

"She knows exactly where you are. She's listening."

Ophelia's laughter came out hollow, reverberating through my head. *Isn't he cute? Trying to help you out— as though he can! Really, sis, I can't blame you for falling for him—I mean, I did. I took one look at those glorious baby blues of his . . .*

"I am not your sister," I muttered between clenched teeth.

Did he slip up? Call you his girlfriend? Did he whisper, "I love you" in the middle of the night?

My saliva went sour and my stomach lurched. I felt the tears beginning to pool behind my eyes, but I wouldn't give Ophelia the satisfaction of seeing me cry. I breathed deeply, blinked away the tears.

Face it, Sophie. You're second best. Again. First Daddy, and now Alex. Sorry, sis. Stings a little bit, I bet, huh? Poor thing. Really, it would be easier for everyone if you just . . .

"No." I gritted my teeth.

Ophelia started to hum softly, an eerie unnatural lull-aby running through my mind.

"Sophie, don't let her get to you. Alex, we have to do something. Sophie's going crazy."

Alex's voice was even. "Ophelia is dangerous and as long as she can get into your head, Lawson, we're at her mercy. You've got to try to block her out."

"Great. So now we have to get Ophelia out of my head and the Vessel out from my . . . wherever it is. Geez. What else is in me?" I had an image of my empty skin, heaped on the floor in front of me.

Alex took my hand. "Okay, Sophie, I need you to think. There is always something that we think about, sometimes when we concentrate hard enough or go somewhere where we can't let anything else into our mind."

"Like . . . having a one-track mind?"

"I guess. Is there something you can think about that is all consuming?"

Nina raised her hand, grinning salaciously. "I've got mine."

I clamped my eyes shut and was pleasantly surprised when my mind rolled out a blank, black canvas. But little by little, at the edge of my periphery, images rolled in. There was Ophelia, and when I saw her in my mind's eye I felt myself stiffen sharply. I worked to push her out and focus on something else when I felt a tightness at my throat, a deep pressure ringing my neck. I coughed, feeling the prick of the individual hairs of rope as they scratched my skin, tightening, making it hard to breathe. I felt the rope as it rolled upward as though someone were—were—hanging it? Tears sprang to my eyes and I opened them, clawing at the imaginary rope around my neck, gasping. I blinked, feeling the stolid air in the car, Nina and Alex's eyes on me, swimming with concern.

"Sophie?" Nina asked.

"I'm okay," I lied, opening the back window and relishing the cool wind crashing over me. "I'm okay."

Alex took my hand when we got back to the apartment. He squeezed it gently. "Are you sure you're okay? In the car you were—"

"It was just a lot to take in," I said with a calculated sigh. "I'm okay, really."

Alex's eyes were intent on mine and I could tell he wasn't convinced. I threw in a smile filled with forced happiness. "Really."

"Do you need me to stay? We could talk about this—make some coffee, figure out some sort of plan?"

"That's very Dr. Oz of you, but, to be honest, I just want to go to sleep. Besides, the fate of the world might hang in the balance, but polyester pants wait for no one. I just want to go to sleep for a little while—just for a little while—before I have to face my new job." And before I had to face my new family.

Chapter Nineteen

My new position at People's Pants may not have offered a 401(k), but it did offer hour upon hour of mind-numbing, repetitive duty. I worked to keep my mind focused on the People's Pants–approved tri-fold technique and not on the events of last night—particularly, that my family tree seemed to be getting bogged down with more and more rotten fruit. I had slunk into my bedroom last night feeling betrayed and alone. Ophelia had known about me, but I hadn't known about her. Who else did?

I folded another pair of pants and the silver button fly caught my eye. Four shiny buttons. My mouth went dry and I quickly glanced around, then hunched closer to the pants. "Grandma?"

I heard the snap of gum behind me and a burst of grape-scented air. I whirled, and Avery was behind me, her lips dyed to match her gum, her eyebrows raised. "Were you talking to the pants?"

I wagged my head furiously. "Of course not."

She gave me a look of skepticism and disbelief and turned on the platform heels of her black plastic boots, popping another bubble as she went.

My cell phone chirped and I gasped, clasping my hand

over my heart. "Geez!" I slid it out of my People's Pant blue smock pocket.

"'Lo?" I answered, dropping my voice and dipping my head behind a mammoth stack of painter's pants.

"I'm taking you to lunch," Alex said.

I dropped the pair of pants I was folding and peeked around, periscope style. I watched Avery unwrap another chunk of gum and stick it into her mouth, then settle at the register with a rock magazine. Aside from the two of us, the store was empty.

"Okay, but I only get a half hour. I wouldn't want to upset my teenybop supervisor."

I clicked my cell phone shut and hurried for the break room, peeling off my smock and fluffing my hair as I went. I yanked out my shoulder bag—excessively heavy due to my new Taser—and dumped the black plastic case back into my locker. No need for a stun gun with Officer Angel by my side. By the time I made it out to the main floor Alex was leaning against the front counter, examining a pair of god-awful one-off chinos while Avery swooned behind him.

"We have them in slate, charcoal, verbena, and cherry, too," she cooed. "Or I can show you something in a soft-weave nylon."

Alex's eyes met mine and I watched Avery immediately stiffen. "I'm going to lunch now, okay?"

Avery's dark eyes went from mine to Alex's; she used her thumb and index finger to rub the bridge of her nose as she let out a long, aggravated sigh. "Fine. Just make sure you're back on the floor by one. My moon is in the seventh house and I can already feel my chakras backing up—I really need to meditate. And you have that entire pile of side-zip capris to mark down."

I pasted on a smile. "Can't wait."

Alex ushered me out the People's Pants doorway and

pointed to his white SUV, parked across the street. I looked at him, impressed. "Someone has parking karma."

San Francisco, while loaded to the gills with gourmet restaurants, killer fashion boutiques, and the best donuts on the planet, is sadly sparse on parking spots. Last I heard there were six.

Alex grinned and opened his coat, his badge glinting in the sunlight. "This isn't just a fancy piece of jewelry."

I gaped. "You flashed your badge to get someone to move?"

He shrugged. "I consider this official police business."

We pushed through the double glass doors of the diner. The V-shaped restaurant was fronted by big glass windows looking out on the city and the bay, and sported dark wood booths with tall dividers that made patrons feel cozy as the swirls of fog rolled in just beyond the glass. Inside the restaurant was slightly dark, reflecting the afternoon sky, and the homey scents of meatloaf and French fries greeted me and made my stomach growl. We stood in the foyer waiting to be seated and I hunkered back, certain that everyone was staring. As the waitress led us to our table, I stared at the ground, focusing on the toes of my shoes rather than the questioning eyes I felt boring into me. I slid in the booth and looked around nervously.

"You're paranoid," Alex said.

"I am not." I bit my thumbnail. "But everyone was looking at us, right? They were staring?"

"No more than usual, Lawson."

Another waitress came by with a carafe and filled up our coffee mugs, handing us two laminated menus. We scanned our menus and she took our order—two burgers, two fries. I watched her disappear behind the counter while Alex studied me.

"You're completely paranoid," he said finally.

"Okay, if I am—which I am not—don't I have the right to be?" I tried to keep my voice hissing and low, but I could feel my voice rising. "I am the Vessel, Alex. Everyone wants me!"

The diner patrons had the uncanny ability to drop into silence at the most inopportune of moments—like this one. All heads swung toward me, appraising. The waitress strolled back over and gave me an uninterested once-over, then sloshed coffee into Alex's mug, ignoring my own.

I hunched lower in the booth and began to whisper, spitting dirty looks at Alex, who sugared and stirred his coffee with that stupid smug grin on his face.

"I mean, everyone wants the Vessel. And it seems that a whole lot of people are onto my little secret. So excuse me if I'm just a little jumpy."

We were silent while the waitress slid our plates in front of us. I examined my sandwich like a crime scene investigator examines a crime scene—I checked the bread, both top and bottom, poked at all the fries, tore the burger in pieces. I waited for Alex to take a bite of his burger. He did, chewed quietly. No maggots. I took a tentative bite of my lunch. Once I felt my teeth sink into the moist meat—no squishing of maggots or crunching of rat bones—I chewed happily, licking the caramelized-onion grease as it spilled over my fingers. "This is the best lunch ever," I said with a mouthful.

Alex sat forward, his voice low. "The number of people who know about the Vessel of Souls—let alone are searching for it—is miniscule."

I swallowed my bite. "Fabulous! So only a *small* number of people want to kill me. I feel so much better now."

"All I'm saying is that you don't have to operate like there are snipers on every corner. I'm here."

"For now," I said, staring at my plate.

"And besides," Alex continued, ignoring me, "you have your stun gun."

I thought of the weapon in its hard plastic case, nine blocks away, casually thrown in the locker of a discount clothing chain.

"Right," I agreed.

Alex picked up a French fry and popped it in his mouth. "How's that working out for you, anyway?"

"Excellent. I electrocuted three people on my way to work this morning and then I used it to warm up my morning coffee."

The waitress stopped in front of our table, thought better of it, and kept walking. I gaped and Alex grinned, pointing at me with a fry.

"People might not like you, but they're not trying to kill you."

"Be honest. You stole that from a Hallmark card, didn't you?"

I was in a groove rhythmically folding a stack of 2XL peach terry sweatpants at the store when I felt eyes on me. I turned slowly, and Avery was behind me, her made-up eyes focused hard, the little silver hoop in her pierced eyebrow raised and angled.

"Can I help you?" I asked her.

She snapped her green-apple gum. "You've got a dark aura right now. Like danger, evil."

I looked down at the pair of sweatpants I was folding and held them out. "I think you're catching the aura of the pants."

Avery wagged her head. "I know you don't believe in

this, but there definitely is something about you that attracts evil."

If you only knew the half of it, I thought.

The bells above the front door tinkled and we both turned to look as a handful of scruffy-looking teenagers loped in. They nonchalantly poked around the racks of one-off brand-name jeans and lounge pants. Their collectively unkempt hair was scraggly and served to disguise their faces as they pretended to study the merchandise, but instead kept eyeing Avery and me.

"Look at them," I said in a low voice. "They look like they're up to something."

Avery blew a bright green bubble and then sucked it back in and crossed her arms in front of her chest. "Hooligans," she said, wagging her head so that her royal-blue dreadlocks swung. "They just ooze misdemeanor."

I scanned the racks of merchandise, eyeing the sea of sailor pants, capris, and walking shorts in an array of barf-worthy colors. "I can't see what anyone would want to steal from this place," I muttered.

Avery shrugged. "Not my problem. Everything has security tags on 'em anyway."

The bells tinkled again and I felt my mouth form an O, then a huge grin. "Lorraine! Kale!" I said, racing through a rack of acid-washed shortalls. Lorraine pressed her hands to her face in that Miss America-winning-the-crown way and Kale stood back, smiling.

Lorraine broke into a smile as she rushed toward me. We all exchanged hugs and then I stood back, appraising. I looked at Lorraine's earth-dyed crinkle skirt and at Kale's upscale business slacks. There was no way they were People's Pants shoppers out for a casual lunch-hour spree.

"Kale, I don't think I've ever seen you outside of the UDA."

"Oh, I get out. I've even been to your house." Kale, who looked adult in her business trousers, blushed a heavy pink and she looked like the teenager she was again, shadowing Lorraine for her witch's license. "I was hoping Vlad would be there."

I nodded, still smiling. "What are you guys doing here?"

Lorraine looked at my smock, at my trainee name tag, and a flash of sadness marred her lovely features. "This is where you're working now?"

I flushed with embarrassment. "It's just temporary, I hope. Not even Nina knows I'm here though—how did you two?"

Lorraine slung her arm around Kale proudly. Kale grinned. "My first locator spell was a success," Kale said.

"Congrats. But, why were you looking for me?"

Lorraine frowned. "Because we miss you."

"And because the UDA is going to Hell in a hand basket," Kale supplied.

"It's nothing like it was when you and Sampson ran it."

I leaned against the acid-washed jeans. "Aw, thank you. But I didn't really run the UDA and Sampson has been gone for a long time." It still stung every time I said it. "I'm sure Dixon and his guys are doing a good job."

Lorraine snorted. "Are you kidding? They've got Los handling transfer records now."

"What's wrong with that?"

"Los? The goat boy? We're overloaded with demons because so far, Los has eaten sixteen files."

"Sixteen?"

I heard a snicker from the group of hooligans who came in earlier. I looked over my shoulder at Avery, who had been watching us and then busied herself folding pink corduroy pants, effectively ignoring her customers.

"Excuse me, guys," I said, putting my hand on Lorraine's arm.

I headed over to the gang and pasted on a smile. "Welcome to People's Pants. May I help you find something?"

One of the boys—who seemed to be the leader of the group—stepped forward. He towered over me by at least two feet and as I scanned the group I realized that they were all unnaturally tall. Which wasn't completely unusual, given that I am unnaturally short. They all seemed to share the same carved features, too—upturned noses with slight angles, sharp cheekbones, skin so translucently pale it looked oddly luminous under the harsh fluorescent store lights. The five other members of the group sunk back behind the tallest, forming a narrow triangle.

The boy up front seemed to be sizing me up. His eyes were smoke grey and sharp as cut glass. His smile was cocky, bordering on menacing.

You know what we're looking for.

I staggered back when his voice reverberated through my head. His grin lost all cockiness and was fully menacing—and it mirrored the five other kids behind him.

"You must be Sophie," he said. "I'm Adam. We've been looking for you."

My stomach lurched. My throat was dry and my breath came in short, hot gasps. "What do you want?"

"We have something for you," Adam continued. "A little gift from your sister."

I dropped my voice. "Can we not do this here?"

That seemed to amuse Adam.

"Sophie?" Lorraine came up over my left shoulder. "Is everything okay here?" She bristled when she looked at Adam and I could see that she sensed danger.

Adam's eyebrows rose with interest. "A witch?" He raised one arm and quickly flicked his wrist. "I don't like witches."

I felt the draft from Lorraine's body as she was flung across the room. "Lorraine!" I cried as she crashed against the back wall and crumpled to the floor. I tried to run to her, but something was pulling me back. It felt as though my bones were magnetized, pulling behind me, tearing against my skin. Pain seared through me. I whimpered and slumped just in time to miss a fireball that leapt from Kale's outstretched palm and hurtled toward Adam and his gang.

The gang scattered and the fireball hit a rack of rayon palazzo pants; they instantly went up in flames, an impressive plume of choking black smoke snaking toward the ceiling. It took a millisecond for the fire alarm to screech its warning, for the sprinklers to start their meager shower from the ceiling. The water, the screech of the alarm, or the fire must have distracted Adam and his goons because I was able to grab Kale and run toward Lorraine. Kale leaned down and was shaking Lorraine's shoulder; I looked up and coughed through the grey haze of smoke, then saw Adam materialize just behind me, grey eyes glittering, wide smile unfaltering.

"Get her out of here," I called to Kale.

Adam lunged for Kale and Lorraine, but I intercepted him, kicking over a rack of cargo pants that he swiftly jumped over. I looked over my shoulder to see Kale helping Lorraine up and I heard the crack before I felt it. Adam had punched me square in the jaw and I reeled back, stumbling over a topless mannequin wearing bedazzled jeans. My nose stung and my eyes watered as the star of pain spread through my jaw. My teeth seemed to throb; I pressed my hands to my face in a futile effort to quell the pain.

I squinted through the growing haze of smoke and was able to make out Adam swiftly approaching me. I huddled back into the pale arms of the mannequin, then pried one off and lurched toward Adam, swinging blindly. I heard the *thwack!* of a plastic arm hitting fleshy calf and Adam's loud "Oaf!" as he fell flat on his back.

I dumped the mannequin assault arm and crab-crawled backward, then dove behind the front counter, where Lorraine and Kale had gone and where Avery was huddled, her blue smock pulled over her head, her hands wrapped around the purple quartz.

"This place is going to go up like it's the Fourth of July!" she yelled.

I clasped my hand in hers. "No, it's not. I'm not going to let that happen."

Water from the overhead sprinklers drizzled down the cash register and over the front counter in a steady stream. Kale tried to move her, but the rivulet drizzled on Lorraine's scalp and down her forehead. The water seemed to be reviving Lorraine; she started coughing and blinking in Kale's outstretched arms.

Avery pulled the smock off from over her head and there were dark black railroad tracks down her cheeks where her makeup had smeared. "You don't understand. There isn't a natural fiber in this entire store. You saw how fast the palazzo pants went up. This place is a powder keg! How are we supposed to get out of here? We have to get out!" Avery scrambled on her hands and knees and poked her head over the counter. She yelped as Adam and his goons closed in on us.

"Who are these guys and why do they hate our merchandise?"

I could think of several hundred rayon and candy-colored reasons why, but I remained silent. Instead Kale put her hand up. "The fire was my fault, actually," she said apologetically. "I'm really sorry. My aim isn't great."

"Don't apologize; your fire probably saved my life," I said.

Avery gaped at me. "This is all your fault? Those guys are after you?"

I peeked over the counter and saw that Adam and his gang were pushing through the fire-strewn racks of clothing, not flinching as the white-hot flames licked at their bare arms and legs.

"Let's play the blame game later, okay? We don't have much time."

"What are we supposed to do?" Avery asked.

I looked at Lorraine—who was starting to blink away the sprinkler water and was working to sit up—and Kale. "You've got to get out of here. All three of you."

"What about you?" Kale asked

"Just go!" I jabbed my index finger toward an open aisle snaking out the back of the store. "That way." The heat of the fire was starting to press on my chest and I labored to breathe. "Now!" I ordered.

Kale hurried the two women out and I stood up, coming face-to-face with Adam.

"Let 'em run," he said, jutting his chin in the direction the girls had gone. "It's you we want anyway."

For the first time, I noticed the squat handle of a bowie knife tucked into Adam's waistband. I swallowed hard and let out a relieved squeal when I remembered my shiny new stun gun in its black plastic case. Then I winced as I remembered the stun gun and its case, both fitted snugly in my purse, all three ingloriously dumped in locker number forty-three, *Hell=People's Pants* scratched into the red metal. Adam seemed to read my distress; his face looked grotesque as he grinned, his cold eyes raking over me.

A bead of sweat inched its way down my back, and I wondered how Adam and his gang weren't being singed by the heat from the fire. He took one step toward me, and I took one step back, my fingers desperately searching the register counter for some sort of weapon.

"Just get her, dude," one of Adam's henchmen called. "Get her and let's go."

My fingers walked the length of the counter, knocking over useless mugs of pens, a receipt pad, the can of Diet Coke that Avery had been drinking.

Adam leered at me. His eyes were bright, alive, the yellow flame reflected in them. "Ophelia wants you for herself," he reported, pulling the knife out from his waistband, "but I know what you are and there is no way I'm turning you over to her. She won't be in charge for long."

The smoke was stinging my eyes, but I could see Adam's arm raised above him, the blade held aloft, aimed at my chest. My hands closed around a stapler on the counter and I gripped it, walloping him on the side of the head, stapling and screaming manically. My tirade must have been enough to startle or confuse him because he stumbled back and I scrambled over the back counter, sprinting in the direction I had sent the girls. I pushed through the back door of People's Pants and emerged into the alley, coughing and taking in large gulps of city-fresh air. Kale ran toward me and over her relieved wails I heard the howl of fire engines.

"Are you okay?" Kale looked over my shoulder. "Where are they? Are they still in there? Who are they?"

My head was buzzing and my eyes were stinging from the combination of smoke and the sooty water that dripped from my sopping hair. My blue People's Pants smock was clinging to me, and I shivered as I stumbled around the alley.

I was dazed and a paramedic came and pulled Kale

away from me. A second paramedic sat me down on the edge of the ambulance and shined a penlight in my eye, asking me questions. I mumbled answers robotically— my name, the date, where we were—as the paramedic slung an itchy blanket over my shoulders and slapped a blood pressure cuff on my arm. I watched with bleary eyes as another medic hustled Kale, Lorraine, and Avery to a second ambulance, and a stream of firefighters came out of the People's Pants building, announcing it clear and turning the fire hoses on it. I stood up, shrugging the blanket off me.

"There was no one else in there?" I asked the paramedic.

"Ma'am, you need to sit down."

"There was no one else in the building?" I repeated, this time shouting.

The medic put his hands on his hips. "Ma'am!"

"Hey!" I yelled at the sooty back of a fireman's head. When he turned, I felt myself gape. "Will?"

Will grinned, his teeth blaring white against his dark, soot-streaked cheeks. "Now who's stalking who?" He took off his helmet, revealing his spiky blond hair.

"You're a fireman, too?"

He leaned the ax he was carrying against his shoulder. "No. I just like to dress up and rush into burning buildings." He spun the helmet in his hand. "And the hat's pretty cool, too."

Just then another firefighter clapped Will on the shoulder, jutted his chin toward the remains of People's Pants. "We're going back in, Sherman."

"Wait," I said to both men. "Did everyone get out?"

"There was just the four of you, right? No customers inside prior to the fire?" Will's eyes were suddenly dead serious and focused hard on me.

I paused for a beat and then shook my head no. "It was just the four of us."

I was refusing to go to the hospital when I spied Alex's white SUV speeding up the street. He parked crookedly in the back alley and sprinted out toward me, enveloping me in his arms. He held me tightly against him; I could feel the erratic beat of his heart. "I was so worried," he told me.

I wiggled out of his embrace. "I'm fine," I said to Alex and to the paramedic. "We're all fine."

Alex used his thumb to wipe the soot from my cheek, then smiled that cocky half-grin. "Geez, Lawson, I knew you hated your job, but burn the place down? Arson is a crime, you know."

"So is floral-print polyester. And I didn't burn the place down." I slid off the tailgate and the medic strode toward me, frowning.

"Ma'am!"

"She's okay," Alex said, turning to the medic. "I'm taking her home."

The medic shrugged and began packing up his things. "Whatever, man."

Alex held me at arm's length as if examining me for breakages. Then he pulled me aside and squinted into the darkness. "Hey, isn't that Will?"

I blew out a sigh and nodded without turning around. "Yeah. I'm getting my own fan club. Can we just get out of here?"

"You're sure you're okay?"

I touched the pads of my fingers to my cheeks. "I feel a little sunburned, but that's it." I left out the part about how every other sound made my heart do a double take while my breath constricted in my throat. I left out the part about wanting to curl up under my comforter and pretend this whole thing—the Vessel of Souls, Ophelia, the devil—didn't exist. My shoulders slumped and I trudged to the car, sinking myself into the front seat.

Alex slid into the driver's seat, and the slamming of the car door brought me back to the cool interior of his SUV.

"So tell me about these guys," he said as the engine purred.

I took a deep breath, my lungs feeling ragged with lingering smoke. "Just a group of kids."

"Kids?"

"I don't know—teens, maybe early twenties. The head guy said his name was Adam. He said he had a message from Ophelia."

Alex turned toward me as we coasted to a stop. "What was the message?"

"Gee, I don't know. I was a little bit distracted by the fire and the giant blade hurtling toward me."

"What else?"

"I don't know, I don't remember. It happened so fast."

The muscle jerked in Alex's jaw. "Think."

I sighed. "Um . . . he said he knew what I was, that he wanted to keep me for himself. He wanted to stab me."

"And?"

I shrugged. "I don't know. Uh . . . they had bad hair. I should have known something was off about them. I should have known they were evil. One of them was actually looking at the poly-blend clam diggers. Like, looking to *buy* them, Alex." I shuddered.

"Anything beside their odd fashion sense stand out?"

"They were really tall. All of them. Like, really tall."

This got Alex's attention. "How tall?"

"Freakishly tall. Like an NBA team in to rob People's Pants. Although we do—did—carry a large assortment of big and tall."

"All of them were tall?"

I nodded. "And they all kind of looked alike, too. And the fire didn't seem to bother them. And"—I sat forward in my seat, remembering—"they disappeared. They couldn't have gone out the front of the building unless they went directly through the fire. They would have had to come out the back, but they didn't. No one did except for us. The firemen said the place was empty." I shrugged. "No bodies inside." I blew out a sigh. "I don't get it. Before, Ophelia showed up herself. Now, suddenly, she's bringing in the B-squad to do her dirty work?"

"Maybe she had other plans."

I forced a smile. "Well, at least we know killing me isn't her first priority if she's outsourcing."

Alex's lips were pursed, his hard eyes focused on the road.

"What?" I asked him. "What aren't you telling me?"

"They're called Nephilim."

"Nephilim?" I let the word roll over my tongue. "Are they angels, too?"

Alex shook his head slowly. "No. They're half-angel, half-human."

"I take it they're evil?"

Alex's nostrils flared. "Vile."

"Well, now they're working for Ophelia."

I watched Alex's Adam's apple bob as he swallowed. "And now they know where the Vessel is."

"How do we stop them?"

Alex shifted to a stop and looked at me. "I don't know if we can."

Chapter Twenty

I sunk my key into my lock and pushed open the front door. ChaCha came vaulting toward me in a series of yips and barks. She took one whiff of my smoke-scented jeans and backed away, then snuggled back into her bed and began licking her toes.

"Behold the unconditional love of man's best friend."

"Can I get you something?" Alex asked, helping me out of my jacket. "A cup of tea, something to eat?"

"Stop fussing over me, Alex. I'm fine."

He tucked a lock of hair behind my ear and I shivered at his gentle, warm touch. "Don't take this the wrong way, but you don't look fine."

I glanced down at my soot-streaked blue smock, at my red plastic trainee name tag that had melted to a warbling glob. There were scratches and bruises on my forearms that I didn't remember getting, and the knee of my jeans was torn wide open, brown-red blood staining the denim.

I smiled. "Geez, the one time I could really use my People's Pants discount, the place burns down."

Alex stepped back. "Why don't you go take a shower and I'll make us something to eat." He went to the kitchen and pulled open the fridge, then frowned over his shoulder at me. "Okay, which do you prefer—two tablespoons of cottage cheese, half a blood bag, or a moldy lemon?"

My stomach lurched. "Your choice."

Alex poked the mushy lemon. "Maybe I'll order out."

I peeled off my smoke-stained clothes and dumped the whole mess—smock and all—into the bathroom wastebasket. I ran a shower as hot as I could stand it and worked hard to scrub the day—soot, death threats, and all—from my skin and hair. When I stepped out of the shower the bathroom was choked with a breath-stealing haze of steam. I slunk into my robe and glanced at the steamed-up mirror from the corner of my eye, half expecting to see my grandmother's disappointed face, half glad when the only reflection staring back at me was my own.

"Sophie Lawson!"

I stopped dead, my hand hovering over the shiny doorknob. My grandmother's face was stretched over it. Her brows were drawn, her wrinkled lips puckered. "Oh, my sweet girl, are you okay? I heard about the fire."

I ran my hands through my damp hair, winding it into a weak bun. "I'm fine, Gram. We all got out okay." I sank back. "How did you hear about it?"

I watched Grandma's hand—her nails manicured an improbable tangerine—squeeze her chest. "Never mind. I was just so worried about you. What happened?"

"Where have you been? I've been trying to get a hold of you for days. Isn't there some sort of heavenly paging system?"

"Sophie, the fire. Tell me what happened."

I thought of the swirling stacks of polyester smoke, of Lorraine, Kale, and Avery hunching under the counter—

of Adam's clear, cut-glass eyes and his dagger. I bit my lip. "Grandma, what do you know about Nephilim?"

Grandma's eyes widened, milky and blue in the doorknob reflection. "Sophie, what is this about?"

"It's about the goon gang that tried to barbeque me and my friends this afternoon. They weren't normal, Gram. They weren't people."

"Well, Sophie, you know how rare it is we run into actual 'people' in the city. Are you sure they weren't—"

I crossed my arms. "They weren't Underworld, either."

Grandma tapped her nail against her lip.

"What do you know about me?"

Grandma's eyebrows rose. "About you, darling? What are you talking—?"

"Please, Grandma."

The reflection in the doorknob wobbled and started to fade. I crouched down. "Grandma! Grandma! Geez!"

I flung open the bathroom door and Alex stood in front of me, grinning. "Something you want to tell me?"

I crossed my arms. "I don't know. I just spent the last twenty minutes talking to a doorknob."

Alex held up a bulging plastic takeout bag. "Me, too. But I think they got the order right."

Alex and I were halfway through our dinner when he leaned back on the couch, wiping his hands on a napkin.

"Are you planning on actually eating anything, or just pushing it around into fun patterns?"

I rested my plate on the coffee table and sighed heavily. "I'm sorry, Alex. I guess I'm just not that hungry. I can't stop thinking about . . . everything. With all the stuff that has happened, I feel more lost than ever. I don't have a single answer."

"Well, at least you know that you're the Vessel," Alex tried helpfully.

I shrugged. "Another question. Why? And how? And, what am I supposed to do about it? And, two weeks ago I barely knew who my father was. Now I know he's Satan. And I still don't *know* him, know him."

"Maybe that's a good thing."

"Do you think—if my dad is . . . him—that he could have had something to do with my mother's death?"

Alex swallowed. "It wouldn't be the first time he was involved with someone's death. That could explain why your grandmother is so against you searching for him."

"Do you think she's protecting me?"

"Of course she is. She doesn't want you to find him because he's the man who abandoned you. He hurt you once. Whether or not it's because he's the devil, too, well, she might be protecting you against that, as well. Maybe she could at least give you some information about the Vessel—how you became . . . it."

"And then there's Ophelia."

I watched the muscle in Alex's jaw twitch as he looked at the food remaining on his plate and pushed it aside.

I looked down, tracing a pattern on the couch. "I don't know how to protect myself against Ophelia."

Alex took my hand; his grip was firm and encompassing. "You don't need to protect yourself against Ophelia. I'll do that."

I felt the burning prick of tears behind my eyes. "I'm not sure you can."

"I brought her into your life. I promise, I'll find a way to get her out. And as for your father and the other stuff, we'll tackle it, too. Together."

I looked into Alex's earnest eyes and call it exhaustion or trust, but something broke and I wanted to believe him. I wanted to live the rest of my life drowning in those eyes, believing in the safety of his firm arms, feeling the warmth from his chiseled chest. I wanted the only sound I heard to be his heartbeat.

"Will you stay with me tonight?" I asked.

"Anything," Alex said.

I woke up to the delicious warmth of midmorning sun and Alex Grace. He slept soundly, his naked chest rising and falling in a perfect, slow rhythm, his arms wrapped tightly, safely around me. I snuggled closer to him and he shifted, his full lips brushing across my forehead in a gentle feather of small kisses.

"Morning," he murmured.

I felt the smile spread across my lips, reaching all the way to my earlobes. "Morning," I repeated.

Alex's fingers trailed through my hair and the gentle tousle made me break out in delighted gooseflesh. Alex grinned. "What are you thinking about?"

I should have said something sexy, something sensuous or Carrie Bradshaw chic, but when I opened my mouth, I heard the word "donuts" tumble out. I felt my face flush pink.

I shook against Alex's chest as he laughed. "See, Lawson? That's what I love about you. You're a real woman with a real appetite." His fingertips danced lightly over my neck and shoulders. "And you have a very good taste."

"Don't you mean I have very good taste?"

Alex raised one eyebrow slyly and grinned. Then he gently slid out from under me, resting my head on my pillow. I pretended not to watch as he leaned down and slid into his worn jeans and then slipped his snug white tee over his head. He grabbed his keys from the nightstand, leaned down on his elbows on the bed, and pressed his lips against mine. "Donuts it is."

I watched him rake a hand through his disheveled curls and slip out my bedroom door, then heard the lock on the front door tumble as he stepped out. I sunk deeper into my pillows letting the contentment of the night and of this sun-drenched morning wash over me. I breathed in deeply the comforting scent of laundry detergent and Alex Grace from my pillows.

Donuts it is, Ophelia mocked.

The millisecond of surprise at hearing Ophelia's voice reverberating in my head was instantly replaced by searing anger. "This is my morning, Ophelia," I said between gritted teeth. "Get out."

Sophie, Sophie, Sophie, she intoned, *you are so easily played. Do you really think you're special?* Suddenly my mind was filled with images of Alex again, of his strong naked back. A pair of female hands slipped over his shoulders, raked blood-red nails across his taut skin, leaving prickly red trails. There was a low, feral moan and Ophelia appeared, her pink lips nibbling and biting along Alex's shoulder, the corner of her mouth turned up in a sly grin.

"Stop that," I spat. "It's not true." I buried my head into my pillows, breathed Alex's warm scent, flooded my own mind with memories from last night, with the sweet, salty taste of Alex's skin, with the way his lips tasted on mine—plump, bee-stung, juicy—like ripe strawberries. I felt his fingers glide over my body, felt his palm pressing against mine. I heard his heartbeat, heard his breath as it went ragged, hungry in my ear. I felt his skin on mine, his chest pressed against me. I snaked my legs over his.

He doesn't love you, Ophelia tried again. *You're a means to an end and you know it.* I could feel Ophelia trying to work her way into my mind, but the memory— the real memory—of Alex and me was too strong and

Ophelia was losing power. Her voice was softer, more distant but still hard: *I'm tired of these games. It's just me and you now, Sophie, and I'm coming to get you.* I smiled in spite of Ophelia's ominous warning. When I felt her leave, I slid into a hot shower.

When I padded into the living room Alex was in the kitchen with a huge, grease-spotted white bakery bag and two plastic-lidded paper cups filled with coffee. He held one out to me. "Skinny mocha, half whip, extra cocoa and a shot of hazelnut." He reached into the bakery bag and balanced a chocolate glazed donut on a napkin. "And a donut."

I took both and grinned. "You really are an angel."

He raised one brow salaciously. "I aim to please."

I felt myself go red from toenails to the top of my head.

"Did I miss anything while I was gone?" Alex asked, mouth full of maple glazed.

I pried the lid off my coffee and took a large, sweet, hazelnutty swig. "Not a thing," I said.

I grinned and realized I was ravenous. We took the bounty to the coffee table and set out our spoils. I was halfway through my second chocolate-glazed Bavarian cream filled when I felt the cold prick of fear slink up my neck. I cocked my head, listening.

"What's up?" Alex took a slug from his paper coffee cup, then finished a second maple bar in two bites.

"Listen."

Alex plucked a pink-sprinkled number from the box. "To what?" he said as I stared at him, eyes wide. He picked at a stripe of pink frosting while I watched him. "I'm secure enough in my masculinity to eat a pink donut."

"It's not that." I stood up and ran to the bench by the door, pawing through the heap of purses, shopping bags, and jackets that Nina and I had discarded there. "A phone is ringing."

Alex sat back with his pink donut, nonplussed. "Life was so much simpler before the invention of that thing. I gotta say, I was pretty sure it wouldn't catch on. Boy, was my face red. . . ."

"Shut up, Alex," I said, "I need to listen."

I tore through the entire pile of bags and then followed the sound on hands and knees. "Ah ha!" I reached under the couch—all the way to my shoulder—and slid out the offending phone. It stopped ringing immediately and my stomach dropped. I held up the phone.

"This is Nina's phone."

"So?"

I held the phone aloft. "Nina doesn't go anywhere without her phone. Nowhere. If she showered, she'd take it there."

"So, maybe she forgot." Alex patted his flat gut. "I've got room for a third."

"You don't understand. If Nina's phone is here and Nina is not, then something is wrong." I tucked the phone in my robe pocket and ran to Nina's closed door. "Something is seriously wrong."

"Nina?" I knocked spastically, then pushed the door open, plunging inside her room.

To call Nina's room a bedroom is misleading; show-room would be more apt. Along with the occasional naïve neck, Nina's fangs were deeply entrenched in all things fashionable and she wore every decade of her life with that fashionable fervor. Thus, her room was lined with boutique-quality couture all the way back from the 1800s; Victorian corsets mingled with Juicy hoodies, hand-hewn necklaces and tatted lace from the Edwardian ages merged seamlessly with hip-huggers and love beads.

"She's not here," I said, my mouth going dry.

I jumped—and so did my heart—when the phone rang again. I dove into my pocket.

"Hello? Nina?"

There was laughter on the other end of the line and then a piercing, primitive scream. "Hey there, sis," Ophelia said. "I think I've got something of yours."

Ophelia continued to giggle and I heard the wailing scream again. Then heaving tears. Then the phone went dead.

"Who was that?" Alex asked.

I turned to him, suddenly feeling leaden. "That was Ophelia. And she's got Nina."

"What? What are you talking about?"

I shook the phone as if an explanation would fall out. "Ophelia has Nina. She's hurting her." I slapped my palm to my forehead. "That's why she sent the Nephilim. She wasn't trying to scare me, she was trying to distract me, get me all wrapped up in the fire at People's Pants." I swallowed a sob. "And it worked."

Alex took both my hands and led me to the couch, trying to get me to sit down.

"No," I said, dodging him. "We have to go. Now. We have to save Nina."

"Where is she?"

I frowned down at the phone, my vision blurred with a fresh wave of tears. "I don't know."

"It'll be okay. Nina's an immortal; there's not much that Ophelia can do to her, right?"

I gaped. "Except drive a stake through her heart, cut off her head, light her on fire, send her out in the sunshine, shoot her with a silver bullet . . ."

"I thought that only worked with werewolves."

"Oh, now you're paying attention to legendry?"

"Lawson—"

"No, now." I peeled off my bathrobe and yanked yesterday's (pre-Pants fire) clothes off the floor. I was hopping on one foot, trying to get into a pair of jeans, when Alex stopped me.

"Calm down, Lawson, you're going to give yourself a heart attack."

"Better me than Nina!" I shrieked, finally getting the blasted pants over my hips.

"Let's sit down and figure something out first."

I yanked a semi-clean sweatshirt over my head. "Why can't you see how serious this is?"

A giggle roiled through my head. Ophelia's ghostly laughter. *Alex has a secret. . . .* she sang.

I stepped back. "What are you hiding?"

"What?"

"Why don't you want me to find Nina?"

Alex's brows drew together. "I'm not hiding anything and I do want you to find Nina. I want to help you find Nina, but you just can't go off half-cocked like this. Ophelia is dangerous and—and—for all we know, this could be a trap. You could be walking right into a trap."

"I don't care, Alex. I don't care. I'm not going to risk Nina. I'm not going to put anyone else's life at risk because of me, especially not my best friend's."

"I'm just saying we need a plan."

I stood nose to nose with Alex, the fury rolling off me in waves. "And I'm saying we have to look for Nina, now."

"You have to know that out of any of us, Nina is the one best prepared to take care of herself," Alex said as he followed me out the door.

"Yeah," I said, taking the stairs two at a time. "But that doesn't mean she should have to."

Chapter Twenty-One

My mind was racing as I sat in the front seat of Alex's car. "Why Nina?"

"Ophelia wants to get to you."

"That's fine, but she wants me, right? She wants the Vessel. We don't even know where she took Nina. Wouldn't it be easier for her to have left a note or something?"

"Like what? 'I've got Nina tied to the train tracks, come get her'? I don't think this kind of thing works like that."

I gulped. "Tie her to the train tracks? You don't really think she'd do that, do you?"

"Not unless she has a cartoon hat and a handlebar mustache."

"This is not a time to joke!"

Alex stretched his arm along the backrest, his hand gently massaging my neck. I squirmed away.

"I know. But going into hysterics isn't going to help Nina, either."

I glowered in cross-armed silence until we made it to the police station—which we did in record time. Alex was shrugging out of his jacket when I pressed him down in his desk chair and handed him Nina's cell phone. He stared at the phone in his palm as though he had never seen a pink Swarovski Crystal–bedazzled Motorola.

"What am I supposed to do with this?"

"Trace the call!" I screamed. "Dust it for fingerprints. There was obviously a struggle. Nina would never leave her phone under the couch—"

"And she wouldn't leave it behind," Alex said, taking the phone.

"Yeah. So go all *CSI* on that phone's ass."

Alex clicked the phone shut and turned on his computer. "Okay, first of all, this is SFPD, not *CSI*. Tracing takes a little longer than a commercial break."

I slumped into the red pleather guest chair, defeated. The reality of Nina's disappearance—and the realization that she was with Ophelia—finally began to sink in. I sniffed, then started to cry. "We're never going to find her, are we?"

"Okay, got it," Alex said, clicking shut his laptop and grinning.

"Got what?"

"Come on, Lawson, get moving." He stood up, shook me out of the chair. "The call came from an address up north."

I abruptly stopped crying and sprang up. "You were able to trace it? Did you triangulate the cell phone towers to pinpoint their location?"

Alex snatched his coat from the back of his chair. "No. I Googled the phone number."

Alex peeled out of the police department parking lot with sirens blaring. The few cars on the city roads eased to the side to let us pass, and Alex kept the gas pedal flush with the floor of the car the second we hit the freeway on-ramp. He gestured to the flashing lights and sirens above us as we overtook a Yellow Cab, slow with wide-eyed tourists and their world of luggage.

"These things are so convenient."

"Let me guess—another perk they didn't have when you were here last?"

"Something like that."

We sped down the freeway in silence; Alex hadn't mentioned the exact address from which Ophelia's call originated—he didn't have to. We both knew it had come from my father's house in Marin County. My heart started to thunder in my throat as we took the Sir Francis Drake exit and wound through the quaint city of Marin, most of its residents barely roused, despite the sunny morning.

"She'd better not hurt her," I muttered, gritting my teeth until my temples hurt.

"It's you that Ophelia wants," Alex said, his knuckles white on the steering wheel. "She's just using Nina to get to you."

"Does that mean she won't hurt her?" I asked hopefully.

"No."

We turned down the tree-lined street to my father's house. Alex parked skewed in the driveway and leaned over me in the front seat.

"What are you—"

He popped open the glove box and pulled out a handgun, slipping it into his waistband. He slipped a short-handled knife with a fat blade into a leather sheaf wrapped around his ankle. Then he looked at me.

"Do you still have the stun gun?"

I shook my head miserably. "No. I lost it in the fire."

He sucked in a breath and then ducked between my legs. I had heard that life-and-death situations made people randy, but personally, I really wasn't in the mood. "Alex! Now?"

But Alex came up with a small black gun in his hand.

"I always keep a spare," he said, checking the magazine. He handed the gun to me and pushed the black metal gun box back under my seat.

"Remind me not to use the vanity mirror," I said as we crept out of the car. "What does it do—launch a hand grenade?"

"No, cyanide powder."

I wasn't sure if he was joking, but I made a mental note not to check.

I tried to tuck my small loaner gun in my waistband like Alex had done, but one too many donuts prevented that. Besides, I had the kind of luck that meant I would be shooting off my privates halfway through our daring rescue. Instead, I slipped the gun into my sweatshirt pocket. The butt of the gun was already damp from my sweating palms.

"What are we going to do?" I whispered to Alex as he steered me flat against the garage. "Do we knock?"

Alex's brows rose. "Really? You ask me if I triangulated a cell phone call to pinpoint Ophelia's location, and then you ask if we knock?"

"Right. We barrel roll through the front window."

"No more cop shows for you. I go check it out, you stay right here." Alex put both hands on my shoulders, pushed me down about four inches so I was mostly ducked into a pittosporum bush, and then repeated himself. "Stay right here. Got it?"

I nodded, though I had no intention of hanging back. Nina was my best friend, and her afterlife was in my hands. She would have happily been sucking on a blood bag and reading an *InStyle* magazine if I hadn't come along. I sniffed, feeling the tears start again.

Alex looked at me and softened. "Just stay here. We're going to get Nina."

He tiptoed out across the driveway, hugging as close to the shadows cast from the house as possible. He disappeared around a clutch of flowering bushes and I assumed he had gotten onto the front porch, but there was no sound.

I counted to twenty-five and then tiptoed from my pittosporum hiding place, picking my way along the shadows of the driveway, following in Alex's footsteps. I held the butt of my gun in both my hands, arms outstretched. I couldn't remember if that was the way Alex told me to hold the gun or if I saw it on *Cops*, but either seemed good enough so I took a few more tentative steps, letting my gun lead the way. When I reached the front porch it was empty.

"Alex?" I whispered, lowering my gun a half inch. "Alex?"

I scanned the surrounding landscaping for any sign of Alex, and then I noticed the front door was slightly ajar. I gently shouldered it open just enough to squeeze through, and promised myself that should I get out of this alive, donuts were strictly off-limits. Well, off-limits right after my "I survived this rescue attempt" donut party.

The lights were off in the foyer; all the curtains were drawn, casting the room into shadows. The house was ungodly still, and the only sound anywhere was the thunderous beating of my heart, the ridiculously loud rush of my blood through my veins. I held my breath and paused before blinking, certain that both would come out as loud as a snare drum, causing Ophelia to rouse from her hiding place and slit all of our throats. When nothing happened for a thirty count I tiptoed farther into the house, calling out for Alex in my mind. *If I was going to get any additional powers*, I prayed, *now would be the time.*

I had to stop and get my bearings. *Okay.* I thought to myself, *if I had kidnapped a vampire and was holding her hostage, where would I take her?* I blinked in the near darkness, letting my arms and my gun fall to my sides as my arms started to ache. I prowled farther down the hallway, using one palm against the wall to guide myself through the relative dark. When my fingers stumbled on the cold plastic of a light switch cover I instinctively went to flick on the light and then paused—Ophelia would come toward the light. Or, she had the whole house wired to this very light switch, and when I flicked it on we would all go up like a powder keg. I jammed my hand in my sweatshirt pocket and moved on.

I found my way to my father's office and pressed my back against the wall, holding my gun *CSI* style. I peeked through the slightly open door and slumped considerably when I saw an obsessively clean desktop, a plastic plant, and a flat-faced computer screen that looked like it was made out of cardboard. The entire office looked like the bland cardboard cutout of an office supply store.

I heard the far-off trill of laughter, the sound of footsteps creaking over hardwood. I silently prayed that the spastic fluttering of my heart wouldn't give me away.

"Alex?" I tried, my voice barely audible. "Nina?" I looked around, suddenly feeling very alone in the darkness. The house had fallen into an ominous silence again, and I slunk against the wall and then slid the whole way down, sitting on my butt. I pressed my forehead to my knees, sucked in a deep breath, and tried to channel Ophelia.

Ophelia, I called out in my mind. *I'm here. Let Nina go. Let Alex go. It's me you want, right? I'm the Vessel; I'm what you want. So, if you're so badassed, come out and get me.* With no immediate answer, I started to feel bolder. *Come on, sis*—I hissed the word—*come out, come out wherever you are* . . . I pushed myself to my feet and made my way back down the hallway to the broad, sunken living room right off the kitchen. I walked with a little more sass, holding my gun in one hand and tapping it against my thigh as I continued the baiting call in my head.

Ophelia . . . I heard the creak of footsteps again and I snapped to attention, my whole body stiffening. I didn't have time to react when I saw the flash of movement reflected in the sliding glass door in front of me. I thought I could make out a face and I heard the footsteps speed up as they came rushing toward me. I tried to turn around but was pushed back with a crushing, full-body blow. I felt arms tense around me, squeezing; I felt my breath leave me, felt my feet leave the ground and then the icy pricks of glass showering my shoulders, shredding my arms.

We went crashing through the sliding glass door and slid onto the grass below. I felt my ribs cracking, felt a fist clenching against my lung as the breath went out of me. I arched against the crunch of glass that pierced through my clothes. Once we stopped I dove for Ophelia's neck. She slapped my hands away and brought my hands to my sides; I was amazed at how freakishly strong she seemed. I blinked at her.

She was Alex.

"What the hell?" I screamed.

Alex scrambled up from the ground and carried me with him, pulling me tightly against his chest. I squirmed and kicked out against him, tasting blood in my mouth, feeling the dampness of the earth that had seeped into my clothes.

"Stop it, stop it, Alex! You can have the Vessel! You can have it!"

Alex had carried me less than ten feet from the house

and heaved me to the ground when we heard the explosion. He threw his body over me, but not before I was able to peek out and watch the fireball that was my father's house mushroom up to the sky. Alex rolled off me and we both blinked at the black bones of the house as they were spat out from the flames.

"Thanks for offering me the Vessel," he said with a lopsided, far-too-calm-for-the-situation grin.

"What happened?" I choked out a panicked sob. "Where's Nina?" I tried to stand up but found that everything hurt. "We need to get in there!" The smoke from the fire was choking me and making my eyes sting. I started to cry and hiccup, kicking at the ground to get my feet to push the rest of my body up.

Alex pinned me down. "She wasn't in there, Lawson, I promise. I checked every room. Ophelia set us up; it was another trap."

I sniffed, feeling the energy drain out of my body as I slumped against Alex and cried. My tears made cold tracks down my cheeks and I wiped at my face with a hand that was caked with dirt and grass. "Then where is she?"

"I don't know, but she wasn't in there. I should have known. Ophelia wouldn't give up that easily."

I sunk back into the grass—and into Alex's arms—and we watched the fire for a millisecond before the wails of the fire-engine sirens droned through the morning light.

"Can you stand?" Alex asked.

I nodded, and got up gingerly. Alex took my hand and led me to the front of the house, where firefighters and uniformed police officers were ushering pajama-wearing neighbors behind wooden barricades and dousing the flames.

I heard the sharp cut of Will's words before I saw him. When we turned the corner he was there, standing in front of one of the fire trucks, barking orders at the firemen, who scattered in perfectly organized chaos, dragging fat hoses and lining up at the edge of the burning house. He was wearing his uniform and again his big yellow coat was streaked with black lines of soot and debris. His helmet had a nick in it and was almost totally blackened. He stopped midsentence when he saw me and strode toward Alex and me, nudging in just before the paramedic made his way toward us.

"Sophie?" The playful lilt he'd had when we talked the other day was gone from his voice.

I nodded, too stunned to speak.

"Are you okay? What are you doing here?"

I saw a glint—of what, jealousy?—in Alex's eyes as he sized Will up. "You're the guardian?" he asked finally.

Will straightened a bit and looked over his shoulder, then stepped closer to us. He nodded.

Alex used the end of his shirt to dab at a cut on my cheek. "Hell of a job you're doing, buddy."

I put my hand on Alex's arm and stepped aside, just out of his reach. "It's not his fault."

Will and I exchanged glances and Alex put up his hands, palms out, and sucked in an exasperated breath. "Okay, fine, whatever. We need to find Nina. If your buddy here wants to come along, he can follow us."

"I'm looking after Sophie," Will said.

"So am I," Alex replied.

The men exchanged staunch, tight-lipped glares and under any other circumstance I would be updating my Facebook status, letting the world know that two incredibly hot men were fighting over me. Instead, I stepped between them.

"We have to find Nina. Now."

Another fireman ran up to us. He looked from Alex to me and then expectantly at Will. "Are you taking care of this, Sherman?"

Will nodded curtly. "The detective here was just telling me what happened."

"Fire bomb," Alex reported, his eyes focused on the second fireman, who wore a water-slicked yellow coat with the name ALLEN sewn on it. "Thrown from the outside when Ms. Lawson was inside."

Allen nodded and Will raised a suspicious eyebrow. "And Ms. Lawson was inside because?"

Alex cleared his throat. "She was with me. I was escorting her back to her apartment after a second round of questioning when a call came in about a suspected burglar at this address. I asked her to stay in the car. It's not like anyone was guarding her though." Will's eyes flashed as Alex continued. "She must have just slid in behind me."

I watched the gold flecks in Will's eyes glitter angrily at the bit of smile that hung on Alex's lips. Allen looked at the three of us, oblivious to the volumes of subtext going on, and nodded. "Looks like you fellas have got this under control. Just make sure to escort the lady home."

Will stepped toward me and Alex cut him off, blocking me with his body. He clamped a hand on my upper arm. "I've got this under control," he told Will.

Will went eyebrows up but stepped back. Alex steered me away from the clutch of firemen and flashing lights, and when we were out of earshot, I shrugged him off.

"What was that? You've got this under control? Don't you mean you've got *me* under control? And what was the stare-down for?"

"Really, Lawson? We're going to do the woman's lib thing here in the shadow of your father's raging inferno?"

"I guess not," I relented. "But that doesn't mean it's over!"

"I wouldn't expect anything less," Alex said.

I glanced over my shoulder at the smoldering house, at the firefighters working to tame the huge flames that thrust out of windows and licked the tops of nearby trees. I felt an odd sense of loss; I had just found my father— I saw his collection of books, what he kept in the fridge (nothing), the way he decorated a room for his daughter— and now it was gone. Going up in smoke.

I walked up to the neighbors pushing against the wooden barricade. A woman in a velour housecoat was clutching her lapel. Her eyes were so intensely fixed on the fire that I could see flicks of yellow flame reflected in them.

"Did you know the family that lived there well?" I asked her. "What were they like?"

The woman looked down, blinking at me as if I had just materialized out of thin air. "The family that lived there?" she asked. "No, honey, nobody lives in that house—and thank God, now. It's the model home for the new development going up just over there." She pointed to a clutch of houses one street over, all glaring with brand-new beige stucco and eco-friendly trim.

"What? But I went inside. It was furnished."

"Yeah," the woman said, turning back to watch the flames, "they decorate the house as if someone lives there, but everything inside is fake. Fake plants, fake books, even fake computers and TVs. They just put it up so people feel comfortable, so they can see what their houses will look like once they're lived in."

"Oh," was all I could manage.

I let Alex lead me to the car. He all but clicked me in my seat belt as I gazed dumbly ahead of me.

"It was all made up," I mumbled.

"What are you talking about?" he asked, plugging his key in the ignition.

"The house. Everything in it. It was fake."

Poor, poor baby sister . . . Ophelia whispered. *Losing the childhood home she never even had. No home, no daddy, and now, no best friend.* Ophelia giggled in my ear while the fury reawakened in me. I tensed.

"You're shaking, Lawson. What's going on?" Alex asked, coasting to a stop at the light.

"Ophelia. Get her out of my head." I could feel the unattractive flare of my nostrils, feel the ache in my jaw from gritting my teeth. "She's always going to be one step ahead of us as long as she's in my mind. If we're ever going to save Nina, I have to get her out."

"Okay," Alex said, staring through the windshield.

I grabbed his shoulder, feeling my fingers digging into his warm skin. "Tell me how, Alex. Tell me how to get rid of her. You have to know a way."

"Well, there is one way. The mind reading—"

"Mind-hijacking is more like it."

"Well, it's not an exact science. Every time she gets in your head, you're generally on your own, right?"

I frowned. "Or with you."

Alex ignored me and continued. "The more people who are around—the more distraction—the more difficult it will be for Ophelia to get a handle on your thoughts. She'll find it difficult to find you and get in your mind."

"Okay, fine, so we go somewhere with a lot of distraction."

"Somewhere with a lot of people. Generally, people who won't notice a stray or weird thought poking into their head. There needs to be something entertaining them."

I crossed my arms in front of my chest. "Okay, but I don't think we can make it down to Disneyland before Ophelia lays waste to my entire life."

Alex remained silent, thinking. Suddenly, he jerked the car toward the highway on-ramp, wheels squealing as he took the corner at full speed. "I know a place."

Chapter Twenty-Two

I fiddled around with the car stereo and finally found a soccer game being broadcast on the Spanish channel. I turned it up to earsplitting level, hoping the hiss of the crowd would drown out any Ophelia-influenced thoughts. We were inching our way through the Golden Gate Bridge toll plaza when Alex turned the volume down and looked at me.

"Since when do you like soccer?"

"It's called football," I murmured.

"Okay. Since when do you like football?"

Since I've had a psychopath taking up valuable real estate in my brain. Since Will walked into my life and try as I might, I can't get the soft English lilt of his voice out of my head, can't deny the knight-in-shining-armor way he looks in his firefighter uniform. I thought. I was stabbed with a pang of guilt when I glanced at Alex, at the sincere worry in his eye.

He's not staying around. . . . This time the voice in my head was my own, and the truth of the words squeezed at my heart.

"I just want to focus on finding Nina," I said to the windshield.

"Where would Ophelia take Nina?" Alex mumbled.

"Vlad."

"What?" Alex cut behind a Muni bus, causing the man in the Zipcar behind us to lay on his horn. "Do you think Vlad might have a better lead on Nina? Vampire connection or something?"

I rolled my eyes. "No, Vlad is right there."

I pointed, and Alex followed my gaze out the driver's side window to the garish lights of the Roxie Theater. Vlad and his fellow VERMers—all dressed in the standard-issue velvet smoking jackets and ascots—were marching in a neat oval, their wooden-stake signs illuminated by the red and yellow lights of the Roxie. There was a small group of teenagers gathered around them, and when Alex rolled down his window we could hear their faint chant as they thrust pale fists into the air.

"What's he doing?"

I unhooked my seat belt. "Protesting." Before Alex could say anything I was bundling myself against the late-afternoon city fog and dodging cars. I crossed the street and made a beeline for Vlad, who, while marching, was clearly being followed by an adoring clutch of teenage breather girls.

"Vlad," I said when I saw him.

He glanced over his shoulder at me, a kind smile spreading across his lips. "Are you joining us?"

I felt thin fingers clutching at my elbow, and I whirled, only to go face-to-face with a young girl, her cheeks ruddy and shiny, her forehead broken out and partially covered by a failed attempt at Sandra Bullock side-swept bangs.

"You know him?" the girl asked, her grey eyes heavy with awe.

I rolled my eyes.

Vampires, as a whole, are an attractive lot. Vlad, immortally sixteen, and with the wiry, smooth muscles, chiseled jaw, and brooding countenance of the attractive, misunderstood, teenage ne'er-do-well, was all but irresistible to the under-eighteen female set. It wasn't the first time I'd witnessed girls falling all over themselves to brush a finger through his thick black pompadour while attempting to lose themselves in his black-as-coal eyes. Since his last crush had tried to kill me, I was wary.

I shook off the girl. "Trust me, you're better off." I turned back to Vlad. "This is the theater you're protesting?"

Vlad shrugged. "As a warm-up. We thought the Roxie would be sort of a dry run before we took on the big guns."

"The Metreon?" I guessed. I felt the fingers on my arm again, and when I glanced back, the teenage girl was nearly pressed up against me, eyes glazed and fixed firmly on Vlad. I looked back at him, saw the sly smile creep across his lips.

"Well, hello," he said over my shoulder.

The girl's grip on my arm tightened and I stared at her fingers in awe. "Who are you?"

She ignored me. "I—I want to be with you," she said to Vlad, her voice breathy.

Vlad raised an interested eyebrow.

"I know what you are. I understand you," she continued, seeming to muster courage from her ever-tightening grip on my arm. I shrugged her away a second time and she simply pushed past me and went directly to Vlad.

"I get you."

The smile disappeared from Vlad's lips. "You get me?"

"I know you don't want to be this way."

"Oh, here we go," I muttered.

"We can be together. I want to help you." The girl yanked up her sleeve, exposing the fleshy part of her arm, pink with youth and baby fat. "I want to be a donor."

I watched Vlad's nostrils flare. "Then go to Red Cross." He hitched up his sign and glanced over his shoulder at me. "Later, Soph."

I grabbed his shoulder. "Have you seen Nina?"

Vlad shrugged. "Not since last night."

I felt the grip of fear starting at the pit of my stomach. "She's missing."

"What do you mean, missing?"

I leaned closer, turning Vlad from the group of glamoured teens who were trying to inch their way toward the other VERMers. "Ophelia. Ophelia has kidnapped her."

The teenage angst/smugness dropped from Vlad's face all at once. Fear shot through his eyes and his expression was soft, a momentary glimpse into what he may have looked like, pre-fang. He dropped his protest sign and gripped my arm, pulling him along with me.

"Where's the angel?"

Vlad and I piled into Alex's car and Alex pushed the gas pedal to the ground. We hit thirty-five before being cut off by a trolley stuffed with grinning wedding guests, their cheeks ruddy with champagne and the cold grey air.

"I hate this town," Vlad muttered.

"We need to get Sophie somewhere where Ophelia can't get into her head. Loud noises, lots of action—it'll confuse her."

Vlad climbed over the center console and turned down the blaring radio. "Is that why you're broadcasting the soccer game?"

"It's called football," Alex and I said in unison.

"Do we have any idea where we're going?"

"I know a place," Alex said, expertly weaving through traffic. He skidded into a parking spot and I gripped the car door to save myself from sliding across the seat.

"Parking karma," he said with a shrug when I gaped at him. "Are you coming?"

I slammed the car door shut and looked up, the flashing lights from the two-hundred-foot-tall sign glaring down at me. The yellow chaser lights spelled out BIG AL'S, the words platforming an enormous, angry-looking mobster in a pinstriped suit carrying a tommy gun.

Vlad snorted—although whether it was a snort of disgust or humor I couldn't tell.

"Really?" I snarled at Alex. "Really? This is the *only* place in the entire city that you could think of that would offer distraction?"

Big Al's was an adult superstore, housing all manner of sexual vices and advertising each one in bold, multicolored neon lights. The lights pulsed to the sound of a thrumming bass coming from somewhere inside, and the sidewalks were littered with throngs of people zigzagging their way through sidewalk displays of half-naked women arching wantonly on glossy poster board. Interspersed were big, angry-looking men with crossed arms who guarded darkened doorways, and the occasional few who danced around out front, slapping fliers in the hands of unsuspecting passersby and yelling things like "Ladies always free!" and "You fellas like to dance, don'tcha?"

"Just come on," Alex said, threading his arm through mine.

To my relief, we passed Big Al's and its gaudy assortment of neon-colored paraphernalia. I yanked on Vlad's arm, dragging him behind me as he started to slow down, his dark eyes going big and wide at the splashy photography. He may have been of age—way, way of age—but to me he was still my best friend's sixteen-year-old nephew and I was in charge.

"Stop staring," I muttered to him, pulling him along.

Alex dodged the ladies who pranced around us in garter belts and plastic heels and I did my best to keep up with him, growling, "This is not going to help." I stepped around a weaving crowd of beer-soaked bachelors. "How do you expect this to help? My best friend has been kidnapped! She could be dying and we're here at"—I paused, looked up— "The Roaring Twenties?"

The Roaring Twenties was Big Al's slightly more up-scale neighbor—a throwback to a 1920s speakeasy, complete with dancers in period costumes (when they wore costumes) and heavy, carved double doors. The outside walls were lined with sepia-toned prints of the San Francisco of yesteryear, interspersed with the women of Saturday night. Even the doorman—a burley black guy with a bald head and a puffy black mustache—was dressed in authentic-looking 1920s garb.

At The Roaring Twenties, you got some history with your lap dance.

Vlad grinned, his fangs catching the reflection of the blinking lights of Broadway. "I loved the twenties. Pretty girls, lots of neck action."

I shot him a look and his gleeful smile faded. "Sorry," he said with a disgusted groan.

I squeezed Alex's arm and steeled myself. "I'm not going in there. What are you thinking? That Ophelia sold Nina into white slavery and now she's working as a naked historian?"

"I'm thinking that you should trust me and keep walking." Our train shimmied through the thickening crowds on the busy streets and my head throbbed with the pulsing lights and the heavy bass that thumped behind the closed doors. My legs were aching from the gradual uphill climb and still stung from the shower of soot and glass at my father's house.

I just wanted to find Nina. I felt a hopeless lump rising in my chest as Alex grabbed my arm and steered me around a sharp corner, then hustled me through a set of double glass doors. I instinctively clamped my eyes shut and sputtered, "I don't want to see any naked ladies!"

I was greeted with a wall of silence and the bitter smell of coffee, tinged with the slightest hint of brown sugar. I opened one eye and saw the bakery cases, the round black tables scattered with tea drinkers staring curiously up at me. I glanced around, seeing the flashing lights of Big Al's in the distance, reflected on the plate-glass windows.

"We're not at a strip club?"

"Sorry to disappoint you, Lawson," Alex said with a smug shrug.

I felt a flood of embarrassment from hair follicles to toenails. "Oh." I dropped into a chair. "Can you get me a cannoli then?"

Vlad sat down next to me. "I don't understand what any of this has to do with finding my aunt."

Alex ordered a round of cannoli and coffee, then sat down.

"Hopefully, it's buying us enough time to confuse and annoy Ophelia. It'll be harder to read Sophie's mind with everything going on—the crowds, the lights on Broadway—"

Vlad scowled. "Well, if that was working, why are we here?"

Before Alex could answer, the mournful wail of a harmonica cut through the cinnamon-scented air, followed by a smattering of applause and the tuning of a guitar.

"Chaotic enough?"

The hum of quiet conversation raised to a din, punctuated by the clattering of dishes and live music. I looked around nervously, locking eyes with a heavyset man behind the counter. When he bent down to take something out of the dessert case, I nudged Vlad.

"That guy's staring at me. There's something about him. Can you get a scent on him?"

Vlad's nostrils flared and he nonchalantly sniffed at the air, then shrugged. "Not unless he's a cinnamon scone or a caramel macchiato."

I rubbed my temples with my fingers. "Okay, we've got to find Nina. If you were a raging lunatic with a vampire captive, where would you go?"

"Someplace private," Vlad suggested.

"Someplace that means a lot to you. That's why she took you to your dad's house."

Vlad's eyes widened. "You went to Hell?"

"No—Marin. I can't think with all this distraction."

Alex put his hand on mine. "We need the distraction. As much as it's bothering you, it's worse on her end. We can't let her know what you're thinking. So, focus."

A slim waitress with an apron double-tied around her waist deposited a plate of cannoli in front of us. I took one and chewed absently.

Vlad tapped his finger on the table, the sound adding to the roar. I glared at him and he stopped. "This really isn't doing us any good," he said.

Alex's eyes were intense as he stared me down. "Where would she take Nina that would get to you?"

I polished off the first cannoli and was reaching for my second. "I don't know."

"Come on, think. What place means a lot to you? Where do you go a lot?"

"Target. But I doubt she'd hold Nina there. Or Philz Coffee."

Alex blew out an exasperated sigh. "Someplace that means something to you."

"Cheap clothing and great coffee *do* mean something to me."

Alex glared at me.

I thunked my forehead on the table. "This isn't working. Look, Alex, I appreciate you bringing me here, but besides the sugar shock and ooginess of walking down Broadway, nothing has changed. Ophelia can't read my mind because there is nothing in it. I have no idea where she could take Nina that would really get under my skin."

"Home," Vlad said simply.

Alex and I both swung our heads to look at him. "What?"

"She got you out of the house, right? And she kidnapped your best friend. She's aiming at things that are close to you."

Alex picked a lone chocolate chip off the plate. "Doesn't take a genius to figure that out."

"She takes up space in your head and it drives you crazy. Doesn't it make sense that she'd try to invade your home, too?"

Alex and I shared eyebrow shrugs. "He makes a good point," I said. I felt a mild flush of panic. "She could have been there the whole time, but just made us think that she wasn't."

"All right." Alex pulled his keys out of his pocket and we stood up. Just before we left the table I snagged the remaining cannoli and mashed it in my mouth.

What? It's not like it was a donut.

We were waiting to pull out into the slow traffic on Broadway. Alex had one hand loosely draped on the steering wheel, was using the other to stroke the soft stubble on his chin. "Does your building have security cameras?"

"Yeah, and they work, too. But Nina won't show up on film."

Alex bit his lip. "That's right. Neither would Ophelia."

"Really? I didn't know that about fallen angels," Vlad said from the backseat.

"Yeah." Alex looked at his arm, made a fist, and then let it go. "Technically, we're not corporeal."

And yet I had felt his corporeal.

Chapter Twenty-Three

Alex, Vlad, and I were silent, sitting rigid as Alex took the hills of San Francisco with dizzying speed. My heart was thumping painfully by the time we neared my apartment. I thought about Ophelia's last visit, the tornado of destruction she inflicted in the few minutes she was there. My heart started to beat faster and I gripped the car door, ready to run out the second the wheels stopped spinning.

"Do we have a plan?" Vlad asked.

"A plan?"

"You know, what are we going to do?"

I frowned. "I hadn't thought much further than blast through the doors with a fallen angel, a human Tupperware, and an ascot-wearing vampire."

Vlad straightened his ascot and raised an eyebrow. "Who's the Tupperware?"

Alex jerked his thumb toward me and I met Vlad's questioning eyes. "It's a long story."

"So, your sister kidnapped my aunt, your dad is Satan—"

"Might be," I interjected.

"And now you're Tupperware? Man, you've got problems."

I sniffed. If it weren't for me, Nina wouldn't be hurting. She wouldn't be wincing, struggling, her arms and chest singed with holy water.

I *caused* problems.

My mouth dropped open and I clamped my eyes shut, pressing my palms against my ears. "She's doing it again!"

Vlad reached over the front seat and cranked up the radio. Alex pushed the gas pedal to the floor and we were all flung back against our seats. By the time I opened my eyes, we were double parked outside of my building.

My stomach was playing the accordion as we lumbered up the stairs. I hoped that the last image I had of Nina was just another one of Ophelia's throw-offs and that Nina was stretched out on our couch painting her toenails, unscathed; that she had whooped Ophelia into a simpering mess somewhere far, far away. Then we could all go out for a pizza.

No such luck.

The apartment was just as we left it: white grease-stained bakery bag and coffee cups still on the counter, Alex's backpack full of books on the kitchen table, and Nina, nowhere. We filed into the living room and ChaCha ran out to greet us, yapping spastically until Alex and I gave her the obligatory head scratches. She went to Vlad next, flicked her whiskers as she smelled his pant leg, blinked her big brown eyes at him, and then ran off, wriggling under the couch.

"And there goes the infallible security system."

"I have a gun, remember?" I groaned, yanking it out of my jacket pocket as Vlad and Alex dove to the ground.

Vlad looked at Alex, panicked. "Does she know how to use that?"

"Unfortunately, yes," Alex said.

I slammed my gun—with the safety on, thank you very much—onto the coffee table. "Let's find something out."

We had all fanned out across the apartment—Vlad checking Nina's room, Alex checking the windows. There was a knock on the door. I froze.

"Ophelia?" I asked Alex in a low voice.

Alex shook his head. "Not a knocker."

I rolled up onto my toes and looked out the peephole, seeing the chunky cut of Will's sandy blond hair in my fisheye view. "It's Will."

I yanked open the door. "What are you doing here?"

"And it's a pleasure to see you, too, love," Will said, sauntering into the apartment, all smugness and British accent.

I crossed my arms in front of my chest and jutted out one hip. "Look, Will, I'm not in the mood. Ophelia has kidnapped my best friend." My voice cracked and my vision blurred, the hot tears rushing over my cheeks. "And it's all my fault."

Will stepped closer to me, tried to put his arms around me, but I pushed him away, using the back of my hand to wipe my eyes. "And you're a horrible guardian!"

"Isn't she a bit old for a guardian?" I heard Vlad mutter to Alex.

"Vessel thing," he returned.

Then, "Oooh. She's got the Vessel?"

"She *is* the Vessel."

I pushed my palms flat against Will's chest. "Get out."

I felt Alex's palm on my shoulder. "Wait. Lawson, we need all the firepower we can get. As much as I don't like it—or him—he is the seventh guardian. He's avoided Ophelia for this long and kept you alive."

Will grinned, brushing his fingernails on his shirt proudly. "Haven't lost one yet."

"You had to put the 'yet' in there, didn't you?"

"Um, guys? Can we just go find my aunt?" Vlad said from behind us.

We all filed into the living room, filling Will in on what we knew. When we got to the table, Alex unzipped his backpack and started handing out books.

"I thought these just dealt with the Vessel," I said.

"All of these mention the fallen and all of them were stolen from Ophelia. Might give us some insight into where she took Nina."

Vlad took the book Alex handed him and looked at the spine disdainfully. "I don't think this is going to help. I'm sure I can sense her or track Ophelia by her scent."

"You can track a scent through seven square miles?" Alex asked.

Vlad's lip curled and he huffed into a chair, pulling open his book angrily.

I pushed away from the table and looked out the living-room window, staring into the slate grey of the sky as it edged into night. Everything was still outside; the world stood motionless. I blew out a sigh.

"Everything okay?" Alex asked, coming up on my left shoulder.

I wagged my head, feeling waterlogged and exhausted from the tears I'd already shed. "It's going to take forever to get through all these books, and even then all that's going to happen is that we'll have an *idea* of where she may have taken Nina. We won't have Nina."

"We're going to find her," Alex said solemnly.

"I just feel like Ophelia is constantly one step ahead of us."

"Well, right now she is. But"—Alex gestured back at the guys, Vlad snapping pages angrily, Will silently moving his lips as he read—"we're gaining on her."

I looked hopelessly on.

"We need to do more." I tapped my index finger against my lips and paced. "I think I have an idea. I think I know a way to get one over on Ophelia."

I took Alex by the hand and led him into the hallway. "You need to get the Vessel."

Alex raised an eyebrow. "What are you talking about?"

"If you have the Vessel of Souls—if you return it— then Ophelia won't be after me anymore. She'll release Nina and everything will be fine."

Alex put his fists on his hips. "Everything will be fine? We don't know that Ophelia would release Nina, and anyway, Lawson, you'll be dead."

"We all have to make sacrifices."

Alex grabbed my shoulders and gave me a shake. "Do you hear what you're saying? No. No, I'm not going to do it."

"It's the only way to get rid of Ophelia and keep Nina safe."

"It is not."

"Come on, Alex. If we go up against Ophelia, it's likely I'm going to—"

"Don't you dare say it," Alex said between gritted teeth. "Don't you dare."

"Maybe this is why you found me."

"I found you so I could protect you and I sure as hell am not going to let Ophelia win. We'll figure out another way."

"I'm beginning to believe there is no other way."

"This isn't worth your life."

"Nina is."

"We are going to find another way."

I stepped back, put my hands on my hips. "Okay, so what else do you propose we do?"

"I'm not sure yet."

Alex followed me back into the dining room, where Will and Vlad were turning pages. Vlad groaned. "Can't we just go to her house or something? Doesn't anyone know where Ophelia lives?"

We all wagged our heads.

"So far she's blown up my father's house—"

Will knitted his brows. "Oh, I'm sorry about that, love."

"Don't be. It wasn't actually his house. And anyway I think my dad is Satan. Oh, and Ophelia's my sister."

Will's eyebrows shot up. "Now that wasn't on your getting-to-know-you form. Hell of a family tree."

"I just need to think," I said, sitting down on one of the dining room chairs and holding my head in my hands. I tried to concentrate, ran my fingers through my hair. I heard the whisp of a name—*Sophie*—run through my mind. *It's you. . . . It's always been you. . . .* I closed my eyes and saw two pinpricks of light flicker behind closed lids. They came into focus and I recognized birthday candles, a fat chocolate cake, pink cheeks pushed out and ready to blow. . . . I saw myself on my fifth birthday, strawberry-red pigtails bouncing as I tore the wrapping off a Barbie Dream House.

It's always been you, Ophelia's breathy voice came again.

The image warbled and I saw Nina's face, drawn and bruised. Her eyes were red-rimmed and tears dribbled silently as her head lolled, chin on chest.

Sophie, Ophelia sang, *won't you come out to play?*

"I think I know where she is," I mumbled to myself.

"What was that?" Alex asked me.

"A shower. You know"—I shook myself—"this soot and dirt. I think better near water anyway."

Alex followed me as I headed to my bedroom. I turned

around at the threshold, heart pumping. "I'm just going to clean up. I'll be right back." I forced a smile. Alex and I had an unspoken agreement that his angelic mind-reading abilities were strictly off limits when it came to me. He let his fingers trail over my bare arm and I knew that his focus was not on my mind.

Alex brushed his lips over mine. He wrapped his arms around me, pushing me into my room, and kissed me hard. I pulled away, licking my lips.

"That doesn't feel like the kiss of someone who's expecting me to come back," I told him. "I'm just getting in the tub."

Alex pulled me toward him again and nibbled on my bottom lip, flicked his tongue over my ear. "No, that's the kiss of someone who not only expects you to come back, but who intends to pick up where he left off this morning."

I felt a delicious shiver in spite of my fear. When I pulled back I looked into Alex's eyes. "Good to know."

Chapter Twenty-Four

I closed the door and rummaged through my underwear drawer, finding the gun Alex had given me a year ago. It was now nestled between a lacy thong with the tags still on and a pair of fuzzy socks with polar bears on them. The gun used to live in the freezer, but after an unfortunate accident with a Skinny Cow Mint Dipper, I decided to move it to a safer location. I pulled my bathrobe from the peg by the door, slipped it on, and tucked the gun in my pocket. I trudged out past the guys, head down, shoulders hunched under the guise of girlish modesty—and just as I suspected, they all did their best to look away.

The one benefit of undead men—they've got all that old-school chivalry.

I locked the bathroom door behind me and turned the tub on full bore. Then I slid out of my bathrobe, unrolled both of my pant legs, and yanked my discarded sneakers from their "I'm going to get rid of these tomorrow" spot on the floor. I threw my well-thawed .22 into my shoulder bag and added a couple bars of soap for good measure. I wedged the bathroom window open, sucked in my stomach, and launched myself through.

My apartment was on the second floor and my hefty rent gave me a priceless view of a well-tagged brick wall and a bank of Dumpsters—not so useful for romantic dinners on the fire escape, but excellent for a midnight sojourn with destiny. In my own Nadia Comaneci move I vaulted from the end of my fire escape to land in an inglorious belly flop on a pile of bagged garbage. I bit my lip to keep from screaming as I picked my way through splitting bags of God knows what, cursing my neighbors for buying cheap garbage bags and Cala Foods for selling them. I swamp-walked through the trash, willing myself not to breathe, reminding myself that all the slimy hands that I felt reaching out for me were either banana peels or burger wrappers.

When I mercifully reached the rusted metal side of the Dumpster I hauled myself out, landing with an impressive thud on the cement below. I dared a look up to my illuminated bathroom window to check if Alex and the guys were on to me—nope. I took off running then, the sound of my sneakers slapping the pavement echoing through the dark alley.

Halfway to my destination I was heaving and certain my lungs were going to explode; I hailed a cab and paid the shameful $5.65 to go the next six blocks, then tore through the police-station parking lot, mashing my fingers against the elevator's down button.

"Come on, come on," I moaned to the molasses-slow machine as I danced from foot to foot. "Come on!" As I waited, I scanned the lineup of menacing-looking mug shots in the MOST WANTED photos and shivered. If Ophelia was just your basic, everyday homicidal maniac or computer hacker, I'd feel a lot better. At least then I'd have the whole police force behind me and she'd stay out of my head—and her mug could be plastered all over the streets of San Francisco, making everyone on high alert.

I stepped inside the elevator and watched the doors close on the safety of the police station vestibule. "I have to do this," I told myself out loud. Suddenly, the thundering beat of my heart was all I could hear. My mouth went dry and my palms were wet; my stomach seemed to drop with every floor. I dipped my hand into my shoulder bag, fingering the comforting coolness of my gun.

"Everything is going to be okay," I whispered.

When the elevator's big steel doors opened, the UDA waiting room was dim, the empty furniture and deserted kiosks bathed in an eerie yellow glow from the room's flickering emergency lights. The UDA was technically closed, but since the standard lock-and-key method did little to deter the undead who wanted in, the company was locked up tight with a magical charm, courtesy of the higher-ups at Underworld corporate. The supernatural padlock method was ingenious for keeping out curious breathers and impatient demons, but it had one weak spot—me. My magical immunity wasn't just a fun parlor trick; it occasionally came in handy, too. I breathed deeply and tried to convince myself of my confidence.

Ophelia may have the supernatural powers of the otherworld behind her, but I had a gun, a handbag full of soap, and a team of mythical defenders who thought I was taking a bubble bath.

I gulped.

"Ophelia?" I called out.

I heard her giggle—this time it was out in the open and not in my head.

And then I heard a scream.

I tore down the hall, screaming for Nina and kicking open doors. When I got to the last one—the room the

UDA used for storage—I paused, until I heard Ophelia's laugh again. I yanked open the door.

I lost my breath when I saw the storeroom. Just like the rest of the UDA, the lights were off, the only illumination coming from the sickly yellow glow of the emergency lights. The storeroom furniture had been pushed back and heaped up against the walls, so towers of used office chairs and obsolete phones were stacked in precarious mountains all around me—everything except for one wooden desk and one chair. The desk had been pushed to the front of the room and Ophelia was stretched out on her stomach on top of it. Her fingers were knitted and her chin rested in her hands. Her long, bare legs were kicked up and she would occasionally kick her bare foot like a child watching fireflies. She was dressed in a red cotton sundress with crisp white piping—inappropriate both for the situation and for San Francisco weather—and her long blond hair looked flawless, held back by a thick white headband. Her curls trailed over her bare shoulders and spilled down to her elbows. There was a jaunty straw purse sitting on the desk next to her. If her arms and shoulders hadn't been streaked in blood, she would have looked like a teenage girl lounging on a summer day.

"Sophie!" Ophelia squealed gleefully when she saw me. "So glad you could make it!" She waggled her bare feet and grinned at me, a shiny prom-queen grin that morphed into a pouty frown. "I don't think Nina wants to play with me anymore."

Ophelia stretched one arm, her talonlike nail pointing to where Nina was tied against one wall.

My stomach sank and I had to bite down hard on my lower lip to stop myself from crying.

"Nina?" I breathed.

My best friend was sitting on the missing desk chair, bare ankles double-roped against the legs of the chair, her arms tied behind her. She was wearing the slip dress I had last seen her in, except now it hung listlessly on her and her once-glossy hair was snarled in a series of rats-nest knots. There were large tears in the silky fabric of her dress and the elegant lace that edged the bodice was torn and hung around Nina's neck like a noose; one strap hung ineffectually around her upper arm, right next to it a series of oblong purple bruises. Her exposed skin—usually marblesque and perfect—was pockmarked with angry red gashes, burn marks, and cuts. Splatters of blood marched across her chest and arms, and long, bloody rivers dripped down each leg.

"Oh," I whimpered, feeling the sting of tears that wanted to fall, feeling the tension in my spine as it crawled up the back of my neck.

Nina's head lolled to the side and I saw that her lips were puckered and had a handful of tiny cut marks on them. There was blood caked at the corner of her mouth and under her nose and one eye—usually decked out in a luxe MAC eye shadow palette—was nearly swollen shut. Half-empty blood bags were torn open and leaking all around Nina. I cringed.

"Oh my God," I whispered, swallowing hard against the lump in my throat.

"You know what's neat?" Ophelia said, hopping from her spot on the desk like an excited school child. "I can hurt vampires! And if I feed them just enough to get their system going—but not enough to gain their strength—I can make them bleed." Ophelia was downright giddy and she clapped her hands, her straw purse bobbing jauntily as she wound it around her arm. "Isn't that fun?"

My jaw tightened and my stomach went leaden.

"Great. You can hurt a vampire when she has a quarter of her powers. You're real tough."

Ophelia's eyes narrowed and she went on, ignoring me. "I wanted to tell you—I tried to get in your mind to show you all the fun stuff that Nina and I had discovered but your mind was closed completely. It was clogged by all the others around you." She frowned a pouty little girl's frown. "It made me sad. Where were you—the mall?"

"Broadway." My voice was barely audible to myself and I didn't want to raise it. I thought of us wandering aimlessly through town, and Alex and I rolling around in bed, all the while, Ophelia was learning—and hurting Nina.

"Don't cry!" Ophelia said. "There's plenty left for you, too!"

I backed up, slipped my hand into my shoulder bag. Ophelia's eyes followed the line of my arm.

"You know what else is different?" Ophelia asked. "I can't read your mind in here." She held her arms open, blue eyes grazing the ceiling. "Must be something about the Underworld—protects their own or something? No, that can't be it because you don't belong here." She grinned. "You don't belong anywhere."

I gritted my teeth. "Are you through?"

"No. Like I said, I couldn't read your mind—it was frustrating. Imagine how I felt, having to cart around that bag of bones"—she inclined her blond head toward Nina—"on the off chance that you'd be where I wanted you to be."

I licked my lips. "So you took a chance?"

"No, silly." Ophelia paused then, her eyes wide and dripping spurious innocence. "I couldn't read your thoughts, so I read Alex's."

Ophelia smiled serenely, stepping back toward Nina. She gingerly slipped her fingers under the strap of Nina's dress and lifted it back up to her shoulder, smoothing it carefully. Then she trailed her fingers slowly through Nina's hair, playing with the few strands that weren't snarled and blood caked.

"You get away from her," I spat.

Ophelia just smiled and sweetly patted Nina's unmoving head. "That's okay. I'm done playing with her. Now I'm ready to play with you."

Nina's body lurched forward in the chair and Ophelia slapped her back. I sucked in a breath, praying that my best friend wasn't dead. I kept my eyes fixed on Ophelia, but gingerly kicked one of the blood bags closer to Nina.

Ophelia kept up her lament.

"You know, Sophie, I should be really, really jealous of you. Alex loves you in a way that he never even considered me." The soft lilt of Ophelia's voice took on a hard edge. "He thinks about you so often, he doesn't even know he's doing it."

Ophelia walked slowly, closing the distance between us. "He's been so worried that I'm going to hurt you. He thinks about it constantly. He's even thinking about it now as he drives to your grandmother's old house."

"What?"

"Alex was right when he said it was easy to hijack your mind—the maggots, Daddy." Ophelia pressed her manicured fingers to her lips and giggled. "But it wasn't too hard to put a few suggestions into his mind. Especially since they seemed to be the same thoughts that your ragtag bunch of supernatural friends were having. And because I wrote your grandmother's address in the margins of all my books. I would have included a Google map, but I thought that would be just a little too obvious."

I nudged closer to Nina, trying to eye her through my peripheral, to see if she was alive.

"But that Alex—" Ophelia clasped her hands and batted her eyelashes innocently. "Try as I might, I just can't get over him. I guess it's a girl thing—or maybe it's those sweet baby blues of his." She licked her lips as if the memory was a delicious one and winked at me. "You know how mesmerizing those eyes are. I still love him, Sophie; a part of me still wants him back. I just can't do anything to hurt him. So, you don't have to worry. I'm not going to hurt you."

I let out a breath I didn't know I was holding and Ophelia smiled.

"I'm just going to kill you."

Ophelia's face fell when mine did. "Oh, honey! Don't take it personally. I mean, we are sisters after all, and I've always wanted a kid sister. But you know what I want more? Complete control."

I took another step back, the hammering of my heart so dramatic it hurt as it thumped against my rib cage. I blinked and Ophelia was right in front of me, standing on the vacated desk. She held her hands out, palms up, like a scale.

"Have a kid sister to control"—she sank her left hand down a quarter of an inch—"or have the entire world to control." Her right hand thudded downward, and Ophelia cocked her head, looking genuinely sad. "Sorry, sis, looks like you lose."

Ophelia lunged for me and I skidded out of the way, winding my way back to the storage-room door. I heard the slap-slap-slap of Ophelia's bare feet on the concrete; I heard them gaining on me. I crouched, snatched my .22 out of my bag, and then used my bag to wallop Ophelia on the side of the head. The bars of soap made a satisfying thunk as they made contact with Ophelia's pretty blond curls.

"Ow!" she howled, looking stunned. "What the hell do you have in there?"

I took the opportunity to lunge closer, arm outstretched, gun aloft, finger firmly on the trigger. I tried to focus, but the barrel trembled, and so did Ophelia's shoulders.

She pressed her fingers to her mouth and I felt a bead of sweat make its way down my back.

Ophelia couldn't hold my gaze—because she was laughing so hard.

"Really, Sophie?"

I swallowed, my throat constricting. I was afraid if I opened my mouth I'd vomit, so I just nodded, hoping the movement looked cool and certain.

Ophelia laughed harder and skipped toward me. She flicked my hand, then pressed her forehead against the barrel of the gun.

"Go ahead."

"I will," I said with every ounce of confidence I could muster.

"I'm waiting." Ophelia's ice-blue eyes locked on me and her lips turned up into a mocking smile. "You wouldn't. I'm your sister—the only family you have left. And you're a complete wimp." She stepped back, crossing her arms in front of her chest.

A pinprick of pain started behind my eyes and began pulsing, coursing through every fiber of my being. The room dropped into stony silence. A drop of sweat fell from my hands in achingly slow motion and then the world cracked. Loudly. There was a spit of fire and I was vaulting backward.

"You bitch!" Ophelia was a hairbreadth away and she smacked the gun from my hand. "You shot me!"

I didn't notice any blood on Ophelia so I hurriedly glanced at the ceiling and floor (my two usual targets). Nothing.

Ophelia grinned at my confusion. "Not corporeal," she said, thumping her chest. "There is nothing inside here!"

I'll say.

I took off running toward the waiting room with Ophelia close behind.

"Come on, Sophie," Ophelia yelled. "Don't you want to be a part of something bigger? Don't you want to be something greater than yourself?"

I stopped and held my ground. "Like a Vessel?" I said, my own voice a fearsome snarl.

Ophelia giggled—a sweet, completely inappropriate giggle. "Oh, you know about that."

I snatched a metal ruler out of Pierre's *I Heart Tuscaloosa* penholder mug in the waiting room and brandished it like a sword. "And I know about our father."

Ophelia paused, her eyes wide. She pulled herself up on a desk and sat down, crossing her long bare legs. "What do you know about Daddy?"

Hearing her say the word *daddy* tugged at my heart. Ophelia cocked her head and stuck out her lower lip. "What's the matter, Sophie-pie? Feeling a little abandoned since Daddy left you and Mommy couldn't stand you?"

I felt that snarl of anger roil through me again.

"Shut up, Ophelia."

Ophelia bobbed her foot playfully. "Don't worry; it probably wasn't you at all. I mean, Daddy did have me at home and your mom, well"—Ophelia looked at me, her eyes sharp and icicle blue—"he always said she was a regular nutcase."

"That's not true!"

"Oh come on, Sophie! How many people who are square in the head go out and kill themselves?"

I bit my cheek hard, feeling the bitter taste of my blood.

Ophelia jumped off the desk and landed, sure-footed, on the ground. "Okay, enough with the family reunion crap. I'm impatient. I'm ready to rule." She snapped her fingers. "Come here, chop, chop!" Ophelia giggled at her own horrible pun. "Or shoot, shoot." She dug into her prissy straw purse and pulled out a gun. I gulped, the sudden thunderous beat of my heart—corporeal as I was—nearly choking me.

"Um, will that really work to release the Vessel?"

Ophelia looked at the gun in her hand and frowned. "Yeah, why?" She acted confident, but I could tell by the tone of her voice that she was unsure. I sucked in a breath and stood a little taller.

"You have to know that something with"—my eyes flicked over the barrel of the .357 Magnum she held— "that kind of firepower runs the risk of shattering the Vessel."

Ophelia faltered for a split second, the barrel of the gun dropping a fraction of an inch. "You don't know that."

I shrugged. "Suit yourself. But, being the Vessel, I think I pretty much know how this works."

Ophelia narrowed her eyes. "You didn't even know *what* you were until I came along."

I raised my brows. "Really? Is that what you think? The Vessel of Souls—a divine vessel used to hold the souls of the recently departed until their fate is decided. Desired by the fallen, protected by the righteous. The holder has the power to tip the scales and control both worlds. Hidden in plain sight. The guardian of the Vessel must do anything in her power to ensure the safety of the

Vessel." Even as I said it—a definition made up from snippets I had heard from Alex, read in my father's journals—things were becoming clearer. I couldn't let Ophelia see me falter.

I put my hands on my hips, jutting my chin toward the butt of Ophelia's gun. "So, you tell me. Do you really want to risk it?"

Chapter Twenty-Five

Ophelia lowered the gun slowly and I felt the race of my pulse begin a miniscule slowdown. I kept my eyes fixed and watched her every motion: she slid her purse strap off her shoulder, daintily laid it on the desk. Carefully laid the gun next to it. And then her eyes were fierce and sharp as she bared her teeth, fisted her hands, and launched herself into me. I skidded back with a pained thud and felt my limbs flailing uselessly as I kicked, punched, and scratched in every direction, Ophelia laying on top of me, working to pin me down.

I felt her knuckles as she landed a blow to my chin that made my teeth rattle. I reached up and grabbed a lock of her pretty blond hair in my fist and gave it a fierce yank. She howled but didn't let up, and her next punch caught the side of my head as I flopped like a caught fish.

"If I can't shoot the Vessel out of you," Ophelia huffed, "I'll choke it out of you!"

I slapped at Ophelia's hands as they dove for my neck; I felt my feet slide uselessly against the industrial carpet as I worked to gain footing. I scratched and tried to bite at her arm, but Ophelia found my throat, used her nails to get a tighter hold. My breath caught in my throat as she gripped my neck, her thumbs pressing against my windpipe. I huffed and squirmed against her body, pinching my eyes shut against the bruising pain threading across my throat. I reached behind my head and felt the metal ruler, gripped it hard, and brought it down on Ophelia's head with a loud *thwack!*

Ophelia frowned, loosened her grip on me, and felt the tiny beads of red velvet blood that bubbled from the cut on her forehead. "You hit me! You bitch! My own sister."

I gasped, sucking in all the air I could with painful, hollow breaths and clawing at her hand that stayed clamped on my throat.

"You're trying to kill me! You're my sister and you're trying to kill me!" I wriggled like a centipede and Ophelia lost her balance, tumbling over. Scrambling to my feet, I scanned the office for something to use as a weapon. Ophelia lunged for me, her hands missing my ankles by a hair. I sprinted toward the bank of waiting-room chairs and grabbed one, then tossed it with all my might like I had seen stuntmen do in the movies, but Ophelia swiftly dodged it. I threw a *Time* magazine at her and she smiled maniacally, watching the glossy pages flutter in front of her. I tossed a cup full of pens, a potted plant, Nina's wireless radio.

The radio hit Ophelia squarely in the chest.

"Ow!" She rubbed the rapidly reddening spot. "Now I'm mad," she growled.

I stepped back and she lurched forward. There was a loud *snap!* and a pair of tattered, tar-black wings sprung from Ophelia's bare back. The wings were sharply angled with a shadowy black gossamer that stretched between jet-black bones and was fringed with anemic-looking black feathers.

"Oh my God," I muttered, stunned.

Ophelia's lips curved up into a grotesque smile; her eyebrows took on a sinister arch. Her wings flapped and she was almost on top of me. I bobbed, tumbled to my knees, and crawled into the main waiting room vestibule, then crawled to my feet.

"Come'ere!" Ophelia sneered. She sprinted behind me, the wide berth of her wings slowing her down as I wound around the waiting-room chairs and velvet ropes. She had to angle herself to follow me or risk being dragged down by the furniture.

Finally, I was where I needed to be. When Ophelia saw my back pressed against the wall her smile widened and her wings gave an anticipatory flap. "I win!" she sang.

"Okay, Ophelia. You want me? You want the Vessel of Souls? Come and get it."

Once again Ophelia lunged and I danced out of the way, snagging the trident left in the UDA wall as I did. I turned on Ophelia and now her back was up against the wall.

The last time I looked into her eyes, they were wide and ice blue as she saw the trident coming at her chest, pinning her to the wall.

I stumbled back when she finally stopped seething and writhing. I dropped to my knees and hung my head, trying to catch my breath, trying to will my heart to start beating its usual rhythmic pace again.

The cheerful ding of the elevator arriving caught my attention and I turned to look, the huge metal doors opening on the drawn, concerned faces of Alex, Vlad, and Will. All three men were in fighting stance, weapons drawn.

"Sophie!"

"What happened here?"

The men all gathered around me, Alex kneeling low and gingerly rubbing my back, Vlad staring at the ruins of the Underworld waiting room, and Will eyeing Ophelia, wings splayed, head lowered as she lay pinned to the wall.

"How did you know where to find me?" I managed to say through parched, blood-caked lips.

"You mean after you snuck out the window?"

Will puffed out his chest. "I am the guardian. I knew you left."

Alex's nostrils flared. "He knew you left when the water started coming in under the bathroom door. You forgot to take out the stopper and the tub overflowed."

"Oh." I tried to straighten, but pain raged through me. "Nina. Save Nina."

Vlad crouched down in front of me, dark eyes huge. "Where?"

"Storeroom."

Vlad turned and took off down the hall; Will and Alex hovered over me, glaring at each other. I pushed at Will's leg "Please help Vlad. I don't think Nina can walk."

Reluctantly, Will turned, casting one last glance over his shoulder before running after Vlad.

"Are you okay?" Alex asked, his voice soft as his fingers picked bits of flowerpots and Bic pens out of my hair.

I had never considered the idiocy in that question before now. Every inch of me ached.

"Okay?" I repeated absently.

Dried blood mixed with dirt stung my eyes. I tried to move my lips, to form another word, but my throat was dry and my tongue felt heavy, immovable. I worked to raise up from my hunched position, but every motion—breathing included—set off a series of wailing pains, every one a reminder of my fight with Ophelia.

"I think I'm okay," I was finally able to whisper.

Which was more than I could say for Ophelia.

Though struck through with a trident, oddly, she wasn't bleeding. Her body seemed small and crumpled with one leg bent, her arms hanging limp at her sides, head bowed. Her lovely blond hair was streaked through with dirt and blood—apparently, mine. There was a gunpowder-black penumbra cast on the wall around her.

"Is she dead?" I asked softly.

Alex went to her and used a single index finger under Ophelia's bowed chin to lift her head. I couldn't bear to look into her eyes and I imagined Alex reverently thumbing them closed.

"Not dead, exactly," Alex said.

I involuntarily stiffened, wincing as my rib cage protested. Alex hurried to me, carefully sliding his strong arms underneath me, raising me gently to my feet.

"What do you mean, not exactly?"

Alex steadied me and I took a few sharp, shallow breaths—each one making my head spin—and then I looked at him and repeated my question.

"You can't kill someone"—he glanced over his shoulder, back at Ophelia, as if making certain she was still there—"or something that is already dead."

I stepped back. "Then she can come back?"

"No, she's not coming back. The black shadow there? That means she's been called back."

"Called back?" I asked. "Where?"

Alex just raised his eyebrows.

"Oh," I said softly, feeling strangely sad. "She was my sister."

Alex led me to the employee break room, where he doused a dishtowel in warm water and gently touched it to my face. I winced.

"Sorry," he said.

"It just stings a little bit."

"I don't mean about that," Alex said, dipping the towel back into the sink.

"I'm sorry I failed you."

I felt my brow furrow.

"Failed me?"

Alex touched the cool towel to my head again, worked at the dried blood. "I should have been there for you. I should have protected you. I should never have let Ophelia into your life."

I wrapped my fingers around Alex's wrist. "This isn't your fault," I said sternly.

"If I hadn't been around, Ophelia would never have known what you are."

Chapter Twenty-Six

Alex and I sat in silence as he worked the dried blood and dirt from my face. We both stiffened when we heard the clunk of the storeroom door opening, the slap of feet racing down the hall. I was relieved when I saw Nina zip by the break-room door, Vlad and Will right behind her.

"Oh my God!" Nina howled.

Alex helped me to my feet, and when we emerged in the UDA waiting room, Nina—her lips a fresh, healthy blood red, the cuts and bruises already growing faint—was sitting on her knees among the rubble, desperately crying, clutching an Alhambra water jug to her chest and rocking it gently.

"Sophie, Sophie, Sophie," she was murmuring. "We failed you, dear Sophie. Poor, sweet Sophie."

Alex put one hand respectfully on Nina's shoulder and crouched down. "Are you sure that's Sophie?" he asked.

The offense washed over Nina in waves. She looked incredulously at the water bottle and then at Alex. "Of course this is Sophie. I would recognize her anywhere, in any form. Alex, she was my best friend. Our friendship

transcends any physical manifestation." She held out
the empty jug. "Look at her. Look at her!" She cuddled
the bottle again. "Sophie . . ."

"Um, Nina?"

I stepped through the rubble and Nina stiffened.
"See?" she said. "If you listen carefully, you can hear her
talking. Hello, my Sophie," she called into the jug. "You
may now be an empty Vessel, but you will forever be our
Sophie."

I stomped my foot—then wished I hadn't, as the pain
seared through me. "Hey! It's me. I'm here." I picked my
way to Nina, Alex, and the jug. "I'm not a jug."

Nina's eyes were wide as saucers; Vlad and Will
stepped aside.

"We tried to tell her," Will said.

"Sophie!"

Nina came toward me, flinging the not-me plastic jug
aside and throwing her arms around my waist.

"Ow," I whimpered.

"I'm so glad you aren't an Alhambra bottle," she said
softly.

"I'm so sorry I let her hurt you," I said back.

Nina shrugged. "No biggie."

I patted Alex on the shoulder when he turned toward
Ophelia. "I'm sorry about that," I told him.

I watched Alex's Adam's apple bob as he swallowed
slowly. Finally he turned to me, cobalt eyes clouded, and
said, "I'm not. She wouldn't have stopped hunting you,
ever. Fallen angels are inflexibly determined in their mission. Obstinate in their evil."

I pushed a lock of Alex's dark hair across his forehead.
"Not all of them."

Alex caught my hand and kissed my fingertips. "Right.
Not all of us."

"Hey—how did you find me here?"

Vlad stepped forward. "We pored through all the books."

"We were on our way to your grandmother's old place when Alex realized that Ophelia was probably just baiting him—again," Will said. "It wasn't my choice of locales, but you heard the man—fallen angels, their mission, blah, blah, blah."

Will came closer and Alex dropped my hand, the muscle in his jaw flicking as I stood between them. He picked a clod of dirt off my shoulder, flicked it in Will's general direction. "You really can't fault someone for taking their life's mission too seriously."

Vlad piped up, "I don't know about you guys, but all of this drama has made me incredibly hungry." He patted his gut. "I think my blood sugar is low."

Nina nodded. "I need grease. And fat. I so want to eat a fat guy right now."

Will blanched and Alex clapped him on the shoulder proudly. "You'll get used to it."

The cool night air was heavy with fog, and the city seemed oddly quiet. Alex led me out to the parking lot with Nina, Vlad, and Will in tow, but I felt completely alone. I looked back over my shoulder at the closed door of the San Francisco Police Department and expected to hear Ophelia's hollow giggle. All I heard was the lonesome whoosh of wind as it pushed the fog toward the bay.

"You're going to be okay, Lawson," Alex said, resting his coat on my shoulders. I felt heavy and alien in my own body. When we pulled up in front of my apartment building, we sat in silence for several minutes, watching the traffic pass.

"You ready?"

I twisted my hands in my lap. "I appreciate everything you've done tonight, Alex, but I think I would like to be alone, if you don't mind."

Alex put his hand on my thigh and squeezed gently. It was probably the one part of my body that wasn't sporting a flower of purple bruises.

He nodded. "Of course. But you promise to call me if you need anything, okay? Anything at all."

"Sure."

I turned as Alex rested his hand on my shoulder. "Hey, about what I said the other day, about me not being around?"

I sat back. "Yeah?"

"It's not that I—I don't want to be around. It's not that I don't want to be with you—"

I forced a smile; the pain seared all the way through me. "You don't need to explain."

"If I could . . ."

I took his hand off my shoulder and patted it gently. "I know, Alex. If you could—if there were any way to make this work—you would, right?"

Alex swallowed hard but nodded, avoiding my gaze. "So, are we good?"

"Good friends? Yeah."

Alex's head bobbed, and then he turned to me, his blue eyes catching the light. "You know I love you, Lawson."

I nodded my head. "I know you do, Alex." I slammed the car door and turned away before he could see the tears welling in my eyes.

I slowly made my way to the apartment vestibule. I was met at the door by Will, who was balancing a pizza in one hand and paying the pizza man with the other. His profile was illuminated in the building's lights and he had changed into sweatpants and an Arsenal T-shirt. He raised the pizza box when he saw me.

"Hey, love, how you feeling?"

I wagged my head and shrugged. "I don't really know."

"Fancy a slice?"

"No thanks. I just want to go to bed."

Will looked like he was going to make a smart reply but thought better of it. Instead, he patted my shoulder awkwardly, then leaned down and brushed a soft kiss over my cheek, his lips soft as they tickled my ear. "Sorry you have to have such a crap guardian."

I heard the rev of Alex's engine as he sped away.

I opened the apartment door and Nina was stretched out on the couch, barefoot and dressed in a silky violet robe. There were a dozen empty blood bags crushed on the coffee table.

"Couldn't find a fat guy."

"Where's Vlad?" I asked.

"Took off with the VERMers," Nina said. "Apparently, a T-shirt shop on The Haight has committed some egregious crime against Count Chocula. Besides, I thought we could use a quiet night. Just you, me"—she held up the paper bag that was next to her on the couch—"and a couple dozen marshmallow Pinwheels."

I grinned and lowered myself gingerly to the couch.

"You wouldn't believe how hard these were to find. The corner market was totally sold out."

"Weird. You're starting to look better."

"A full meal will do that to you."

I poked the stack of blood bags with my toe. "A full meal? Looks like you had a full football team."

Nina grinned and burped softly. "No offense, but you're not looking so hot."

I frowned and glanced at myself in the hall mirror. My hair was ratted and streaked with dirt and dried blood. There was a noticeable bald spot that flared red and angry when I touched it. My mascara was running and my lower lip was split and fat. Scratches and cuts crisscrossed like raised red train tracks over my legs and arms. It seemed that every part of me that wasn't covered in blood was smeared with dirt and ballpoint-pen ink.

"I look like I got in a fight with the Office Depot guy."

"And lost."

I glared and Nina grinned, the tips of her fangs still sporting a deep red hue from her recent feeding.

"I think I'm going to take a shower."

I ran the shower water as hot as I could get it and stood under the stream, scrubbing gently and whimpering each time I found a new ache. I stepped out and dried myself off, being careful not to look into any shiny surfaces. Ophelia's gleeful laughter at my mother's suicide still rang in my head and I wasn't ready to face my grandmother.

I stiffened, thinking back to when I confronted Grandma about my being the Vessel. "Being a Vessel isn't the worst thing, but dying to protect it is."

Dying to protect the Vessel. Dying, to protect . . . me.

I clamped my eyes shut and lost my breath. I saw the glare from the sun on the blond hardwood floor. I felt my mother touching me, nuzzling me, her hands seeming so big as they stroked my hair. "This way they'll never find you, Sophie. They won't know where to look." A sob choked in my throat as the image became a memory, a thought. My tears mingled with the shower stream, flooding over my cheeks. I remembered that voice. I remembered that moment.

"It's the only way."

I started to nod my head despite the ache the movement caused. "Don't do it," I whispered. "I need you here."

I stood still, letting the hot shower water wash over me.

When I finished with my shower I flopped on the couch in my bathrobe. ChaCha curled up next to me and Nina dumped two whole boxes of marshmallow Pinwheels on a plate and set it on the coffee table in front of me.

"I feel like I should be taking care of you," I told her. "I practically got you killed."

"But you rescued me," Nina answered from the kitchen. "You came and found me. I've never had a friend who would do that for me." She curled up on the couch next to me, folding her legs neatly underneath her.

"So, what happens now?"

"Well, I don't have to be afraid of Ophelia anymore."

"Does that mean it's over?" Nina wanted to know.

I looked into her dark eyes and took a deep breath, trying to banish the image of Ophelia's crumbling wings, her solemnly bowed head from my mind. I thought of Alex, of our night together, how I had run my fingers over the four-inch vertical scars just under each shoulder blade. He had stiffened, ashamed of the marks left from losing his wings.

"No, it's not over. Not by a long shot."

Nina rested her head on my shoulder, wrapping her cold arms around me. "It's just the beginning, isn't it?"

I may have been safe from Ophelia, but that was all. "I keep wondering how long it's going to be until someone else comes hunting for me. And then there's Alex. . . ."

"Alex isn't going to come hunting for you, Sophie. He's in love with you."

"He's a fallen angel."

Unrepentant in her mission . . . Alex's words rang in my head. I closed my eyes and prayed for sleep to find me.

Chapter Twenty-Seven

The sun was streaming through my curtains when I woke the next morning at seven. ChaCha was snuggled up beside me and she opened one marble-brown eye when I shifted; she let out a sound halfway between a growl and a moan. I let out a sound halfway between a whimper and a cry, fairly certain that most of my bones were on backward. When I stepped out of bed and caught sight of myself in the mirror I sucked in a shocked— albeit not surprised—breath. Bruises pockmarked every bit of skin that was exposed. In between the quarter-sized blue and greenish orbs were scratch marks and cuts already beginning to scab over. I figured today would be a whole heck of a lot of Cover Girl and just enough Advil to get me through. *But then again*, I thought as I slumped back onto my bed, *where do I have to go, anyway?*

I chased the negative thoughts out of my head and gave myself a pep talk: Today I was going to find a job (preferably one with fire-retardant clothing), and possibly one that included access to painkillers and gauze, and I was going to get my life back to normal. I might be a supernatural Vessel of Souls, but I was still Sophie Lawson, right down to my lime-Jell-O green eyes and my frazzled red hair—at least, what was left of it. I pulled a baseball cap low over my eyes and slid into a pair of sweatpants and a hoodie, marching to the front door. As I reached out for the knob, there were three short raps on the other side. My heart did a double-thump. Theoretically, the danger was gone. But in my life, staking the maniac du jour meant nothing. I rolled up on my tiptoes and cautiously peeked through the peephole.

"Dixon," I said to myself. I yanked open the door and peered out. "What are you doing here?"

Dixon dipped his head in a supremely eighteenth-century manner. "Hello to you, too, Ms. Lawson."

"I'm sorry, Dixon. Hello. What are you doing here?"

"May I come in?"

I looked Dixon over—tall, commanding, even standing in my reconstructed doorway. I didn't notice any bulging holsters or daggers poking from his slick black suit and his eyes had the flat look of a satiated vampire. I decided he was safe and stepped aside. "Yes, come in."

Dixon stepped around me and the little waft of cold air coming from his skin made me shiver.

"Nina told me what happened. Are you okay?"

I nodded, retracting my bruised hands into my sweat-shirt sleeves. "It's not as bad as it looks. We—breathers—just haven't gotten that superhuman speed-healing thing down." I tried to smile, but a drying cut at the side of my mouth prevented it. "Sorry about the state of the office."

Dixon shrugged. "Our janitorial staff is used to much worse."

There was a beat of companionable silence. I sucked in a slightly nervous breath. "No offense, but is there a reason you're here?" I paused. "Do you want me to pay for the cleanup? Because my new job"—I twisted my sweatshirt in my hands—"burned down. So, I'm a little strapped for cash right now."

Dixon's usually slick smile looked kind. "No, of course we don't expect you to pay for the damage."

"Then . . ."

I wouldn't have thought it was possible, but the six-foot, four-inch Dixon Andrade, all fangs and broad shoulders, looked bashful. "I wanted to offer you your job back."

My stomach flip-flopped. "What?"

"I mean, if you're still interested."

"I am, yeah, of course. But—but Nina and Anson have pretty much taken over my old job and I'm not going to take Nina's job. I guess if you have to let Anson go though . . ."

Dixon shook his dark head of perfect, slick-backed hair. "Oh no, of course not. Nina will remain"—Dixon straightened his tie—"under me. This whole situation—with Ophelia and Alex—opened my eyes to a sect of the supernatural world that is currently being underserved. Sophie, I would like you to head up the Underworld Detection Agency's Fallen Angel Division."

I felt my cheeks push up into a grin. "Wow, sir, that sounds great. Except, I'm still the Vessel of Souls. Isn't this going to be . . . kind of dangerous?"

Dixon shook his head. "You will have full knowledge of any fallen angel activated anywhere in Northern California—likely before they even know you exist. Alex and I discussed how it would work."

"Alex. Oh."

"Besides, I think it's best to always be one step ahead of the demon—or other—in the Underworld." He grinned, his fangs catching the light. "So, will you come back to the Underworld Detection Agency, Ms. Lawson?"

I looked at Dixon's outstretched hand, then glanced

back up into his dark eyes. "One step ahead of the demons, huh?" There was a glint from the mirror across the room, and I grinned, then shook his hand. "Well, my grandmother always told me I should keep my friends close and my enemies closer."

Please turn the page for an exciting sneak peek of
Hannah Jayne's
next Sophia Lawson urban fantasy novel,
coming in May 2012!

You'd think by the time a guy had earned immortality, he'd tire of copying his butt on the office copy machine.

Not so.

I was pulling out the third paper jam of the morning— and tossing fistfuls of copies of a weird combination of butt cheek and hoof—when Nina poked her head in, scanned the room and asked, "Is she gone?"

I flopped back into the sea of crumpled paper and blew a few strands of my hair (done up in Clairol's Red Hot Rhythm) out of my eye. "Who?"

Nina shimmied into the copy room and straightened her vintage boat-necked Balenciaga dress. She had paired this little number with black and purple lace tights and those peek-a-boo booties that made me look like a poor lumberjack and supermodels (and vampires) look amazingly chic.

I guess living through two world wars and umpteen clothing revolutions would pique your fashion sense.

"What do you mean, who? Mrs. Henderson. This dress," Nina did an elegant twirl, "is not only vintage, it's irreplaceable. I wore it when I nabbed a bite of John

Lennon." Nina batted her lashes and grinned, her small fangs pressing against her red lips.

I cocked an eyebrow and Nina blew out an exasperated sigh.

"Fine. It was Ringo. So, is she gone?"

Mrs. Henderson—the UDA's resident busybody dragon and all-around most obnoxious client—and Nina have a bit of a history together. One that most often left Nina nicely singed from head to toe, her vintage couture du jour in ashes, and Mrs. Henderson hiccupping smoke rings and apologies.

I looked down at my watch. "Oh my gosh, I'm totally late. Thanks for reminding me."

I thrust the last of the hoof-and-butt Xeroxes into Nina's hands and beelined to my desk—hopping over the burnt-hole remains of a wizard who blew himself up and averting my eyes when the fairies from receiving headed down the hall. Lorraine—resident witch and finance whiz—tried to stop me by waving a folder full of invoices in front of my face, but I was able to dodge her, thanks in part to the seminar that HR held on "Respecting Your Co-Worker's Personal Space."

I flopped into my ergonomically questionable chair and eyed the clock, blowing out a deep, comforting breath and lacing my fingers over Mrs. Henderson's files. In addition to being a fire-breathing, St. John's Knit–wearing dragon, Mrs. Henderson was a divorcée hell-bent on squeezing her cheating ex-husband for every last dime. As our agency detected all supernatural movement within our region, Mrs. Henderson dropped in monthly for updates and liked it especially when we were prepared for her with Mr. H.'s paycheck stubs and warm, fuzzy stories about his current financial woes.

Fifteen minutes later, Mr. H.'s statements were still

safely tucked into my file folder and Mrs. Henderson was nowhere to be found.

I buzzed the reception desk and Kale answered—I could hear the murmur of the iBud she kept continually tucked in her left ear. "Reception," she said, "what can I do you for?"

"Hey, Kale, it's Sophie. Did Mrs. Henderson call in? She's almost twenty minutes late for her appointment."

I heard Kale muss some papers on the other end of the phone and then the snap of her gum. "No, nothing. Are you sure she was scheduled today?"

"Positive. It's the fifteenth."

"Ooh, alimony pick-up day. She's usually a half hour early."

"That's what I was thinking."

"'Kay. Oh!"

I rapped my fingers on my desk, suddenly impatient. "Yes?"

"Um," Kale started to stutter and drift off and I could almost see her biting her lower lip, curling the telephone cord around her finger.

"What about Vlad?" I asked.

Vlad was Nina's nephew—current UDA employee, leader of the San Francisco chapter of the Vampire Restoration and Empowerment Movement, and permanent fixture on our couch. He had the bright eyes, video game fetish and disdain for folding clothes that most sixteen-year-olds had.

Except that he was 116.

"Do you know if he's seeing anyone?"

Kale had been in love with Vlad since he first blew into the city—moody, restless, and dressed like Count Chocula. The Vampire Restoration and Empowerment Movement (VERM for short and for annoying Vlad incessantly) required that its adherents stick to the "classic" dress code of the fearsome vampires of yesteryear (more Bela Lugosi, less Edward Cullen) and also preached a staunch code against non-demon mixing. That left Kale—a Gestault witch of the green order—to pine relentlessly and call me on numerous occasions to ask about Vlad's dating status.

"No, Kale, I don't think so."

She let out a loud whoosh of relief. "That's what his Facebook status said. I just wanted to make sure. Bye Sophie!"

The dial tone droned in my ear and I pulled up Mrs. Henderson's phone number. I was in mid-dial when Nina stalked in, slamming the door behind her. "So what did the big lizard have to say today? She need more money for crickets?"

I hung up the phone and rubbed my temples. "She's a dragon, not a lizard, and she still hasn't shown up. That's not like her."

Nina whipped out a nail file and gave her perfectly manicured nails the once-over. "Maybe she lit herself on fire." She snorted, her smile lingering. "One can only hope. I want to go shopping. What do you think: boutique in the Haight or mainstream on Market?"

I frowned. "I'm kind of worried about Mrs. Henderson."

"So send her an edible arrangement. Don't they have one with staked mice or something? Anyway, boutique or mainstream?"

I pulled out my calendar and flipped back a few pages. "Last week I had two other missed appointments."

Nina pouted. "Are you doubting your popularity at UDA now? You know everyone here adores you and we don't even consider your . . . issue."

I felt a blush rise to my cheeks.

My "issue" was my breath. Not that it was bad (at least I don't think it is); it is that I have some. The Underworld Detection Agency not only caters to the demon community—providing transfer papers, tracking paranormal activity in the city, detecting demon activity and protecting from demonic or human threats—it is also staffed by demons.

Except for me.

Which is why there is currently a bologna and cheese sandwich wedged between two blood bags in the office fridge and why there is a constant CAUTION: WET FLOOR sign in front of the hobgoblin receiving line (hobgoblins are constantly slobbering). The Detection Agency has a severe non-discrimination policy so every centaur, vampire, werewolf, zombie or *other* applies for the cush jobs at the Agency. We boast great healthcare, excellent dental (especially since Dixon Andrade and his vampire cronies took over), and four weeks paid vacation (because apparently, if you're going to travel to Hell, you need to stay "at least three weeks" to make it worthwhile). So what's a pretty little breather like me doing in a place like this?

Besides the overwhelming need for good dental and the fact that with my English degree the only companies interested in me were Starbucks (as a barista) and the Kitty Kat Klub (don't even ask), a paper-pushing job at the UDA was a godsend—even if I did run into the occasional amorous troll or disembodied zombie finger dropped in my morning coffee. Aside from that, my humanity was a bit tainted.

My grandmother was a seer—of the crystal balls, crazy scarves and playing mah-jongg with a pixie in the living room kind. She raised me after my mother passed away—I was five, then—and although I hated being linked to her as a brooding teenager, she was the closest thing to a family I had ever known. She died just after I'd graduated college and just after she had talked the then-president, Pete Sampson, to get me a job at the UDA. After my grandmother died, the members of the UDA became like a second family. Like a second family with fangs, hooves, and the occasional stinking odor of bleu cheese.

Hey, I never said we were the Waltons.

I missed my grandmother terribly after her death and the fact that she'd occasionally pop into half a cantaloupe—yes, after death—to scold me didn't really make it any easier. Anyway, my mother was a seer as well, and my father . . . well, there's a good chance he's Satan.

And that's a long story.

So, with a blood family tree that included a cantaloupe and the devil, you can see why I found comfort in a company that offered life insurance—insurance you collect should you come back to life.

But even with the strange fruit on the family tree, I am, pretty decidedly, normal. I'm five-foot-two if I stretch (and stand on a phone book) with a shock of hair so naturally red I could pass for Kathy Ireland (in her pre-Kmart days) or Carrot Top's kid sister. I'd love to call my eyes emerald or smoky jade but they're more accurately lime Jell-O green and if you ask me, a little bit too small. I can't see the future—I'm lucky if I can set the DVR—or read minds. Though there is the very minor chance that I'll inherit the powers of Hell from dear old dad, there really is nothing else remarkable about me.

Oh, except for the Vessel thing.

I recently found out not only that angora comes from bunnies (bunnies!) but that I am a supernatural vessel that holds the souls of the recently departed before they make their way to the angelic planes. Also, I think I'm lactose intolerant.

I know, no ice cream.

As for the Vessel, it's within me—the angels like to do this "hidden in plain sight" thing when it comes to big whopping things like the Vessel of Souls. Other than the fact that fallen angels and some general baddies have been seeking the Vessel forever and that the job comes with a wise-cracking, annoyingly lovable English guy as my guardian, the Vessel thing doesn't really have that much play in my daily life—except of course for throwing a serious curve in my dating life—you know, if I had one. Oh, my other X-Man skill? I'm immune to magic.

I rolled my eyes. "I know no one cares about me being human. I've been working here forever. It's the missed appointments. No cancellations, no phone calls, nothing. I called the last two for follow-ups and couldn't reach anyone. No messages returned, nothing."

Nina shrugged. "Who cares?"

"Where do you think they're going? It's not like there is another company out there protecting demons."

"Like a demon Wal-Mart undercutting our fees?"

I crossed my arms in front of my chest and cocked an eyebrow. "Yes, Nina, I'm really worried that we're losing business to Wal-Mart."

"Bring it up with Dixon."

I gnawed my bottom lip. "I guess I could. We do have an all-staff meeting at four."

Nina's coal black eyes went wide. "I had totally forgotten about that."

"Cuts into your shopping time?"

"No," she clapped a hand to her forehead and started a vigorous massage. "Do you know how awkward that's going to be? Me and him in the same room together after what happened!"

I leaned forward. "What happened?"

"Ohmigod. You're my best friend—and my roommate, Soph! Have you not paid any attention? Me and Dixon?"

she annunciated, "The whole dating thing? It totally didn't end well."

"Oh, right. That's probably because it was all in your head. Nina, he's our boss. It's expected that he'd call you. And asking you to collate his copies means just that. The man needs staples."

Nina narrowed her eyes. "Oh, and I suppose you're going to tell me that him asking me to boot up his hard drive was completely innocent, too!"

I groaned.

Nina leaned over to gather her coat and enormously gaudy Betsey Johnson bag. "So, you never told me. Shopping on Market or Haight?"

"I don't know. Both. I can't make a decision."

Nina raised an eyebrow and grinned salaciously. "Ain't that the truth?"

I pursed my lips and straightened the already-straight selection of Post-it notes and general office supplies on my desk. "Bite me."

Nina dumped herself into my office chair again and lolled back; she kicked her Via Spiga booties up on my desk, crossing her ankles. "Hey, I'm not judging. If I had two hot otherworldly creatures ready to duke it out to save my afterlife," and here she splayed a single pale hand against her chest, "I'd have done my best to keep them both around, too."

She swung out the nail file again. "So, about that shopping trip . . ."

I gathered a few files from my cabinet. "Give me a half hour and I promise to be your couture sherpa all the way through San Francisco. Deal?"

Nina cocked her head, her long, ink-black hair swishing to her elbow. "Deal."

I shooed her out the door and shook the mouse, making my computer screen whiz back to life.

I typed in Mrs. Henderson's name, and up popped her list of appointments—the one she missed flashed an alarming red—and her address. I scrawled it down on a Post-it note and tucked it in my folder, heading out to find Dixon.

Though it's been over a year, walking into Dixon Andrade's office still pricked a little pang of sadness in my heart and gave me a small shudder of fear. I don't think I'll ever be able to walk into this part of the UDA again and not think of Pete Sampson, not think of the day I walked in to find my desk smashed to smithereens and his office—including the steel wrist and ankle cuffs used to hold him through full-moon nights—destroyed. The worst thing about that night was that Sampson was missing, blood was spilling in the streets, and Sampson—my Sampson, who had given me my first job, took me under his wing, and brought me more morning donuts than my pants could stand—was the chief suspect.

"Hey, Eldridge, I need to see Dixon."

Eldridge was chic with a white-blond ponytail that hung halfway down his back, high over-arched eyebrows and a slight sweep of make-up on his pale face. I could tell he was wearing a hint of shimmer on his pursed lips and when he clasped his hands together I realized that his manicure—French, of course, with squared-off fakes—was better than mine. I mashed my free hand into my pocket.

"Do you have an appointment?"

I rolled my eyes. "Of course not. It's important."

Eldridge sighed. "Mr. Andrade is a very busy man."

"I understand that."

"And so am I."

"Right," I put a single finger on Eldridge's desk and slid the *Cosmo* out from under his stack of official-looking documents. "And what exactly is your sexual style, Eldridge?"

If Eldridge had any blood in his body, his cheeks would have darkened. Instead, he just pursed those glossy, passion pink lips and pointed a well-manicured finger toward Dixon's office.

I knocked on the door frame. "Dixon, can I have a moment?"

Dixon looked up and grinned. "Ah, Ms. Lawson! Come on in."

He stood up when I walked in and stayed standing until I made myself comfortable. One great thing about older men—and I mean centuries older—is that they tend to retain that old-fashioned sense of politeness and chivalry. I might be stuck in a room with a blood-sucking demon but I felt every inch the lady.

"Thank you," I said.

Dixon sat and steepled his hands. "Now, what is it I can do for you?"

It was hard not to like Dixon Andrade. He was tall—imposing at six feet four inches, especially to my meager five foot two—and looked an awful lot like he just sauntered out of a Calvin Klein ad. He wore impeccably tailored suits in muted colors—charcoals, navy blues—that offset his pale features incredibly. When he fixed you with his sharp, glass-cutting eyes, it was nearly impossible to take a steady breath.

While Nina swooned the moment Dixon took over the UDA, I had my doubts. And I continued to have them once he fired me and I burned down my second place of employment. I felt a little better after he rehired me and dubbed me head of the Underworld Detection Agency's

Fallen Angel Division. While it's true that I am the one thing that fallen angels spent their low life lusting after, Dixon saw my newly found, life-endangering knowledge of them and the Vessel of Souls a business bonus. And, happy to have medical insurance and unlimited access to office supplies again, I agreed.

"I suppose it's not really a big deal yet, but in the last two weeks I've had three missed appointments."

Dixon's thin lips broke into a patronizing smile. "And?"

"And I think that's a bit odd."

Dixon opened his arms as if to remind me that working in an office thirty-five floors *underneath* the San Francisco Police Department was odd on its own.

"I know," I continued, "it's just that these are demons who never miss appointments. And none of them have called to reschedule and when I called them to check in—nothing. No return calls, no rescheduled appointments. I even checked with Kale to see if there were any messages or I just missed something. Don't you think it's fishy that three demons in two weeks would miss appointments? Especially Mrs. Henderson."

"Miss Lawson, while I truly appreciate the concern you have with our clientele, you must remember that demons are a volatile bunch. And often nomadic."

I gritted my teeth. "That's what the *Detection* part of our agency does, sir. We detect demons, even when they are volatile and nomadic."

Dixon sucked on his teeth and held out his hand, palm up. "Why don't you leave the files here with me and I'll take a look at them. If there is anything that raises any red flags for me, I'll have Eldridge and Stella look into it." He grinned a pacifying, annoying grin that showed off his long fangs. "Okay?"

"Brilliant. I feel much more confident knowing that

the Wonder Twins are on the case," is what I wanted to say. Instead, I shot back my own pacifying, annoyed grin and said, "thank you."

It was just after 5 pm and the demon clientele had faded to a trickle. I stamped my last Fallen Angel registry form and plodded into the elevator with a couple of pixies and a zombie who kept staring me up and down.

"Did you need something?" I finally asked.

The zombie's face broke into what passed as a smile for the undead, his greying skin crinkling at the corners of his toothless mouth. "Sorry. I've never seen one of you up close before."

I was rolling my eyes when I bumped—smack dab, chest to chest—into Alex Grace in the police station vestibule.

"Hey, Lawson." Alex grabbed my arms to steady me and I wanted to crawl back against him and sink into those arms.

"Oh, hey, Alex. Sorry, I guess I'm just a little bit distracted."

I blinked, then looked up into those cobalt blue eyes of his. Oh, yes. I was definitely distracted.

Alex Grace was heaven. His milk-chocolate dark hair curled in run-your-fingers-through waves that licked the tops of his completely kissable ears. Those searing eyes were framed by to-die-for lashes; his cheeks were tinged pink and his lips were pressed into his trademark half-smile that was all at once genuine and cocky, with just a hint of sex appeal. A man like this was otherworldly.

And Alex had the two tiny scars just below his shoulder blades to prove it.

Alex was an earthbound angel. Fallen, if you want to

be technical. But he lacked the certain technicality that made other fallen angels so annoying—*he* didn't want to kill me. Most of the time.

I tried to tear my eyes away from his beautiful, full lips—lips that I distinctly remembered kissing—and focus hard on my rogue clients, but even though we had decided to be "just friends" almost six months ago, there was still a sizzling something between us. Call it forbidden love or my addiction to Harlequin novels, but Alex Grace was not an easy man to get over.

After all, he was an angel.

"What's going on?" Alex asked me.

I popped out of my revelry and shrugged, feeling my bottom lip droop. "Nothing. Just a long day at the office."

Alex sighed. "Me, too."

Since fallen angel-ing didn't come with a paycheck or a 401(k), Alex spent a good chunk of his mortal life working as an FBI field detective, generally stationed in a back office at the San Francisco Police Department. The vagueness of his actual job title or description allowed him to come and go as he pleased, attending to official police—or angel—business whenever necessary. And also, he really liked donuts.

"Want to grab a drink?" Alex asked.

"Herbal tea?"

Alex raised a questioning eyebrow and before he felt my forehead for a fever, I rolled my eyes and explained. "I'm on a cleanse."

"A cleanse?"

I shrugged. "Yeah. After spending a year running from baddies I figured I should probably go on some sort of training regime. You know, cardio and . . . stuff."

Alex wasn't convinced.

"Fine! I'm holding together my fat jeans with a rubber band, okay?"

"Enough said. How about Java Script?"

"Sounds good."

Ten minutes later we were sitting at a slick, back table at the back of Java Script, the whirl of cappuccino frothers drowning out the canned jazz music. I was frowning into my bar-code mug when Alex said, "All right, out with it."

"Out with what?"

"With whatever it is that's making you look like someone kicked your puppy. You can't hide it. I *am* an angel, you know."

"Correct me if I'm wrong, but aren't your only angelic powers wolfing down a pizza in one bite?"

"And the occasional mind reading." Alex's grin was sinful and I wanted to crawl under the table. He never said it outright but I had the overwhelming suspicion that Alex had done the occasional mind dip when my mind was . . . indisposed. Generally indisposed with images of Alex Grace greased up with coconut oil and reclining on a beach.

Why couldn't I fall in love with an inmate like a normal woman?

I worked to avoid the blush that I knew was creeping over my cheeks. And here's the thing about blushing: on those chestnut brunettes a bashful crimson makes a pretty glow; ditto on those sun-kissed blondes. But when you're red-headed and have the kind of skin that people politely refer to as "porcelain" (meaning glow-in-the-dark white), a "hint of blush" equates to looking exactly like an overcooked lobster in a Gap sweater.

I clapped my hands over my cheeks and balanced my chin in my palms. "I think there's something going on in the Underworld."

Alex broke a hunk off his mammoth chocolate chip cookie and chewed thoughtfully. "Something like a vampire with an overbite or something like Armageddon?"

I frowned and picked at my own cookie (I was having herbal tea with Splenda; which cancelled out the cookie). "Something in between."

"Spill."

"Okay, so, over the last two weeks, I've had three clients not show up for appointments." I held up my palm, stop-sign style. "And before you make some comment like 'it's not them, it's you' or 'maybe it's just a coincidence,' one of those demons who didn't show for an appointment was Mrs. Henderson."

Alex chuckled. "Not them, it's you. That's good."

I crossed my arms and pursed my lips. "I don't even know why I bother talking to you."

"Chiseled pecs, coconut oil . . ."

"We're done here."

I stood up and Alex grabbed my wrist, sending a delicious shiver up my entire arm. "Hey, I'm just kidding. Tell me again why you're concerned."

"Demons don't miss appointments. Well, zombies do, but everyone knows they are completely disorganized. It's weird that our clients would suddenly stop appearing."

Alex knitted his fingers across his abdomen and leaned his chair back. "How do you know she hasn't gone on vacation?"

"The other two—a witch and a minotaur—sure. But Mrs. Henderson? She doesn't do anything without a publicity statement and a check from her ex-husband."

"Has anyone else had missed appointments?"

I shrugged. "I haven't really checked."

"I'm sure it's nothing. Maybe Mrs. Henderson met

someone. Wasn't she talking about going on Match-dot-com?"

I gave Alex a half nod and worked a chocolate chip free from my cookie.

"I think it's too soon to consider anything sinister. Besides," he added with a snide grin, "don't you know that all that Underworld malarkey is made up?"

I glanced up, lips pressed into an annoyed line and Alex flashed me his million-dollar grin. He was holding a thick, hard-backed book wrapped in a glossy black jacket, the title *Angels, Demons and Other Things that Don't Exist* in three-inch raised lettering across the cover. He opened the book, thumbed through a few pages and snorted while I snaked the last of his cookie from the plate.

"*Angels are the mythological heavenly messengers and stories of their assistance and comfort have been reported across all Western religions, and often by those who have experienced near-death situations.*" Alex grunted, shaking his head. He continued reading in a pompous orator voice. "*The so-called white-winged angel is nothing but our humanistic need to find a sense of comfort in the face of unexplainable tragedy and death. The angel myth is a direct result of humanity's unwillingness to grasp the finality of death.*" Alex snapped the book shut and tossed it on our table, the huge tome making our tea slosh. "This guy really knows his stuff."

"Does he have a chapter on missing dragons?"

Alex slid a bookmark out from the front of the book. "Don't know. But according to this you can ask ole' Harley Cavanaugh himself. He'll be signing copies of this fascinating ode to idiocy tomorrow night."

"Ooh, meet an Underworld debunker straight up and in person? Sign me up!"

Alex grinned at me, his eyes flashing a sexy combination of mischief and glee. "Sounds like a date."

I was halfway out the door when Alex snaked an arm around my waist and pulled me toward him, my back against his chest. He buried his nose in my hair, his lips a hairbreadth away from my ear. "Don't get involved. Promise me you'll let Dixon handle the dragon thing," he whispered.

My entire body—hormones to hair follicles—was humming. "Uh-huh," was all I could muster.

I sat in my car in front of Mrs. Henderson's house, her check balanced in my lap. I wasn't getting involved, I was making a friendly delivery.

Besides, any statement made under duress or against an incredibly chiseled chest was useless, right?

Mrs. Henderson and her two obnoxious teenagers lived in a gorgeous old-Hollywood-style house in a quiet neighborhood off 19th Avenue. The house, usually resplendent with an impeccably manicured lawn and showy dusting of baby-pink impatiens, was hardly recognizable. The lawn was overgrown and the impatiens were leggy and capped with drooping brown blooms. I continued up the stone walk and stooped on the porch to gather up at least a week's worth of *Chronicle* newspapers and local circulars advertising great prices on everything from fertilized duck eggs to tripe. Clamping my mouth shut against a wave of nausea, I rapped on the door, then waited. The hairs on the back of my neck slowly started to rise, as did the suspicion that I was being watched. I pressed the newspapers to my chest and slowly turned to look over my shoulder. The Hendersons' overgrown lawn and shaggy plants remained as they were and the street was empty—but I couldn't shake the creepy feeling. I stepped off the porch and glanced up and down the street. Mainly deserted, except for a few parked cars—ticketed, of course—and an old man walking a basset hound four houses down.

"I'm just jumpy," I muttered to myself. "Jumpy."

I went back up the walk and I rapped again, harder this time. The door swung open. I stepped in tentatively. The prickly feeling was still there, so I slammed the door, then pasted on a smile, ready to greet Mrs. Henderson or one of her annoying teens.

"Thank you so much," I started, "Sorry to drop in but I have your check." I waved it spastically. "Hello?"

There was no one in the foyer and it was dim. All the curtains were drawn and the little wedge of outside light that came in through a small crack in the fabric illuminated dancing dust mites.

"Mrs. Henderson? It's me, Sophie. From the UDA. You missed your appointment today . . ." I stayed pressed up against the door, the chill from the wood seeping through my sweater. "Is anybody home?"

My instinct told me that something was terribly wrong. That I should turn around and leave, drive straight to the police department and talk to Alex.

But I was never very good at trusting my instincts.

About the Author

Hannah Jayne lives in the San Francisco Bay Area. In addition to the Underworld Detection Agency series, Jayne writes cozy mysteries, young adult fiction, and grocery lists that she never remembers to bring to the grocery store.

When she's not battling the demons of the Underworld, Jayne shares a house with two neurotic, feet-attacking cats and, like her character Sophie Lawson, has a Kryptonite-like weakness for donuts.

You can find her at www.hannahjschwartz.com or at *Hannah Jayne* on Facebook.